PENGUIN BOOKS

Behind Dead Eyes

Behind Dead Eyes

HOWARD LINSKEY

PENGUIN BOOKS

PENGUIN BOOKS

UK | USA | Canada | Ireland | Australia
India | New Zealand | South Africa

Penguin Books is part of the Penguin Random House group of companies
whose addresses can be found at global.penguinrandomhouse.com.

First published 2016
001

Text copyright © Howard Linskey, 2016

The moral right of the author and illustrator has been asserted

Set in 12.5/14.75 pt Garamond MT Std
Typeset by Jouve (UK), Milton Keynes
Printed in Great Britain by Clays Ltd, St Ives plc

A CIP catalogue record for this book is available from the British Library

ISBN: 978–0–718–18034–8

www.greenpenguin.co.uk

For Erin & Alison

Letter Number Three

Perhaps you think I'm a monster. Is that it?

Maybe that's why you've not been in touch. Have you read terrible things about me, Tom? Heard stories that disturbed you? None of them are true.

I've done bad things of course, who hasn't? None of us are saints. Let's not bother to pretend we are. I know the one thing you truly understand is human frailty, Tom. I've had to account for my actions and I've paid a very heavy penalty for my misdeeds but I can assure you I never killed anyone.

Did you believe the poison that drips from the pens of those so-called reporters? They're not interested in the truth, none of them. They spend their lives wading through other people's trash looking for dirt, turning over rocks to see what crawls out. And they have the nerve to call me names.

The Lady-killer.

What chance did they give me?

Please see me. I'd visit you but clearly they won't allow that. If we were to meet face to face, I'm certain I could convince you I am not the man they say I am. If you can look me in the eye and actually believe I am capable of such savagery, then I promise I won't blame you for leaving me here.

I think you are a truth-seeker, Tom, but you don't seem to be at all interested in my truth. That's disappointing.

You are my last and only chance, Tom Carney. Please DO NOT continue to ignore me.

Yours, in hope and expectation.
Richard Bell

1995

Chapter One

Tom Carney was having a very bad day. Maybe it was the new kitchen cupboard doors and the way they refused to hang straight or the boiler going on the blink again or perhaps it was the letter from a convicted murderer.

No, it was definitely the boiler.

He hadn't owned the house long but it seemed virtually every part of the offending boiler had failed and been replaced at great cost, only for another of its components to buckle under the strain and cease to function. He should have got a new boiler when he bought the creaking old pile but funds were short then and virtually non-existent today, so he'd opted for the false economy of replacing it bit by bit instead of wholesale. How he regretted that now, as he stood tapping the pipes with a wrench in an attempt to knock the ancient thing back into life. Tom exhaled, swore and surveyed the stone-cold water tank ruefully. It came to something when a personal letter from a man who had beaten someone to death with a hammer was the least of his concerns.

He went back downstairs and tried to phone the plumber again but the guy didn't pick up. If events ran their usual course, Tom would have to leave several messages before the plumber eventually got back to him. He might then grudgingly offer to 'fit him in' towards the end of his working week. If Tom was really lucky, the bloke might even turn up on the actual day but he knew this was far from guaranteed.

Tom recorded a message then picked up the letter from the hall table. The words 'FAO TOM CARNEY' had been scrawled on the envelope in large block capitals with a marker pen, above an address handwritten in biro. It was disconcerting to realise one of the relatively few people who knew where Tom lived these days was a murderer.

For the attention of Tom Carney? Why not some other reporter? One who was actually still reporting, and not so disillusioned he'd turned his back on the whole bloody profession, to plough what was left of his money into renovating a crumbling money pit? This was the third letter he'd received from Richard Bell. Tom had read then studiously ignored the previous two, hoping one of the north-east's most notorious killers would eventually tire of contacting him but, just like his victim, Tom had clearly underestimated the killer's resolve.

Bell was a determined man, but was he a psychopath? He read the letter again, surveying the handwriting for evidence of derangement but this wasn't some rambling, half-crazed diatribe, scrawled in crayon and inspired by demonic voices. It was angry, and there was an undeniable level of frustration at Tom's failure to engage with him, but that was all. Having singled Tom out, Bell presumably felt the hurt of rejection. The handwriting was neat enough and it flowed evenly across the page. Tom couldn't help wondering if this really was the same hand that brought a hammer crashing down repeatedly onto a defenceless woman's skull until she lay dead in the front seat of her own car? A jury thought so and the judge had told Bell he was a monster. Tom remembered that much about a case that dominated the front pages for days a couple of years back. Was Richard Bell insane, or was he really an innocent man; the latest in a long line of miscarriages of justice in a British legal system discredited by one scandal after another?

Tom took the letter into his living room, if he could still accurately call it that with the carpet ripped up and tools scattered everywhere. He sat in the armchair and read it once more. Richard Bell's message in all three of his letters was consistent and clear. He wasn't mad and he wasn't bad. He hadn't killed his lover. Someone else had done that and he was still out there.

Chapter Two

Detective Sergeant Ian Bradshaw stared at the woman's face and wondered what she had looked like. Was she pretty once? He couldn't tell from this photograph. No one could. Someone had done one hell of a job on her.

All of the woman's teeth had been pulled out with pliers and the flesh on her face burnt with a strong acid; sulphuric most likely, of an amount sufficient to scorch away the lips, nose, eyelids and the flesh from her cheeks, leaving discoloured skin that looked like it was part of a melted waxworks dummy. In a final brutal act, the tops of her fingers had been snipped off with pliers to prevent the collection of prints.

Thankfully, these horrific injuries had all been inflicted post mortem. According to the report, the cause of death had been strangulation with a ligature of some kind. The victim would have had no knowledge of the gruesome things done to her to erase her identity. This might be some small comfort to her family but, since they would probably never be able to positively ID the body, tracing them seemed an unlikely prospect. In the absence of teeth, they'd had to resort to scientific analysis of the bones in order to put an approximate age to the corpse, which was estimated at somewhere between fifteen and nineteen years of age, according to the experts. This was all to do with the amount of cartilage present in the joints of the limbs, which transforms into bone as a body develops. The corpse was not yet fully matured, so they were attempting to identify a relatively young woman.

The body had been found three months ago, following a tip-off about illegal goings on at a scrapyard with suspected links to some of the region's shadier 'businessmen'. The officers who attended had hoped to find drugs or money, but figured they would more than likely have to settle for stolen goods or perhaps the discovery of a hot car awaiting the crushing machine. They didn't expect to find a body. They certainly weren't ready for one missing its face.

Predictably, the guy running the scrapyard swore he knew nothing about the body found at the back of his premises. The place was a vast out-of-town site with cars piled up all round it, so a heap of dead bodies could have been hidden in one of its messier corners without anyone spotting them. It didn't stop them giving the guy a thorough going over.

He had no idea why anyone would dump a body at his scrapyard.

He had not been asked to dispose of it.

He had no clue as to its identity, nor did he ever hang out with known criminals.

Nobody believed him of course. Nathan Connor was a shifty and feckless loser with a minor-league criminal past, presumably granted custody of the yard for those very reasons. He would do as he was told without asking questions, but was he actually a killer? It seemed unlikely and, aside from the fact that he oversaw the yard where the body was dumped, there was nothing to link him to the murder.

Efforts to trace his employer proved frustrating. They were able to interview one other man who was described as the owner but under questioning from the police he couldn't remember too much about the place. It wasn't long before he was dismissed as a front man, whose name was on the door and ownership papers, with no actual involvement in the day-to-day running of the enterprise, which was ideal for laundering cash and ridding its real owners of awkward items like a body. The detectives gave up trying to get anything more out of either man and they were released on police bail. The threat of a lengthy prison sentence was not as frightening a prospect as grassing up whoever really owned that scrapyard.

Usually senior detectives in Durham Constabulary vied with one another for murder cases. They were rare in these parts and a successful conviction would be a feather in the cap that could ultimately lead to promotion. However, an unidentifiable victim meant the usual enthusiasm for a murder case was absent.

The Detective Superintendent placed responsibility for the case with DI Kate Tennant, a newly promoted outside-transfer who was the only female detective on the force with a rank higher than Detective Constable. She was also bright enough to realise she had been stitched up like a kipper. Nothing in those intervening months had altered Tennant's view, even if she steadfastly maintained an outward conviction that her team, which included DS Bradshaw, would ultimately solve a case that saw them plodding through a seemingly endless number of box-ticking enquiries for more than three months, with nothing in the way of concrete leads.

How could they hope to solve this murder, Bradshaw wondered for the umpteenth time, if there were no witnesses, nothing from the usual public appeals, zero intelligence from sources in the criminal world and they could not even identify the victim?

'What are you doing?' he hadn't noticed DC Malone's approach until she was standing over his shoulder. He could tell she was perturbed to find him staring at images of the *burned girl*, as she had become known to them.

'Looking at her photos.' He deliberately included the word *her*.

'*Why* are you looking at them?' Bradshaw knew DC Malone thought he was just being ghoulish.

'To remind myself,' he said eventually as he stared at the blackened skin on the disfigured face, 'that she used to be a person.'

Letter Number One

You don't know me, Tom, but I suspect you know my name. I'm infamous I suppose, ironically for something I did not do. I did not kill my lover and I think you can help me prove that.

Two years ago I was convicted of murdering Rebecca Holt; a woman I was seeing. We were both married, so when the police told me she had been beaten to death I panicked and said we were simply friends. I have deeply regretted that lie ever since – because it was used to discredit me. I lied about that, so I must have lied about everything else, or so the story goes.

There was no real evidence against me though. I was arrested by police officers too lazy to search for another suspect, prosecuted by a CPS who thought motive was everything, my name was blackened by journalists jealous of my success with women and I was convicted by a jury who wanted to punish me for my lifestyle.

I read your book, Death Knock, *and was mightily impressed. You solved a sixty-year-old mystery that baffled everyone else and it gave me hope. I haven't had much of that lately.*

Visit me at HMP Durham. You're only round the corner. Hardly anything of any real substance ended up in the newspapers and most of that wasn't true. I can give you something no other writer has had: access to the truth. All I ask in return is that you keep an open mind.

Yours sincerely
Richard Bell

Chapter Three

The radio was on but it always crackled inaudibly in Tom's car, unless it was tuned to a particular local station that only played adult-oriented rock. As Tom drove, Foreigner were loudly pleading with him to explain what love was.

An upbeat jingle was followed by the affected transatlantic voice of the local DJ, who sounded part-Geordie-part-American as he read out a series of local events 'coming your way this weekend'. Tom listened to a predictable weather forecast for autumn; *cloudy and overcast, chilly with a strong likelihood of rain later* then a traffic bulletin explained why he'd barely moved; road works in Durham city centre. It was the change of tone from the talk show host that captured his interest.

'Our next guest is no stranger to this show,' he announced solemnly. 'Well-known in the region before he resigned as leader of Newcastle City Council earlier this year, Councillor Frank Jarvis has placed politics firmly on the back burner to undertake a very personal quest and he is here today to tell us all about it.' The radio host paused. 'Frank, a very warm welcome from everyone here and thanks so much for coming on,'

'Thanks for having me, John.'

'Would you like to tell us why you're on the show?'

'I'm looking for my daughter.' The councillor spoke slowly, as if he was trying to control his emotions.

Tom may not have been a journalist any more but he still

devoured the news and recalled reading something about the politician in Newcastle who was worried about his teenage daughter. He was aware of Frank Jarvis too. The man was something of a firebrand, with an old-fashioned opposition to big business and unrestrained urban development that set him aside from the modernists in his party.

'Your daughter, Sandra?' offered the talk show host gently, as if coaxing the details from his guest, 'who is nineteen?'

'That's right.'

'And she has been missing for some time now?'

'Eight months,' answered the politician flatly.

That didn't sound good. If she had been missing for that long the very best you could say was that she really did not want to be found. The worst-case scenario wasn't worth contemplating. Tom didn't hold out much hope for poor Sandra or her father.

The radio host sighed in sympathy at the councillor's plight. 'That must be incredibly difficult for you and your family?'

'It is,' said Jarvis, 'it has been a terrible time for my wife Elsie and I. I can't tell you . . .' He seemed to falter then and there was a silence for a moment. The dead air time seemed to stretch out and Tom found himself concentrating hard while he waited for the councillor to speak once more.

'Take your time, Frank,' his host told the former councillor but he was really urging him to say his piece.

'I'm sorry.' And Tom's heart went out to the poor man. A politician lost for words? It would have been comical if it hadn't been so tragic.

'That's absolutely fine, we all understand what you are going through right now,' the host assured him. How could you, Tom wondered? 'Perhaps you could begin by describing her.'

There was another pause while Jarvis attempted to find the words. 'Sandra is five feet five inches tall with long blonde hair. When she was last seen she was wearing jeans and a blue T-shirt, with white trainers and a dark brown coat.'

'Now why don't you tell us, in your own words, what happened on the day she disappeared?'

'My daughter told us she was going out with some friends,' he began. 'She was in her second term of her first year at Durham University and was home with us in Newcastle during reading week. We thought she was staying with a friend and were expecting her back the following night but she never came home.' When he said that Tom could clearly detect the disbelief in his voice, even after all this time.

'And what do you think has happened to Sandra?'

'We don't know,' Jarvis admitted, 'we just don't know. It turned out she hadn't stayed with the friend and no one close to her had seen Sandra for a couple of days before she finally disappeared but there were a number of sightings of her in the city during that period.'

'And when was the last time anyone did see your daughter?'

'That was on the eighteenth of February, when she bought a rail ticket at Newcastle Central Station.'

'Do you have any idea where she was going?' the host asked.

'No,' admitted Jarvis.

'And I understand there was no particular reason for her to run away like that? She didn't have any problems?'

'None,' he said and Jarvis sounded surprised again,

'nothing, no reason at all. Sandra was always such a happy girl who had no reason to run away from home. She wasn't in any trouble.' Then he added quickly, 'she *isn't* in any trouble. We just want her to come home.'

'And the police have been investigating but have no leads at all?' the DJ questioned. 'Even after eight months?'

'We can't fault the police. They have done everything they can. They have spoken to dozens of people about the disappearance of my daughter and kept us fully informed.'

'And yet there have been no sightings of Sandra since that day when she boarded a train out of Newcastle?'

'There have been numerous sightings,' Jarvis corrected the host, 'all over the country, but we have no way of knowing if they are genuine. We are just hoping and praying she is safe and one day will come back to us.'

'This is a difficult question, Frank, but I know you want to give out as much information as possible.' He paused. 'Might someone have taken Sandra and could they perhaps be holding her against her will?'

Tom guessed the question had been pre-agreed between them.

'It is possible,' admitted Jarvis. 'Sandra is not the kind of girl who would just run off, so the police say they can't rule anything out. If someone out there knows something, anything at all, please come forward so you can help us to find my daughter.' He cleared his throat once more. 'Until that day comes, I will continue with the Searching-for-Sandra campaign,' and he went on to give the campaign's phone number.

'And what kind of person is Sandra, Frank?' asked the radio host when he was done.

'Sandra is a kind and loving human being who lights up

any room she walks into. She's fiercely intelligent, has done well at everything she's ever turned her hand to but is still a caring person with lots of friends. She would help anyone, absolutely anyone. She is our world,' he concluded, 'and I don't know how we are managing without her.'

'And if, by some chance, she is listening now . . . ?'

'I'd say please just get in touch, Sandra; you can phone home or call this show or the nearest police station but please just let us know you are safe. We're not angry, we're not upset, we just want you to come home.'

'Frank Jarvis,' the radio host sounded genuinely moved this time, 'thank you so much for coming on the show today and being brave enough to talk about your daughter. If there is anyone out there who knows anything about the disappearance of Sandra Jarvis, please give us a call.'

Chapter Four

Helen Norton breezed into the restaurant, pretending to be in a hurry, a borrowed mobile phone clamped to her ear for effect. A panicked waiter belatedly noticed the attractive young woman then attempted to escort Helen to a table of his choosing but she sat down before he could reach her, as if weary from a morning conducting important business deals. Helen made a show of placing her handbag on the table, which she opened with one hand before extracting a pen and a notebook, all the while mumbling, 'Yeah . . . yep . . . aha . . . okay,' to the imaginary person on the end of the line, as she jotted down fictitious notes from her fake phone call. She wanted to be impossible to budge.

When the waiter reached her she said, 'Just a moment,' into her phone, in a brusque tone she hoped would intimidate him. She moved the phone away from her ear and told him firmly, 'A Greek salad and a large glass of white wine,' before adding, '*anything* but Chardonnay. I'm waiting for someone,' she concluded before returning to her pretend call while the waiter scuttled off to fetch her order.

Normally Helen would never have dreamed of speaking to anyone in such an imperious manner but today she was somebody else. Helen Norton was working undercover and acting on a tip-off she prayed was reliable. Her table had been carefully chosen because it faced the bar and the front door of the restaurant but, crucially, also afforded Helen a view of the discreet alcove favoured by Alan Camfield.

The words at the bottom of the anonymous note sent to her newspaper were clear, 'Camfield is meeting someone he shouldn't.'

Helen had ordered the cheapest thing on the menu but still felt giddy at the prospect of the bill from one of Newcastle's few shamelessly upmarket restaurants. She hoped her editor would let her claim it back on expenses but knew she would need to write a good story to justify that. Helen worked for a 'daily' these days, not a 'weekly', but the paper wasn't made of money.

Her hand shook slightly as she took off her scarf and placed it on the table. She reached inside her handbag and slowly drew out the tiny camera, another expensive item borrowed for the occasion. She positioned the camera so that it faced the table Camfield favoured but was obscured from view by her scarf. Next, she pretended to drop her pen on the floor and bent low to pick it up. As her head rose again she stole a quick look into the camera, lifting the scarf a fraction of an inch so she could adjust its angle till it provided a clear shot. Satisfied, she straightened and hid the camera beneath the scarf once more.

Helen's wine arrived in a large, heavy, crystal glass and she took a sip just as Alan Camfield walked through the door.

The Chief Executive, Chairman and majority shareholder of Camfield Offshore was a rare north-east success story, the head of a business that was actually expanding while the manufacturing base of the region was contracting alarmingly, thanks to competition from cheap foreign imports and an indifferent government, which always favoured the free market.

Camfield was bucking the trend with fingers in numerous pies and an empire built on cheap borrowed money and what was sometimes referred to as *entrepreneurial zeal*. He was a developer, with a mission statement that promised the realisation of maximum potential for underutilised, often brown-belt land in the north, but his business had numerous sub-divisions. There was also a 'service provision' arm that competed for government contracts in the expanding private sector. The services provided included care for the sick and elderly, plus catering operations in hospitals, prisons and large works' canteens.

Helen had her own opinion of Alan Camfield's business acumen. It seemed he had managed to amass a considerable fortune, of some several hundred million pounds, by taking advantage of other people's misfortunes. If a council, particularly a northern one, received insufficient funding from central government to run a service, then Camfield would graciously step in and save the day, by taking the employees and assets off the council's balance sheet. He would then 'streamline' this 'inefficient' business, which in practice meant getting rid of a number of employees while the remaining ones, who were desperate to keep their jobs, would be forced to sign new contracts with fewer rights and benefits in order to provide 'flexible' working practices. Cut to the bone, this new subsidiary of his business would then provide the barest minimum level of service to the council's dependants, who were often the most vulnerable in society, so their complaints were ignored. Somehow this new, lean and efficient business would then manage to bank large profits, while paying its employees the lowest possible wage for their 'unskilled' labour. As far as Helen could make out, neither the people providing these services nor those dependent upon them were benefitting from their privatisation. The only one who did gain from the new way of doing things was Alan Camfield.

Helen leafed through a copy of *Tatler* for the first and only time in her life, occasionally stealing furtive glances at the millionaire, who was frowning at the menu as if it was not entirely to his liking. At that point, the second half of her story helpfully walked into the restaurant. A fawning maître d' personally escorted Joe Lynch, leader of Newcastle City Council, to Camfield's table, with whispered platitudes about how wonderful it was to see him again. So much for the democratically elected representative of the working man, thought Helen.

Councillor Lynch took his seat opposite Alan Camfield and they began to talk quietly to one another. Helen wasn't close enough to hear them, but her tip-off had been accurate. The leader of the council, who could steer opinion either way on the upcoming Riverside property tender, a deal conservatively estimated to be worth more than one hundred million pounds to the successful business, was being entertained at an expensive lunch by one of the main bidders. That fact alone, placed into her story, would be enough to cause consternation. Readers would undoubtedly wonder what else Councillor Lynch might be receiving from Alan Camfield in return for his influence.

Helen checked the waiters were busy then she lifted the end of her scarf with one hand and activated the camera with the other. The sound made by the click of the shutter could not have carried much beyond her table but she waited for a moment to see if either man reacted to it. When they showed no sign of comprehension she repeated the manoeuvre once more.

'Gotcha,' she whispered softly to herself.

At that point the front door of the restaurant opened abruptly and there was a loud bang as it slammed into the wall. The man who swung it open looked puzzled, as if he didn't quite know his own strength – which was entirely possible, judging by his bulk. Along with most of her fellow diners, Helen had looked towards the noise and been shocked at the sight that greeted her. She had never met the man before but knew him instantly. The maître d' stepped quickly out of his way and the waiter let the man pass without a word. Almost everyone in the restaurant recognised the new arrival or had heard of his exploits. He was the most dangerous man in the city and he was heading straight for Helen.

Photographs of the latest batch of missing persons filled every surface of Ian Bradshaw's desk at headquarters, arranged neatly in rows from left to right. More than a dozen faces stared up at him and he gazed back at them, not hearing the sounds of his colleagues going about their business; phones ringing, the tapping of keyboards as yet another report was prepared, laughter at the usual office banter. Ian Bradshaw was completely oblivious to all of this.

He had already examined the cases of every female reported missing in the north-east of England dating back years before the corpse of the burned girl was found but come across nothing to link any of them to her. Like Tom, he had listened on his car radio as Councillor Frank Jarvis appealed for information on his own missing daughter and Bradshaw was reminded of a brief period when they had wondered if she might be the burned girl; a theory that lasted as long as it took to compare their measurements. Sandra Jarvis was almost four inches taller than the burned girl.

Bradshaw widened the radius and asked for help from all

over the country, even though his gut instinct told him this girl was local. These pictures had been sent from North Yorkshire and he read all of the reports carefully, dismissing them one by one. Some were too short or too tall, some he could exclude from their skin tone or other distinguishing characteristics and others had gone missing after the date their victim had been found. He was beginning to come to the inevitable conclusion that, whoever she was, the burned girl had never been reported missing – but how could a young woman just disappear like that without anyone noticing?

Bradshaw looked at her photograph again, taking in every mark and blemish on her charred skin. He knew he was becoming obsessed but he just couldn't help himself. He had to know who she was. His eyes followed the scorched boundaries on her face and neck where the acid had robbed her of an identity. Then he noticed something. There was a tiny blemish, which was a slightly different colour from the larger marks on her face and neck. He was still peering at it intently when DI Kate Tennant's voice snapped him out of his private thoughts as it carried across the room.

'Stop what you are doing for a moment,' she called and the four other members of the team transferred their attention to her. Tennant's squad had been steadily dwindling in numbers as detectives were reassigned to more important cases now that twelve weeks had elapsed since the burned girl had been found and no progress had been made.

'I know you are disillusioned,' her gaze seemed to take in each of them in turn, 'it's written all over your faces,' no one contradicted their DI, 'but we *will* solve this case.' So they were in for a probably long overdue pep talk. 'If we follow up each and every lead, no matter how inconsequential it might seem. Sooner or later something is going to give and we will get real, solid intelligence about this victim, but only if we stay on top of our game. That means not allowing the negativity that's setting in to get the better of us,' there were a couple of murmurs of agreement at that, 'because I won't allow *this* to go unsolved.'

She sounded a bit desperate, Bradshaw thought, and he suspected she knew it but he was always willing to cut Kate Tennant some slack for she had more brains than the rest of them put together. A female DI was unheard of in the north-east before she'd been transferred in, during a move rumoured to have been instigated by the top brass because they were desperate to fill a government quota.

'Someone did something unspeakable to this poor girl. Why? Because they are scared,' and she let that thought sink in, 'scared of us and what we might find. You don't do this to a body unless she is part of a very big secret indeed. If we find out who she is, we are halfway to understanding *why* she was killed. So keep at it,' she urged them.

She was right, identifying this poor girl was the key to the whole case but they knew that already. How could you do it though, when there was nothing to distinguish the burned girl from anyone else?

She was a blank canvas.

Almost.

Ian Bradshaw focused again on a tiny area in the photograph that was subtly different from the rest. A second later, he was up from his seat and tugging on his jacket. Bradshaw was out of there before anyone could ask him where he was going.

Helen watched helplessly as Jimmy McCree marched towards her. The most notorious gangster in Newcastle had to be mixed up in this somehow. It was too large a coincidence for him to be entering the restaurant independently of Alan Camfield and Joe Lynch. Had he somehow spotted the camera jutting out from beneath Helen's scarf and was about to snatch it, taking all the evidence with it? She was torn between leaving the camera on the table beneath the scarf and trying to pretend it wasn't there and an almost overwhelming urge to snatch it and run from the restaurant, but how could she do that when the big man was between her and the door?

Jimmy McCree had to be at least six feet four, with a broad chest and the kind of physique that only comes from endlessly pumping iron. The absence of hair on his bullet head seemed only to highlight two dark brows furrowed above menacing eyes that were staring straight at her. As he reached her, Helen realised she was holding her breath.

And then he was gone. The moment he reached her table he passed it without a word, going straight to the councillor and the businessman. For a brief second she pictured him pulling out a gun and shooting them both, as if she was suddenly part of some American gangster film, but instead he nodded a greeting, then pulled out a chair and sat down between them. For some reason neither man seemed to find the presence of a known criminal at their table disturbing.

Jimmy McCree had his back to the wall, which looked like an instinctive move to avoid presenting it to the street, but this meant he was also facing Helen's camera. Only when they were deep in conversation did she slowly reach out an unsteady hand until it slipped beneath her scarf. With the little finger of her left hand she lifted the material slightly to uncover the lens then used her index finger to depress the shutter. She repeated the process twice more to ensure she had a perfect shot.

As Helen was taking the third picture she risked a side-long glance towards their table and realised Jimmy McCree was staring straight back at her. The expression on his face told her everything she needed to know. He knew exactly what she was doing.

McCree said something to the other men and they turned to gaze at Helen. She started to rise from her seat. This was McCree's cue to get up, too. She knew he would reach her before she could escape. He was starting to come round the back of the table and she frantically scooped up her belongings to shovel them into her bag, but it was hopeless. He would be across that room in seconds.

Then Helen got a lucky break. Before she could leave her seat the maître d' swept past her with another man, who was carrying a large silver ice bucket on a stand with a bottle of champagne leaning lopsidedly in it. The waiters made a show of delivering it to the men at the table but, as they fussed and fretted about the positioning of the ice bucket and started the elaborate process of uncorking the champagne they inadvertently blocked McCree. There was frustration and anger in McCree's eyes and there was no doubt in Helen's mind that if they had been anywhere but a very fancy restaurant, the wine waiter would have simply been pushed to one side so he could get at her.

As Helen swept her belongings into her bag, Alan Camfield calmly spoke to the maître d' and indicated Helen. In her haste she dropped the borrowed phone and had to quickly bend to retrieve it. 'Miss,' called the maître d', as she rose with the phone. 'Miss,' he called again, louder this time, somehow managing to make the word sound sinister in these genteel surroundings. She banged her head on the table as she stood and threw the phone and camera into the handbag, while grabbing her purse. 'Miss, could you please . . .' He was heading towards her now, twisting his hips to get through a narrow gap between tables, the restaurant's greed at packing the place with as many covers as possible working in her favour. She grabbed notes from her purse that more than covered the cost of her meal and dropped them onto the table then headed for the door, still with a head start on the maître d'.

She had almost made it when another waiter stepped out in front of her, instantly blocking her escape, saying, 'Excuse me, Miss,' as he held up his hands.

'It's okay,' she said quickly, 'my money's on the table but I have to go now.' But the waiter must have taken his cue from the maître d' and he refused to step out of her way. 'Excuse me,' she said firmly but he reached out a hand until it touched her arm, lightly at first, then his grip started to tighten. Helen was trapped.

'Don't touch me!' she shouted instinctively at the waiter and all heads instantly turned towards them. 'How dare you touch me like that!' The waiter flushed, backing away quickly as if he'd just been slapped across the face. Seizing her opportunity, Helen marched for the door, but not without calling the single word 'Disgusting!' back over her shoulder.

She pushed the door open and bolted through it. As soon as Helen was out of the door, she ran. She moved quickly across the street without glancing back then rounded a corner before losing herself amongst a crowd of shoppers on the high street.

Letter Number Two

Were you alarmed by my correspondence, Tom? Was that it? There was a time when I might have been upset to receive a letter from a convicted murderer – and a famous one at that. I should probably have explained how I found you. It wasn't difficult. People are easy enough to track down. You might want to be more careful in your line of work.

I don't normally trust journalists but I think that you are different. I like your work. I believe you managed to crawl your way out of the gutter and I respect that. Are you 'the repentant sinner' the prison chaplain keeps telling us about, Tom? You might just be.

My appeal against conviction has been refused because there is no fresh evidence to overturn the guilty verdict and they won't allow me to appeal against the length of my sentence. My solicitor keeps reminding me that murder is murder and the sentence is always life, so I am forced to face facts. I'm going to be in here for a very long time unless someone can vindicate me, and the police have no interest in doing that. They probably truly believe they have their man. They don't. He's still out there somewhere, just waiting to do it again – and if that isn't a thought that keeps you awake at night, Tom, then it should.

Yours
Richard Bell

Chapter Five

'What the bloody hell happened here?' demanded Tom.

'New owners,' the barman said by way of explanation. Tom took in the sight of his favourite pub, which had just emerged from a two-week shutdown for 'renovation'. Its walls were now painted bright orange and covered with framed pictures of Cadillacs and Chevys from the sixties that were completely out of place in a Durham city boozer. The long-serving barman was wearing a sombrero, which seemed to move independently of him while he poured drinks or dispensed plates of bar food.

Tom shook his head. 'When I was last in here it looked like a pub. Not a brothel at the Alamo.'

'It's a new Mexican theme to go with the menu. They've got some huge models on order to keep the kids happy outside. A tyrannosaurus and a stegosaurus.' The barman's face told Tom he shared the younger man's distaste. 'But what can you do?'

Tom, who had made it one of his life's rules never to drink in a pub with a plastic dinosaur in its garden, was about to say, *you can go somewhere else* but the barman had already poured a pint of his usual bitter and placed it on the bar in front on him. 'Better enjoy that while you can,' he explained, 'they're ripping out the pumps next week and replacing them with cervezas.'

'Replacing them with what?'

'Cervezas, I think it's Spanish for beer. We are getting

three of them in here on draught. Owners told me that's what the punters want these days.'

'That and plastic dinosaurs?' said Tom doubtfully. 'Are they Mexican dinosaurs?'

'Don't know.' The barman thought it was a serious question.

Since when did drinkers become punters? thought Tom. 'They'll go bust in a year.' He noticed a small machine on the bar which dispensed jelly beans, as if they were a sensible accompaniment to a pint of beer. But this wasn't the final straw for Tom. The final straw was the repainted toilet doors that said 'Senoritas' and 'Hombres' instead of 'Ladies' and 'Gents'.

'Make that three months,' he said sourly as he looked at the new bar food menu, which featured chilli dogs and refried beans, along with tacos and empanadas. 'Is there a remote chance of getting a burger in here that isn't smothered with salsa or guacamole?'

'I'll check with the kitchen.' And he left Tom mourning the loss of his favourite Durham city watering hole. The barman returned and said, 'That's fine, the chef says you can have a burger-with-nowt.'

'A burger-with-nowt it is then.' Tom handed over his money.

While he waited for his burger-with-nowt, he sat in the corner trying to ignore the restlessness that was almost always in him these days. What the hell had he been thinking when he bought that house? It was supposed to be an investment and he was meant to be spending the afternoon searching for 'home improvement solutions', but he had no interest in that any more. Instead his thoughts turned back to Richard Bell.

Madman or no, Bell seemed pretty steadfast in his denials of murder. Tom knew most criminals continued to claim innocence long after they were convicted. It afforded them a sense of injustice to nurture while behind prison walls as they worked on an appeal, but there was something in Bell's words that made him sound more believable than that. Tom wasn't quite sure what it was though; perhaps the claim that the real murderer was still out there or maybe it was the bit about Tom being his last hope that intrigued him? Tom had once known an old lady without hope and witnessed the effect it had on her at first hand.

Tom fished inside his bag and brought out the fruits of his morning's labours, a large number of black and white photocopied articles from the university library's newspaper archive; each one dating back to the court case that ended with Richard Bell receiving a life sentence. He placed them in a neat pile on the table in front of him and began to read.

JULY 20, 1993

MURDER VICTIM'S LIFE PROBED

The investigation into the murder of former model, Rebecca Holt, is 'centring on her complex private life' a police source has revealed.

Rebecca's body was found in her car at a rural County Durham location favoured by courting couples. She had been brutally beaten to death.

Rebecca, 30, was married to multi-millionaire northern businessman, Freddie Holt, 52, who made his fortune in construction. Holt was enjoying a cruise, shortly after the break-up of his 26-year marriage to first wife, Angela, when he met Rebecca who was working as a cabaret singer on the ship. They married following a whirlwind courtship.

A neighbour of the couple, who did not want to be named, said, 'Freddie is away a lot on business. It must have been very lonely for Rebecca in that big house all on her own.'

Police are working on the theory that Mrs Holt may have been planning to meet someone at Lonely Lane on the day of the attack. 'We would like to speak to anyone who may have information regarding Mrs Holt's private life,' said Detective Chief Inspector Kane who is leading the investigation. 'If you were due to meet Mrs Holt or know someone who was, please come forward so we can eliminate you from our enquiries.'

Police have already questioned several men who knew Rebecca Holt. Asked if Mrs Holt could have been attacked by a stranger, DCI Kane said, 'We cannot rule anything out at this stage. Our enquiries are ongoing.'

JULY 28, 1993

MAN ARRESTED FOR LONELY LANE MURDER

A man has been arrested on suspicion of murdering Rebecca Holt. The 32-year-old, who has not yet been named, is thought to have known her intimately, according to a police source. He is currently undergoing questioning.

JULY 30, 1993

MURDER SUSPECT CHARGED

A local man has been charged with the murder of Rebecca Holt. Richard Bell, 32, was known by the victim and is a member of the same sports club. Bell is married with two young children. He has been remanded in custody awaiting a trial date.

MURDER SUSPECT A 'LADY-KILLER'
SAYS HIS OWN LAWYER
ASTONISHING GAFFE FROM
DEFENCE BARRISTER

The long-awaited trial of Richard Bell took a bizarre twist yesterday when his own lawyer referred to him as 'a lady-killer'.

Martin Nixon told a jury they probably would not like his client but this did not mean Bell was guilty of murder. 'Richard Bell is a handsome man who is capable of an easy charm and has perhaps taken advantage of this in his dealings with women,' he said before adding, 'in a bygone era we might have considered him to be something of a lady-killer.' There were gasps from the public gallery at that and the defence barrister immediately added, 'though obviously not in the literal sense.' Richard Bell stared impassively from the dock throughout his lawyer's opening remarks.

Bell is accused of murdering his lover Rebecca Holt, who was found dead inside her car, which was parked in a notorious lovers' lane in rural County Durham. Police said she had been brutally beaten with a blunt instrument, possibly a claw hammer, during what was described as a frenzied attack.

Bell, 32, initially lied to police about their affair but, under questioning, later admitted meeting Rebecca regularly for sex sessions. He denies murdering the former singer and swimwear model because she threatened to expose their affair. Bell worked for his father-in-law's company and, according to the prosecution, stood to lose everything if his extramarital activities were exposed by the woman he had been seeing, giving him a strong motive that 'marks him out as the only credible suspect' in her murder. The trial continues.

KILLER COULD NOT HAVE BEEN A WOMAN

Rebecca Holt must have been murdered by a man, according to an expert witness. Professor Angus Matthews told a court that a woman 'lacked the upper body strength for such a sustained and savage attack on another human being. Only a man could have administered blows of such ferocity with a blunt instrument, possibly a hammer, which caused the severe cranial fracturing that killed Rebecca.'

Richard Bell's wife told the court she was standing by her husband, despite his adulterous relationship with the dead woman and the murder charge that now hangs over him. Annie Bell said she took a share of the responsibility for his affair. 'I was often busy with work and the children. I regret that now. I want to rebuild our relationship and we are both determined to make this marriage work. Richard is completely innocent.'

Earlier, Bell's friend and best man at his wedding, Mark Birkett, confirmed the accused once assaulted a former girlfriend. The police were called when Bell struck Amy Riordan, his college sweetheart, but Bell escaped with a caution and was allowed to continue with his studies.

The trial continues.

OCTOBER 18, 1993

JUDGE CONDEMNS SORDID AFFAIR

A trial judge condemned a murder suspect for 'conducting a sordid affair' with the victim. Richard Bell engineered 'a number of sexual encounters with Rebecca Holt, which showed a level of cunning that could scarcely be credited', said Mr Justice Thurley, who reserved particular scorn for the manner in which the two lovers communicated with one another. Using a complex dead-letter drop, he said, 'was like something out of a John Le Carré novel'.

The judge told Bell he was an immoral man with a cold heart but it was up to members of the jury to decide whether this meant he was actually guilty of murder. They would have to look deep into their own hearts, he told them, in order to decide what lay in Richard Bell's. 'As you hear about his dual life, full of duplicity and lies, do you conclude that this is a man capable of committing a most brutal act of murder without a single moment's remorse?' The jury has retired to consider its verdict.

OCTOBER 21, 1993

MONSTER GUILTY OF BRUTAL MURDER KILLER SENTENCED TO LIFE FOR EVIL SLAYING OF FORMER LOVER

Rebecca Holt's former lover was sentenced to life imprisonment today for her brutal murder. The judge described Richard Bell as a monster.

A jury took just six and a half hours to decide that Bell, 32, was guilty of beating his former lover to death. The married father of two showed no emotion as Mr Justice Thurley told him, 'You were once intimately involved with the victim of this terrible crime but when she threatened to expose the sordid affair to your wife, you decided to rid yourself of her in the most callous manner imaginable.'

Bell was told he would serve a minimum of 24 years. His wife Annie Bell, who proclaimed his innocence and stood by him throughout the trial, wept openly as Bell was led from the court room.

OCTOBER 24, 1993

MY SAUCY ROMPS ON LOVE BOAT WITH TRAGIC REBECCA

The best friend of murder victim, Rebecca Holt, lifts the lid today on their bawdy years together on board a cruise ship nicknamed the 'love boat'. Nicole Andrews has revealed all about her life at sea during two uninhibited, fun-filled years singing professionally for wealthy passengers, including Rebecca's future husband.

In an exclusive interview, Naughty Nicole confessed the girls, then in their mid-twenties, often drank too much following their twice-nightly shows, then slept with fellow crew members or wealthy passengers.

'There was a new set of passengers every week so there were always plenty of opportunities,' admitted Nicole. 'We just wanted to have a good time. The passengers were loaded so we'd get them to buy us drinks after a show.' Nicole admitted one thing would often lead to another. 'We would regularly wake up next to a stranger but I don't regret a thing.'

Naughty Nicole revealed that

- Sleeping with strangers was considered normal on a cruise ship nicknamed 'the love boat' by its young and crazy crew.

- Raunchy Rebecca regularly sunbathed topless on the upper deck in full view of passengers and crew because she 'hated tan lines'.
- When Rebecca met millionaire businessman Freddie Holt she told Nicole, 'He's my passport out of here!'

'Only a handful of guests attended Rebecca's wedding, including some of her friends from the boat,' explained Nicole. She said they were astonished by the contrast between the bride and groom, cruelly dubbing them 'Beauty and the Beast'. 'Freddie is old, fat and bald,' she explained, 'and Rebecca was so beautiful. We all said it was only a matter of time before she began to look elsewhere.' The two women rarely saw each other after the wedding, because they were 'moving in different worlds' by then, but Nicole will always remember her best friend.

Nicole left the cruise ship last year in a row over pay. Currently unemployed, she has no regrets about her wild youth but is 'glad to be out of that world now'. She wells up when talking about her former friend. 'I was jealous of her money and new designer clothes. For a while I wished it was me but then I might have been the one who was murdered. It just proves that you should be careful what you wish for.'

Chapter Six

'Okay, what have you got for me?' asked her editor. Helen placed the large black and white photograph on the table in front of him.

Graham Seaton regarded it for a second. 'Whoa! Where did you get this?' he said, looking at her with something resembling amazement. 'And *how* did you get this?' Helen did not reveal her source was an anonymous note but admitted borrowing the little camera and managing a handful of shots at the restaurant before being spotted. 'And is this who I think it is?'

'From left to right,' she began, 'Alan Camfield, boss of Camfield Offshore, Councillor Joe Lynch and Jimmy McCree.'

'Who needs no introduction,' he said of the latter. 'And just why would these three fine fellows be sitting down to a cosy lunch together?'

'It's got to be the Riverside development.'

Her editor knew all about the region's biggest property deal, involving acres of prime, council-owned, former ship-building land on the banks of the Tyne, currently up for grabs via a tender. 'The councillor has no business sitting down to a cosy lunch with one of the bidders – and that's even before you throw in the inexplicable presence of Jimmy McCree. The man's a gangster and a very scary one. How the hell did they think they'd get away with this?' he mused.

'They weren't expecting a journalist,' she reminded him. 'Not everyone in the restaurant spotted McCree. I'd be willing to bet hardly any of them recognised Camfield or Lynch. We live in a bubble.' Helen meant that public awareness of politicians was staggeringly low. Most people could not even name their local MP.

'Jimmy must be offering up his security firm,' said Graham. 'He's supposed to be going straight these days but the boys in blue aren't having that.'

'So how are we going to run this story?'

'Carefully,' he told her. 'No matter how bad his reputation is, Jimmy McCree has never actually been convicted of any criminal offence. He's been arrested on countless occasions, even charged a few times, including once for murder, but was acquitted every time. Everyone knows he controls a lot of the crime in this city but we can't risk being sued,' he grinned at her, 'and I want to be able to walk round without fearing for my life.'

'Do I call the leader of the council?'

'To ask him what the hell he is playing at? Leave that to me if you don't mind, Helen. Councillor Lynch has a right to reply on this,' he glanced at his watch, 'but not just yet. If we give him too long he'll be making frantic phone calls to the owners of this newspaper and I'll get the heavy brigade down here. Right now he probably doesn't know who you're working for. There'll be nothing left of your story if our owners come under too much pressure from the vested interests in this city, and I won't let that happen.' Graham exhaled thoughtfully.

'But how will we run this?' Helen asked him.

Her editor held up the photograph and looked at it closely. 'You know what? I'm a firm believer in that old adage.'

'Which one?'

'That a picture is worth a thousand words.'

*

'For fuck's sake ,' hissed Michael Quinn, 'do you have to use the front door?' Before Bradshaw could answer, the burly man steered him into the shop then shut and locked the door behind them, turning the 'open' sign to 'closed'.

'You haven't got any customers, Michael. I checked.'

'You call it checking,' said Michael, 'I call it door-stepping where anybody could see you.'

'Just tell them I was after a tattoo.'

'You don't look the sort.'

'You see all kinds with them these days; perfectly respectable lasses getting little tattoos on their ankles or the small of their backs. I prefer the good old days when we used to call tattoos barcodes-for-criminals.'

'Times change, Detective Constable.'

'It's Detective Sergeant, actually.'

'Gone up in the world have we? Who did you nick to get that promotion?'

One of my own colleagues thought Bradshaw, but he didn't tell Michael that, or the fact the man hadn't lived to do prison time.

'It's alright,' Bradshaw reassured him, 'it wasn't the case you helped me on.'

'Could you not say that out loud, please.' Quinn winced, even though there was no one else in the shop.

'You did the right thing, Michael. You could have carried on covering up gangsters' tattoos and done time for perverting the course of justice but, instead, you shopped them, retaining your liberty and the right to continue earning your livelihood.'

'And those people on the inside still have friends on the outside. One careless word from you and I'm history.'

'Is that right?' said Bradshaw nonchalantly.

'Yes.'

'Then you'd better stay out of dark alleyways,' said Bradshaw, 'and on my good side.'

'I don't know nothing else. I swear it. I haven't done any of those cover-up jobs since you blackmailed me.'

'Blackmail is a very strong word, Michael. I just gave you the chance to do the right thing, but I'm not looking for you to shop anyone, at least not today. It's your professional expertise I am after.'

Bradshaw produced the photograph of the burned girl then and placed it face up on Quinn's tattoo bench.

'Jesus,' said Quinn, 'what the fuck happened to . . . it?'

'*It* is a *she*, Michael, and the answer to your question is undiluted sulphuric acid.'

'Oh my God.'

'We are having a problem identifying the poor victim, which is where you come in.' Bradshaw pointed at the photograph. 'Take a close look at this,' he ordered the man, 'and tell me what you think.'

Reluctantly Quinn bent lower and squinted at the area of the photograph Bradshaw had indicated. After a moment he said, 'It could be.'

'I know it could be but is it?'

'Most of it has gone. It's just a tiny smudge really,' and he swung round a desk lamp with a magnifying glass attached to it so he could take a closer look. Bradshaw watched as Quinn turned on the lamp, peered through the glass and examined the light blue mark on the burned girl's neck. 'But it does form an angle.

'I think it *is* a tatt,' he said eventually, 'but it could be almost anything.'

This was not the answer Bradshaw was hoping for. 'What do you *think* it is?'

Quinn looked again. 'Well it could be a number, a letter or the shape of an animal or possibly the corner of an emblem of some sort.'

'Bloody hell, Michael, I could have told *you* that.'

'Well, I'd need a bit more time if I'm going to examine it properly and compare it.'

'How much do you need?' he asked.

'I dunno,' Quinn shrugged helplessly, 'a while, possibly quite a while.'

Bradshaw folded his arms. 'I'm in no hurry.'

'Look, I don't mean this disrespectfully, but could you at least fuck off for a bit and come back later?'

'No, Michael, I couldn't.'

'Christ,' hissed Quinn, as if Bradshaw was standing there in full uniform and not a suit.

'So if you want me gone, you'd better get a move on.'

'Alright, alright.' And Quinn did get a move on. He started dragging catalogues containing tattoo designs over to the bench and opening them near the photograph of the burned girl so he could compare the smudge to them.

'Take your time, Michael,' said Bradshaw, 'but I'm expecting great things from you.'

'Don't hold your breath,' said the flustered tattooist as he leafed through the catalogues. Bradshaw killed time looking at the myriad of designs on the tattoo parlour's walls before deciding that none of them were remotely appealing to him.

It took Michael Quinn some time before he felt confident enough to look up from the catalogues and share his findings with Bradshaw.

'If it is a smudge from a tattoo then it could be just about anything but . . .'

'But what?' pressed Bradshaw.

Quinn pointed to an area on the photograph just inside the portion of skin that had been virtually destroyed by the acid, 'you can just make out what remains of a very faint line.'

Bradshaw peered through the magnifying glass at the area Quinn was indicating. 'So you can,' he agreed, 'just.'

'That could be a line that moves outwards into an edge, ending here and joining up with this more pronounced line that's still partially visible,' said the tattooist and he pointed at the blue mark on the burned girl's neck. 'I think this mark you found might just be the curve of a sword or the outer edge of the wing tip of a bird.'

'Really?'

'Take a look,' said Quinn, and he slid the images he had found along the table so they were close to the photo of the burned girl. 'These designs are very popular and small enough to go on your neck, ankle or an inner thigh. I've done a few of those.' He smiled at the memory. 'The positioning of the smudge would tally with a tatt at the base of the neck and to one side so it's discreet. You can have it on show or not. Lasses like that.'

Bradshaw surveyed the images closely then glanced back at the picture of the burned girl.

'Maybe,' he said uncertainly.

'Hang on,' said Michael and he peeled a transparent design away from a pile of images and placed it right next to the smudge. Bradshaw could now more easily compare this tattoo and the mark on the burned girl. 'It's not quite to scale but . . .' Michael slid the image of a dove towards the smudge until its edge slotted into its corner. Now that it virtually overlapped, Bradshaw could tell the faded edge of the tattoo could easily be a match to the outer edge of the dove's wing.

'Bloody hell,' said Bradshaw, 'you might just be on to something there, Michael. How did you manage that?'

'I just picked the dozen or so most popular designs and this one is the closest match.'

'Well done.'

'Aye, well, I'm glad you're pleased and there's a very simple way you can repay me.'

'Go on,' said Bradshaw assuming he wanted money for his time.

'By telling no bugger about it.'

'Have no fear, Michael,' said Bradshaw, 'my lips are sealed.'

'They'd bloody better be.'

Helen's Norton's newspaper ran a front-page lead story about the Riverside tender. It stressed the need for openness and transparency during the bidding process and the importance of getting the very best deal possible from the sale of publicly owned land. Next to it they printed the photograph she had taken, with the caption, 'Council leader Joseph Lynch enjoys lunch with Camfield PLC owner Alan Camfield and well-known-local-businessman James McCree in a high-class, city centre restaurant.' The hyphens in McCree's title were her editor's idea. They were not quite as blatant as punctuation marks but they ably highlighted the ironic nature of their description of the local gangster

For anyone outside the region, that photograph would have seemed innocuous. However, if you were from Newcastle the image would have been shocking. The leader of the council was sitting down to a cosy and expensive lunch with a multi-millionaire and one of the city's best-known criminals.

Councillor Lynch used his right to reply to offer a flustered and angry response, which Helen's editor included at the foot of the article. 'I absolutely deny I had lunch with Mr Camfield and Mr McCree. I was there to meet someone else. Mr Camfield was already at his table. I went over to say hello to a prominent local businessman I have known for many years. While I was speaking to Mr Camfield, Mr McCree arrived at the restaurant to discuss opportunities for his security business, should Camfield Offshore be successful in their bid for the Riverside development scheme. At that point I left both the conversation and the table.'

'I should have waited till the food arrived,' said Helen, 'I've given him an out.'

'Do you think anyone is going to believe that?' asked Graham. 'The people of Newcastle have legendary bullshit detectors. Lynch has been banged to rights. We have done some serious harm to his credibility.'

'Was he angry?' Helen asked.

'No,' said her editor, 'he was apoplectic.'

'So will he try to . . . ?'

'Ruin our lives? Oh yes. If I know anything about Councillor Lynch he will not rest until I'm fired, this paper's closed down and the building we are standing in demolished, but do you know what? Fuck him. That's journalism. Sometimes you just have to roll the dice and print the story, otherwise what's the point?'

Helen Norton may have been a reporter but right then she would have struggled to put her admiration for her editor into words. 'Print and be damned, eh?' she managed.

'Print and be damned,' Graham repeated firmly.

Chapter Seven

'Tom Carney?' The prison officer called his name and Tom, having waited for what seemed like an eternity, was suddenly snapped out of his private thoughts. He got to his feet and followed a burly man in a blue jumper with epaulettes on his shoulders.

He had expected to be fobbed off. He figured there would at least be a number of bureaucratic hoops to be navigated before he was able to come to the prison. Instead it was almost as if they were expecting him and, to his genuine surprise, he was given an appointment that same day.

Tom was led into the visiting area. He had assumed he would be among the friends and families of dozens of inmates but instead of a crowded room full of wives and children at visiting time, he found himself alone in a room filled with empty chairs and small tables. Tom chose one and sat down. He didn't have to wait long for Richard Bell to appear.

The heavy metal door at the opposite end of the room swung open and the murderer stepped inside. He smiled broadly at Tom and there was a disconcerting excitement in his eyes. Tom was glad of the presence of the barrel-chested prison guard who took up a position a little way from the table Tom had selected. No one else followed Bell through that door. It seemed they really would have the room to themselves.

Bell walked towards him. He was still a handsome man but those famous looks had been diminished by two years in prison. The effects of an inadequate diet and being locked up for most of the day were obvious. Richard Bell had traded a life of expensive restaurants and foreign holidays for one of extreme stress, poor nutrition and perpetual confinement and it showed. His face, starved of sunlight, was pale, his hair straggly and uncombed, but the most startling alteration to his appearance was the vivid scar on the side of his face. It wasn't entirely new but fresh enough to provide a stark contrast to the rest of his skin, running in an almost horizontal dark red line across his right cheek. This was a mark Bell would be forced to carry for the rest of his life.

Tom stayed in his seat because it didn't feel right to rise for a murderer. He felt decidedly on edge. Seeing Bell in the flesh prompted him to fully recall his crimes. They no longer had the distance created by bland words in a newspaper article. Tom checked Bell's hands to ensure they were empty but Bell wasn't carrying anything.

The killer stretched out an arm to shake his visitor by the hand. 'Thanks for coming, Tom. I can't tell you how much this means.' Tom did not react. Bell's smile dissolved into a slight frown but it was one of bemusement, not anger.

'I don't think we've reached that stage,' Tom told him.

Bell seemed to ponder this for a moment before withdrawing his hand. 'Fair enough. I appreciate you taking the time to visit me.'

'You were very persistent.'

'Three letters?' recalled Bell. 'I'd have written thirty-three if that's what it would have taken to persuade you,' he reflected. 'You are just the man to help me.'

'I didn't say I was going to help you,' Tom told him firmly. 'I'm here to listen to you. I'll hear you out but I'm promising nothing.'

'Of course, you've not heard my side yet. I understand

your caution. I'd have been disappointed if you'd promised me cooperation without hearing what I have to say. That would have meant you were more interested in making money out of me than clearing my name. I don't want the kind of reporter who's only interested in *an-interview-with-a-killer*.' Bell said the last words ironically.

'You *are* a killer,' Tom reminded him.

'I'm a convicted murderer,' Bell admitted, 'but I didn't kill anyone, Tom. That's what I've been trying to tell you and if you'll just keep an open mind . . .'

'What happened?' Tom interrupted and when Bell didn't comprehend his meaning, he stroked a finger along his own cheek, mirroring the scar on Bell's face.

'Oh, that.' Bell actually smiled then. 'One of my fellow inmates fell in love with Rebecca during my trial.'

Like those doomed rock stars of the sixties and seventies, death had done little to quell Rebecca Holt's popularity with the opposite sex. 'Unfortunately for me, he happened to be a particularly vicious London gangster with a bit of an entourage. He got one of his men to come at me armed with a toothbrush,' his smile turned grim, 'with a razor blade attached to it. I was actually quite lucky. He was aiming for my throat but I saw it coming and at the last moment I managed to duck. The second slash caught me on the cheek and it opened me right up,' he said brightly. 'There was an awful lot of blood and I had a second mouth for a while until they managed to stitch me up.

'I was quite proud of myself though,' continued Bell. 'After he slashed me, I managed to punch the guy right in the face. I don't know who was more surprised by that; me or him. Most people go down, you see. They clutch their wounds and beg for mercy but they won't get any in here. Not me though.

I just got angry and thumped him. I think it was all the months of stress and carrying this huge feeling of injustice around with me. I was just waiting to take it out on someone. It's funny, I used to spend all that time in the gym just to look fit, but I'd been doing weights for so many years that when I finally put those muscles to good use, I dropped that guy on the spot. It might actually be the single most impressive thing I've ever done. I mean if a criminal attacked me in the street with a knife and I decked him like that they'd run a story in all of the newspapers, wouldn't they?'

'I suppose they would,' Tom conceded.

'But not in here. They ran stories alright, but it was "Ladykiller slashed in face by vengeful inmate", as if the guy actually knew Rebecca. There was no mention of the fact I knocked my attacker senseless. They gave him solitary for that but he didn't give a shit. Lifers,' he added ruefully, 'you just can't control them.' Bell added, 'I don't regret it though.'

'You don't regret hitting him or being slashed open with a razor blade?'

'Either of those things,' Bell said calmly. 'He did me a favour, in fact. Up until that point I'd been sharing a cell with two other men,' he explained. 'After they stitched me up I had a few days in the hospital under crisp white sheets. Then, when they put me back, I got a cell on my own far away from the nut-jobs and gangsters – because they heard there were several people in here still keen to kill me. Rebecca has quite a fan club. Anyway the governor knew he would look very foolish if anything else happened to me.' He pointed to the vivid scar on his face. '*This* made the nationals and he doesn't like newspaper reports that make it seem like he isn't entirely in control of his own prison. So I am also in a form of solitary confinement, for my own safety, which I appreciate.'

'Is that why we are on our own right now?'

Bell nodded. 'My solicitor wanted to sue the arse off them but I persuaded him not to. Let's just say the governor appreciated my discretion. I get certain unspoken privileges as a result; one of them is time alone with you here today, as long as Andrew is in the room with us,' he indicated the prison guard. 'A cell to myself is another – they can't guarantee my safety any other way,' he shrugged. 'I get a little privacy, I feel safer, my cell doesn't stink of other men; every cloud.'

'That's pretty extreme.'

'Well I'm in an extreme situation, Tom,' Bell made a point of looking around the place, 'haven't you noticed? They used to hang people here, you know. Out there in the courtyard; imagine that. The last man to be hanged in Durham jail was a twenty-year-old soldier named Brian Chandler, who killed an old lady . . . with a hammer,' and he widened his eyes ironically at the coincidence. 'I suppose they would have hanged me if Rebecca was killed back in 1958 but, as I keep telling everybody, I didn't do it.'

'You do keep saying that,' said Tom, 'but nobody seems to believe you.'

'My wife believes me,' he said, 'but you're right, nobody else does, despite the fact there is very little evidence against me.'

'Did you study English at college?' Tom changed the subject.

'Business studies, why?'

'I was remembering your letters,' and he quoted from them: '*The poison that drips from the pens of those so-called journalists?*'

'Are you mocking me, Tom?'

'No,' Tom said, 'I'm just noting you have a way with words.' He quoted the other man once more: '*Are you mocking me* not *Are you taking the piss?*' and he looked at Richard Bell intently. 'I wondered if you were a writer in your spare time, that's all.'

Bell shook his head. 'Not a writer, no, but I can appreciate a good turn of phrase and spare time, as you call it, is all I have these days. I chose my words carefully because there was a great deal resting on them. I read a lot. That's the one thing they are pretty good about. They don't mind us having books and I devour them. There really is nothing else to do in here. We are locked up for twenty-three hours a day, so books are all I've got. I read yours in a day. I thought it was exceptional.' Tom ignored the compliment. 'I reckon I could tell a pretty good story, given the chance.'

Tom leaned forward. 'Then why don't you tell me yours.'

Richard Bell began his story with the words, 'I'm trapped. I don't just mean in here. I am trapped in another way. Do you know what is meant by an innocent man's dilemma, Tom?'

'I think so, yes.' But Bell regarded him as if he was a student who had not yet provided a satisfactory answer, so Tom continued, 'You've been sentenced to life in prison for murder but life does not necessarily mean life. You could qualify for parole once you've served around a third of your sentence. Most murderers don't serve their full term. The average is around fifteen years but if a man is of previously good character, if a parole board can be persuaded that he snapped for some reason or was provoked and is highly unlikely to kill again, he could be out in less than ten.'

'That happens to around one in ten convicted murderers,' confirmed Bell. 'They are released back into the community to resume their lives,' he said, 'just like nothing ever happened *but* . . . and it is a very big *but* . . .' He paused and allowed Tom to complete the point.

'The murderer has to admit guilt.'

'Precisely.' Bell nodded his approval at the journalist's knowledge of the legal system. 'To qualify for parole, a prisoner must first confess his crimes. He must show sufficient remorse for the pain and suffering he has caused. He must have paid his debt to society and be fully rehabilitated.' He spread his palms in front of Tom. 'But what if he didn't do it? If he is innocent. What then?'

'He may not wish to admit to a crime he didn't commit, so he will never qualify for parole and must serve his full sentence.'

'Life,' agreed Bell, 'which in my case is twenty-four years, according to the judge. I've done two, so only another twenty-two to go,' he said brightly. 'I'll be fifty-six when I get out of here, assuming I don't conveniently die before then, which is a distinct possibility.'

'But you won't admit guilt?'

Bell shook his head.

'So you're stuck in here.'

'Trapped in an innocent man's dilemma,' and he snorted, 'I'd be treated far better as a self-confessed killer than a man who continues to protest his innocence. Even my lawyers have advised me to say that I did it.'

'Ever cross your mind to take their advice?'

'Why would I? I didn't kill Rebecca.'

'So you say, but your lawyers must have had their reasons for urging you to admit guilt.'

'And those reasons have nothing to do with justice.' When he realised Tom did not understand he grew impatient. 'They don't care whether I'm guilty or not. They just think we have run out of options. The authorities will not allow me to appeal against the guilty verdict or the length of my sentence. There is a lack of evidence to contradict the verdict and the normal sentence for murder is life, with the exact tariff at the judge's discretion, which is then reviewed after a time by the parole board.'

'But you can't qualify for parole,' Tom reminded him, 'unless you admit guilt.'

'Exactly,' said Bell, 'and that's why I had a falling-out with my lawyers. I asked them what my options were and they said, "You don't have any, why not just admit you're guilty and see if you can get parole."' Then Bell pretended to talk casually: '"It's not like you killed a bunch of people, Richard. This was a crime of passion. If you admit it, you'll probably only do nine or ten years in total. You've already served two."' The look on Bell's face said it all. His legal team were morons who did not understand the two years he had already served were a living hell and that seven more would be a lifetime.

'I can understand your reluctance to do that but,' and Tom chose his next words carefully, 'nine years is better than twenty-four. If you don't admit to the killing, the parole board will never recommend you for release. You'll be . . .'

'Officially classed as *In Denial of Murder*,' Bell said. 'I should keep my head down, maybe do an Open University course, develop a sudden interest in God. If I behave like a model prisoner then I could be out of here in another seven years, as long as I take responsibility for my actions and admit my terrible crime. Just say the word and serve a third,' he added dryly, 'but if I continue to maintain my innocence I'll do the full tariff. So let's say I admit to killing Rebecca, hypothetically.'

'Hypothetically,' agreed Tom.

'What then? What happens to me?'

'You serve the rest of your sentence, then leave.'

'Where do I go? What do I do?'

'You go home; assuming your wife will have you. What you do then is up to you.'

'That's where you're very wrong, Tom. It's not up to me. I know Annie would take me back but I'd have no job and no way of getting one. Not many blue-chip companies employ murderers and I don't think my father-in-law could be seen to be taking one back either, even if he felt inclined to.'

'You were his Sales Director?'

Bell nodded. 'Whatever would his clients say?'

'I'm not saying it would be easy . . .'

'Easy? It would be impossible.'

'But . . .' Tom ventured '. . . better than this?'

It was as if Bell hadn't heard him. 'What would I do for the rest of my life? Take walks in the park every day, go to the library, read even more books, then maybe meet my girls from school?' And he chuckled, but without humour. 'Can you imagine the looks in the playground? Let's face it; my life is over as soon as I say I did it.'

'I'm not sure you have an alternative.'

'*You* are my alternative, Tom. I want you to clear my name. I need you to use all of your skills to take a fresh and un-biased look at Rebecca's murder and find out what really happened. The police did a rushed investigation under a great deal of media pressure. As soon as they found out I was seeing Rebecca and had everything to lose if she told on me, they never seriously looked for another suspect. Most people are killed by someone they know so it was all about me from the off. The police were convinced I was their man, the press went for my jugular and the judge bloody hated me. As for the jury, there were a couple of women who looked at me like they wanted to give me a life sentence just for cheating on my wife. There was no one on my side. I need someone to find the truth and that someone is you. When you've uncovered the truth, you can write another book about it, with my blessing. It would be quite a story, wouldn't it? Journalist frees innocent man wrongly imprisoned for murder? You'll have another bestseller on your hands.'

Tom wasn't in the mood to contradict Bell on the sales figures of his book. The last time he'd seen *Death Knock* it was in a bargain bin, covered in large red 'sale' stickers and marked down to £1.99. His publisher's only comment when he had enquired about sales was a rueful, 'It's been a tough year for true crime'.

The publisher had been enthusiastic at first. 'This could launch you!' he gushed, as if front-page leads in national newspapers didn't count for anything. When firstly the book stores then the public failed to share this enthusiasm for the investigation into the murder of Sean Donnellan more than five decades earlier, they quickly lost interest in Tom and the half-promised offer to write a second book somehow failed to materialise.

'I'll be brutally honest with you, Richard, I'm not sure I can afford to spend weeks looking into a cold case on the off chance I find something that might be strong enough to reopen it for you.'

'And I wouldn't expect you to,' Bell said, 'which is why you will be paid.'

'How would that work?'

'My wife has money, enough to give you a weekly retainer while you look into this, with a bonus at the end should you discover fresh evidence strong enough to re-open my case – which you will, because I didn't do it. There will be a further, generous bonus for you when my conviction is finally overturned.' And Bell proceeded to spell out the terms of his offer. The weekly amount alone was extremely tempting to a man in Tom's parlous financial state and the additional bonus at the end, should Richard Bell ever walk free, was the kind of cash injection any hard-up journalist would dream of.

'And your wife is happy with this arrangement?'

'She has agreed to it,' Bell confirmed, though Tom couldn't help feeling this wasn't exactly the same thing.

'You make it sound very easy, but it could take months for me to find something and I may not come up with anything at all.'

'Time is all I have, Tom. I'm not going anywhere. You can work at your own speed. Just keep me posted. If you draw a complete blank we can review things, but I honestly don't think it will come to that. You do have a distinct advantage over the police.'

'Do I?'

'They thought I was guilty. We know I'm not.'

'But I don't know that,' Tom reminded him, 'I could be helping a cold-blooded killer.'

'You could be,' admitted Bell, 'but if you are going into this with an open mind then you may have to give me the benefit of the doubt on that.'

'Particularly if you are paying me.'

'*If* you want to get to the truth,' Bell corrected him.

'Okay but what if I can't find the truth?'

'There is only really one thing I need to get through my days here, Tom, and it's not food, visitors or books.'

'Hope,' said Tom instinctively.

'You see,' said Bell admiringly, 'you're good. I knew you would be.'

'I can usually put myself in the other man's shoes,' said Tom, quietly.

'A useful quality in your profession,' said Bell, 'if I can believe that a man like you; a good man, a clever man, is trying to find out what really happened, then I can go on.' When Tom said nothing in response, Bell's shoulders seemed to sag. 'Look, I'm a realist. I have to be. I know you are busy and I don't expect you to work every hour of every day on it, just take some time to look into it for me; a couple of weeks at least, please? Just a little paid work looking for the truth, until you choose to look no more? Do it for Rebecca, if you won't do it for me.'

'Where would I even start?'

'I'll give you a list of names, everyone that matters. Go and see everybody connected with the case.'

'I'd have go a lot deeper than that.'

'I think I understand a little of the way you go about your work. Did you bring a pen?' Tom reached automatically into his jacket pocket and brought out his pen and a notebook.

'Right,' the guard's voice boomed in the large visiting room, 'wrap this up now.'

'Just a few more minutes,' pleaded Bell, 'we're writing a list . . .'

'No lists, no writing, wrap it up now.' Bell looked like a child who had woken on Christmas morning to find no presents under his tree.

'No lists then,' he conceded, 'but you'll come back tomorrow.' It was more of a statement than a question and when Tom did not look entirely convinced, he added the word, 'Please.'

Chapter Eight

Councillor Jarvis hadn't made an appointment – but then Frank Jarvis didn't need to, not when he simply wanted to see a Detective Chief Inspector, and particularly when he had known that DCI since he was a beat bobby. All the same, Kane was a little perturbed when the politician produced a bottle of Scotch and placed it on the detective's desk.

'Bloody hell, I'm supposed to be driving home,' but he still went to the cabinet in the corner of his office, opened it and produced two glasses.

'Get one of your lads to drop you off,' Jarvis told him. 'There's plenty would be willing to do that small favour for a DCI,' he said, unscrewing the top from the bottle and beginning to pour. 'I'm being picked up later.' And Kane wondered which young member of the local party machine had been singled out for that honour.

'This isn't the bloody seventies,' Kane scolded him half-heartedly as he watched the whisky go into the glasses. 'Can't have detectives getting arseholed in their own offices in the afternoons anymore.'

'One drink isn't going to hurt you and no one can see,' countered Jarvis and he was right. The view into Kane's office was obscured by an ancient set of grubby venetian blinds, permanently blocking the windows.

When the whisky was poured they both raised their glasses to each other and drank silently for a moment while Kane waited for Jarvis to say his piece.

'My wife is struggling,' he told the policeman, 'I mean she's *always* struggled . . .' and he looked away for a moment because that struggle was an embarrassment to him, 'but this . . . this is . . .' and Jarvis turned slightly so that he was facing towards the window '. . . something else entirely.'

'No joy from our friends up north?' asked Kane. They both knew he was referring to Northumbria Police, the force that had led the investigation into the disappearance of the councillor's daughter, Sandra Jarvis, since her whole family was from Newcastle. It was their patch, but Durham Constabulary, DCI Kane's force, had assisted in the hunt for the missing girl from the beginning. She was studying at Durham University when she disappeared so there were lines of enquiry pursued by both forces without any positive outcome.

The rivalry between them was friendly enough for the most part, though officers based in Newcastle tended to view their County Durham counterparts as slightly bumbling, country bumpkins who spent most of their time investigating gentle crimes like vandalism or burglary, whereas their opposite numbers in Durham saw Geordie officers as out-of-control city dwellers, who were only mildly better behaved than the gangsters and drug dealers they were paid to lock up. When it came down to it though, there was a good deal of 'cross-border' cooperation between them, particularly if murder was involved or, as in this case, a disappearance that could have involved foul play.

'There's nothing,' answered Jarvis. 'That new bloke.' And he shook his head dismissively. Kane knew he meant the recently installed Chief Constable, who must have been foolish enough to be less than fully cooperative when Councillor Jarvis came knocking. He was surprised some-one could actually become a Chief Constable without understanding the influence a man like Jarvis held in the region. He might be the *former* head of Newcastle City Council but one word in the right ear could still mean a favour granted, a problem solved. A whisper in another could cause a major problem for a senior police officer with ambition. Simple passive resistance from key politicians round here was enough to derail a promising career on its own. Kane was certain the new guy would soon learn who the real power brokers were in his own back yard.

'I don't know what to say to you, Frank, I really don't. We have tried everything. We've spoken to everyone who had even the vaguest dealings with your daughter.'

'And come up with nothing,' the councillor reminded him sharply, 'which smacks of incompetence.'

Kane's silence was his answer. Jarvis was a man suffering the worst possible grief combined with uncertainty. His daughter had been missing for six months without a word from her or a single confirmed sighting. DCI Kane knew by now that her chances were not good.

Eventually Jarvis sighed, 'I'm sorry. I didn't mean that.'

'I know.'

'It's just . . .'

'I won't say I understand, Frank, because I don't. No one can begin to comprehend how you are feeling but we know you are in a very dark place right now. We are doing all we can, I assure you.'

'So you're leaving no stone unturned? You can look me in the eye and promise me that.'

'We're doing everything in our power to find your daughter.'

'What about things that aren't within your power?'

'How do you mean?' asked Kane.

'I'm just saying there are limits to what you can achieve, given that you are bound by a code of conduct.'

'We're bound by the limits of the law, Frank,' Kane observed, 'that's all. I hope you're not thinking of doing anything foolish.'

'I'm just saying there are lines of enquiry that can't easily be pursued by the police. I'm not suggesting anything dodgy.'

'Not another private eye?' Jarvis shook his head at this. 'I mean, seriously, did he actually give you anything you didn't already have?'

'Apart from his bill?' Jarvis admitted, 'No.'

'Well, then.'

Jarvis didn't seem to want to argue the point so there was a momentary lull in their conversation until he said, 'What about this other fellah you told me about a while back?'

Kane seemed to stiffen at that but simply answered, 'Which one?' while privately regretting he had ever mentioned Tom Carney's name, even in passing, for he realised the bloody reporter was undoubtedly the reason for Jarvis' visit.

'That journalist.'

'That was a very different case, Frank.'

'It was a missing person.'

'It wasn't that simple.'

'But you said he was a real asset.'

That was before he stabbed me in the back, thought Kane, whose opinion of Tom Carney had plummeted since the days immediately following the resolution of the Michelle Summers case. 'Don't go down that route, Frank, I'm begging you.'

'Why not? He's a good investigator, isn't he? You said so yourself.'

'He's also a self-centred, arrogant, egotistical, cage-rattling, pain-in-the-arse.'

'Sounds like he's just the man I'm looking for then.' Jarvis leaned forward and poured another generous measure into Kane's glass.

DI Tennant left her office an hour later and peered out at her team. Her gaze settled on Ian Bradshaw and her eyes narrowed. 'Bradshaw,' she called, 'DCI Kane wants you.'

'DCI Kane wants *me*?' he parroted back at her in surprise. Bollockings from senior officers had been a regular occurrence during Ian Bradshaw's police career but he had hoped that was no longer the case. He'd been keeping his head down and his nose clean as Kane once advised him.

'Yes,' she said curtly, 'he wants you to drive him home.'

This was the cue for some hilarity from the team, including DS Cunningham reciting gleefully, 'Kane and Bradshaw sitting in a tree, K.I.S.S.I.N.G.'

'Fuck off, Cunningham,' might not have been the wittiest answer Bradshaw could have come up with but he offered it anyway. He was troubled now. It wasn't Cunningham's comment that bothered him though or the banter that continued as he was leaving the room, it was the look on DI Tennant's face as she watched him go, as if he'd just farted at the dinner table.

DCI Kane felt quite hammered. Not falling-down-drunk-on-a-night-out-with-the-lads pissed but drunk enough for a school night and certainly in no condition to drive, which was why he had phoned Katie Tennant to commandeer Bradshaw. It made obvious sense for him to kill two birds with one stone.

Katie had asked him why he needed to speak to one of her officers and his first reaction had been to tell her to mind her own bloody business but he bit his tongue. She was one of the new generation, he supposed, trained to use their initiative, not blindly follow orders like he had been. He would never have dreamed of questioning a senior officer. It wasn't the way to get ahead.

Had he been entirely sober he might have said, 'I'd like a word with him,' but because of the whisky he'd been a little too honest and said, 'I need him to drive me home,' and by the time he'd realised that was probably not the most impressive thing he could have told his subordinate, it was too late.

'I see,' she clearly wasn't impressed, 'I'll send him over.'

He was glad he had the Polo mints. God knows how long they'd been in his drawer but he didn't care about that now. He shovelled four into his mouth and crunched on them, managing to swallow all of the minty fragments before Bradshaw showed up at his door.

'Ah, Bradshaw,' he said, 'good lad. My car's playing up and I wanted a word with you anyway. Be a good man and give me a lift home then you can knock off, eh?' he said brightly. 'After we've had our chat.'

'Yes, sir,' said Bradshaw, who was still baffled as to why he had been summoned to act as his DCI's taxi driver, though he did at least understand the reason why Kane wouldn't be driving himself home. He noticed his boss discreetly palm a packet of Polos into his jacket pocket and there were two empty, recently rinsed glasses on a nearby cabinet. There was something solid wrapped in an old carrier bag that had been placed in the waste paper basket too, which could have been an empty spirit bottle. Bradshaw supposed he should be grateful there were two glasses.

'Let's get going then.' Kane put the palm of one hand firmly against Bradshaw's shoulder as he steered the detective sergeant to the door and Bradshaw got a strong whiff of mints as they left the office.

Katie Tennant was fuming. She normally had an 'open-door' policy but not that afternoon. Now her door was very firmly shut against an unfair world. God help anybody who tried to disturb her before this day was through.

Durham Constabulary's solitary female DI should have seen it coming. She half expected there'd be a spy in the camp, reporting back to DCI Kane on her competence and fitness for leadership but she hadn't expected Kane to be so bloody blatant about it.

He hadn't liked it when she bridled then asked him why he needed to see one of her team so he had invented some bullshit story about needing a lift home. There was something else that was bothering her about the whole thing: Bradshaw. She'd actually thought he might be different, that he could, quite possibly, be one of the good ones and Lord knows there weren't many of them. Well, at least now she knew differently.

In the morning she would challenge Bradshaw, maybe even ask him outright if he was Kane's spy and see if that put the wind up him. If he wavered for an instant, she would never trust him again.

Chapter Nine

'Working late again, I see.' The words were spoken like a reprimand, as Graham Seaton surveyed the rows of empty desks in the newsroom but, as usual, there was a smile behind her editor's eyes. 'Aint you got a home to go to?'

'So are you,' Helen reminded him, 'working late I mean – and you do have a home to go to.' Graham was married with children, not returning to an empty one-bedroom flat like she was.

'I'm planning on being there very soon and I didn't put the hours in that you do when I was your age.' This sounded funny, coming from her relatively youthful boss. Graham was still in his early thirties, which was very young for an editor on a daily.

'I bet you did.'

'Mmm, well maybe,' he admitted, 'but back then I was keen,' he was heading back to his office, 'not a cynical, clapped-out old veteran who never gets out of the newsroom anymore.'

'I wouldn't say you never get out of the newsroom.'

'Oi, watch it, Norton,' he grinned back at her, 'or I'll transfer you to the obituary page.'

'Then who would get you all your exclusive crime stories?' she asked. 'You know you'd be lost without me.'

He pretended to ponder this for a while. 'Maybe I would be.' And their eyes locked for a moment. 'Don't stay too late though,' and he disappeared into his office.

Oh God, did she just flirt with her boss? Was that flirting or was it blokeish banter? There was no innuendo; but maybe it wasn't what she said, but the way she said it. Her editor was good-looking, but it wasn't just that. What really made him attractive was how damned capable he was. Helen felt she was learning something new every day here and the six months she had been in the job had flown by. Graham was such a contrast to her old editor on the *Durham Messenger*. Malcolm had been lazy, and sleazy with it, which was never a winning combination. After that experience anyone would have been an improvement but Graham had trusted her from day one, despite her lack of experience, handing her plum assignments and letting Helen follow her own judgement. He provided wise counsel to ensure she didn't drift into territory that could prove ruinously expensive for the newspaper if somebody sued but he was never less than encouraging. Now she actually had a boss who behaved like she always imagined a newspaper editor should.

He was also married with kids, she reminded herself again, but even if he hadn't been, Helen Norton was in a relationship; a long-standing and committed relationship she almost jeopardised once before by becoming too close to a colleague and she told herself she was never going to allow that to happen again.

There was no one else in the newsroom and the light from her editor's open office door was enticing. More than once she had gone to see him at the end of the day with a question about a story. He would answer in his usual, unhurried manner and this often lead to a more general chat until they both realised time was getting on. She glanced towards that open door again now and found herself thinking of an excuse to knock on it.

That would be a bad idea.

Helen decided to take her editor's advice and go home.

'Do you know Frank Jarvis?' asked Kane as Bradshaw steered his car through the traffic.

'The politician? Of course,' answered Bradshaw, 'though I've never actually met him.' Bradshaw had followed up leads on the councillor's missing daughter but hadn't played a major role in the investigation. Later, when he was assigned to the burned girl case, Sandra Jarvis had been one of the first possibles but thankfully she was much taller than the murdered female.

'I need a favour from you,' Kane said as Bradshaw drove them out of the city, windscreen wipers working overtime against rain that had shown no sign of abating all afternoon. He must have seen something in Bradshaw's face. 'It's nothing dodgy, so don't get your knickers in a twist, Bradshaw. I'd hardly be asking *you* if it was, would I?'

'No, sir,' answered Bradshaw, even though the question was more than likely rhetorical and the accompanying compliment hugely backhanded.

'You're like bloody Florence Nightingale.' The DCI realised he had probably said far too much. He wound down the car window for some air, despite the rain. 'That journalist friend of yours,' he began.

'Which one?'

'You know which one; Tom-bloody-Carney.'

'I haven't seen him in ages, sir,' said Bradshaw, 'not since . . .' And he wanted to say *not since he blotted his copy book with us* but left the sentence incomplete. The last thing he wanted Kane to think was that he'd carried on a cosy little friendship with someone considered *persona non grata* by Durham Constabulary.

'You don't meet up with him now and again?'

'God, no,' protested Bradshaw and he began to wonder just what he was going to be accused of. 'We cooperated on the Michelle Summers case . . .' Was *cooperated* too controversial a word? 'I was at school with him but we were in different years . . .'

'Not even for a quick pint,' Kane persisted and Bradshaw wondered how he knew that, 'from time to time?'

Bradshaw sought refuge in a semblance of the truth. 'I haven't bumped into him in a while. He was a useful source of information for a bit but after that article . . .'

'Yes,' Kane seemed to sigh inwardly, '*that* article.' And his brow creased at the recollection. 'So you're not exactly best mates then?'

'No, sir,' he answered quickly, 'barely on nodding terms these days.' He hoped that was enough to get him off the hook. Tom Carney had obviously capitalised on a leak from somewhere but it had nothing to do with Bradshaw and he certainly wasn't going to take the rap for it.

'Pity,' said Kane.

'What?'

'I was hoping you did,' Kane explained, 'meet up with him that is.'

Bradshaw was baffled. All he wanted to do was distance himself from the accusation that he had been fraternising with Kane's least favourite journalist but now the DCI seemed disappointed.

'Could you, do you think?' asked Kane quietly.

'Sir?'

'Take him for that pint and have a little chat, if I asked you to?'

'Well, I could get in touch if that's really what you want me to do?'

'It is.'

There was a gap in the conversation while Bradshaw took this on board and Kane failed to enlighten him further. Finally the Detective Sergeant asked, 'What do you want me to say to him?'

'I've got a proposition for our Tom Carney.'

Outside, the evening air was crisp and Helen buttoned her coat as she walked across the car park. There were only a handful of cars left but Helen liked her job and often found herself staying late. When she got the call informing her that her application to join the newspaper had been successful she had moved to Newcastle as soon as her notice would allow, leaving the *Durham Messenger* with Malcolm's words ringing in her ears, 'The grass isn't always greener you know,' while neglecting to add any thanks for her hard work on his newspaper. Helen knew she would never be forgiven for leaving the place. It was as if ambition was a dirty word there and her departure some form of calculated snub.

Perhaps she should have spent more time looking for a flat though. Her place in Newcastle was tiny and more than a little depressing, another reason she was never in any hurry to go home.

She noticed the two young men then. They were crossing the car park from the opposite direction as if heading towards the newspaper's offices but they didn't look like cleaners or security men. They were both too young and dressed too casually for that. They were doing that lazy, exaggerated shoulder-rolling walk, trying to look like gangsters. Helen knew it was a form of prejudice to be immediately distrustful of young people but she couldn't help wondering if they were there to break into cars. She kept her eye on them both as they drew nearer but avoided directly crossing their path. Thankfully they showed no interest in her, staring straight ahead as they swaggered up the centre of the car park.

Helen was glad of this. More often than not, when she encountered youths like these two they felt the need to verbally abuse her. Young women were routinely heckled on the street in a way men rarely encountered and seldom understood; receiving judgemental comments about looks, figure or dress. Helen had been called a slut and a whore then, in the same breath, a frigid bitch for ignoring the abuse she was receiving. She wasn't sure how she could be both of those things.

So why wasn't she grateful that these two rough-looking young men were ignoring her?

Because something didn't seem right.

Despite her suspicions, she wasn't expecting what happened next. As they drew alongside Helen, the furthest from her suddenly nudged his friend hard with his shoulder, which sent the other man stumbling towards her at speed. It was a deliberate act and his friend used the shoulder barge as an excuse to collide with Helen, knocking her off her feet and sending her crashing to the ground. Helen hit the cement hard and narrowly avoided striking her head against the nearest car. Her handbag slipped from her arm and bounced onto the floor, upending itself and spilling its contents in the process.

Before she could react the thug who clattered into Helen was already standing over her. 'What the fuck do you think you're doing!' he roared.

'Watch where you're going, you slag!' the second man bawled and she rolled over to face them, turning to look up into two twisted, hate-filled faces. She could feel the rawness on one knee where it had scraped against the cement as she fell and the palms of her hands were sore from the impact as she tried to protect herself.

'Get away from me,' Helen demanded, her voice wavering as she tried to climb to her feet.

'Who do you think you are, bitch?' And the man who knocked her to the ground leant in close as she got to her feet. She could smell his breath, rank with the stale smell of beer and cigarettes. The second man closed in on her and Helen began to fear they would attack or even try to rape her here in the car park. She was looking around for anyone who might be able to help her but there was no one. She could run but wouldn't be able to get far with two young men in trainers chasing her. She'd never be able to reach her car.

When the second man spoke, she instantly understood why they were here. 'That'll teach you to stick your nose in.' This wasn't some random assault on the first young woman they found. These thugs had actually targeted her because of the stories she had been writing. They'd been waiting for her to come out of the newsroom and now she really was frightened.

'Oi!' The male voice was deep and angry. 'Get away from her!' It was Graham and she had never been happier to hear him. He was standing on the office steps some distance away. Her editor started to march towards them and she prayed they would think they'd done enough and melt away. Graham hadn't hesitated to come to her aid but could he really fight them both off? They looked like the kind of young men who were used to violence.

71

'You've been warned,' the second man told her, 'it won't happen twice.' Then he shoved Helen violently. She shot backwards and fell hard against the bonnet of the nearest car, pain shooting through her spine.

Both men took off at a casual jog as Graham ran towards her. She was vaguely aware of them laughing, swearing and turning back to mock the older man, giving Graham the finger. Sensibly he did not pursue them, deciding instead to halt by her side. They ran from the car park then, whooping excitedly at a job well done before they vanished into the night.

'I'm alright,' she told her editor, 'I'm alright.'

Graham took one look at her, his face all concern. 'No Helen, you're not.' Then he bent low and deftly scooped the spilled contents back into her handbag, handed it to her and said, 'You're not alright. Come on.'

Graham took her back into the newsroom, sat her at her desk and disappeared for a moment to the tiny kitchen area, which was little more than a fridge for sandwiches and a vending machine next to a row of cupboards. She heard a cupboard door open then close and this was followed by the sound of a tap running. Graham returned, bent to examine her knee then gently pressed a wet cloth against it. 'Does it hurt?' he asked.

'A little,' she said though in truth it hurt like hell. As well as the sting of the cloth against broken skin, she could feel her whole knee beginning to stiffen as it swelled.

'Who the hell were they?' Graham was gently attempting to clean her knee without hurting her and although it felt strange to be sitting alone in the darkened newsroom with her editor while he sat on the floor and tended to her like this, his concern was touching.

'A couple of morons,' she said dismissively. Although it was tempting to tell him the truth; that they had been sent to warn her off, she couldn't afford to be sidelined by a well-meaning editor trying to protect her.

'What did they say to you?' He looked up as he asked this.

'Nothing but abuse,' she told him. 'I'd rather not repeat all of the words, if you don't mind.'

'So you'd never seen them before?'

'Never,' she replied honestly.

'And they didn't know you,' he said it almost to himself and she decided to treat the question as if it didn't need an answer, 'so I guess you were just unlucky.' And then he got to his feet. 'All clean,' he said. 'We should call the police now.'

'Oh no, really, let's not,' she urged him. 'What's the point?' she had already lied to her editor by omission and didn't want to compound the sin by misleading the police as well. 'It was dark and I could barely describe them. The last thing I need right now is a few fruitless hours down the police station.'

At first it looked as if he was about to argue the point. 'I'm fine,' she said firmly, 'really.'

'Okay,' he said uncertainly, 'if you're sure?'

Helen got to her feet then and instantly regretted it, crying out in pain. He grabbed her as her knee gave way and helped her stand straight again. 'I'm alright,' she said but he did not let go of her arm. Instead he steered her to the door, supporting her as they went. 'I'll drive you home,' he said. 'Your car will be fine here overnight and I'll pick you up again in the morning.'

'That will set tongues wagging,' she told him.

'I don't mind if you don't.'

'I don't,' she told him.

Chapter Ten

As he drove into the prison, Tom Carney knew deep down he was kidding himself. This was a one-off job, he had reasoned, which would probably only last for a week or two but it didn't mean he was back in journalism and he certainly wouldn't be writing another book. Financially, it made sense at a time when he desperately needed an injection of cash and he absolutely wasn't giving up on the house renovation. Perhaps now he would be able to afford to get someone in to help him finish some of the trickier jobs.

The one thing he didn't admit was the truth. Tom was experiencing something he had not felt for some time: a surge of excitement. He was intrigued by the Rebecca Holt case. Tom was convinced there were secrets here, and he wanted to be the one to uncover them.

'What do you think of me, Tom?' Richard Bell asked abruptly as soon as they were seated in the visiting room. 'Be honest.'

'Think of you?'

'I'm sure you've done your homework and we spent time together. What impression did you form of me?'

'I'm not sure, yet.'

'Do I look like a murderer?' Bell probed.

'Very few people look like murderers.'

'Strike that then. Do you *think* I am a murderer?'

'I honestly don't know, Richard.'

Perhaps he had hoped for more. 'Well, at least we are on first-name terms.'

'You *are* capable of violence though,' Tom reminded him.

'I was attacked,' Bell protested. 'It was self-defence.'

'I don't mean in here. I'm talking about the ex-girlfriend.'

'That was years ago. Christ, we were kids.'

'You were twenty.'

'Don't you remember what it was like to be that age?'

'I never punched a woman.'

'It was a slap,' Bell replied, 'not a punch, and I'm not proud of it either way.'

'It did you some damage in court.'

'Look, it was a very long time ago and I got run ragged by the girl in question. I lashed out and I have regretted it ever since. Ask Mark . . .'

'Your best man? The character witness that didn't work out the way you intended?'

'That wasn't his fault,' said Bell, 'the prosecution lawyer tied him up in knots, but he'll tell you the truth. What happened with Amy doesn't make me a murderer.'

'I won't lie to you,' Tom said, 'I could look into this case for you but I won't sugar-coat what I find.'

'I did not kill Rebecca Holt. I did not beat a woman I cared for over the head with a claw hammer. I know that saying it out loud won't make you believe me but I will not give in until I have cleared my name.'

'Who said it was a claw hammer?' asked Tom, fixing his gaze on Bell.

'Well,' was there a slight stammer in his reply, 'the prosecution had an expert witness . . .'

'He said it was a blunt instrument.'

'Which was most likely a hammer,' Bell corrected him firmly, 'because of the dimensions of the impact marks on Rebecca's skull.'

'A hammer yes but he didn't say it was a claw hammer.'

'Do you own a hammer, Tom?'

'Of course.'

'Usually they have a flat bit at one end of the head to bang in nails and a claw at the other end to pull them out again,' and he looked Tom right in the eye, 'hence my use of the words, *claw hammer.*'

'Okay,' said Tom, letting it go, 'so you were saying . . . about wanting to clear your name.'

'Freedom without exoneration is meaningless to me. How can I look my daughters in the eye and tell them their daddy is a killer,' Richard asked, 'or try to explain that he isn't but had to admit to being one just so he could get out of jail?'

'I understand.'

'Do you? I seriously doubt that. It's not as if saying it would even change anything. I'd still be in here with no hope of release for years. What are you planning for the next five years, Tom; meet a girl, settle down, have some kids, get a home, a better job maybe with nicer prospects? That's what people usually do. They try to improve their lives. All of that is on hold for me until this nightmare is over. No women, no booze, shit food, nothing to look forward to. What do you think most people would say if they knew what my life was really like?'

'That you deserved it,' offered Tom, 'for killing Rebecca.'

'Yes,' he admitted, 'you're right. I think that's exactly what most of them would say – but I did not kill Rebecca. You've got to believe me.'

'No, I don't,' Tom told him, 'I don't have to do anything,'

and before Bell could contradict that he added, 'but I've decided I will look into your case. I'll do some digging and I'll see if I can come up with something new and, with permission, I'll speak to your nearest and dearest to see if they can shed some new light on the events of that day – but you won't be able to control my opinions or conclusions and you might not like what I find,' warned Tom. 'If it's something about Rebecca that you didn't know or I discover the real reason she was killed . . .'

'Tom, I assure you I can live with anything if the alternative is to stay in here for the rest of my life.'

'And what if all the evidence I uncover still points to you?'

'Then I'll be no worse off but I have every faith you will find the real killer.'

'How do you want to play this? Do I keep visiting you here with updates?'

'The governor isn't too keen on that idea.'

'Why not?'

'Because he knows that sooner or later one of his guards will sell the story to the newspapers.'

'What story?'

'Journalist reopens Rebecca Holt murder case,' Bell explained. 'You can keep my wife informed. Annie visits regularly and this way nobody will ever know you are working with us.'

Tom liked the sound of that. Working for a convicted murderer wasn't something he was keen to include on his CV. 'I still have a lot of questions.'

'Then you'd better ask them.'

She'd asked for a couple of days off and Graham said she'd earned them. He'd told Helen it might be a good idea to keep her head down anyway following the incident which, in the

77

cold light of day, Helen was able to shrug off, particularly as the damage to her knee was less serious than she first thought. Aside from painful stiffness when she went up and down stairs, it was already on the mend. The time off was to accommodate her boyfriend, who had been granted a couple of free days by his father in return for all the hard work he had put in lately at the family business – a small chain of carpet stores in Surrey that Peter had been wholly dismissive of when they first met. He was not going to work for the old man, Peter had told her firmly. He was going to start up his own business. She had believed him.

A year after graduation, reality set in and Peter told her he was going to work for the business after all. It seemed the prospect of entry-level jobs while he saved up and planned his own venture was not that appealing. 'This way I get proper hands-on experience before branching out on my own,' he'd enthused. A few years down the line and Peter no longer talked about his own dreams, only the intricacies of the carpet retailing business he was being groomed to take over, and Helen no longer asked about them.

They were walking down by the river together. A bracing breeze travelled along the Tyne towards them. 'Isn't it a beautiful city?' she remarked about her adopted home.

Her boyfriend snorted, 'What's beautiful about it? Half of it's a building site.'

'They're regenerating the place. When it's done it will look amazing. They are going to build a massive concert hall on the banks of the Tyne and they reckon they can get funding from that new lottery. They're going to convert the Baltic Flour Mill,' she pointed across the river to the imposing old building, 'into an art gallery.' When Peter offered no further thoughts, she continued, 'Of course, that will take years . . .'

'If it ever gets beyond the planning stage.'

'But when it's done it will be fantastic. Anyway I still think it's beautiful, down here by the river beneath the bridges.' And she did. As well as the famous Tyne Bridge there was Robert Stephenson's High Level Bridge, a wrought-iron engineering miracle that still supported both road traffic and the trains from the railway in a single, two-tier construction, which had spanned the river since the days of Queen Victoria. She was about to tell him this was the bridge they used in *Get Carter*, but he might ask her how she knew that and it had been Tom Carney who told her, as they had raced over it on the way back from seeing the key surviving witness in the Sean Donnellan case. Peter didn't like her mentioning Tom. He wasn't jealous, he told her, he just didn't like her 'banging on' about the guys she worked with and anyway, Peter wasn't looking at the bridges. He was frowning at some young girls in short skirts who were laughing raucously on their way to a pub.

'Does anyone *ever* wear a coat round here?'

She wondered if he was going to say they would all probably catch their deaths. When she didn't immediately answer him, Peter turned to look at her as if he'd been slighted somehow. 'Just because I don't find this northern outpost at the end of the known universe beautiful,' he was doing his exaggerated I-was-only-joking voice with accompanying winning smile, the one that had worked on her the night they first met in the bar of their student union, 'doesn't mean I'm not happy to be here. *It* might not be beautiful but *you* are.' He put his hands on her waist then kissed her on the forehead, which she supposed was sweet but it did have the effect of making her feel like a little girl being counselled by a man who considered himself older and wiser, even though they were the same age.

'I'm also bloody freezing,' he told her then he shivered melodramatically, 'so can we *please* find a pub or something?' He was still talking in that breezy manner, as if everything was just too silly to get upset about. 'You know, one without sawdust on the floor.'

She wanted to say she had never been to a pub in Newcastle with sawdust on its floor but Helen knew he would sigh and say, 'I was *joking*,' before going into one of his sulks, so she agreed to go for a drink, since that was easier than an argument, even though their walk had barely lasted a hundred yards along the river bank.

As she headed for the pub she found herself wondering whether Tom Carney would have wimped out of a bracing autumn walk like that. No, she thought, he wouldn't, but he would probably have been just as dismissive of Helen's romantic view of its post-industrial landscape, with its cranes and heavy girders in perpetual motion on the south side of the river. Tom was like a lot of people she'd met since she'd moved up here: fiercely defensive of the north-east to outsiders but just as likely to do the place down amongst themselves for its lack of opportunities. Absent-mindedly, Helen found herself wondering what Tom Carney was doing right now.

Chapter Eleven

'When the police first questioned you, you denied you were having an affair with Rebecca Holt.'

'Yes,' admitted Bell and Tom waited for an explanation. 'Well you would, wouldn't you? I panicked. At that point I thought I was only putting my marriage in jeopardy but denying it at the beginning made me look bad later when it was mentioned in court. I understand that now. The prosecution made it sound like I was an effortless liar who wasn't even upset to learn the news of Rebeca's death.'

'And were you?' Tom said. 'Upset, I mean?'

'Of course!' Bell said. 'I couldn't believe what I was hearing. I cared for Rebecca deeply, and when the police told me she'd been killed, well, it was a complete shock.'

'What did they say?'

'That Rebecca's body had been found in her car. That it was parked in a lovers' lane and she had been murdered.'

'Did they say how she'd been killed?'

'Not at first but I asked them.'

'And what did they say?

'With a blunt instrument.'

'How did you feel when you heard that?'

'How do you think I felt?' Bell snapped.

'I have no idea,' said Tom calmly. 'Maybe you were shocked and completely devastated or perhaps you were worried the police thought you'd done it. Possibly you were panicking because you didn't want your wife to find out about your secret lover, maybe you were worrying about everything you could lose: the job, the money, the house, the family. I don't know, Richard, because I don't know you. That's the point and it's why I'm asking these questions . . . and if you want me to help you then you really should consider answering them.'

Richard Bell held up a hand to placate Tom. 'I'm sorry, you're right, you don't know me or anything about me apart from what I've told you and the stuff you read about in the newspapers.' He was quiet then and seemed to be recalling the moment when the police knocked on his door. Eventually he spoke: 'It was like someone had punched me in the guts. I remember having to make a conscious effort of will just to stay standing and not crumple to the ground in front of them.'

'Did they question you right there on the doorstep?'

'Pretty much; they asked me about my relationship with the victim. I told them we were friends who had met at the sports club. They then asked me if we were *just* friends and I assured them we were.' And he shook his head, 'I didn't know they already knew. Otherwise . . .' Richard shrugged.

'You would have confessed to the relationship?'

'Yes, of course – but at that point I was still hoping it wouldn't all come out. I was in damage limitation mode.'

'How did they know?'

'One of my notes,' he answered. 'Rebecca stuffed it into the glove compartment. She must have forgotten to destroy it. Obviously they found it straight away. I don't think the police ever seriously looked beyond me as a line of enquiry from that day to this.'

'Why not?'

'I don't know,' and when Tom looked unconvinced, 'I really don't. You'd have to ask them. I honestly can't think why they would assume I'd killed Rebecca and not her husband say or some random nutcase.'

'Oh yes, the nutcase theory,' said Tom.

'Why do you say it like that?'

Tom quoted from Bell's letter: *'He's still out there, waiting to do it again.'*

'Got your attention, didn't it?' Bell smiled grimly.

'That the only reason you wrote it in your letter?' asked Tom. 'To get me out here?'

'There have been reports of a man roaming the area near the lovers' lane for years. Numerous incidents have been attributed to that man or possibly several men. The police don't know if it is the same person and it is a wide stretch of land, which is why people meet there for . . .'

'Sex?'

'I was going to say *privacy*,' Bell replied, 'but yes, if you are going to have sex with someone in a car then Lonely Lane is as good a place as any.'

'Back when I was a teenager it was known as "Shaggers' Alley".'

'With some justification,' conceded Bell. 'The lane stretches for miles across fields between two arterial roads, with deep woods on both sides. That combination is always going to attract lovers, plus all manner of sleazy individuals. It was only when we got into the case against me that we discovered there were guys out there doing all sorts of things in the woods and fields surrounding the lane.'

'What kind of things?'

'Voyeurism, for starters,' he began. 'One guy was arrested with a camera and a zoom lens. He'd been taking photos of people having sex in their cars. They don't know if he was a blackmailer or just an old-fashioned pervert. Most people have no idea what goes on in the woods. I certainly didn't know. There's been more than one rapist,' Bell told him, 'some have been caught and some haven't. It's the ones that haven't you should be looking for.'

'But Rebecca Holt wasn't raped,' Tom reminded Bell.

'No,' said Bell, 'she was beaten to death by a madman,' and he looked Tom directly in the eye.

'Okay,' said Tom, 'let's say it wasn't you and it wasn't a madman. Who else could it be?'

'Her husband,' said Bell without hesitation. 'I'm serious. Who had the biggest motivation? If he found out about us . . .'

'Perhaps,' agreed Tom, 'but why didn't he kill you instead?'

'I don't know. Because I can fight back? Perhaps he didn't fancy his chances against another man. Maybe he just couldn't bear the thought of his property being handled by someone else so he had to destroy it.'

'His property?' repeated Tom. '*It?*'

'That was the way he viewed her,' said Bell.

'She told you this?'

'In so many words.' And when Tom looked unconvinced Richard added, 'She didn't have to tell me explicitly but she mentioned things.'

'What kind of things?'

'He was jealous and possessive,' said Richard.

'Sounds like he had cause to be.'

'Not from day one.'

'So he drove her to it?'

'He didn't like her going out on her own. He didn't want her to have friends at all. He'd complain if she dressed nice when she went somewhere without him or if she wore something too revealing when he was with her. He once told her all he wanted to do was keep her in a box. He thought *that* was a compliment.'

'Okay,' said Tom, 'I'll look into it.'

'You'll speak to her husband?'

'Yes.'

'Then be careful. Tell people you're going to see him then make sure he knows you told them. I don't want to read about you being washed up on the banks of the Tyne.'

'That's not going to happen.'

'Freddie Holt is a very ruthless man who does not like to be crossed,' said Bell. 'He had some union problems once, a long time ago. He made them go away.'

'How?'

'The old-fashioned way, using big guys with pickaxe handles.'

'How do you know this?'

'Everybody knows it. I'm surprised you've not heard the stories.'

'I've not,' Tom admitted, 'but I'll check them out.' And he thought for a moment. 'If he's the kind of man who sends men with pickaxe handles after his enemies, wouldn't he do the same to you if he found out you were shagging his wife?'

'I've thought about that. If he knew I was having sex with Rebecca behind his back he might have been tempted to break every bone in my body,' said Bell, 'but bones heal and this kind of punishment lasts a lifetime, quite literally.'

'Are you actually saying he framed you?'

'I'm saying it's a possibility. I don't know but it certainly suited him, didn't it? He got rid of an unfaithful wife without having to pay her a penny in alimony and had his revenge against her lover at the same time. I'd say that was a bit of a result, wouldn't you?'

'Assuming he didn't love his wife,' said Tom.

'It wasn't what I would call love,' Bell assured him.

'Explain the dead-letter drop to me,' said Tom. 'Why go to all that trouble?'

'It might sound like a lot of trouble,' said Bell, 'but I couldn't phone Rebecca at her house because I never knew when her husband would be around. There are only so many times you can say "Sorry, wrong number." She didn't own a mobile phone. Why would she need one? Rebecca was basically a housewife. She could hardly justify asking him for a mobile when she didn't have any cause to use one, except to go behind his back with somebody. He would have suspected her straight away. He didn't keep regular hours like normal guys. Sometimes he was away for days at a time or he'd show up suddenly without warning. We wondered if he did that just to test her. If she was at home when he came back then fine, but if she was out, she'd get the third degree; *Where had she been and who was she with?* If she was alone, which stores did she go to, if she was with friends who were they, if they went to lunch together what did everybody have? It used to drive her crazy, he was so controlling and he never trusted her.'

'So you used your dead-letter drop to arrange meetings down Lonely Lane.'

'Yes, but I didn't arrange to meet her that day.'

'Then why would she go there?'

'I don't know.'

'Was she seeing someone else?'

'God, no.'

'You're certain about that?' Bell nodded. 'And you definitely didn't arrange a meeting for the day she was murdered?'

'Positive. I wouldn't forget a meeting with her. They took some setting up for one thing and . . .'

'Go on.'

'Well, they were memorable.'

'Because of the sex?'

'Yes,' Bell answered defiantly, 'but not just that. We had a connection.'

'Did you love her?'

'Rebecca?'

Tom nodded. 'It's a legitimate question. I'm not just being nosey.'

'I suppose I did.'

'You suppose you did?'

'I'm not sure I know what that word means. I'm not convinced I ever did. There were times when I was meeting Rebecca and I would be so excited I could actually feel my heart beating in my chest – but is that love or was it lust? Then afterwards I'd be driving away from her, feeling completely content except for wondering when I would be able to see her next. Is that love? Perhaps it is.'

'And did she love you?'

There was no hesitation this time. 'Yes.'

'She said so?'

'She used the word.'

'And did you use the word?'

'Is this relevant?'

'I don't know yet – but I suspect I may have to ask you far more embarrassing questions than this before we are through, so why don't you just answer?'

'No, yes, in a way.' And he sighed, 'I used to routinely answer "Me too" or "So do I" and on occasion maybe "Love you too."'

'But you'd say it quick, like you were making light of it?'

'Perhaps,' he admitted.

'Women notice that kind of thing,' Tom told him.

'I know,' answered Bell, 'I understand women, believe me. I just always associated the word *love* with something permanent and I didn't see how we could ever be a permanent thing.'

'Why not? I'm serious. If she loved you, she could have left her husband and you could have asked your wife for a divorce.'

'You make it sound very simple.'

'It could have been.'

Bell shook his head. 'What would we live off; fresh air? If I tried to divorce Annie I'd be out of a job like that,' and he clicked his fingers. 'If Rebecca left her old man he'd tangle her up with lawyers for years. He has money squirreled away all over the place, some in bank accounts in Jersey, property abroad, that kind of thing.'

'You still could have done it though,' Tom persisted, 'made a clean break, started somewhere else, if you really wanted to.'

'Yeah, well, perhaps we were just lazy then.' His voice softened. 'And I had the girls to think about.'

'And how do you feel about them?' asked Tom. 'Your girls, I mean.'

His reply was instant. 'I love them more than life.' Tom decided not to pursue Bell further on that.

'Wasn't it all a bit elaborate though?' he asked instead. 'Leaving messages for each other in a wall?'

'I could hardly write letters to her or leave notes next to the frozen peas in her local supermarket.'

'But you used to see her down the sports club?'

'That's how we met, but I was never really alone with her there. There's always someone around. If a married woman is seen at the bar or on a tennis court more than once with the same guy everybody just assumes they are screwing. They love a bit of gossip down there. They have money, they don't work and they're bored. They love to catch someone doing something they shouldn't.'

'What made you think of it?'

'You can blame Annie for that. She bought me a spy novel for Christmas. The hero had to contact his agent in a hostile country, so they worked out a dead-letter drop. Basically you write a note then find a place to leave it but it has to be somewhere no one else is likely to stumble on by accident. There were loads of loose stones in the walls around the fields. I just had to mark one so Rebecca could find it. I got one of those tester pots and put a small splash of white paint on the stone then left my first note behind it when I put it back. It was easy.'

'How did Rebecca know when to collect it?'

'Up until that point we were trying to see each other every two or three days at the same time in the same place, but half the time it didn't happen. If her husband was home or if Annie's old man called a client meeting I couldn't get out of, one of us would be left sitting there, so I promised I'd find a better way. Every morning on my way to work I'd pull over for a couple of minutes, scribble a note to Rebecca and leave it behind the stone in the wall. Sometimes it would say I could see her that day and what time, or at least I was able to tell her I couldn't make it.

'Rebecca would go out later that morning, pick up my message and leave one for me. I'd nip out in my lunch hour or on my way somewhere and pick up her reply. Sometimes it confirmed our appointment, sometimes she said she couldn't do it, which was always disappointing but at least I would know and I wouldn't waste my time hanging around waiting for her.'

'Was that all you wrote? Just times to meet up?'

'At first, but sometimes we would leave letters for each other. Rebecca started that.'

'What was in the letters?'

'Just, you know, how we felt about one another, how we

wished we could be together and not trapped with other people. It was our way of keeping the flame burning when we couldn't see each other.'

'But you both destroyed these letters?'

'Of course.'

'Except the one Rebecca left in the glove compartment,' he reminded Bell. 'Must have been stressful though, all that sneaking around.'

'It was but you know what; it was exciting too. We were creeping round like a couple of teenagers whose parents didn't approve of us being together. Like it was us against the world, you know. It was part of the game.'

'I get it,' Tom told him, 'so what happened on the day she was murdered?'

'I don't know,' Bell told him, 'we weren't meeting up that day. She wasn't supposed to be there.'

'That's the bit I'm struggling to understand,' Tom told him. 'If you were saying she was killed by some passing maniac, that she was somehow in the wrong place at the wrong time and that you got there five minutes later then frankly even that would be pretty hard to swallow but it would be more believable than your story.'

'It's not a story, Tom,' said Bell, 'it's the truth.'

'Then what was she doing there if you didn't arrange it? Did anybody else know about the dead-letter drop?'

'No.'

'You're sure about that?'

Bell nodded. 'I was very careful. There was never anyone around when I put the letter in the wall. No one else knew about it unless . . .'

'Unless what?'

'Rebecca told them about it.'

'And why would she?'

'She wouldn't,' Bell said. 'I've thought about it a lot. Even if for some inexplicable reason Rebecca wanted to tell a friend about it, if she felt the need to boast or confess or ask for advice, there would be no reason to reveal the exact location of our messages, would there?'

'No,' agreed Tom, 'there wouldn't, which leaves you with a problem and a big gap in your story. If this was the only way you communicated with one another, apart from the times you were physically together, then why did she go to your usual spot that day if you didn't summon her?'

'I don't know,' Bell admitted.

'Could she have got the day or the time wrong?'

'Maybe. I wish I knew, believe me. It has been eating me up for more than two years.'

'Could someone have followed her and seen her leave a message there?'

'It's possible, I suppose, but I told her to be really careful, not to stop if she thought she was being followed or saw anyone else she knew. Even then the wall is set back away from the main road. You couldn't just follow a car up that trail without being seen so I don't understand how it could have happened.'

'Then you have a very big hole in your story, because I don't see how she could have been there that day if you didn't arrange it.'

'I know,' Bell said and he placed his elbows on the table and put his hands up to his face in frustration. 'I've driven myself half-crazy thinking about it.'

'Then there's your alibi,' said Tom, 'or lack of it. You told the court you went to see a former lover.'

'I wouldn't describe her as that.'

'But you did have sex with her.'

'She was a waitress at the sports club and it was only a two-time thing. Just a bit of fun, you know.'

'And yet she summoned you to an urgent meeting and you dropped everything to go to her flat.'

'She wrote to me at my office and told me she thought she was pregnant.' Bell was exasperated. 'Can you imagine how I felt when I got that note? She told me she had to see me. I was worried she was going to tell the whole world the baby was mine if I didn't go.'

'And when you called on her?'

'She wasn't there. She'd cleared out and the house was empty.'

'She'd been gone a fortnight by then,' said Tom, 'off travelling the world, which rather blows a hole in your claim that she thought she was pregnant and desperate to see you that afternoon.'

'I know,' admitted Bradshaw, 'the police couldn't trace her either, though I don't think they really tried.'

'How do you explain her letter?'

'A prank from one of her friends or a cruel trick she played to shit me up because I wasn't interested in seeing her again?' Richard shook his head. 'I don't know what her motives were.'

'You couldn't produce the letter when the police asked you for it.'

'I put it in the shredder,' said Bell. 'I could hardly keep it in my briefcase, could I? What if Annie found it?'

'And the timing of this meeting roughly coincided with the time of Rebecca's death.'

'Within an hour or so.' And he sighed. 'I realise how it looks, believe me.'

'Yeah,' said Tom. 'It looks bad. It looks like you killed her.'

'Why are you still here then,' challenged Bell, 'if you reckon I did it?' He sat back in his chair and stared at the reporter.

'I'm waiting for you to convince me otherwise,' Tom told him. 'Perhaps I want to believe you, maybe I feel there is something not quite right about this whole case. You could be telling the truth, and when I look at the evidence against you it all feels a bit convenient; a few small things that add up to not that much but it made the jury rule against you.'

'Go on.'

Tom started counting the points off on his fingers while Bell listened to him, 'One; they didn't like you. They saw you as an arrogant womaniser. Two; you can't reasonably explain why Rebecca was there on the day she died if you didn't summon her. Three; the judge completely disregarded the notion that Rebecca could have been killed by a stranger. Four; you have no alibi but her husband and your wife do, which rules out two other people who might just have had cause to kill her, particularly the husband since we know the killer's blows were so strong they could only have been delivered by a man but alibis can be bought or concocted, particularly by wealthy businessmen.'

'Exactly,' said Bell.

'Though how the hell we can prove that, I don't know.'

'It's the injustice that makes me so angry,' said Bell. 'I tell you, Tom, I have even contemplated killing a man in here, just so I could say I actually deserve the punishment I've been given. It's not as if there aren't a large number of suitable candidates. You wouldn't believe the vermin in here. They would chill you.'

Tom regarded Bell closely. He didn't seem to realise that the words he had just uttered made him sound like a man capable of anything.

Chapter Twelve

'Isn't the Metro fantastic,' announced Helen as they emerged blinking into the light of a chilly but bright afternoon, 'a couple of stops and we're back in Jesmond. The trains are always half empty too.'

'That's because they're all still in bed,' Peter countered, 'unless it's collect-your-giro day.'

Peter had been doing this more and more lately, believing every regional stereotype and cracking lame jokes about them; Scousers were thieves, Scots were alcoholics, Yorkshiremen never bought their round and Geordies were all unemployed. These were views he would have never have spouted at college but it was as if he had abandoned any notion of open-mindedness on the day they graduated.

'We went to university with people from different parts of the country,' she reminded him, 'including the north-east.'

'They don't count,' he'd told her with a glint in his eye. 'They escaped and I bet none of them returned.' Before adding, 'No jobs to go back to.'

'Most of the people up here have jobs, you know.'

'If you say so,' he said as if he was humouring her.

'Not everybody gets the chance to work for their dad.' The words were out of her mouth before she could prevent them. She could feel his whole body stiffen. A few steps later he let go of her hand, which signified the beginning of one of his sulks. She was supposed to apologise then. The withdrawal of the hand was a clear signal, which Helen chose to ignore. He didn't say another word until they were back at her flat.

They ate the dinner she cooked then watched a video he had chosen from her local Blockbuster. She gave up on it during the second car chase and read a book instead. It was all about organised crime in the north-east in the sixties and seventies and was full of infamous characters, most of them long dead. It told of beatings, protection rackets and wars over the control of slot machines in pubs and working men's clubs. There were bent coppers, corrupt politicians, unsolved murders and links with London gangsters like the Kray twins. Helen felt as if she was immersing herself in the history of the criminal world she was now reporting on. Even with the noise of the idiotic action movie in the background she couldn't put it down.

'That's a cheerful read,' Peter told her at one point, between shootouts.

Later, they went to bed. 'Do you mind if we don't?' she asked and he sighed as if this was the most unreasonable thing he had ever heard.

'No,' he said simply, which of course meant *yes* and she wondered if he was about to remind her of the cost of his rail ticket.

He couldn't have been too bothered though, because he was asleep and snoring in minutes, leaving Helen wide awake and restless. Half an hour later she gave up on sleep, went into the living room and began to read her book once more.

The following morning Tom drove into the private underground car park, ignoring the warning signs about wheel clamping being the likeliest option, unless he was a legitimate client. The building housed a number of legal firms and nobody could possibly know who he was here to see.

He climbed the stairs to a second floor that opened out into a reception area with soft leather chairs in front of a handful of glass-walled offices. The reception desk of Stone, Nixon and Stone was manned by an unsmiling guardian who regarded him suspiciously as he advanced on her.

'I'm here to see Mr Nixon,' said Tom with what he hoped was an air of complete confidence.

The receptionist's face darkened. 'Do you have an appointment?'

'I've phoned several times but nobody returned my calls so I thought I'd drop by.'

'You're the reporter,' she said as if it made sense now, 'Mr Cardey.'

'Carney,' he corrected her, 'Tom Carney. I'm working on a story that features Stone, Nixon and Stone. Mr Nixon will want to know about it before it goes to press.'

'I hardly think so,' she said, 'or he would have called you back. We don't speak to journalists.'

'Even ones who are about to put your firm on the front page of a newspaper read by four million people?' He was bluffing but she looked a little less self-assured for a moment before quickly regaining her composure.

'I'm afraid I will have to ask you to leave,' she told him icily.

There was a small heap of glossy brochures on the reception desk and Tom picked one up. 'Background reading,' he told her.

'If you don't leave this minute I will have to call the police.'

'Okay,' Tom said, irked by the woman's sense of superiority, 'see you on the front page then,' and he glanced at her name badge, 'Carol.'

Her face flushed at this and she hissed, 'Get out.'

Tom gave her his best disarming smile then left.

*

'I think you should know,' the old man warned him, 'that I called the police.' He took a step back when Bradshaw turned to face him, as if to avoid an imaginary blow from the man standing on his neighbour's driveway.

'I am the bloody police,' Bradshaw told the wiry old man behind the hedge that lay between them. He produced his warrant card and showed it to Tom Carney's neighbour.

'Oh,' he flushed, 'well, how was I supposed to know you weren't a burglar?'

'Do you know the owner of this house?' asked Bradshaw.

'Yes. Well, no, not really. I don't know him but I've seen him about,' the old man said.

'Is he around, usually, I mean?' asked the detective.

'Most of the time. He's doing the place up, always coming and going with one thing or another: planks of wood, pots of paint.'

'Do you reckon he'll be back soon?'

'More than likely,' said the man. 'Is he in trouble then?'

'Not at all,' said Bradshaw, 'he's just assisting us with our enquiries.' Which had been true once, though not for a while.

'Well,' said the old man with foreboding, 'you always say that don't you, right before you slap the cuffs on.' He walked back inside his house and Bradshaw heard him lock and bolt the door then slide the chain across.

Bradshaw walked back along the driveway towards his car. When he was halfway down, two uniformed officers he vaguely recognised suddenly appeared at the other end of the driveway and began to walk towards him. They stopped when they realised who he was.

'You beat us to it,' the young one said.

'We had a call,' his older colleague explained, 'a sighting

of, quote, "*a highly suspicious-looking person who is very probably up to no good*", unquote.'

'That would be me,' Bradshaw told them and he had to commend the old man on the accuracy of his description.

The charity golf day was about to commence as Helen arrived. The contestants, all well-heeled businessmen, were there as guests of Camfield Offshore. They had arrived at the annual event for an early tee-off and been rewarded with bacon rolls, coffee and fresh orange juice served by a bevy of teenage girls dressed in crisp white blouses and dark skirts with hair tied back in ponytails. Helen noticed there wasn't a girl over twenty among them and each waitress was strikingly pretty. It seemed Camfield had very specific requirements about who could wait on their middle-aged, entirely male clientele.

The men filed out of the room towards the first tee but Helen's quarry was not among them. A well-built man in a dark suit approached her. 'Can I help you, miss?' he said in a tone that made it clear he was not interested in helping her at all. The absence of a white blouse and ponytail had been a giveaway, she realised, and she was past the retirement age for a Camfield waitress.

'I'm looking for Alan Camfield.'

'And you are?'

'Helen Norton from the *Record*,' she explained, 'the newspaper.'

The man took out a notebook and pen from his inside jacket pocket, made a note of something, presumably Helen's name and employer, then smiled mockingly at her.

'I'm not working undercover,' she explained, 'I'm here legitimately to speak to Alan Camfield in my capacity as a journalist.'

'Mr Camfield rarely grants interviews but if you would like the opportunity to write a profile on him you can submit a written request to our press office,' he told her.

'I'm not interested in a profile piece.'

'You'd rather harass him at a charity event.'

'Oh it's a charity event, so why did he invite a gangster?' she asked. 'Unless you're going to tell me that wasn't Jimmy McCree I saw in the car park, getting out of a big black BMW.'

'Right, that's it, Miss Norton,' and he grabbed her by the arm. 'I asked you nicely to leave and you refused to comply, so I'm escorting you from the premises.' He started to tug her by the arm towards the entrance.

'Get off me,' she demanded but he didn't break stride. 'You didn't ask me to leave . . .'

'Then I'm asking you now.'

'You can't do this,' she told him, 'you're hurting my arm. This is assault.'

'Is it?' He could not have sounded less interested. 'Mr Camfield has hired the whole course for the day. This is private property and you are trespassing at an invitation-only event.' He'd already marched her out through the main door and was pulling her across the gravel driveway towards a row of cars. 'Yours, I presume,' he said nodding at the little Peugeot parked at the end of a row of Mercedes, BMWs and Jaguars.

Helen saw a group of men on the horizon to her left, heading out towards the first tee. She shouted, 'Get off me!' as loudly as she could causing some of them to stop and turn to see what was amiss. They were greeted by the site of a young woman being dragged towards her car by a be-suited security man.

'Scott.' The word was delivered with just the right amount of calm authority to halt the security man, who let go of

Helen's arm. She scowled at him and clutched the spot he had gripped. Then she turned to look at the half-dozen men staring back at her. At their centre stood Alan Camfield, watching her intently. Next to him was the unmistakable figure of Jimmy McCree. It crossed her mind to march over to Camfield and protest about her rough treatment, while firing off some questions about his choice of guests and possibly even his plans for the Riverside development.

'Don't ... even ... *think* ... about ... it,' hissed Scott, enunciating each word slowly through gritted teeth and she realised the security man would probably relish the chance to harm her if she shamed him twice in front of his boss. 'On your way.'

The golfers had already turned their backs and were marching over the horizon to their golf day. She wondered what Camfield would tell them about her. Was she merely a reporter demanding an interview at an inappropriate time or perhaps she was an anti-capitalist environmentalist who thought profit was a dirty word.

Helen climbed into her car and steered it down the driveway. She could clearly make out the surly figure of Scott in her rear-view mirror, watching her until she passed through the gates of the golf club.

Tom waited in the underground car park for nearly ninety minutes, hoping that Nixon would eventually emerge. He had not really expected to be admitted to the inner sanctum and was fully prepared for a lengthy wait. On the passenger seat next to him was the firm's brochure, opened on the double page entitled 'Partners'. Martin Nixon's bespectacled face stared out from it self-importantly.

Tom read then re-read the copious notes he had taken,

glancing up occasionally when the lift doors opened and another serious-looking individual departed. He occupied his time making a list of people to talk to, not including the lawyer who was eluding him. Top of that list was Annie Bell, the loyal, long-suffering wife who still stood by Richard. Was she too good to be true? Tom wanted at least to know why she was so convinced her husband did not kill his lover. He'd like to speak to her father too; the man who had employed his son-in-law as his Sales Director. Tom had to wonder if that appointment had been based solely on merit. Then there was Freddie Holt, the supposedly ruthless millionaire who'd been cuckolded by Bell and humiliated when the newspapers printed every detail of the case. Mark Birkett was an old friend from college who had been summoned by the defence as little more than a character witness. That had not gone as well as they might have hoped when Birkett had been forced to confirm a violent incident from Richard's past involving his old girlfriend. Then there was Nicole – or 'Naughty Nicole' – as the press had christened Rebecca's supposed best friend in her exclusive, confessional interview. He wanted to speak to Richard Bell's ex as well. If anyone knew what the man was capable of in a dark moment it was her. He surveyed the list:

1. Martin Nixon – lawyer
2. Annie Bell – loyal wife
3. Annie's father – employer
4. Freddie Holt – Rebecca's husband
5. Mark Birkett – Richard's best man
6. Nicole – Rebecca's friend from the cruise boat
7. Amy Riordan – Bell's ex

It seemed enough to be going on with for now.

Finally, a man emerged from the lift who looked a lot like Martin Nixon. Tom glanced again at the photograph in the brochure then back at the man in the raincoat who was walking briskly towards an enormous silver Mercedes, brief-case in hand.

It was him.

Tom got out of his car before Nixon could elude him.

'Mr Nixon!' he called and the figure stopped in his tracks and turned to face Tom. 'Could I have a quick word?'

If Tom was hoping that Nixon might not at first realise who he was he was soon disillusioned. 'I don't speak to reporters,' said the lawyer, who had obviously been well briefed by his receptionist.

'You're clearly a man in the know,' Tom told Nixon as he began to climb into his car, 'so you will be aware of who I write for.'

'I have no interest in who you write for Mr . . .' He had clearly forgotten Tom's name already. 'I simply do not speak to *reporters*,' he said that last word like it was an infectious disease, '*ever*. Is that clear enough for you?'

At this point the lawyer was climbing into his car, giving him a look that clearly said 'Back away,' but Tom didn't move. Instead he replied, 'It certainly is but I really would advise against that,' his tone was conciliatory, 'unless you want a fine reputation built over years destroyed overnight. I'll be making some pretty strong claims. If you don't respond, people will assume you have no problem with my allegations.'

Nixon took his leg out of the car. 'What allegations?'

'My argument will be that an innocent man may be serv-ing a lengthy prison sentence because he failed to get satisfactory legal representation from your firm. It's my responsibility as a journalist to give you the right of reply but it really doesn't matter. I can simply put that you refused to comment. It would certainly make my life simpler.' And when Nixon hesitated, Tom said, 'Sorry to have taken up your valuable time,' then he began to walk away. He'd taken a few steps and begun to question whether his bluff had failed when he heard a single, slightly panicked word from Nixon.

'Wait,' he urged. Tom turned back to face Nixon, who looked decidedly uncomfortable now, 'which case?'

Tom made a show of looking round the underground car park. 'I don't think it would be proper to discuss it down here, do you?'

When the lift doors opened, the receptionist was surprised to see her boss again so soon and at first she wondered what he might have forgotten. When she realised Tom Carney was walking calmly behind him, her surprise turned to shock as they both headed for Nixon's office.

'Coffee, Carol,' Nixon told her curtly then added, 'and biscuits.'

Tom grinned at her then and enjoyed the look of indignation on her face as she was dispatched to provide him with refreshments.

Chapter Thirteen

Bradshaw waited for an hour, hoping Tom had just nipped out for a tin of paint, but he did not return. He decided to give the reporter ten more minutes but realised he faced a frustrating day, involving repeat visits to Carney's small semi-detached house until he finally nabbed him.

While he waited, Bradshaw's thoughts idly turned to his girlfriend. He and Karen were an unlikely couple. She was tall, blonde and beautiful with a gym-toned figure that would normally have been enough to keep her well out of his league, but when Karen met Ian for the first time, he was at his absolute best, for he was unconscious. There was no way he could mess things up with a terrible opening line and nerves were never going to get the better of him. Karen was a WPC sent to check on him at his hospital bed by a concerned DCI Kane when Bradshaw nearly drowned. She had brought him fresh clothes from his home and instead of being disgusted by the mess in his flat, had decided he was like a lot of single guys: hopeless without a woman in his life. He later discovered the nurses had done half the work for him by assuring Karen he was a bloody hero. Although he had done everything they claimed he had done, he still couldn't help feeling like a bit of a fraud. When he eventually came round to find this angelic figure smiling down at him he had been quick to dismiss his achievements and she, naturally, assumed he was just being modest.

Bradshaw's unease did not stop him asking her out for a

drink when she popped round to his flat a few days later to 'see how he was doing'. Later she freely admitted she hoped he would invite her on a date.

The past eighteen months had been a bit of a whirlwind for a man who hadn't had a girlfriend in a long while. As well as numerous visits to pubs, restaurants and cinemas there had been, he had to admit, some pretty amazing sessions in the bedroom.

It was true that Karen was not his usual type and they did often run out of things to say to each other, having quite different views on the world. She tended to care a lot more than he did about station gossip, frivolous TV shows and the need to get down to the gym four times a week as an absolute minimum. He went with her though and Karen assumed he was as obsessed with burning calories as she was. In truth he exercised because he always felt better afterwards and it helped to banish the low moods before they took a hold. He didn't tell Karen about this because he instinctively knew she would never understand.

There was still no sign of Tom Carney and Bradshaw figured he had better get back to the rest of the team. The very last thing he wanted was to be in DI Tennant's bad books. As Bradshaw drove away he noticed a curtain twitch at the house next door to Tom's.

'Here comes trouble,' remarked her editor as Helen walked into the newsroom.

'What do you mean?'

'A certain high-powered London-based PR agency has been on the phone to me. They represent Alan Camfield.'

'Oh,' she said.

'I got a pretty lengthy lecture about not allowing my

reporters to intrude on property that has been privately hired for a charitable event, namely a very fancy golf course not too many miles from here.'

'I see.'

'Yes,' Graham went on, 'words like *trespass*, *illegal*, *unethical* and *Press Complaints Commission* were mentioned.'

'Right,' she said unsurely and waited for the telling-off that would naturally follow.

'I used a few choice words myself; including *freedom of the press*, *public interest* and finally *fuck off* and *don't ever bother me again*,' he told her. 'Don't worry, Helen, I've got your back.'

Her smile was warm. 'Thanks, Graham. I really appreciate it and sorry for the hassle I caused you.'

'It's fine. If you're treading on toes then you must be getting close to something,' he told her, 'so what have you got for me?'

'From the golf course? Nothing,' she admitted.

'Nothing? I was hoping it was something.'

'I couldn't get near the man himself,' she said, 'too much security, but I did see him walk over the horizon with a bunch of bigwig businessmen and Jimmy McCree.'

'McCree again?' And he frowned at this. 'You know what bugs me, Helen?'

'What?'

'When a gangster becomes a household name and suddenly everybody wants to be their friend. You start seeing them at parties with their arms around actors and footballers. Now it's rich businessmen and even the head of the council who conveniently forget the victims. At least when Frank Jarvis was leader he was openly critical of McCree, now there's no one willing to take him on. Jimmy McCree has left widows and orphans for God's sake.' Then he took a breath. 'I'm ranting now, sorry.'

'I agree with every word,' Helen told him.

'It's partly our fault, I suppose. We write about them.'

'Only to hold them to account.'

'Do you really think they care about that?' asked Graham.

'Yes, I do.' And she wanted to say 'If they didn't, they wouldn't send their thugs to knock me over in the car park,' but she couldn't admit that to Graham; not without running the risk he might tell her to stop investigating McCree, Lynch and Camfield. Maybe he would even hand the task to somebody more experienced, probably a man, in a mis-guided attempt to protect her. The attack proved her investigation was beginning to worry someone and she was determined not to allow those thugs to deflect her from reporting the truth. 'I do have something else,' she said quickly, 'take a look at this.' And she handed him a folder containing some photocopied documents. 'They're from the land registry.'

Her editor blinked at the papers she placed in front of him. 'What is it?'

She pointed at an address on the first document. 'That's a house that used to be owned by Councillor Joe Lynch.'

'Right.' And he scanned the details.

'It forms part of the information openly available to potential buyers of the property, which incidentally is up for sale again. It's now owned by a Mr Cooper, who has had it for just over a year.'

'So it's back on the market,' he said, 'and was previously owned by Lynch?'

She nodded. 'Mr Cooper bought it from Councillor Lynch. What do you notice from the information on that first sheet?'

'Well,' he said, 'the councillor picked it up for a song back in 1979 and he's made a tidy profit on it in around fourteen years, so fair play to him I suppose.' And he looked at his reporter. 'He's not the first to make a few quid on a property in Newcastle. Some of the outlying areas have really come on. I know he's meant to be a socialist, Helen, but I doubt we could run a story criticising him for cashing in on a mini north-east housing boom.'

'No,' she said, 'we couldn't – but I did some digging. Three other similar-sized houses sold in his street at around the same time. They both went for less; a lot less.' She could tell her editor was interested now.

'So the councillor knows how to drive a hard bargain?' he offered.

'He must do,' she said, 'because he managed to get thirty grand more than the market rate for his house when he sold it.'

'Thirty grand?' said her editor in disbelief. 'Are you sure?'

'I'm certain,' she said 'and I have all of the land registry documents to prove it.'

'So what do we know about the man doing the over-paying?'

'Mr Cooper? Very little and, strangely enough, there was no estate agent involved in the purchase. It was an entirely private transaction.'

'Well I never,' he said dryly.

'But Mr Cooper had a change of heart, because he never moved into the place. The property has been standing empty since the day Joe Lynch moved out. I checked with the neighbours. They haven't seen a soul at that house in more than a year. I looked through the windows and there's nothing there. It's a shell.'

'And what does Mr Cooper hope to get for it this time, I wonder.'

'That's the really interesting bit. This time there *is* an estate agent involved so I went down there posing as a potential buyer. I asked about the price and they confirmed it is on the market at the going rate, meaning our man will lose just under thirty grand in a year, if he holds out for his full asking price.'

'That's quite a hit he took,' and her editor smiled, 'considering he never lived in it or rented it out to anybody in the intervening period. Any luck in tracking down Mr Cooper for a comment?' She shook her head. 'Thought not.'

'He's abroad apparently, according to the estate agent. Mr Cooper is a very private businessman and they only deal with him over the phone or by fax machine but of course everything is all above board.'

'Of course.'

And she laughed. 'The estate agent actually said to me, "Don't worry, love, it's all cushty."'

And the editor's smile grew broader. 'So what's your conclusion, as if I didn't know already?'

'Someone paid Lynch off,' she said, 'and whatever he did for them, it was worth thirty grand but Joe Lynch didn't want anything as grubby or incriminating as cash in a brown envelope. So instead they bought his house at a vastly inflated rate and he pocketed the difference. Whoever the buyer really was, they waited a year to avoid suspicion and now they are quietly disposing of their asset.'

'But what did the buyer of Joe Lynch's house get in exchange for his generosity, I wonder?'

'Whatever it was, they got lucky with Lynch because he's leader of the council now and head of the planning committee, so he has a big say in the Riverside development.'

'In that case his price will have gone up considerably.' And he regarded the documents as if he couldn't quite believe what he was holding. 'And this buyer, Mr Cooper?'

'He's probably just a set of papers or a front for someone like Camfield or McCree,' Helen said. 'Who else can afford to blow thirty grand to buy a councillor? Even if we could track an actual person down, it won't get us very far because he'll never talk.'

'So how can we run this story?' Graham seemed to be addressing the question to her while simultaneously mulling it over in his own head.

'Put down the bare facts. The leader of the council has made a very tidy sum out of property while others in the same area had to settle for much less.'

'There's just enough in there for people to draw their own conclusions,' said Graham. 'His own party will want to burn him at the stake when they read this.'

'*Lynch Mob?*' she offered as a joke headline.

'I like that,' he chuckled.

'We should ask Councillor Lynch to tell us all about Mr Cooper,' she went on. 'If he gives us some proper information, we can use it to track the man down. If as I suspect he tells us nothing, we can say he refused to tell us anything about his mystery buyer. I'm hoping he'll say he never met the bloke personally, which will make him sound like those guys who get sent down for possessing stolen goods. They usually say they bought them from a man they met down the pub but they can't remember his name.'

'Even better,' he said. 'Are you going to phone the councillor now?'

'Not yet,' she said, 'a wise man once told me not to give a guilty party too long to come up with excuses or call in the lawyers. I was thinking an hour before deadline. Meanwhile,

I'll write up the rest of the story and leave a gap at the bottom for the councillor's flustered denials.'

'Then get writing and I'll hold the front page.' And he grinned at her. 'Again! You realise I've got grizzled veterans in this newsroom who are beginning to look at you with hostile eyes because you're starting to make them look bad.' Then he placed a hand on her shoulder and gave it a gentle squeeze. 'Seriously, this is really good stuff, Helen. Well done you. I mean it.'

'Thanks,' she said, for his support was beginning to mean a lot to her.

When he had gone it struck Helen he no longer asked where she was getting her stories from. Perhaps he knew she wouldn't tell him about her anonymous source. Someone was very unhappy with the way Joe Lynch was going about his business as council leader and they were more than happy to tell Helen all about it. The latest note to land on her desk had been typewritten, just like the rest. *Ever wonder why Joe Lynch sold his family home?* it asked her. *Or how he managed to get so much more for it than anybody else?*

It took a while for Tom to persuade Nixon to discuss Richard Bell's case at all. In the end he was forced to agree to write his piece with no mention of the law firm, in exchange for their version of what actually happened in court. This Tom did reluctantly but only out of principle. Unbeknown to Nixon, Tom wasn't actually writing a piece for the largest tabloid in the country, merely investigating Rebecca's Holt's murder on behalf of her supposed killer.

'I want to talk to you about the advice you gave your client before the trial,' Tom began.

'I gave him a lot of advice,' said Nixon as he broke a

digestive biscuit into two equal halves with absolute precision, 'some of which he chose to ignore.'

'I'm talking specifically about the revelations surrounding his private life.'

'Oh that.' And he took a tiny bite of his biscuit.

'You got him to admit to a whole series of . . . you called them *assignations* with women other than his wife,' Tom reminded him, 'which did not exactly endear him to the jury.'

The barrister sighed, 'Yes, well, we were between a rock and a hard place there. We quizzed him about his affair with Rebecca Holt and decided there was little point in denying it. The police knew about it already and if he lied about it again in front of a jury, the prosecution could bring proof of the relationship into court – then the rest of his testimony would lack any credibility.'

'I get that,' said Tom, 'but did he really have to stand in the witness box and list every conquest he'd ever made?'

'It wasn't quite like that,' argued the barrister.

'*Serial Shag-Around* and *Lying Love Rat* were just two of the following day's headlines.'

'The gutter press misrepresented him,' said Nixon, 'as they are apt to do. Some of the coverage was scandalous.'

'I don't think they did,' said Tom.

'Well, you're a journalist.'

Tom reached for his notebook and began to read aloud from his shorthand notes of the trial coverage. ' "I've always liked women and very often they have been attracted to me. I enjoy their company and usually find sex easy to come by. I know I should not have continued seeing other women once I was married but I became convinced I was somehow entitled to do this because of the stresses of my life. I enjoyed the thrill of the chase and freely admit I was attracted to the forbidden nature of these affairs. I knew it was wrong but I couldn't help myself. I enjoy sex and, from what I have been told I am good at it. I suppose I must be, because they usually come back for more."' Tom raised his eyebrows at that. 'Now tell me he doesn't sound like a narcissistic prick who thinks he is above society's norms and therefore capable of murdering his inconvenient mistress?'

'On reflection . . .' began the barrister '. . . this is off the record, right?'

Tom nodded. 'Entirely.'

'. . . it was a mistake. You have to understand our biggest fear before the trial was that the prosecution might uncover Richard Bell's double life and use it against him. It seems he was addicted to having affairs left, right and bloody centre and if we could discover this, it was highly likely they would too. If we got him to stand up in the witness box and say he was a family man who had strayed once in having this affair then the prosecution produced evidence of all of his other . . . misdemeanours, we would be dead in the water. We thought it was better to grasp the nettle and get it all out in the open early on, so the jury knew the kind of man he was and maybe they could deal with it.'

'But instead?'

'They hated him,' admitted the barrister. 'I could see it in their eyes the whole time he was up there. We advised him to throw himself on the mercy of the jury, admit he had done some very bad things and beg his wife for forgiveness.'

'But that's not how it went.'

'I think he just couldn't help himself. He'd been successfully seducing all these women on the sly but he had no one to tell it too. I think you're right, Mr Carney, he is a narcissist and he wanted the world to know about it. Once his affair with Rebecca was known, the dam burst and he figured what the hell; might as well be hanged for a sheep as a lamb.'

'You were playing a high-risk strategy,' said Tom, 'but there was logic behind it and Bell didn't help himself.'

'You can only lead a client in a certain direction if he chooses to follow you. Nobody was more frustrated by the outcome than me, I can assure you. I don't like to lose.'

'That alibi of his. You were never able to trace the girl.'

'There were vague reports she may have gone to Ko Samui or Bali but she never told anyone where she was off to. She was just an Aussie girl who'd been all over Britain and was now off seeing the rest of the world. We knew that if we did find her she would probably just say she never wrote the note Richard claimed to have received from her. She was long gone by the time he received it, so it wasn't much of an alibi. If anything she would probably have harmed his case.'

'Who did write it then?'

'If it really existed? Your guess is as good as mine.'

'Thank you for your time. It's been useful,' Tom told him, 'I do have one last question though.'

'What's that?'

'Did he do it?'

The barrister snorted. 'How should I know?'

'Alright then,' Tom corrected himself, 'do you *think* he did it?'

Nixon seemed happier with the rephrased question, so much so that he allowed himself a lengthy period of reflection. Tom became conscious of traffic noises outside then the voices of a couple of teenage girls from several floors below.

Finally the barrister spoke. 'If you are asking me whether I think he did it, then I genuinely don't know. If you are asking if he is *capable* of the act, then my answer has to be an emphatic yes.'

Tom was taken aback by this. 'Why do you say that?'

'Because I think that Richard Bell shows all of the signs,' Nixon said to him, 'the absence of regret or remorse, the inability to play by society's rules, the tacit enjoyment of risk and the lack of inhibition in his sexual behaviour. Most of all, I suppose, his lack of empathy.'

'All the signs?' asked Tom.

'Of a psychopath.'

Chapter Fourteen

Ian Bradshaw was surprised to be summoned straight to DI Tennant's office as soon as he arrived at headquarters. He figured she was about to ask him where he had been that morning and was about to rummage for his excuse when instead she quizzed him about Kane.

'Did the DCI have a reason for nabbing you like that?' She sounded suspicious as if he had brought this upon himself somehow.

'It was like you said, ma'am, he just wanted a lift home.'

'And why was he unable to drive himself home?'

Bradshaw got the impression she already knew the answer to that question. 'He said there was something wrong with his car.'

'He said or there was?' she asked, but he wasn't daft enough to go there.

'Both, I assumed.'

'Mmm. And what did you talk about on the way to his house?'

'Ma'am?' He put deliberate bafflement into his tone, as if he couldn't imagine why she would want to know that. Bradshaw wanted to tell her it was none of her business but he suspected that would get him into a whole new world of trouble. 'Nothing much, but he did ask me about my future and aspirations.' Bradshaw hoped he might be on safe ground with that.

'Did he now? And what did you say?'

'I said I was happy where I was for the time being.'

'Why? Don't you want to get on?' Tennant asked sharply.

'Yes, of course I do.'

'So when a senior officer asks you about your future you tell him you're happy to stay put?' The raised eyebrows told him she was unimpressed.

'I just meant I was in no particular hurry.'

'DCI Kane won't mistake you for an overly ambitious officer then.' And she left that thought hanging. 'So where have you been this morning?'

'Following up on a lead.' He wasn't about to tell her he was staking out Tom Carney's home for DCI Kane so instead gave her his theory about the burned girl having a tattoo. He had been keeping this to himself until now but it was a useful smokescreen

She listened and when he had finished his explanation said, 'That's useful,' though she sounded uncertain, as if surprised he could have come up with it. 'That's good work.'

'Will that be all, ma'am?' he asked stiffly.

Kate Tennant sighed her exasperation. 'Just get back to work, Ian.'

Mark Birkett lived on a building site. His house was the only completed property in a cul-de-sac full of newbuilds. There were twenty houses on the development, in varying stages of completion, and they flanked a curving, half-finished road that had rough foundations but no tarmacadam to smooth it over, so the drainage and manhole covers stuck up out of the road, causing Tom Carney's car to bump all the way along Runnymede Lane. It had rained that morning and slick wet mud clung to Tom's tyres. He parked outside the only house with a roof, got out of his car and knocked on the door.

'You found me then,' Birkett observed sullenly. 'Most people don't.'

Tom had phoned to explain his interest in Richard Bell's case. He got the impression Birkett had allowed him to come round because he couldn't think of a good reason to prevent it but he didn't look pleased to see Tom.

The house was small and neat; a decent starter home for a young family. Tom was invited into a tiny lounge, which barely had room for an armchair, sofa and a TV.

'I understand you and Richard were close,' said Tom.

'Not really.'

'But you were best man at his wedding.'

'Someone had to be. I wouldn't say I was any closer to Richard than a number of blokes who went to college with him. We hung out in the same group of friends, went out drinking together but I barely saw him after university. A couple of years after graduating, he called me up, told me he was getting married and wanted me to be best man.'

'Were you surprised?'

'At the best man bit? Yes, but not about the getting married part.'

'Why do you say that? Seems a bit young these days.'

'It was logical. He already had everything he wanted.'

'So it wasn't just because he was in love with the girl?'

'Who said he was in love with her.' Birkett looked a little uncomfortable then. 'Look, I've nothing against Annie but I wouldn't say it was a normal romance, it was more—'

'A meeting of minds,' offered Tom sarcastically, 'or a marriage of convenience?'

'When he married Annie he got the full package: the woman with the brains and the career, the job with her old man's firm; her dad already got them a big house. I think he bought into all of it, that's all. I think he married Annie because he didn't want to jeopardise things.'

'Are you saying he didn't love her?'

'I have no idea if he loved her or not. I'm saying he married the boss's daughter. The rest of us were out there trying to get a leg-up in our first jobs, paying off student debts, renting tiny rooms in crappy, shared houses. He already had everything. On the rare occasions we did get together it was a bit jarring. He was living in a different world, driving a brand new car with golf clubs in the boot, eating in restaurants I wouldn't dream of going to. He was way ahead of us and it was all so effortless.'

'I see. So tell me about this other girl at college,' Tom said, 'Amy, the one who called the police when he hit her.'

'Oh that,' Mark said as if it was no big deal. 'Well I guess it all came up in court, so it's no secret. In our first year Richard was an absolute hound. He had a different girl every week, or as near as. Most of us were lucky to get one a term but with Richard it was easy. He had the looks, he had the patter, women just fell for him but he never showed any inclination to stop rutting around,' Birkett smiled grimly, 'until he met Amy.'

'Then he changed?'

'We were in our second year by then. We'd moved out of halls and were sharing a grotty place on the edge of town. We threw a house-warming and she showed up with her mate.'

'Is that how he met her?'

Birkett nodded. 'She was a fresher and didn't know anyone but I tell you every bloke in that room stopped what he was doing when she walked in.'

'Good-looking?'

'Stunning.'

'So every guy wanted her but Richard was the one who started going out with her?'

'Predictably so – and to be fair to him he did carry on seeing her. This wasn't a one-night thing for once.'

'How long were they in a relationship?'

Birkett shrugged. 'Six months or so, but back in college that's a lifetime.'

'So what went wrong?'

'Who knows, but one day Amy suddenly called it off.'

'And you don't know why?'

'Who can tell for sure what goes through a young girl's head? I got his side of it, of course. He was devastated. He thought they were a permanent item. Apparently she didn't.'

'Why not?'

'He said she wasn't ready for it. Amy was too young and wanted to see the world *and* other people. She was a bit of a free spirit and Richard was quite old-fashioned in some ways, which is a bit of contradiction when you consider what he was like in his first year.'

'What happened?'

'He tried to get her back,' said Birkett, 'and failed.'

'And took it badly?'

'He lost the plot and a lot of his pride along the way. I don't think he had ever been rejected by a girl before in his life,' Birkett said with some satisfaction, 'and he had no frame of reference. He just couldn't accept or deal with it, let alone move on. Lord knows we tried to persuade him to forget her but he just couldn't or wouldn't.'

'So she called the police on him?'

'That was a while later. He made a fool of himself on more than one occasion before they reached that point.'

'Go on.'

'He'd wait outside the lecture hall so he could intercept her and hassle her; he'd turn up at her house at all hours. She told him to leave her alone but he wouldn't, he even threatened some guy he saw her with and challenged him to a fight. It was all a bit pathetic if I'm honest. We were embarrassed for him.'

'And it clearly didn't win her round.'

'No,' he said, 'but she did sleep with him once.'

'What?'

'He'd calmed down a bit, hadn't seen her for a while and we happened to be out at the same club as her. She was with her mates, celebrating her birthday and they had a big heart-to-heart in the corner.' He put his palms up as if to illustrate how crazy that sounded. 'What can I say? Emotions run high when you're that age but whatever was said, he spent the night with her. The next morning he seemed to think they were back on again but that wasn't her understanding. I think she looked upon it as break-up sex, a way to end it all amicably or possibly it was just a bit of drunken fun on her birthday. You'd have to ask her.'

'Maybe I will,' said Tom. 'Was that when he lost it?'

'Soon after,' said Birkett, 'when he found out she'd shagged somebody else. Then he lost it big style,' confirmed Birkett, 'shouting at her in the street, calling her names . . .'

'What kind of names?'

'Whore, slut, that kind of thing.'

'When did she call the police?'

'When he finally hit her.'

'When you say *hit* . . .'

'He says it was a slap,' said Birkett, 'she said it was worse than that. Either way he was completely out of order and when he'd sobered up he knew it.'

'What did the police do?'

'Cautioned him.'

'Did that have an effect?'

'I think it shocked him back into the real world. They warned him to stay away from her and the college authorities got involved. He was that close to being kicked out.' He showed Tom a small gap between his thumb and forefinger. 'These days he probably would have been, for hitting a girl, but this was back in the eighties and I don't think they knew what to do with him. The university wanted it to go away, to be honest.'

'Did he get back on the straight and narrow?'

'He barely went to any lectures for weeks and he was drinking a lot; and I do mean a lot. We used to go out and get rat-arsed like all students do but this was way more. We tried to get him off it and back into his old routine but in the end we left him to it.'

'So what happened?'

He looked a bit sheepish. 'We gave up on him but she didn't.'

'Who?'

'Annie Bell,' he said, 'or Annie Taylor, as she was back then.'

'So she already knew him at that point?'

'Annie was in our year. He'd known her from day one but she was just about the only girl he didn't shag.'

'Not interested?'

'*She* was,' said Birkett, 'he wasn't.'

'Why not?'

'Didn't fancy her, I suppose.'

'Yet he ended up married to her.'

'Stranger things have happened.'

'So how did they go from him not fancying her to becoming a couple?'

'I came home one day and she was sitting in the kitchen with him. He looked like shit and she had obviously been giving him a long talking-to. I left them to it but whatever she said to Richard, it worked. I hardly ever saw him without her again after that.'

'But how? I still don't fully understand this.'

'Well nor do I really, but she managed to do what nobody else could do back then and she got his arse back in gear. She must have pointed out he was chucking his whole life away and he finally got the message. Then she helped him.'

'With what?'

'Everything. They started studying together in the library and he began to catch up on his uni work. He attended lectures and tutorials and avoided being chucked off his course. She'd turn up at the house with groceries or food she'd cooked for him and even started doing his washing. Honestly, it was like they were already married by the time we started our finals.'

'And he wasn't rutting around anymore?'

'Not back then, unless he was very good at hiding it – but we found out just how good at the trial, didn't we?'

'Was that all there was to it? Annie sorted out the mess he'd made for himself so he stuck with her?'

Birkett shrugged. 'It's my best guess but, honestly, who knows what goes on between two people? I'm not sure how I can really help you.'

'You've been a help,' Tom assured him.

'Look, I agreed to see you because you're helping Richard but I told you we weren't really that close. He's never been down here and he only met my wife once, at his wedding.'

'Not the best at keeping in touch, was he?'

'You could say that,' he admitted. 'I know life gets in the way and everything but we made a big effort that day, stayed in a hotel, bought them a nice gift, but I barely saw him afterwards.'

'Any reason for that?'

'We didn't have a falling-out. I just got the impression he didn't need an old mate from uni and his equally penniless girlfriend hanging around.'

'You don't think Annie had anything to do with it, do you?'

'The murder?' Birkett was shocked.

Tom shook his head. 'No; Richard not bothering to stay in touch with you.'

'I never had a problem with her. I reckon we just weren't part of his world.'

'Okay, well I guess we're done then.' Birkett followed him to the door and Tom made his final question sound like an afterthought. 'So, what do you think about this Rebecca Holt killing? Did he do it?'

'You clearly think he didn't, or you wouldn't be here.'

'I'm keeping an open mind. I've barely scratched the surface yet.'

'I think Richard is an uncomplicated man who knows what he wants,' said Birkett, 'and usually gets it, but when he doesn't he can lose the plot. I saw what happened with Amy. As to whether he actually did it, I have no idea.'

'You wouldn't vouch for him?'

'How could I?' said Birkett as he walked Tom to the front door and opened it onto the unfinished street.

'I persuaded my wife to buy this place,' he said. 'She wanted an old townhouse but I told her we'd get more value for money round here, if we bought a newbuild, off-plan.' He sounded desolate.

'Well you probably will,' Tom assured him, 'once it's finished.'

'Finished?' he said and he looked at Tom as if he was mad, 'Does this look new to you?' And it was not until he'd asked that question that Tom fully noticed his surroundings. A handful of weeds trying to grow through cracks in the pavement was the first clue. Then he realised some of the brickwork on the unfinished houses looked faded and battered by the weather.

'No, it doesn't,' Tom admitted.

'And do you see any work going on? We've been here two years,' Birkett told him, 'and they haven't laid a brick in twelve months.'

'What happened?'

'Developers ran out of money.' He surveyed the cul-de-sac with a renewed sense of disbelief.

'Is there any chance that anyone else could . . . ?'

'Buy the place and finish the work?' asked Birkett. 'It would be cheaper to start afresh somewhere else than pick this mess up. There are properties here that have had the wind and rain battering them for months. You'd have to knock them down and start all over again. No one is going to do that.'

'Won't your insurance company . . . ?'

'They say I have a structurally sound house and they did not insure the surrounding infrastructure for me. They are only interested if I get burgled, experience subsidence, the house collapses or it burns down and, if it does catch fire, they pretty much implied I would be their first suspect,' he concluded, 'just in case I were to get any ideas.'

'That's awful.'

'We're trapped here,' Birkett said. 'I am paying a mortgage every month on a house that is literally worth nothing. Who is ever going to buy it from me when this is what they see when they draw back the curtains? There's nobody else living in this street. We thought it would be a nice place to bring up kids but it's a building site. My wife cries herself to sleep every night.' He smiled grimly. 'We are here to stay. Unless we win the lottery.'

It was dark and getting late by the time Tom finally returned home. He'd stopped at a pub for a pint and some food. He hadn't felt like cooking and wanted some quiet time to re-read his notes and try to draw some conclusions about his client. If anything, Richard Bell looked guiltier than ever.

He walked wearily up the darkened driveway and a burly figure suddenly stepped from the shadows.

'Jesus Christ!' yelled Tom as he flinched from the sudden movement and stepped quickly back.

The man came fully into focus then.

'Where the bloody hell have you been?' demanded an exasperated DS Bradshaw.

Chapter Fifteen

'What were you doing hiding in the shadows like that?' demanded Tom as he handed Bradshaw a bottle of beer. 'I nearly had a bloody heart attack.'

'I wasn't hiding,' protested Bradshaw, 'I was about to try your door bell for the umpteenth time when you came walking up the drive. You should get one of those security lights installed that come on when someone reaches your front door.'

'Good idea, I'll do that in my spare time,' he said dryly so that Bradshaw would notice the chaos in his living room.

'I heard you were doing a place up,' said Bradshaw. 'Big job is it?'

Tom ignored the question. 'How did you find me?'

'I'm a detective.'

'Alright then, *why* did you find me?'

'Because I needed a word.'

'I remember the last time you had a word,' Tom told him, 'there were a fair number of them, in fact. You called me an arrogant, treacherous idiot as I recall.'

'Did I?'

'Yes.'

'Then I should never have called you an idiot,' Bradshaw said reasonably. 'I take that bit back. I've always thought you were very intelligent.'

'For an arrogant traitor,' said Tom. 'Look, Ian, what exactly do you want?'

'Have you heard of Frank Jarvis?'

'The politician? Of course,' said Tom, 'I heard him on the radio recently talking about his missing daughter.'

'Well, pin back your lugholes then, because I've got a tale to tell.'

It didn't take long before the two men became embroiled in an argument. The detective began positively enough, explaining that Councillor Jarvis had asked for help to find his daughter. 'We think a fresh pair of eyes is what is needed here,' he said then he handed Tom a picture of Sandra Jarvis. The ten-by-eight colour photograph showed a pretty young blonde girl with green eyes. Her face was serious, as if she wasn't expecting the camera's presence and resented its intrusion.

Tom listened silently while Bradshaw continued, 'Sandra was a model pupil at school, and left for university with a seemingly bright future ahead of her. But in her second term she completely changed. She missed lectures, shunned her friends and became sullen, moody and introspective, apparently. Then she disappeared during the reading week.'

Bradshaw appealed to Tom's better nature then and asked him to put his feelings about the falling-out with Durham Constabulary to one side. 'We would like you to do what you do best: unravel a mystery. You would be helping a suffering father in the process. There's a fund the force uses to pay for outside experts so we could put you on the payroll. What do you think?'

'You've got to be kidding,' said Tom. 'I mean, seriously?'

'I'm not kidding.'

'After the crap you lot put me through?'

'What crap?'

'Mmm, let's see.' And Tom pretended to think for a moment. 'I've been ostracised by the police contacts I need in order to have any kind of career in journalism, which

128

renders me pretty much unemployable in that profession and this region . . .'

'Well, can you blame them?'

'. . . I have been verbally abused by detectives I've investigated for corruption then threatened with violence by those same men . . .'

'O'Brien didn't threaten you, Tom.'

'Detective Sergeant O'Brien told me he was going to kill me . . .'

'It's a figure of speech. He didn't mean it.'

'I was hauled into your DCI's office and, instead of being congratulated for uncovering serious malpractice within this force, Kane closed ranks, backed his own men and threatened me with arrest for obstruction . . .'

'He has to stand by his men,' Bradshaw protested, 'unless there is concrete evidence, which you couldn't provide!'

'. . . Plus, I've been stopped three times for speeding in the past two months . . .'

'*Were* you speeding?'

'That's not the point!'

'I think it is.'

'Not when I haven't been pulled over once in the preceding ten years!'

'Well,' said Bradshaw weakly, 'we've been having a bit of a clampdown on speeding.'

'I'm a bit late returning my library books this month,' said Tom, 'if you're having a clampdown on that then now is the time to warn me.'

'Trouble with you, mate,' Bradshaw said, 'you're your own worst enemy.'

'How's that exactly?'

'You don't do yourself any favours.'

'You mean I don't do enough favours for the police,' countered Tom, 'like suppressing stories about incompetence or turning a blind eye to corruption.'

'Corruption?' asked Bradshaw. 'If you could prove corruption you wouldn't have left the names out of the stories.'

'I would have thought you'd approve of that approach.'

'No one's perfect, Tom, coppers included. This job has a way of getting to you. Some people cut corners when that happens or they throw their weight around a bit too much, but it's usually because they are under pressure and desperate to get a result.'

'Does that make it right? Do you behave like that?' When he received no answer from the detective Tom added, 'So why should they?' Then he said, 'I spoke to a lot of people.'

'And how many of them were criminals?' Bradshaw shook his head. 'I hope that one day, if anybody questions your conduct, they will give you the benefit of the doubt before they ruin your career on the word of a bunch of crooks.'

'Most of them were crooks, yes,' admitted Tom, 'pissed-off ones: drug dealers who were shaken down instead of arrested, streetwalkers who had to give freebies so they could carry on working for a living . . .'

'So they claim . . .' said Bradshaw '. . . and most criminals will say anything to get a police officer into trouble.'

'You have detectives in Durham Constabulary who use blackmail and extortion on a daily basis, expect a cut of a criminal's enterprise instead of locking him up and that doesn't concern you?' asked Tom. 'Or are you only interested in catching *real* villains.'

'You think we're all the same, don't you? All coppers are bastards, all of us bent and on the take?'

'No!' snapped Tom. 'But what I don't understand is why

honest cops always bend over backwards to save the crooked ones. I don't believe you're all on the take, or even half of you. I'm willing to subscribe to the rotten apple theory. The vast majority of serving police officers are more honest than me but let's just say that five per cent . . . no . . . make it one per cent of detectives are as corrupt as I believe these men were. There are more than one hundred thousand police officers in the UK, so that's a thousand people like them. Get rid of those guys, instead of quietly ignoring the problem, and I'll stop writing the articles!'

'That's exactly what we are doing, Tom.'

'So where are those men now,' asked Tom, 'on remand or bailed to appear before magistrates at some later date?' Bradshaw didn't answer. 'Go on, tell me.'

'Currently off sick,' the admission hurt Bradshaw, 'as if you didn't know.'

'Well, there's a shock. Let me guess: depression? No, stress! You get more sympathy for stress. How long before a guilty man quietly slips away into early retirement? That's what your lot always do, isn't it?'

'Jesus, I hate it when you say *your lot* like we are all in it together!'

'You know that old saying: about being part of the solution or part of the problem?'

'Look, Tom, I didn't come here to have a row with you. I didn't even come here to ask for your help. It's Frank Jarvis who needs that, not us. He's the one who'll suffer if he never finds his daughter. He just wants to meet with you – but if you won't help him because you still bear a grudge against Durham Constabulary, then that's your prerogative.' Tom didn't respond to that. Instead he left the room with the beer he had been drinking and went into the kitchen.

Bradshaw hoped he was thinking it through. He drained the dregs from his beer while he waited and when Tom returned the journalist said quietly, 'It's just . . . I've got a lot on at the moment.'

'I can see how the DIY might be taking up all of your precious time but I'll leave this here just in case.' Bradshaw placed a Manila folder full of documents on the table in front of him. 'There's enough here to give you an overview. Like I said, a man is suffering right now so if you wake up in the morning and change your mind about working with us . . . then I'll see you at the Rosewood café. Breakfast will be on me if you are mature enough to accept it.'

Ian Bradshaw left, but as he was walking down the driveway, Tom appeared at the door behind him. 'Ian,' he called and when Bradshaw turned back to face the journalist, hoping he'd had a change of heart, Tom called, 'you're a sanctimonious prick at times. Has anyone ever told you that?'

'No,' replied Bradshaw cheerfully, 'but I've been called far worse things.'

'I'm bloody sure you have,' replied Tom as he closed the door firmly behind him.

Tom Carney didn't sleep that night. Instead he lay awake while reminding himself of numerous good reasons for avoiding another partnership with Durham Constabulary, even if they had sent a bloke he usually had a high opinion of to act as peace maker.

Tom was busy enough with the Rebecca Holt case. The more he thought about it, the more he became convinced the jury had convicted Richard Bell of murder on the strength of a collective aversion to his personality, coupled with previous evidence of a loss of control against a woman years earlier. The lack of an alibi didn't help either. To be truthful, Tom Carney did not know whether Richard Bell was a murderer or not. Bell could very well be conning him to evade justice but Tom was intrigued enough to probe deeper to find out what really happened to Rebecca.

But, and there was a big but, he would struggle to do this without cooperative contacts in the local police force. In the past he could have called up Ian Bradshaw and asked him to check a fact or give him a bit of inside information, but that avenue was now closed to him. In fact, he knew that if he reopened an old case like the Rebecca Holt murder this would only serve to annoy Bradshaw's superiors further, since they already had their conviction and would not want its veracity threatened by a meddlesome reporter.

There was also his financial situation. Richard Bell's family would pay him a retainer while he worked on the case and he was glad of this, since it might help him to keep his home, but even working on the case part time would rob him of the hours he needed to finish the seemingly never-ending project. If the police were willing to pay him too Tom could hire someone to finish all of the jobs in the house. Then he could sell it and go back to what he was really good at. He couldn't do that while he was embroiled in an ongoing feud with Durham Constabulary though.

Finally, there was the girl to think of. Tom knew a favourable outcome was unlikely at this stage but whatever had happened to Sandra, her family deserved to learn the truth, however painful that might be; rather than see out the rest of their lives in a terrible limbo, not knowing if their daughter was alive or dead.

Tom sat up then, pulled back the covers and climbed out

of bed. 'What's the bloody point?' he asked himself, as he gave up on sleep and trudged downstairs. He made a cup of tea then picked up the photograph of Sandra Jarvis that was next to the file Bradshaw had left him. The girl's unsmiling face gave her an enigmatic appearance, as if she was deliberately harbouring a secret.

'What happened to you?' he asked Sandra's picture. 'Where did you go?'

Chapter Sixteen

The Rosewood café had one of those bells that rang when the front door opened. Ian Bradshaw glanced over at the door's steamed-up window every time the bell made a sound.

On the sixth time it rang, his vigilance was rewarded. 'I didn't expect you to turn up.' Bradshaw looked into a tired face with dark marks under the eyes.

'I'm always happy to take a breakfast from Northumbria Police,' Tom told him.

'I wouldn't want you to think of it as a bribe.'

'Right now, for a double bacon butty I'd sell my soul, along with all of my journalistic principles.'

'What principles?' scoffed Bradshaw then he grinned. 'We can throw in a fried egg if you like and a pot of tea.'

'Coffee,' Tom insisted and he sat down opposite the detective. A moment later a young girl appeared and Tom waited till she had taken their order.

'Okay,' he said, 'I'll help you with your case,' but before Bradshaw could enjoy his small moment of triumph he added, 'but there's one condition.'

'What?'

'You have to help me with mine.'

Kane did not invite Bradshaw to sit down and the younger man was glad of it. He wanted to get out of the DCI's office before Katie Tennant got the hump with him again.

'Did you tell him we'd put him on the payroll?' asked Kane.

'Yes,' said Bradshaw.

'And?'

'It wasn't enough.'

'The greedy bastard!' the DCI flared.

'I don't mean the money,' Bradshaw said quickly, 'it's not about that.'

'What then?'

'He's working on something else,' said Bradshaw, 'and you're not going to like it.' He explained Tom Carney's interest in the Rebecca Holt case then.

'You're joking,' was Kane's response and Bradshaw wondered why people always said that, even when it was patently obvious no one was joking.

'I'm afraid not.'

'Why does he want to open up that can of worms? Richard Bell was tried and convicted.'

'But the evidence was largely circumstantial,' said Bradshaw, adding hurriedly, 'according to Carney.'

'I'm familiar with the case, I was SIO on it,' Kane reminded Bradshaw, 'and there was enough there to satisfy us and the CPS that there was a reasonable chance of a conviction in a murder trial. The jury agreed with us and Bell got life . . . but he's convinced Tom Carney he's innocent?'

'Carney is not saying he's innocent, just that there is some doubt about his guilt. He thinks the jury might have been influenced by Bell's personality.'

'Quite possibly,' admitted Kane, 'the man shagged everything that moved.'

'Bell's family are hiring him to take another look at the case. They want him to discover new evidence that might exonerate Bell.'

'I'm thinking of the shortest verse in the Bible right now,' admitted Kane.

'Sir?'

'Jesus wept,' Kane sighed. 'He won't find anything, we went over it all endlessly.'

'Then it probably won't do any harm,' offered Bradshaw. 'He's promised he'll keep an open mind and if he uncovers anything that Richard Bell won't want to hear, he'll tell him anyway.'

'Including proof that he did it?'

'Including that.'

'So he's too busy to help us?'

Bradshaw hesitated. 'Well he did make one suggestion, but I strongly suspect you are not going to like it.' Bradshaw wasn't sure he liked the suggestion either.

'Go on,' said Kane impatiently, 'out with it.'

'He says he will help us with our case if we help him with his.'

'Ha! He wants us to investigate a case we've already looked into and taken to a satisfactory conclusion, so we can undermine ourselves?'

'Something like that.'

'The cheek of the man.' Kane fell silent for a long while then. Bradshaw knew his boss was pondering Tom Carney's bizarre offer. He was more than a bit surprised when the DCI suddenly said, 'What harm can it do? You said that yourself.'

'So you want us to help him with the Richard Bell case?' Bradshaw genuinely wasn't sure if that was what his boss was suggesting.

'Why not? We can provide him with some inside information, let him read the case files and so on,' said Kane amiably. 'If he has a lead that needs following up, assuming it's a sensible one, then I suppose there's no harm in lending a hand with it, strictly on the QT, as long as it doesn't tie you up for too long.'

'Me?' Bradshaw *really* didn't like that idea.

'Of course you,' said Kane, 'who else?'

'But I'm working on the burned girl case for DI Tennant. Are you taking me off that?'

'Oh no, I couldn't do that. Katie Tennant would rightly see that as a depletion of her already limited resources. No, you'll have to do it in your spare time.'

'Spare time? I haven't got any spare time.'

'Then make some,' snapped Kane. 'If Tom Carney will bring his undoubted skills, along with his hugely annoying personality, to bear on the Frank Jarvis case then it will be worth it – because I am telling you now, he'll not find anything new for Richard Bell. We had some of our best men on it.'

'Skelton and O'Brien,' said Bradshaw before he could stop himself.

'Amongst others.' The tone was a rebuke. 'There were twenty detectives at one point. I put every good man I could find on it in the early days.' That was another putdown, as Bradshaw had never been asked to work the Rebecca Holt murder.

'I'm not sure I will get away with working on the Sandra Jarvis disappearance and re-examining the Rebecca Holt murder in my spare time, without DI Tennant noticing, sir.'

'Oh I get it,' said Kane and his eyes narrowed slyly. 'It's that bit of skirt you're seeing, isn't it? What's-her-name; the fit one, with the blonde hair?'

Bradshaw knew he should have taken issue with his senior officer for describing his girlfriend as a 'bit of skirt'. This was 1995 for God's sake, not the Dark Ages. He also knew his DCI would be completely baffled to be pulled up by Bradshaw on it. Kane would assume he had actually just paid the younger man a compliment. In truth Bradshaw lacked the energy to fight yet another battle and cursed himself inwardly for his cowardice. How the hell did his boss know who he was seeing, in any case?

'Karen,' he answered.

'Yes, her,' Kane nodded, 'you don't want to miss too many nights in with Karen now you're shacked up together.'

'We don't live together!' protested Bradshaw. What the hell had made his boss think that?

'Oh, I heard she'd moved in. Anyway, it doesn't matter.' He waved his hand dismissively. 'Don't worry, you'll still have most of your evenings together, just put a bit of your leisure time into this and I won't forget it. I have a solution that will give you some days away from DI Tennant without Katie getting her knickers in a twist,' he said and he smiled smugly. 'Mentoring.'

'Mentoring?'

'It's a new initiative from the Home Office and championed by the Chief Constable. Senior officers select junior officers with potential and give them mentoring. It'll make you stand out and you might even get fast-tracked.'

'What would I have to do?'

'I'll get you a copy of my diary; you make a note of the things I'm doing, particularly any off-site stuff, leadership courses, visits to other forces, meetings with local brass or politicians, that kind of thing, and you tag along,' he said, 'only you won't be tagging along, you'll be working the other cases. Katie Tennant won't be pleased you're missing days with her team of course but she'll like it a lot more than the truth.'

'But I wouldn't actually be getting any mentoring though, would I?'

'Oh, don't worry about that,' Kane was dismissive, 'it's all a load of rubbish anyway. I mentor you lot every day. Look we can meet up and I'll have a chat with you about your career, your strengths and your . . . er . . . weaknesses, so you can work on them. We'll even map out a career plan for you and I'll get one of the girls to type it up so you can show it to Katie Tennant.' He beamed at Bradshaw. 'The best thing is we can do all of this in the pub. I've always said you learn way more having a few pints with the men above you than you do actually on duty. How does that sound?'

'Great, sir,' said Bradshaw quickly, for he knew this was the answer expected of him.

'But Katie cannot know the real reason you are AWOL from her team,' said Kane. 'It's an off-the-record thing you're doing for me here. DI Tennant will be extremely upset if she finds out about it,' Kane reminded him, 'but her anger will be as nothing compared to my vengeful wrath if you fuck this up,' and he let that sink in, 'got that, Bradshaw?'

'Yes, sir.'

'Good lad,' said DCI Kane, 'now enjoy the rest of your day.'

The statement was terse, short and to the point. 'I do not comment on private family matters,' was all Councillor Lynch offered in his defence, so Helen's newspaper ran the story of his suspicious house sale with that quote at the bottom.

Helen hadn't expected Lynch to phone her back the next morning and threaten her. It was so blatant she had trouble accepting that the words were actually coming from the leader of the city council but when she pushed him a little on whether he had ever met the mysterious Mr Cooper, things rapidly escalated.

'Who the fuck do you think you are?' he snarled at her, and these ferocious words were so unexpected from someone in a position of power that Helen immediately felt queasy. But Joe Lynch was far from through. 'I have worked tirelessly for the people of this city for more than twenty years, then you come along and try to destroy me. Well I won't let that happen, Helen Norton,' and he paused for a second before adding, 'of 14a Monks Walk, Jesmond. Yeah,' he said, 'I know where you live and I know what kind of person you are.' Then he used a stream of foul, misogynistic, four-letter words to describe her that she might have expected from a man like Jimmy McCree but not an elected official.

'Now wait a minute . . .' she began.

'No!' he shouted. 'You've already had your say, now it's my turn. You picked the wrong guy to fuck with, you bitch. I am going to end you, Miss Norton.' And he abruptly hung up.

When he had gone, Helen sat at her desk in complete shock. She realised she was still holding the phone uselessly in her hand when she heard its dead tone. She got up and went to the toilet, ran the cold tap then splashed water on her face.

She had just been threatened by the most powerful politician in the city. *'I am going to end you, Miss Norton,'* he had warned her – but was this the bluster of an impotent man or a real threat from a corrupt official who was friends with criminals? Did *end you* mean her career or her life? She felt sick.

Helen knew this was the point in the Hollywood film when the plucky young reporter vows to take on the all-powerful men at the top, no matter what the cost to her personally – but this was no movie. This was real life, and suddenly Helen Norton was very scared indeed.

Chapter Seventeen

'Mrs Bell is at a meeting,' the lady on reception told him, 'but we're expecting her back around midday.'

Tom glanced at his watch. 'Do you mind if I wait?'

'Not at all; is she expecting you?'

'Yes,' he lied. Tom figured their first meeting might be more fruitful if Annie Bell wasn't entirely on her guard when he arrived.

A little over twenty minutes passed before a brand new hatchback pulled into Annie Bell's reserved space by the front door at the head office of her father's company, Soleil. Tom watched Annie cross the open area towards reception. She was of average height, with what could be described as average looks, but immaculately dressed in a dark business suit. She looked a little older than her years, with a premature touch of grey in her dark curly hair but who could blame her for that?

Tom intercepted Annie before the receptionist could introduce him, 'Mrs Bell, I'm Tom Carney.'

He thought he was being discreet by not mentioning her husband but her first words to him were, 'I thought you would come to the house.'

'I did,' he explained, 'but the cleaner told me you were at work, so . . .'

'. . . Here you are,' she completed the sentence for him. Annie looked around uncertainly.

'I assumed you'd have an office,' he said quietly, 'somewhere private.'

'Alright.' She led him inside. They passed rows of desks, where a surprisingly subdued group of people were working in front of large computer monitors.

Annie Bell's office was at the end of the room. She closed the door behind them and Tom brought a chair closer to her desk so they were facing one another. Annie's office was a curiously impersonal work space, aside from one small, silver-framed photograph of two smiling little girls.

'My two,' she said when she noticed he was looking at the photo. 'I know they look like butter wouldn't melt but they can be a right handful.'

'They're lovely,' he said. 'I apologise if my appearance here is an embarrassment.'

'A surprise, but not an embarrassment,' said Annie. 'I'm a senior manager at a company owned by my father, which employs a large number of people, all of whom know my husband is serving a life sentence for the murder of his lover,' she paused, 'how's that for embarrassment?'

'It must be difficult.'

'It is,' Annie admitted, 'but you know what's more difficult? Knowing he is innocent and not being able to do a damn thing about it.'

'You seem very sure about his innocence.'

'I am.'

'You've never had any doubts? Even during the trial when you heard some pretty bad things about Richard.'

'I have had two years to process the information from the trial. I learned that my husband was a womaniser. Do I like that fact? No. Do I take some of the blame for it? Perhaps but not all. He did what he did and he certainly had a choice not to do it. Does that make him a murderer? God, no. Richard is a gentle soul. I know him better than anyone and I can tell you this from my heart, he did not kill that woman.'

He noticed she did not refer to Rebecca Holt by name. 'So who did? Kill her, I mean.' Then he added, 'Was it you?'

'If that's meant to be a joke, it's not very funny.'

'It's an honest question,' he said, 'and one I have to ask if you want me to look into your husband's case.' When she was slow to respond to that, Tom added, 'Assuming you do want me to look into it, because now's the time to tell me if you don't.'

'I am in favour of anything that might help my husband prove he is innocent, Mr Carney, though I'll admit I was pinning my hopes on a successful appeal – we all were.'

'But you have your doubts,' he asked her, 'about me looking into the case?'

She took a while to answer him. 'I don't want my husband's hopes to be raised without foundation,' she said. 'Richard was devastated when his appeal request was rejected. He went into a big depression for a while,' she explained, 'then he read your book. The next time I visited him, it was all he could talk about. He told me he'd written to you and was hopeful of a reply. I didn't discourage him because I could see what that faint glimmer of hope did for his mood, but I'll admit I'm concerned about the impact on him if you are unable to find anything new.'

'So am I. I'm not even sure I'm the right man to help him.'

'Richard is convinced you are,' said Annie, 'he calls you a truth-seeker.'

'But you think he's clutching at straws?'

'Drowning men do.'

'Is that what he is?'

'Oh yes,' she said, 'I can see the effect that place is having on him. I have to get him out of there.'

'By finding the real killer?'

'Right now that would appear to be our only option, wouldn't you say?'

'It wasn't you then?' he asked amiably.

'No.'

'Convince me.'

She sighed, and looked out of her window for the umpteenth time since they'd been there. 'Not here,' she said and suddenly Annie Bell was on her feet.

Annie marched to the front of the building at speed but Tom managed to keep pace with her as they left the headquarters. 'I can't talk in there,' she said and he understood that. It couldn't have been easy being Annie Bell, even two years after the trial. 'We'll go to the park.'

As they walked past her car he said, 'Nice motor.'

She answered absent-mindedly, 'I drive a different one every week.'

'How do you manage that?'

'I don't own them. It's from the manufacturer. We have a large fleet of company cars. We get demonstrators dropped in every two or three weeks,' she explained. 'The novelty wears off pretty quickly.'

'I'd be willing to risk that,' he said. 'So what exactly does Soleil do?'

'We provide a range of integrated IT solutions tailored to suit the needs of an individual business. We don't just sell unsuitable products then leave you to pick up the pieces. Our sales team act as management consultants who will help a firm with every step, from the purchase of hardware to the creation and installation of tailored software and staff training programmes then we help to set up management information reports.'

'Sounds like a lot of hand-holding; must be expensive.'

'In this life, you get what you pay for.'

The entrance to the park was a few hundred yards from Annie's office. She directed him to a bench in front of some hedges shaded by a large tree whose leaves had started to fall and littered the ground around them. 'I have my lunch here every day,' she said and he got the strong impression she did that alone. 'It's my favourite spot.'

'It's very peaceful.' He joined her on the bench and they sat for a moment in silence until she decided to answer the question he'd asked in her office.

'I might very well have harboured murderous thoughts towards that woman if I had known anything about her,' said Annie. 'Oh, I knew of her existence, even met her once, but I had no idea she was in any kind of relationship with my husband, until the police turned up on our doorstep to tell Richard she'd been murdered. Then it all came out, eventually. They quizzed me about her obviously. I suppose I was even a suspect at first but I had an alibi for the day of the murder . . .'

'You had a day off,' he recalled, 'shopping in town?'

'Yes,' she said, 'lots of people saw me,' adding, 'then later the forensic expert said the blows could only have been administered by a man, so that should convince you.'

'I read that,' he said, 'so who *did* kill Rebecca Holt, if not Richard or yourself?'

'Her husband of course,' she said, as if it was obvious, 'though we'll have a devil of a time proving it. He also has an alibi, for one thing.'

'I'm not one for trusting alibis, Mrs Bell,' Tom said pointedly, 'they can be bought or manufactured.'

'Well I didn't buy mine,' she challenged him, 'there's probably a dozen people who saw me in town during the course of that day.'

'That was convenient.'

'I'm a working mother,' Annie reminded him, 'I rarely have time alone. I run in the mornings though, before I take the kids to school. That's my time. The rest of my day is pretty hectic.'

'So you think Freddie Holt may have done it? You don't subscribe to the mad stranger theory?'

'That's possible too, but her husband had a motive.'

'Mad strangers don't need a motive. It's what makes them mad. Her husband didn't necessarily have a motive either, come to think of it.'

'She cheated on him.'

'He didn't know about that until after she was found dead,' said Tom.

'That's what he said,' scoffed Annie, 'but you don't really believe that, do you?'

'Why not?' asked Tom. 'You expect me to believe the same thing about you.'

'You obviously don't know much about Freddie Holt,' she said.

'What do you mean by that?'

'If ever there was a man capable of murder, it's him.'

They spent half an hour discussing the rumours that followed Freddie Holt while he amassed his fortune. If a tenth of them were true, Rebecca Holt's husband was a fully paid-up member of the ruthless bastard society who was not afraid to bend rules or even hurt people if he thought it was required.

Annie glanced at her watch. 'I have a meeting,' she told Tom. 'If you're finished,' then she demurred, 'for now?'

'Not quite. I do have one last question for you,' said Tom, 'and it's this: why would you care one way or another about the well-being of your cheating bastard of a husband when most women would probably abandon him?'

'*Would* most women abandon him? Perhaps, but I doubt it. This is the real world and he is not just my *bastard of a husband*, as you put it, he's the father of my children. I have two wonderful daughters who miss their daddy very much and want him back. I said I was partially to blame for his behaviour and that was no exaggeration.'

'In what way?'

She looked embarrassed then. 'I wasn't always there for him. Having a full-time job and two small children . . . I was tired a lot of the time . . . We drifted apart. I regret not putting the time and energy into our marriage that I gave to my career and the girls. I think he resented that and sought comfort, if that's the right word, elsewhere. I will always feel responsible for that.'

'Then why work at all? Did you even need to, financially I mean?'

'Because my husband was Sales Director and my father is well off?' She looked disappointed by him. 'Stop being a senior manager in the company and become a housewife instead, living off other people's money, attending coffee mornings and yoga classes? That's not who I am, Mr Carney. It's not who I was brought up to be.'

'I see,' he said. 'I have a list of people I would like to speak to about your husband and his case. One of them is your father.'

She frowned at him. 'Why do you want to speak to Dad?'

'I'd like to get his perspective.'

'I'm afraid he doesn't want to talk to you.'

'Why not?'

'He isn't necessarily in favour of this.'

'I see,' said Tom, 'then it would be useful for me to know his reasons.'

'I have always been one hundred per cent behind my husband. I never doubted his innocence for a moment. My father however . . .'

'Thinks that he did it.'

'. . . Is less convinced than I am. The trial soured his opinion of Richard. My husband's behaviour obviously upset my father. We have clients and investors. My father had to explain that one of his key employees, his own son-in-law, had been found guilty of murder. Obviously that was difficult. He understood Richard wanted to appeal but when that was refused he felt it was the end of the matter. I disagree.'

'So your father thinks you should leave Richard in prison.'

'He doesn't think I have any choice, but Richard wants you to help him and I support my husband's decision.'

'Is Daddy paying my retainer?'

She shook her head. 'I have my own money, Mr Carney. Daddy, as you call him, has no say in this.'

Chapter Eighteen

The multi-storey car park was dark even during daylight hours, thanks to low, grey, concrete ceilings supported on thick pillars, the gloom broken only by light coming from narrow spaces at either end of a long line of parked cars. Helen crossed the ground floor then found the lift had broken down, forcing her to take the stairs, which were lit by bare bulbs strong enough to illuminate the misspelt graffiti covering the walls. As the door closed behind her she was entirely alone and suddenly felt extremely vulnerable in this enclosed space so she moved quickly, becoming out of breath as she took each set of steps without pausing until she reached her floor. This wasn't where she wanted to be right now. Not when she had just been threatened by a powerful man with gangsters for friends, but Helen couldn't spend her whole career hiding in the newsroom. She had just interviewed a youth worker who was helping teenagers avoid gangs by teaching them boxing and this necessitated a visit to one of the rougher parts of the city. Helen had to push the heavy door hard to get it to open and its lowest edge scraped against the ground as it moved. It eventually swung noisily open before wedging itself into the concrete. Once again she was alone and the car park was so quiet every step she made was audible as she crossed the floor.

There was something that didn't feel quite right here, an atmosphere that Helen told herself was caused solely by her overwrought imagination, because she was in an unmanned car park and had seen too many movies where lone women were suddenly pounced on by men who lurked in dark shadows. Nonetheless, she quickened her pace.

Helen was halfway to safety and beginning to feel calmer when there was a sudden loud bang that made her simultaneously start and turn in a panic towards the noise. She almost stumbled, convinced that she was about to be attacked.

But there was no one there.

It took Helen seconds to work out the cause of the noise that had echoed across the car park. The door she wedged open slammed shut with a terrific bang. Helen took two deep breaths before she felt able to resume her walk to her car, which was on the upper of the two levels on this floor. That meant climbing the ramp the cars used, as she could not see a footpath. She did this briskly while looking around her to make sure no one was following. Helen knew she was well and truly rattled now but she couldn't help herself. She vividly recalled the threats from Councillor Lynch and knew the company he was keeping these days. She told herself she had good cause to be nervous.

Helen spotted her car, but as she drew closer, what she saw stopped her in her tracks. Someone must have followed her here – how else could they have known where to find her car? The message had been sprayed on the light-coloured bodywork in thick, dark lettering as unsubtle as the words used: 'Bitch, whore, slag.' It was enough to make Helen feel sick and she was momentarily torn. She had no desire to go near the car but nor did she want to risk going down that dark, enclosed staircase again. She couldn't stand out here in the open either. What if the man who had done this was still nearby? What if he was watching her right now?

Helen decided to move and set off at a normal walking pace

towards her car, noting with relief that at least her tyres remained undamaged. If the vandal was watching her, she was determined not to let him see how upset she was. Helen banished her feelings of revulsion and kept walking. She put her hand into her bag and drew out the keys so she could get into the car and drive away as quickly as possible.

She was only a few yards from her car when it suddenly dawned on her that whoever did this could be inside. He might even be lying in wait for her on the back seat.

She steeled herself and gripped the keys in her palm, ensuring the pointed end stuck out through her fingers. If he was inside and he leapt for her, she swore she would gouge him in the face.

Heart pounding, Helen reached the car and stole a quick glance inside, but saw nothing on the back seat and no one hiding in the foot wells. Instantly her fear of the car was replaced by a desperate desire to climb inside it as quickly as possible and lock the door. She moved the key into a more natural position, opened the door and got in as fast as she was able. Helen slammed the door so quickly she banged her knee, but without pausing, she started the car's engine, reversed swiftly out of the space and drove as fast as she dared for the exit.

The rain was lashing down on Ian Bradshaw as he stood disconsolately on Elvet Bridge, cursing Tom Carney for his lateness. Why had he agreed to meet the reporter in Durham city out in the open? Because the weather had been deceptively warm and sunny earlier that day and it had seemed like a good idea at the time.

'You're late,' he told Tom as he trudged towards Bradshaw with his hands tucked into his jacket pockets.

'Traffic was a bastard. They are digging up the roads

again. I told you we should have met in a pub.' Tom couldn't see the point of meeting at all, since he couldn't imagine DCI Kane agreeing to his little deal.

'I'm on duty,' Bradshaw reminded him, 'it's alright for you.' And the two men walked across the stone bridge together into the old core of the city.

'Then have a bloody orange juice, for God's sake,' snapped Tom. He squinted against the rain that was driven into them by a swirling wind and steered Bradshaw along Sadler Street, which led to the famous cathedral at the top of the hill. They didn't get that far though, as Tom motioned for Bradshaw to follow him into the Shakespeare, an ancient, tiny pub that provided a comfortable nook against the foul weather.

Tom ordered the drinks while Bradshaw removed his sodden coat and hung it on the back of a chair, where it dripped onto the floor.

'Kane has given the go-ahead,' he said when Tom returned with a glass of orange juice and a pint of bitter the detective eyed enviously.

'Really?' Tom could hardly have been more surprised. 'You did tell him my side of the deal?' he asked suspiciously.

'Of course,' snapped Bradshaw. 'Don't worry, you'll get the help you asked for.'

'Oh, so that's it.'

'What?'

'He asked *you* to do the helping didn't he,' Tom told him, 'which explains why you are narked. Well you should have seen that coming.'

'I'm not narked. I'm just dripping wet and you're the one with the beer.' Bradshaw sipped his orange juice then pulled the face a small child makes tasting medicine.

'I thought you'd be happy. You got Kane what he wanted.'

'And you got what you wanted too,' Bradshaw reminded him. 'I'm just the one stuck in the middle.'

'Cheer up. It'll be like old times.'

'I'm just very busy right now but maybe I'll have more luck with another case. So, where do we start?'

Tom shrugged. 'Anywhere,' he said, 'everywhere.'

'That's helpful.'

Tom realised Bradshaw was determined to play the grump, so he began with the case the detective cared about most. 'Okay, answer a question I have about Sandra Jarvis. According to the file you left me, she was seen around the city for a couple of days after her father saw her last. They had an argument, she stormed off and didn't come back, but where did she go?'

'They drew a blank on that,' said Bradshaw, meaning his compatriots in Northumbria Police.

'She didn't crash with a friend?'

'If she did, they couldn't find her . . . or him . . . or someone was lying,' said Bradshaw.

'So if she didn't stay at a mate's, what did she do between rowing with Dad and leaving the city two days later?'

'We don't know, but we got a number of sightings when we appealed for witnesses after her disappearance. She was seen in the Grainger market and Northumberland Street. There were also sightings in the Quayside and one at the Metro Centre.'

'So she went shopping? Doesn't sound like Sandra Jarvis was too stressed at that point then, but she was definitely last seen at the railway station?'

'They have a whizzy new CCTV system. An eagle-eyed detective went through hours of footage until he spotted her.'

'Good for him,' said Tom and he meant it. 'And they say your job isn't glamorous.'

'It has its moments,' said Bradshaw, 'but most of the time it's mundane slog, like the case I'm working on right now in fact.' And he told Tom Carney a little about the burned girl and the problems they were having identifying her.

'And there's no chance your burned girl could be Sandra Jarvis?' Tom asked. 'Not that I'm saying you haven't thought of that, but if you can't identify her?'

'We can rule that out. Sandra Jarvis is considerably taller.'

'This picture of Sandra taken from the CCTV,' Tom asked, 'where is it?'

'It will be in the case files in Newcastle,' said the detective,

'I'd like to see it.'

'I'll get you in there,' he told Tom. 'They're holding a lot of information about her that you'll want to wade through.'

'And while I'm doing that . . .' Tom said slowly.

'Sounds ominous,' replied Bradshaw. 'What do you want?'

'We had a deal, remember?' said Tom. 'I help you with your case and you help me with mine.'

'Yeah, yeah, what do you need me to do?'

'Check out the local perverts for me,' said Tom.

'Excuse me?'

'I need you to look into Lonely Lane,' he told the detective. 'I want to know everything that goes on down there.'

As Tom drove back into Newcastle he kept the radio on out of habit. At this time of the day, between the lunch-time news and drive-time, the local station hardly played any music, having long since realised phone-ins with unpaid members of the general public were far cheaper than paying royalties for songs. In this instance, talk really was cheap.

Today's topic was a popular one, as it involved the region's unofficial religion, football. Newcastle United were top of the league and finally poised to end their decades-long wait for a trophy. They were so far ahead of anyone else that failure seemed a virtual impossibility.

'Howay man,' a caller assured a sceptical radio host, 'even Newcastle couldn't cock this up.'

'Don't bet on it,' muttered Tom as he steered his car into a street full of red-brick, two-up-two-down terraced houses then parked it behind a white van that was so caked in grime someone had used a finger to write, 'I wish my missus was this dirty,' in the muck on its rear doors.

Tom knocked at number twenty. She took so long to answer he assumed no one was in, and was about to walk away when the front door swung open.

'Mrs Jarvis?' he asked the startled-looking woman who answered.

'Yes,' she said in a very quiet voice, as if she wasn't entirely sure.

'I'm here to see your husband,' he told her. 'I'm Tom Carney.' He expected her to ask him in but instead she disappeared into the house without another word, leaving the door open. Rather than wait on the doorstep he followed her inside.

As he entered the lounge she was leaving it through the kitchen door and he heard the heavy back door open. She mumbled something that could have been, 'I'll get him,' but it was barely audible. He was left standing in the living room and he was not alone.

An old lady wearing a white cardigan over a floral-pattern dress was sitting in an armchair, peering at him intently, her face cratered by deep wrinkles.

'Who are you?' she asked accusingly.

'I'm Tom,' he offered, and hoped that might be sufficient explanation.

'And what do *you* want, Tom?' she asked archly, as if everyone who visited the Jarvis household was a con man of some kind.

'I'm here to help Councillor Jarvis.' From her age and the fact she seemed quite at home here, this had to be Sandra's grandmother.

'Help him with what?'

'He has asked me to try and find his daughter.' He knew this revelation could upset the old woman.

'Oh, that one,' she said dismissively, 'she's a little cuckoo.'

Tom was taken aback by the description of her own granddaughter but from the slightly glazed expression on the old lady's ancient eyes she did not appear qualified to comment on someone else's mental stability. She opened her mouth as if she was going to add something. 'It's not as if . . .'

'Be quiet, Mother,' snapped Mrs Jarvis, who reappeared suddenly in the doorway. The old woman didn't seem unduly concerned at being silenced so sharply. The councillor's wife turned her attention to Tom. 'He's not out back. He must be down the allotment.' She said this as if she couldn't quite remember whether he had told her or not.

'Okay,' Tom said, 'could you maybe point me in the right direction?'

'So what can I do for you, Detective Sergeant,' asked Sergeant Hennessey. He was one of those old hands who was always cheerful because he was edging closer to retirement with every passing day.

'I'm after some information about Lonely Lane,' said Bradshaw.

'Shaggers' Alley?' asked Hennessey. 'What do you want to know?'

'It's something I'm looking into for a case.' He felt no need to elaborate but needn't have worried, for Hennessey didn't even feign interest. 'I've heard it's like the Wild West out there,' Bradshaw concluded, expecting the other man to play it down.

'You would not believe what goes on out there after dark,' he offered instead, 'other than the obvious.' Bradshaw assumed he was hinting about darker deeds than teenage sex and extramarital affairs.

'We've not had many arrests though.'

'There's been loads,' said Hennessey and when Bradshaw looked puzzled he added, 'just not many charges. Between you and me, we let most of them off with a caution or a warning.'

'Why?'

'Because, my dear friend,' said Hennessey, 'if we arrested every man down there with his cock out, the cells would be fit to bursting and the Assistant Commissioner would have my guts for garters.'

'I don't understand,' said Bradshaw and he really didn't. 'Surely if these people are caught committing criminal acts we should be arresting, charging and convicting.'

'Oh my poor naïve soul,' Hennessey said to Bradshaw condescendingly, 'it cannot work that way. Why, because all of our recorded crimes would go through the roof in an instant and that's all anyone in authority cares about these days: stats and figures. No, no, no, we give the perverts a slap on the wrist and send them packing, which hopefully deters some of the less determined ones from getting their todgers out in public again.'

'So you're just talking about flashers and the like?'

'I'm talking about everything,' he said. 'We've stumbled across gang bangs and even a group of Satanists once, in flowing white robes. We've had more than one case of bestiality with farm animals and literally hundreds of married men hooking up with gay boys. Do you want me to charge all of them? I'm sure their wives and families don't – and they *certainly* don't.'

'What about attacks,' pressed Bradshaw, 'on women? Do you ever get anything like that?'

'Oh God, yeah,' said the sergeant, 'every other night.'

Bradshaw was staggered. Hennessey made it sound as if they were discussing trivial stuff like an argument in a pub not men preying on women. 'Every other night?'

'I exaggerate of course,' he conceded, 'but we get several cases a month where a woman comes in here claiming she's been grabbed by a man or men in that area.'

'Are you serious?'

'Deadly,' he shook his head, 'but you don't get it. Trust me, I do most of the interviewing. The vast majority of them were off their tits on drink and suddenly decided it's a great idea to walk along one of the dozens of lanes that criss-cross the countryside in that part of the world. They go out in those skimpy little outfits, get pissed and head home on their own or they wander up there with a bloke they've just met and, when they've finished copping off with him, head off by themselves in the middle of the night. I mean, come on, talk about asking for trouble. It's no wonder they get groped and sometimes worse.'

Bradshaw could not quite believe what the old-timer was telling him. Sergeant Hennessey didn't seem to care about any of the women who reported these incidents, but before

Bradshaw could pull him up on this he was off again. 'They usually can't provide any kind of description because the guy has crept up on them from behind. It's dark, they're pissed and scared. I mean tell me, how do you investigate that? Knock on every door in Durham and say, "Excuse me, sir, did you grab a bird's tits last night down Shaggers' Alley and I'm only talking about the ones who didn't want you to?" Imagine the paperwork.'

Bradshaw found himself hoping this waste of space was going to take his pension soon, but had to hold his tongue till he had all the information he needed. 'What about more serious stuff? You ever get men who do more than grope? I'm talking rape or attempted rape.'

'From time to time,' he said calmly, 'but we don't usually report it like that.'

'What the hell do you mean?'

Hennessey clearly didn't like the way Bradshaw had addressed him. 'Listen, son, you don't understand what it is like dealing with these types of crimes. A report of stranger rape sets alarm bells ringing all over the place but the conviction rate for rape is unbelievably low. You deal with murder or assault, the accused doesn't normally say, "It was consensual."' He was putting a stupid voice on now. 'Or, "She was asking for it." You get some pissed-up slapper who's already shagged half the town walking home on her own and she's dragged into a bush somewhere by a stranger. The first thing his defence lawyer is going to say is "You wanted it and now you feel guilty so you're crying rape," and you know what, half the time that's exactly what's happened.' He surveyed Bradshaw to see if he understood his reasoning. 'I'm telling you, ninety-nine times out of a hundred a jury is going to go along with that.'

'So it's the victim's fault?' said Bradshaw. 'Is that what you tell them?'

'No,' he said. 'Look, don't be like that. I'm not callous. I sit them down, make them a cup of tea and give them a biscuit, we even get female officers to have a word with them, but most of the time they end up agreeing with us.'

'About what?'

'That it's not worth pursuing.'

'You're not serious?'

'Of course I am. Look, why put yourself through the ordeal all over again when we probably won't ever find the guy, let alone arrest him. There's all those intrusive examinations from the doctor, you have to go to court and they pick your whole life apart, the newspapers are jotting it all down and the bloke who's done it to you is standing in the dock not five yards away. Far better to put it all behind you and get on with your life.'

Bradshaw picked up the photograph on Hennessey's desk. 'Your daughter?' he asked of the dark-haired smiling girl in her graduation robes.

'Yep,' he said proudly.

'Let's hope she never meets one of the men you've been too lazy to arrest.'

'What did you say?' He got to his feet as if Bradshaw had stepped over the line. For a moment Bradshaw actually thought a punch might be thrown his way but he was ready for that.

'No, you hang on.' Bradshaw towered over the time-server and jabbed him in the chest with a finger. Hennessey hesitated when he saw the look in the detective sergeant's eyes. 'How would you feel if someone gave your daughter the advice you've been giving the women you meet? You could have been putting some of these guys away but they're still out there, thanks to you. You're a bloody disgrace. You've forgotten what you're here for and the sooner you fuck off for good the better.'

Bradshaw was fuming. It wasn't just Hennessey's attitude towards the countless women he'd talked out of making a fuss about indecent assault or even rape that infuriated him. When Richard Bell was on trial no one seriously believed a maniac was roaming the area round Lonely Lane, but Bradshaw knew killers often committed less serious offences before their crimes gradually escalated. If Rebecca Holt *had* been beaten to death by a crazed stranger, it now seemed possible he could have been stopped long before if Bradshaw's own force had taken the situation seriously. Instead the killer might have been let off with a caution or not even pursued at all. That was a thought that genuinely chilled him.

When the older man sat back down again Bradshaw told him, 'You're not a police officer, you're an accomplice.'

Chapter Nineteen

The allotments were set back from the main road behind an old Methodist chapel, three rows of terraced houses and some playing fields. There was no sign of Frank Jarvis here but the allotments covered a substantial area with paths leading to left and right and a third route that climbed the hill ahead of him. A man who looked to be in his sixties was digging into the soil of the nearest allotment.

'I'm looking for Frank Jarvis,' said Tom.

'Are you, now?' He ceased his digging for a moment. 'Well he's right at the top of the pile, as per bloody usual.'

'Sorry?'

The man pointed. 'His allotment's up the hill,' he went back to his digging, 'though it's wasted on him.' And Tom was treated to a rambling monologue about how Frank Jarvis didn't deserve an allotment. Tom tried to interject at that point but the old man wouldn't be silenced. 'Thinks because he can grow runner beans, he knows what he's doing,' he moaned, 'well anyone can grow runner beans but this daft bugger doesn't even know the planting season for potatoes.' Tom opened his mouth then to say something but before he could: 'It's late March at the earliest! April even, you don't plant them in pigging February when you've still got chance of frost . . .'

'Anyway . . .' Tom said but he wasn't finished yet.

'. . . but there's no telling a man like that. He always knows best.'

He finally finished his lecture. 'Not a fan of the councillor then?' said Tom.

The man stopped digging again. 'No, I'm not but I don't discriminate. All politicians are a waste of bloody space.'

'Interesting you should say that,' said Tom, 'some people think he's one of the good ones.'

The man was annoyed at that. 'Do they now? Why? Because he still lives in a council house and he's not on the rob like the rest of them? I doubt they can point to a single thing he's done for his own people. All he cares about is the city centre and the big projects, but nowt's changed round here for nigh on twenty years. Who are you anyway and why are you asking about Frank Jarvis?'

'I'm investigating the disappearance of his daughter.'

'You're a copper?' The man seemed even less impressed now.

'No, I'm not, but they know I'm working on the case.'

His mood seemed to lighten then. 'You're a PI eh? Like that fellah off *The Rockford Files*? I like that show.'

'Not quite. I'm just trying to help Jarvis locate her. Obviously he's very concerned.'

'Aye, well, I wouldn't wish that on anyone, even him. The police asked me all about it at the time like.'

'They asked *you* about her?'

'Yes, but they asked everybody,' he seemed eager to dispel any misunderstanding, 'and I saw her, didn't I? A couple of days before she disappeared.'

'Where was that?'

'Here,' answered the man. 'You never see young lasses on the allotment, so I noticed her.'

'Was she up there long?'

'That's exactly what the police asked me. I don't know but I

164

was probably having my scran,' the man told him. 'My wife always does me a snap tin so I don't have to come back.'

Tom realised he was talking to a former miner as soon as he mentioned his snap tin, which was a sturdy lunch box made of metal that could be taken down the pit. 'So Sandra Jarvis could have walked back down while you were having your butties.'

'I eat them over there.' He jerked his head towards the back of a large, crudely constructed, rickety wooden hut some way from the two of them. 'Got myself a chair and table and I have my tea in a flask,' he said with some pride.

'You just need a bed and you'd never have to leave.'

'Aye, right enough.' He clearly enjoyed that idea.

'Was that all the police asked you?'

He nodded. 'More or less. They wanted to know whether I'd seen or heard anything else.'

'And?'

'Well, I didn't see anything from down here and I heard nowt bar a bit of shouting.'

'You heard shouting?'

'It was only a bit of a row. You hear worse coming from the houses down yonder.'

'So who was doing the rowing?' asked Tom.

'Him and her.'

'Frank and Sandra?'

'I wasn't able to make out the words but they were having a barney of some sort.' And he sniffed.

'No idea what it was about then?'

'Do I look like a mind-reader?' he asked. 'Since she's a teenager and he's her old man I'd say he was trying to tell her what to do and she was giving him a load of lip because she wanted to do the opposite. Isn't that the way it goes?'

'I don't know,' admitted Tom.

'Me neither,' admitted the man. 'Got no kids but that's what I hear.'

'And you never saw her come back down again?'

He laughed. 'No, but I don't think he did her in, do you? The police told me she's been seen around since.'

'She got on a train to London a couple of days later,' confirmed Tom.

'There you go then.'

'Thanks, Mr . . . ?'

'Don't you Mr me,' warned the old man and he straightened then puffed out his chest. 'I'm not one of the bosses. The name's Harry.'

'Then I'll see you around, Harry.'

'Not if I see thee first,' laughed Harry and he went back to his digging.

Jarvis was sitting outside his own hut, staring off into space, when Tom reached his plot of land. He was easily recognisable from all of his local TV appearances. Jarvis spotted the younger man and watched with interest as he ascended the hill.

'Quite a spot you've got here,' said Tom by way of introduction. 'I'm Tom Carney. I understand you wanted to see me.'

'Thanks for coming, Tom.' His handshake was firm and his smile broad, as Tom would have expected from a politician. 'I was hoping you would.'

'So was DCI Kane,' replied Tom, 'apparently.'

'Aye, well, we go back a long way. He told me all about you.'

'And you still wanted to meet me?'

'Yes, I did,' the councillor laughed. 'I suppose I should start by asking you what you know about me, or at least what you think you know.'

Tom shrugged. 'You're a politician, you've been active in local government these past twenty years and up until relatively recently you were the leader of the city council,' he said, 'but you gave that up.'

'To search for my daughter, yes,' he agreed. 'Our mutual friend DCI Kane mentioned you once. It was something about the case of a missing girl you helped him with.'

'Michelle Summers.'

Jarvis nodded.

'That was a very unusual case and I don't see how it could possibly relate to the disappearance of your daughter.'

'It doesn't – but you sounded like a resourceful man who might be able to help someone in dire need, and I am that someone.'

'What exactly did the DCI tell you about me?'

Jarvis took a moment to answer. 'He told me you were a journalist who thought like a copper but had more freedom to investigate things than a police officer does. He said you were clever and you sometimes saw things other people missed. In short, he rates you highly.'

'That doesn't sound like Kane,' said Tom, and the councillor sighed.

'He also said you were a bit of an arsehole. There, I've said it. Happy now?'

Tom laughed. 'Was that all?'

'He added a few other choice phrases,' admitted the politician, 'like stubborn, opinionated, cocky and there was something about a chip on your shoulder "the size of the Tyne Bridge".'

'That does sound like him. Thanks for the honesty.'

'Glad we could clear the air. Look, whatever he actually

thinks, it was Kane who put me on to you. He doesn't suffer fools and nor do I. Now can you help me or not?'

'What do you want me to do?'

'Find my daughter,' Jarvis said simply.

'Just like that?' asked Tom. 'How?'

'Well, if I knew that I wouldn't need you, would I? I don't know how but I want you to use your skills to try to get to the bottom of Sandra's disappearance.'

'And you think she's still alive?' Tom probed. 'I'm sorry, but I obviously have to ask that.'

'Aye, I do, for what that's worth. Call it a feeling, call it pig-headedness but I firmly believe Sandra is alive. She's out there somewhere. If she wasn't, we'd have found her body by now.'

Not necessarily, thought Tom, but he wasn't going to share that notion with her father. 'What makes you think I can succeed where the police couldn't?'

'I might be a politician but I don't live in an ivory tower. We both know there are sections of society, whole communities even, that won't talk to the police, no matter what's at stake. I grew up in the west end of Newcastle and to a lot of people there, the police were the enemy. Now if someone out there knows something but they are into drugs or prostitution or Lord knows what then they aren't going to talk to a detective . . . but they might talk to you.'

'Why?'

'Money,' Jarvis said. 'I haven't got much but I have some and I'm prepared to part with it in return for information on the whereabouts of my daughter.'

'Contacting a journalist wouldn't be most people's first port of call, so who else did you try – aside from the police, I mean?'

Jarvis seemed embarrassed then. 'A private detective. He approached me and said he'd have her back within the month. I wanted to believe him but he got nowhere. Took me for a fool and took my money too.'

'What makes you think I won't do the same?'

'Because I approached you, not the other way round, and you still haven't said you even want the job.'

'The police are going to pay me anyway,' Tom told him, 'from some fund they use for specialists and experts, though I am neither.'

'Oh,' said the councillor, 'I didn't realise that.'

'You can thank your old friend DCI Kane.'

'I will.'

'What if I don't find anything?'

'Then we call a halt but I have a good feeling about you. Kane told me all about that body in the field and how you worked it out.'

'I had help with that,' Tom told him.

'I know; a female reporter and one of Kane's more . . .' Jarvis seemed to be searching for a diplomatic phrase '. . . *unconventional* detectives. I'm happy for you to get help if you need it. I don't care how you do it. Just help me get my daughter back. Please.'

Tom still wasn't sure he could help Frank Jarvis but the man looked desperate.

'Alright.'

'Good man!'

Tom held up a hand. 'I'll ask around and see what I can uncover but it might not be much.'

'I'm prepared to run that risk,' Jarvis assured him. 'So, when can you start?'

'Now.'

The sun suddenly emerged from behind the dark clouds that had been threatening rain again but at the last moment decided against it. The allotment was bathed in bright sunshine and Tom noticed how big it was. Frank Jarvis had obviously spent a lot of time here since he stepped back from front-line politics.

'Plenty to do on an allotment.'

'Always,' agreed Jarvis. 'I've had one for years. Grown most of me own veg since then,' he said proudly.

'My dad used to have one.' Tom surveyed Jarvis's plot. 'Isn't it a bit high for growing stuff?'

'The vegetables don't seem to mind and my bit's sheltered by the top of the slope. You should have said you were coming though,' he told Tom. 'I'd have met you at the house and saved you the bother of trailing up here.'

'It's no problem. I went to your house; your wife said you'd be here.'

'Did she?' He sounded doubtful.

'Yeah,' said Tom, 'I met your mother-in-law too.'

'Well,' said the politician, 'now you know why I have an allotment.' And he did a little grimace. 'No one can bother me up here, including her. If you got any sense out of Audrey you are a better man than me.'

'I only spoke to her briefly but she did say one thing that puzzled me.'

'And what was that?'

'It was about your daughter,' Tom informed him. 'She said she was cuckoo.'

Jarvis snorted, 'She can talk,' then he turned serious again. 'You would have thought her own grandmother might have been a bit kinder under the circumstances but she's always been a malicious old bag that one.'

'Why do you think she said it?'

'I have no idea. There's nothing wrong with my daughter's mental health. She wasn't depressed, mad or suicidal. You're not going to get very far if that's a line of enquiry – I suspect you noticed that if anyone is cuckoo, it's Audrey. Her and her senses parted company many moons ago.'

'So there's no substance in it?'

'God, no. Sandra was as sane as anyone. Her behaviour did change before her disappearance but she wasn't having a nervous breakdown or anything.'

'But that change in behaviour was noticeable enough to cause you concern?'

Jarvis nodded. 'I read up on it, even asked a doctor who's a friend of mine. I didn't tell him I was asking about Sandra. I made out I had a friend who was worried about his son. I told him the behaviour I'd witnessed and he came to a simple conclusion.'

'Which was?'

Jarvis seemed to sag then. 'Drugs. You know, I used to have a very old-fashioned view on drug users. I thought that if parents took the time to outline the pitfalls of drug abuse, if they came down hard on their children if they caught them with a spliff, then they would never lose them to drugs. That's what I used to think.'

'And what do you think now?'

'That I was a fool,' he admitted, 'that it can happen to anyone: your kids, my kids, anybody's kids. If they get a taste for drugs, they'll give up everything for them because nothing means more to them than the next fix. I've seen it, down at the rehab centres and the needle exchanges. We have to provide them, otherwise the playgrounds would be full of used syringes. It's a bloody tragedy.'

'You think that's what happened to Sandra?'

'I hope to God I'm wrong, but it's my best guess,' and he fell silent for a moment before eventually adding, 'though I've imagined worse things.'

'She wasn't gone long though, from home I mean. What was it, a term and a half?'

'It doesn't take long,' he said sadly.

'How do you think she would get her hands on hard drugs in her first year at university, particularly a posh one like Durham?'

'Forgive me, Tom, but that's one of the things I'm asking you to find out, though if you don't mind me saying so, you're being a bit naïve. There's a drug dealer in every city, town and village in this country; they hang round every playground, pub and university campus. They have to; dealers are parasites and the only way they can make a living is to find new users. Drugs are the ultimate growth industry. I've read the reports, I've seen the stats. They call it a war on drugs and I can tell you this, we are losing it.'

'Did she have a boyfriend? Someone who could have got her started with drugs?'

'She never told us about one, but somebody must have got to her. I don't think she would have gone looking for a dealer. Somebody must have taken advantage.'

'That line of enquiry went cold but I'll look into it again.'

Jarvis took out a packet of cigarettes then and offered one to Tom, who shook his head. 'Very sensible.'

'I saw a fellah on the way up here,' Tom said, 'by the name of Harry.'

'Old misery guts?'

'He told the police you rowed with your daughter a few days before she disappeared.'

'I told them that too,' said Jarvis.

'Did she come up here to have a row with you or did one just develop?'

'Why would she come all the way up here to start a row?' asked Jarvis.

'I don't know,' admitted Tom. 'She obviously felt the need to see you. She could just have waited for you to come home but instead she walked all the way up here, so either it was important or she wanted to talk to you in private, away from her mam and grandma.'

Jarvis nodded and gave a grim smile. 'You are a perceptive man. She did want to talk to me in private. It didn't start as a row but soon developed into one, I'm sorry to say.'

'What was it about?'

'The future,' said Jarvis, 'her future, to be exact. She wanted to drop out of college.'

'Why?'

'She wasn't enjoying it, it wasn't what she was expecting, she couldn't see the point of it and wasn't making many friends.' He paused. 'I think Sandra thought I'd hear her out, agree with her reasoning and give her my parental blessing.'

'But you didn't?'

'I told her not to be so bloody stupid. Me and my daughter are both cut from the same cloth. We can be strong-willed, stubborn even, so we clash. She was born several weeks premature you know, so she's had to fight to survive from day one. I've always encouraged her to question everything but she is still a young woman and can be naïve. I was the same when I was her age,' he admitted. 'I was the big idealist who thought I could change the world. She thought she could drop out of college and travel then somehow magically have a career, despite a bloody big hole in her CV and no proper qualifications. I told her she was an idiot for thinking that way after all the hard work she'd put in to get there. Look, if I could go back in time I would handle it differently. I was too harsh on her and she got upset.' He looked downcast. 'She then said some things that I wouldn't tolerate.'

'What kind of things?'

'She was rude to me,' Jarvis seemed embarrassed at the recollection, 'saying I knew nowt about the real world. She started shouting at me so I shouted back. I'm not proud of my behaviour or hers but I was worried she was throwing her life away.'

'What brought the argument to an end?'

'She did,' he said. 'She stormed off.'

'And you let her go?'

'I thought it might be for the best,' Jarvis said. 'Let her cool off and try to talk some sense into her later.' Tom could tell he was hurt by the implication he did not care enough to go after his daughter. Maybe Frank Jarvis wondered if Sandra might still be here now if he hadn't let her go. He visibly slumped then. 'I never realised it would be the last time I'd see her,' he said, obviously fighting back the tears.

'Not the last time,' Tom assured him, for he was embarrassed by the man's discomfort and the fact he had caused it. Tom never liked to plant false hope in anyone but he couldn't help himself now. 'We'll find her.'

Chapter Twenty

He'd started the argument but it was only now he realised Karen was right. He *had* been an arse. When Bradshaw saw his girlfriend that night after a long, tiring day he was still feeling righteously indignant, which is why he greeted his girlfriend with the words, 'How come everybody thinks we are shacked up together?'

'Eh?'

'What have you been saying to make them think that? Even Kane said it to me.'

'I haven't been saying anything,' said Karen, 'and I certainly haven't been talking to your DCI about us.'

He had intended the conversation to be a relatively mild one, during which he would tell his girlfriend he didn't appreciate people discussing them behind his back. Unfortunately, he had not foreseen the conclusion Karen would naturally come to.

'Oh, so you're ashamed of me, are you?'

'What? No, of course not!'

'I'm good enough to be seen with, good enough to be shagging – but not good enough for anyone to think we might be in a proper relationship.'

'Don't be daft. We *are* in a proper relationship.'

'Yeah, course we are . . . just so long as it doesn't involve me staying over too many nights a week and I take my tooth-brush with me when I go?'

While he usually felt he might be a little more intelligent than his girlfriend, Bradshaw had to admit he was absolutely no match for her in an argument. They rowed for over an hour and she seemed to effortlessly move between all of the emotional states: from anger, to sadness and despair then back to rage, via tears and some highly imaginative industrial language. Karen even threw cushions at him at one point while he desperately tried to placate her. In the end she opted to leave and Bradshaw belatedly realised this had been a problem entirely of his own making, so he very quickly went into reverse gear and apologised – a lot.

'I hate it when we row,' she said as she snuggled up to him in bed an hour later, following make-up sex that had somehow pleasingly evolved from the high state of adrenalin they were both in by the end of their argument.

'Well we don't do it very often, Karen,' he said as he drew her closer to him.

'I can see why people might get confused by us though,' she said. 'We do spend a lot of time with each other but that's cos we're good together, babe.' She laughed again. 'I mean I do *practically* live here.'

'I s'pose you do,' he admitted. 'You've got a key, you're here more nights than you're not.'

'Yeah, I know,' she said. 'You get your meals cooked for you all the time and sex on tap. It's not all bad, is it?' They both laughed at that. 'And there's me paying rent on a place and I'm never there.'

He knew she was hinting, but just this once he didn't mind. He'd been an idiot. Karen was a cracking lass but his fragile ego had been dented by the idea of people at work talking about them. Where was he going to get another girl as nice as this one, as good-looking as this one, as accommodating in bed as this one?

He didn't mind her folks either, not really, although her

mum did have an annoying habit of mentioning Karen's ex every time she saw him, since the bloke still lived close by and wasn't over Karen.

'Come on, Mum, we were eighteen,' blushed her daughter the last time the former boyfriend came up in conversation. 'It was years ago and I'm with Ian now.' And she held Bradshaw's hand as if to assure him when she said that.

'I know that,' her mother replied, as if he wasn't in the room, 'I just think it's nice that he always speaks to us when he sees us. He even came round last Christmas to see how we were doing.'

'To see how Karen was doing, more like,' said her father without looking up from his newspaper, 'and I told him, she's got a boyfriend.' He said that bit as if he had seen the other bloke off with his shotgun.

All the same, Bradshaw didn't like to think of Karen with this other man, this first love that must have been so significant her parents kept mentioning him.

He remembered that moment now and how jealous he had been at the thought of Karen with another man, even if it had been years before, and realised he would be gutted if she went with someone else – not that he gave her much incentive to be faithful, with his commitment-phobic attitude. He would just have to grow up.

And just like that, all of his resistance to their relationship was suddenly swept away.

'You might as well, you know,' he said it lightly, 'move in, I mean. There's plenty of room here and, like you said, it's not all bad is it?'

'Oh my God,' Karen said, 'do you mean it?' And there were tears in her eyes then. 'I can't tell you how happy you've just made me. I just never thought we'd end up as a permanent item.'

Neither had he, until she put it like that.

Moving in together didn't necessarily mean forever in Bradshaw's eyes but clearly Karen thought otherwise. 'Yeah,' he said, 'well, there you go.'

'Good to see you, Tom.' There was a brisk handshake at the door of the newsroom. 'It's been a while,' Graham Seaton reminded him as they walked briskly across the newsroom.

'It has,' agreed Tom and he tried not to think about their divergent career paths. Since Graham Seaton and Tom Carney last worked together at the *Durham Messenger* more than five years earlier, Seaton had gone on to become a reporter then a senior reporter for his Newcastle daily and finally, in a move that no one saw coming but Seaton, its youngest-ever editor. Meanwhile, Tom could, at best, describe himself as a failed author, former journalist, part-time amateur builder and 'property developer'. Tom was grateful when Seaton didn't ask him how his life was just now. Instead he was immediately business-like.

'You're looking into Sandra Jarvis's disappearance?' he said. 'Well we've run a lot of stuff on that in the past six months. Her father never lets up, poor bastard. You're welcome to take a look at it all.'

'I will, thanks,' Tom said, 'but it's background I'm after, which is why I want to speak to your best crime reporter, if he can spare me the time.'

'Fair enough.' Graham nodded towards the frosted glass door of the conference room. 'Don't take all day though, mate, we've got an edition to get out.'

'Half an hour, tops,' Tom assured him.

'We keep her in here,' said Graham, as if she were a cell mate of Hannibal Lecter, and he opened the door to reveal a solitary figure sitting at the far end of the conference table. The woman's head was down but there was no mistaking her. She was busy writing notes on a pad. He might have known she wouldn't sit staring out of the window while she waited for him, even for a few minutes.

'Bloody hell,' he said and she looked up, 'small world.'

'I was about to say, "This is Helen Norton, our resident crime expert,"' said Graham, 'but I can see your paths have already crossed. I hope you remembered your manners, Tom.'

'He was the perfect gentleman,' said Helen.

'We worked on the Sean Donnellan case together,' Tom told her editor.

'Of course, the book! How's it doing?'

'Great.'

When Tom offered nothing further, Graham took this as his cue. 'Okay, I'll leave you to it then.'

Tom drew out the chair next to her so they could sit at right angles to one another,

'How are you, Tom?' she asked a little stiffly.

'Surviving.'

'I haven't seen you since . . .'

'Mary Collier's funeral,' he said. 'You stayed for one drink.'

Mary Collier wasn't quite Eleanor Rigby; when she died and was buried people came, but not many. There was the vicar of course, her housekeeper who 'did for her' as she used to say and three elderly ladies who had known Mary their whole lives and hadn't allowed the gossip that followed her in later years to prevent them from paying their respects. One of the few pleasures of elderly widowhood was the opportunity to dress in Sunday best to attend the funeral of one of your peers, gaining a visceral thrill at having outlived them.

Other than that small gathering and Tom, the funeral party

consisted of two people; Detective Sergeant Ian Bradshaw, who sat quietly at the back of the church, and Helen, who had donned a black dress she last wore for a job interview at the paper where she now worked. Both of them attended the funeral service partially out of respect but also because Mary Collier's death marked the end of something more than just her life. It effectively brought down the final curtain on the Sean Donnellan case, which would then become the subject of *Death Knock*, because Tom had agreed with Mary that his book would not be published until she was gone.

'Thought you might have made it to the book launch,' he added, trying to sound like it was no big deal.

'I was going to,' she stammered. 'I wasn't sure you if you wanted me there.'

'How can you say that?' he asked. 'I invited you and you were in the bloody book.'

'I know, I'm sorry. It was stupid . . . I read it though.'

'Really?'

'Of course. I thought it was brilliant,' she said this with such earnestness that he actually let out a laugh.

'Well I'm glad someone did.'

'I wasn't the only one,' she said, 'the reviews were great. Was it a good event? The launch, I mean. Bet you had loads of people there.'

'Ian Bradshaw came,' he said quickly, 'with his girlfriend, Karen. I think he wanted to know what I'd written about him.' He could have admitted that a little piece of him had quietly died when she hadn't shown up, but he wasn't quite ready for that level of honesty. In truth he didn't have too many people to invite. There were his sister and brother-in-law, a handful of friends from school or the pub but precious few fellow journalists. He later found out that Malcolm had issued an unofficial fatwah on him, meaning colleagues from his old job at the *Durham Messenger* lived in fear of being spotted at his book launch. So Tom had said a few thank yous and signed a handful of books before retiring to the nearest pub to drink too much while trying not to wonder where Helen was.

'What are we going to tell our grandchildren when they ask me why you didn't turn up to my book launch?'

'You don't want kids,' she reminded him.

'Yeah, well not this minute but who knows? I could change my mind, one day.'

'Can't see it,' she chided. 'You'd have to evolve into a functioning adult first.'

'Ouch.'

'Sorry,' she said, 'I've been hanging out with the blokes in the newsroom and the banter is just vicious here. It tends to rub off.'

'I can take it,' he said. 'They treating you well then?'

'It's been great.'

'Surprised to see you cooped up in the conference room, not out and about exposing wrongdoing.' He was joking but it struck a nerve. After her experience in the multi-storey car park Helen felt safer in the office even though she knew she couldn't hide herself away forever.

'What brings you to our door then?' she asked. 'I could tell by your face you weren't expecting to see me, so it can't have been a social call.'

'I used to work with Graham, so I called him and asked if I could speak to his best crime reporter,' said Tom. 'I was expecting some middle-aged hack but he brought me to you.' And Tom went on to explain to Helen the sequence of events which led him to the *Record*'s office, including his interest in the Rebecca Holt murder and his agreement to help Frank Jarvis find his missing daughter.

'And what do you need from me?' she asked when he was finally through.

'Well,' he seemed hesitant now, 'nothing necessarily . . .'

'Tom, I'm happy to help,' she said firmly, 'any time.'

'Thanks,' he said, relaxing a little, 'it's just that I don't have a newspaper behind me these days, so anything you come across on either of the cases I'm looking into would be really useful. We'll probably end up going over the same ground but . . .'

'That never stopped us before.'

'No, it didn't.' It was how they had first met, in fact. 'Thanks, Helen. I appreciate it.'

'Least I could do.' Tom took this as a form of apology.

'So how are things with you?' he asked.

'Good,' she said. 'Graham has been great.'

'Who wouldn't be, compared to Malcolm?' he asked.

'Even so,' she replied, 'he has been letting me write some interesting stuff about local politicians and their links to some pretty ropey people.'

'Newcastle has always had its fair share of gangsters,' he smiled, 'some of them in City Hall. You must be pissing people off.'

'There is that possibility,' she conceded.

'Be careful,' he told her, 'articles on corruption tend to upset people.'

'You ought to know,' she reminded him.

'Yeah, well, just don't do anything I wouldn't do. I'm not preaching. I realise you know what you're doing. Things are going well then? You're okay, I mean?'

'Yes, thanks.'

He noticed she hadn't mentioned the boyfriend. He had to assume he was still on the scene though.

'You seeing anyone else?' she asked and he must have

looked a little surprised by the directness of the question. 'Today I mean, while you're in town,' she added quickly.

'I'm going to the Highwayman on the Quayside. Sandra Jarvis worked behind the bar there part time and in the holidays. Maybe I'll find someone who worked with her. They might know something.'

'I don't know it,' she said, 'but the name rings a bell.'

'Then I'm going to Northumbria Police HQ to read the case files, though that might take a while as there are loads of reported sightings.'

'You'll be there all day by the sound of it.'

'There is one thing I would appreciate from you,' he told her.

'Name it.'

'I'm missing a bit of background on Frank Jarvis. There's a lot in the public domain but I could do with a little gossip.'

'You mean dirt?' she asked.

'Possibly,' admitted Tom, 'if he's dirty; but his reputation says otherwise.'

'And you believe that?'

'He's a politician – so I'd say the odds are stacked heavily against him, wouldn't you?'

Helen watched him for a moment to see if he was serious. 'Okay, I'll do some digging,' she said, 'and don't worry, I'll be discreet.'

'You know what, don't be,' he replied. 'I wouldn't mind him knowing I've been asking after him.'

'Why?'

'Two reasons: one, it shows I'm doing my job properly.'

'And two?'

'I'd quite like to see if it rattles his cage.'

Chapter Twenty-One

The two Julies lived in a small student house with a couple of other girls. When Ian Bradshaw told them he was a police officer involved in the Sandra Jarvis investigation, Julie One, whose surname was actually Elliott, nervously invited the detective to sit at the kitchen table with them.

Julie Two, whose real name was Morrison, offered to make him a cup of tea.

'Yes please,' he said and Julie One looked worried.

'We've only got herbal tea left,' she admitted, as if confessing a serious felony.

'Then I'll pass. I won't be long. This is just routine.' He didn't normally try to put people at their ease before questioning them but these two looked guilty and nervous in a way that only the entirely innocent can. Up until Sandra's sudden disappearance they had probably never had any dealings with the police.

'We're not suspects or anything?' asked Julie Two.

'Suspects?' he repeated.

'In Sandra's disappearance?'

'I don't know,' he asked amiably, 'are you?'

'God, no,' protested Julie One and she gave her friend an angry look, 'we had nothing to do with that.'

'Then you have nothing to fear. We haven't been able to locate Miss Jarvis and it has been some time since she went missing. When that happens we like to go over everything again, piece by piece, to see if there is anything we've missed or if someone remembers something in the meantime they didn't mention previously. Okay?'

They both seemed visibly relieved at that.

'You lived with Sandra Jarvis for how long?' asked Bradshaw, reaching for his notebook and pen. He wrote their full names at the top of the new page but from that point simply put 'Julie 1' or 'Julie 2' next to relevant comments they made.

'From the beginning of the first term,' said Julie One.

'Right up until . . .' Julie Two looked a little alarmed as if she might be about to say something incriminating.

'She disappeared?' he offered helpfully.

'Yes,' confirmed Julie One, 'that was in reading week last year.'

'Last year? I thought it was February of this year?'

'She means the academic year,' said Julie Two.

'Of course.' He let Julie One continue.

'We went home to our families then but when we all came back to halls Sandra wasn't there.'

'And you never saw her again?'

'No,' said Julie Two.

'Let's go back to when you first met. What did you think?'

'Think?' asked Julie One, and Bradshaw couldn't help but wonder how these two had landed places at such an esteemed academic establishment as Durham University. Perhaps his DCI was right when he repeatedly told Bradshaw, 'You can't learn everything from a textbook.'

'What was your impression of her?' he clarified.

'She was really nice,' said Julie Two quickly, as if defending the missing girl against an accusation from a third party, then she added, 'at first.'

'But she changed?' Bradshaw prompted.

'After Christmas,' explained Julie One. 'In the first term

we all got along great in our halls. The girls on our floor shared a kitchen and we went out in groups. She was as friendly as anyone else.'

'But you noticed a change in her in the second term.'

'It was very noticeable. I remember when she came back to halls after the Christmas break, she barely acknowledged anyone.'

'Sandra stayed in her room all of the time,' said Julie Two, 'and on the rare occasions we did see her she seemed really sad.'

'Did anyone talk to her about this or did you just leave her to it?'

'Of course not.' There was a defensiveness from Julie Two that might have indicated some guilt. Perhaps she felt they could have done more to help?

'We tried to get her to come out with us like before. Every time we went into town or the union bar one of us would knock on her door.'

'But she always refused?'

'She'd make excuses at first; she had to work or study or was going to do something else instead, like her laundry or buying groceries. After a while she didn't even bother with excuses, just said she didn't want to go out. Some of the girls resented that.' She sounded as if she was one of them. 'We gave up in the end. I mean there's only so many times you can ask, isn't there?'

'There is,' Bradshaw agreed. 'And she never gave any reason for the way she was feeling?'

The two Julies both agreed she had not. 'Sandra just shut everyone out,' said Julie One.

'Problems at home, boyfriend troubles, drugs?' he offered as explanations.

'We got the impression she was happy at home. She didn't have a steady boyfriend. At least I never saw one and she never looked . . .' She was searching for the right word.

'High,' offered Julie Two, 'she never seemed like she was on something.'

'So, no drugs, no boyfriend, no going out and she got on okay with her old man, even though he is a politician, which must have been a bit embarrassing for her.'

'No, I think she approved of her father,' said Julie One. 'One of the girls teased her about him once and she said, "At least he tries to make a difference."'

'So she's proud of the old man,' he conceded. 'What do you think caused her to change then?'

'I really don't know,' said Julie Two.

'It must have been something that happened back in Newcastle,' said Julie One. 'I mean, she was okay when she left at Christmas, but when she came back she was a different person entirely.'

'Did she dress differently after the Christmas break,' he asked, 'change her appearance in any way?'

Bradshaw had met victims of rape and sexual assault who dressed down afterwards. If Sandra Jarvis had taken to wearing shapeless, sexless clothes perhaps this would be a clue as to what had happened to her.

'No,' said Julie One, looking confused, 'why do you ask that?'

Bradshaw ignored her question. 'Did she ever talk to anyone,' and when they looked blank, 'or have a particular friend she was close to? We all need someone to confide in.'

The two Julies exchanged glances.

'You could try Megan,' offered Julie One, 'couldn't he?'

'He could,' agreed Julie Two.

'Yes,' said Bradshaw, 'I could,' even though he didn't have the faintest clue who Megan was.

Freed from the need to be discreet, Helen went to her editor. 'Who's the best person to dish the dirt on politicians in this city?' she asked. 'Stuff that dates back a few years.'

'That person is right here,' replied her editor. 'No, not me. I mean he is in this building – or at least his desk is. Brian Hilton has been our political correspondent since . . . oh probably about 1920.' And he gave her that boyish grin again. 'He actually started on the paper in the early sixties. He's your man.'

'I don't think I've met him,' Helen admitted.

'Not in the office that much, comes and goes as he pleases. I should object to that but he always provides good copy and it's on time so I cut him some slack. Brian is a bit of a grumpy bastard,' he conceded, 'but we'd be lost without him and his contacts.'

'Won't he mind the new girl tapping him for information?'

'He might not,' said Graham, 'if you follow the official procedure.'

'Which is?'

'Wait until his working day is over, then buy him a pint,' said her editor. 'He likes the Crown Posada on the Quayside. You can usually set your watch by him.'

Tom was already standing outside a pub on the Quayside but he quickly realised his walk down here had been a complete waste of time. Sandra Jarvis had worked at the Highwayman before departing for college and returned there to do shifts during the Christmas holidays. Since her personality had changed entirely following that break between college terms, there was a reasonable chance her time at the pub might have had something to do with it. He had gone over the possibilities in his mind as he made his way there: Sandra had been bullied, harassed or possibly even assaulted, she'd had a relationship that had suddenly turned sour leaving her depressed, or perhaps she had been enticed by drugs sold on the premises. None of this sounded entirely plausible to him, but then neither did her sudden disappearance.

Any hopes Tom may have had about getting a lead from the pub were instantly dashed, for the Highwayman was no more. Despite a prime spot on the north bank of the river a short walk from the Tyne Bridge, it had ceased trading. The door was locked and boarded up, the windows already pasted over with bill stickers advertising gigs. Tom peered through a gap and saw that all of the pub's furnishings were still there, including tables, chairs and even the beer pumps behind the bar. Whoever ran this place must have left it in a hurry.

Realising he was going to get nowhere standing outside the abandoned pub, Tom left and arrived very early for his prearranged appointment at police headquarters. They didn't seem to mind. A helpful junior detective handed him several thick folders. These were full of witness statements, background information on Sandra Jarvis's life and her movements plus a large number of reported sightings of the missing girl from all over the country, many of which could probably be classed as wishful thinking or mischief making.

He was allowed the use of a small room to examine the files in private and they even brought him a mug of tea. It had been some time since he had experienced that level of cooperation from the police and he had to admit he was glad of it. They left him to it and he began to read.

The pub in the market place wasn't a typical student watering hole. It was an old-school, local boozers' pub and, when she was not attending lectures, Megan Aitken worked behind the bar there.

Bradshaw showed her his warrant card and asked her if she had a minute. 'No,' she told him in a granite-hard Glaswegian accent, while eying him suspiciously, 'I've lunches to get out.' There were less than a dozen customers in the pub and none of them looked like they were there for the food.

'I'm sure this strapping young man here can cope without you.' Bradshaw stopped a rake-thin barman as he passed by and said, 'You can manage on your own for five minutes while Megan helps me with an important police matter.'

The youth didn't seem to know if this was a question or an order so he simply mumbled, 'Sure,' while Bradshaw indicated Megan should follow him to a table in a far corner.

When he told her why he was there, she said, 'Well I didn't think it was cos I hadnae paid my council tax but I've already had the polis asking me about Sandra, and her disappearance had bugger all to do with me.'

'And we are going over old ground so we don't miss anything.'

'Good luck with that,' Megan said sarcastically. 'Who sent you my way.'

'Some girls that knew both of you. They said you might be able to shed some light on the reasons for Sandra Jarvis's disappearance.'

'Was it Tweedledum and Tweedledee?' Though he was poker-faced in response Bradshaw knew she was referring to the two Julies. 'I bet it was. Why the hell would I know anything about it?'

'They thought Sandra may have confided in you, since you were such good friends.'

'Did they now? Well she didn't and we weren't that close.'

'Why did they think you were then?'

'No idea – except they probably thought we were bestest buddies because we were the only two girls on our course who weren't posh and minted.'

'Really?'

'Well, I don't see anyone else doing bar work to survive. There are girls here who spend five hundred a month just on clothes.'

'That must be annoying.'

'It is what it is,' Megan said as if she didn't care but she evidently did.

'Did Sandra work here too?'

'We did some shifts together at weekends during term time. She worked in a place in Newcastle during the holidays,' she thought for a second, 'the Pirate?'

'The Highwayman.'

'Aye, that was it.'

'Did she like bar work?'

'There are worse ways to get by but you only do it for the money. I'd rather be on this side of the bar but there you go. Sandra felt the same.'

'And when you did these shifts together, when you had a drink afterwards or went for a fag break, she never told you anything about herself?'

'Not really. Certainly nothing that would make me understand why she suddenly disappeared like that,' said Megan. '*If* she disappeared.'

'What do you mean by that?'

'I mean, if she had just upped and left wouldn't someone have found her by now?'

'Not if she didn't want to be found. You think something happened to her? Someone hurt her, maybe?'

'Well it seems likely, doesn't it?'

'It's certainly a possibility but who would want to harm Sandra?'

'How should I know?'

Bradshaw was beginning to seriously question the wisdom of interviewing Sandra's college friends. It seemed the missing girl hadn't bothered to open up to anyone.

'I don't suppose there's anyone you can think of who might know something about Sandra that nobody else does.' He was clutching at straws.

Megan shook her head. 'You'll have already spoken to her room-mate,' she said, as if that was obvious.

'She had a room-mate?' The case files hadn't made that clear.

'She shared a room in halls with Olivia Barrington but that only lasted for the first term.'

'Why? Did they have a falling-out?'

Megan shook her head. 'Olivia wasn't used to sharing things, was she, so she kicked up a fuss until they moved her and she got her own room.'

'I see,' said Bradshaw, 'so where does this Olivia Barrington live now?'

'The Castle.' Megan said the words quickly and her strong Scottish accent led Bradshaw to assume he misheard her.

'I'm sorry, for a second there I thought you said she lived in a castle.'

*

Helen had to walk down Dean Street to get to the pub on the Quayside, a road so steep she was forced to tread carefully to avoid accidentally stumbling into a run. She almost walked past the Crown Posada at first, an ancient, Victorian watering hole with a stone façade, dark stained-glass windows and a single sign above the door to denote its presence.

Once inside the pub, she headed for the bar while scanning the room for any sign of Brian Hilton. She spotted him soon enough. He was sitting on his own in an alcove not far from the front door. Though they hadn't met, Hilton was one of the few journalists at her paper who merited his own photo byline and, except for a few extra lines on his face since it was taken, he looked exactly like his picture. The unfashionably long mane of silver hair was recognisable enough even in the subdued light of the Crown Posada's wood-panelled bar. Helen ordered herself a bottle of beer and 'a pint of whatever he's drinking' and she gestured towards Hilton. The barman poured her a pint of bitter and she took it over, placing it on the table in front of Hilton.

He glanced at the pint, seemed to take a moment to register it, then looked up at the woman who'd delivered it. 'Now then, bonny lass,' Hilton said, 'what are you after?'

Chapter Twenty-Two

While Hilton drained the remnants of his last pint and started on the next one, Helen explained she was a journalist with the same newspaper, because he clearly hadn't recognised her. Helen wondered when and where he wrote his copy; on the back of beer mats? Perhaps he phoned it in to one of the editors, like the football correspondents when they reported on away matches. She recounted a respectful, heavily edited version of the conversation with Graham about Hilton's in-depth knowledge of the local political scene. Next she explained her specific interest in Frank Jarvis and the fact that she was helping Tom Carney look into Sandra Jarvis's disappearance on the councillor's behalf.

When she had completed this explanation, Brian Hilton nodded sagely and said quietly, 'Well, I might be able to help you out there.' Then she noticed he had almost finished the pint, so she got him another, even though her own drink had not been touched.

Hilton took a sizable gulp of beer and Helen realised this conversation was likely to be expensive. 'Frank Jarvis,' he spoke the name like he was trying it on for size, 'the kingmaker.'

'Is that what they call him?'

'Amongst other things,' he said, 'but that probably sums him up. If you want to know someone who can actually get things done round here who isn't all mouth and no trousers then look no further than him.' He drank some more. 'There are people in politics who can get themselves elected; able campaigners who can muster up support from the grass-roots of the party – and there's only one party round here of course – those are the people who climb the ladder.' And he counted off the stages on his fingers. 'Town councillor, borough councillor, county councillor, MP, government minister, and that's ultimately what they want. Most politicians will tell you, "I came into this so I can change things, so I can make a difference,"' another huge swig of beer and Helen waited patiently, 'but that's bollocks.' Hilton thought for a moment. 'I have seen dozens of politicians come and go and they all want to be important. They love that feeling even more than money or sex. It's all they care about in fact,' there was another long sip of beer then he put his pint back on the table, 'except Jarvis.'

Helen waited for him to elaborate and when he failed to do so she said, 'So what does he want?'

'Well, contrary to everything else I've just told you, pet, I have formed the impression that this guy actually does care about the city he lives in. Sure, Jarvis likes the sound of his own voice, they all do, but I don't think he's that bothered about people kowtowing to him.'

'Is that why he never stood for parliament?'

'Partly,' he answered, 'I think that went a long way towards it. He figured he could get more done if he stayed in the region.'

'Better to be a big fish in a small pond?' she asked.

'Maybe.' His eyes narrowed just a little.

'But there was something else,' she said, 'wasn't there?'

'Ooh,' Hilton said dryly, 'very good. You should be a reporter.'

She ignored his mocking tone and noticed his glass was

two-thirds empty, 'I'll get us another drink,' she said, 'and you can tell me all about it.'

Improbably, Olivia Barrington did live in a castle and not just any castle. She lived in *the* castle. Ian Bradshaw had grown up just miles from Durham city and been on countless day trips there as a child; ambling up the hill to the famous cathedral and castle, which towered high above the River Wear. All this time he had no idea it was possible to live in the actual castle but Megan Aitken assured him it was home to more than a hundred hugely privileged students.

Bradshaw was still wondering if Megan was winding him up when he arrived at the ancient Norman castle and climbed the steps by the main door. Would this be the student equivalent of one of those tricks played on young apprentices where they were sent for 'a long stand' or some 'sparks for the grinder'? However, when Bradshaw asked a male undergraduate if he knew Olivia, he struck lucky and was directed to the keep's highest floor.

Her room had two doors; the heavy outer one was wide open, with the inner one ajar. Bradshaw could hear the B52s on the radio. He knocked loudly enough to compete with 'Love Shack' and she called, 'Come in!' Bradshaw found Olivia working at a desk by a leaded window, which gave her a stunning view of the Romanesque cathedral opposite and the Palace Green that lay between the two ancient buildings. He wondered if she took it for granted.

Olivia peered over the top of her glasses at Bradshaw in confusion, having presumably been expecting a friend, not a detective sergeant. Once he told her who he was she immediately stopped what she was doing, got to her feet and gave him her full attention.

If the two Julies possessed public school accents, Olivia's seemed to inhabit an even higher plane, as if educated for future employment at Buckingham Palace. She apologised for her unkempt appearance, explaining she was revising for exams and hadn't even had time to 'have a shar' that morning, 'let alone wash my hair'. Bradshaw found himself mentally translating her words before writing them down and was usually a beat behind her as a result. He wondered how Sandra Jarvis had found sharing a room with a girl who made the two Julies seem almost working class by comparison.

'Sandra was *rilly* nice and it was very jolly sharing for a time but I'd simply die without my own space,' she explained.

Bradshaw nodded and began the same round of questions he'd asked the other girls. The first ten minutes of his interview were routinely repetitive, with Olivia confirming Sandra had never mentioned particular problems with home, love life or academic studies. Bradshaw was already planning which pub to visit so he could grab a pint after a fruitless day, but Olivia was still talking about how *rilly* intense university could be. When he happened to mention it was even more pressured for Sandra because she worked in a bar as well, Olivia said, 'Oh yah, and she worked through the holidays too,' with the wonder of someone who has never had to work a day in her life. 'And there was her other job as well.'

'Her other job?' asked Bradshaw as, once again, there had been no mention of this in the case files.

'Yah, that *did* sound rather stressful.'

'What other job?'

'The one looking after those poor people,' she explained, 'who have had such dreadful lives.'

*

'What do you remember about 1976?' Hilton asked, when Helen returned with two more beers.

'It was hot?' she offered and he frowned.

'Yeah, the heatwave,' he said, 'the hottest and driest summer since records began. That's all anyone ever remembers.' He seemed deeply disappointed by this. 'But what else happened in 1976?'

Helen realised she was being tested. Why would the date mean something to Brian Hilton? She would have been barely five years old, but since they were talking politics she opted for, 'Harold Wilson resigned?'

'Good lass,' he replied, and she felt like she was back in her politics tutorials. 'In March 1976 Harold Wilson resigned as Prime Minister, so there was an election. There was much talk at the time about the new order replacing the old and Frank Jarvis was already seen as the coming man. He was in his thirties, young for a politician but many people thought he was a dead cert to take over from the old MP who was retiring and it was one of the safest seats in the country.'

'So what happened?'

'The seat went to someone else.'

'Why?'

'Because he turned it down. When you're a politician, everything you say or do is fair game. You're in the public eye, particularly at a national level. Round here it's bad enough but we don't jeopardise long-standing relationships with the local party by reporting every piece of gossip we're given and there's always the possibility we'd get sued, which can put a local paper out of business. Down there it's different.' She realised he was referring to London. 'The tabloids don't have to worry so much about staying on the good side of some new MP and they can survive a few libel cases because they sell a lot more papers than we do. Scandal is their bread and butter. A politician's career can be over like that.' He clicked his fingers to show how quickly it can happen. 'We expect MPs to behave impeccably, even though we know they bloody don't.'

'Are you saying Jarvis had something to hide,' she prompted him, 'and that's why he couldn't become an MP?'

'Partly, but it was more complicated than that. Let's just say he was trying to repair something that couldn't be fixed by swanning off to London.'

Helen instantly knew what he meant. 'His marriage.'

Hilton smiled. 'Go to the top of the class, pet.'

Chapter Twenty-Three

Tom had almost finished reading the case files when he noticed something was absent from them. The last sighting of Sandra Jarvis in the north-east had been at Newcastle Central railway station, one of the first places to invest in the relatively new, not inexpensive technology of CCTV, because large railway stations had more than their fair share of trouble from drunks and fights between rival football fans. The still from one of the cameras that showed Sandra Jarvis buying a rail ticket was missing from the file, which was odd since it was a crucial piece of evidence.

Tom was then told he had a phone call, which was a surprise, since hardly anybody knew he was at the police HQ.

'It's me,' Helen said, 'thought you'd still be there.'

'I'm nearly done,' he told her.

'Can you pick me up at the Quayside?' she asked him. 'I got that dirt you wanted.'

'Blimey, that was quick.'

Helen was standing directly under the Tyne Bridge, sheltering from the rain but putting herself in even greater jeopardy from falling bird shit, which was a hazard for anyone walking beneath its girders. He flashed his lights and she quickly jumped in next to him.

'You've gone up in the world,' she said.

'Eh?'

'Your car,' she remarked on the two-year-old black Renault he'd finally upgraded to.

'It's not that flash,' he said shortly, and drove away.

Helen had grown used to the need to play everything down round here. It seemed the biggest sin in the north-east was to become too big for your boots.

'I would never accuse you of being flash,' she said, 'just, you know, it's good to seeing you doing well. You deserve it.'

'What makes you think I'm doing well?'

'Oh I don't know,' she said brightly, 'perhaps it was the several front page leads in national newspapers a while back, followed by the critically acclaimed non-fiction book of the year.'

'I don't remember picking up that award.'

'You know what I mean!' She mock-punched him on the shoulder.

'Have you been drinking?'

'I have been *working*,' she announced grandly and she told him about her drinks with Hilton and everything she had learned about Frank Jarvis..

'It seems Mrs Jarvis had a major wobble when Frank was about to be selected as a Newcastle MP and he turned down the nomination at the last minute.'

'He rejected the chance to become an MP?'

'To save his marriage,' said Helen. 'Alan heard rumours of an affair, which he said was highly likely. A lot of young women used to volunteer to help the Labour Party campaign back then. He told me it was because of "women's lib". He reckons Jarvis probably had a fling with one of the party's "dolly birds".'

'How refreshingly old school,' deadpanned Tom.

'Mrs Jarvis must have found out about it because Frank disappeared for a few days at a critical point then he turned down the nomination.'

'Wanted to spend more time with his family, eh?'

'He may have been forced to do that, otherwise someone would have leaked it. This was nearly twenty years ago, when people were a lot less tolerant of that sort of behaviour.'

'Any idea which "dolly bird" he had an affair with?'

'I'm afraid not,' she said, 'but there was one other thing that will interest you.'

'Go on.'

'It seems Mrs Jarvis has always had a bit of a drink problem,' Helen explained. 'She has it under control most of the time but during that period she was drinking more heavily than normal and she crashed her car.'

'Blimey,' he said, 'was she done for that?'

'No charges,' said Helen.

'What did she do? Abandon the car and stagger off?'

'Not exactly. The story goes that she spun off the road and skidded into a wall somewhere out in the sticks. She wasn't badly hurt and she just stayed there and waited for someone to come along. A police officer attended the scene but when the report was filed it stated the driver was sober and must have skidded on a wet patch in the road.'

'He covered it up?'

'That has always been the rumour, because back then Mrs Jarvis was rarely sober.'

'Bloody hell,' said Tom, 'he's probably Chief Constable by now.'

'Whoever it was,' she said, 'he recognised Jarvis was the coming man and decided it would be sensible to help him out of a big mess.'

'I keep hearing how incorruptible Jarvis is. I was beginning to believe it and you managed to dispel that myth in about five minutes.'

'More like an hour and a half – and I wouldn't say it made him corrupt necessarily.'

'What would you call it then?'

'It's not the same as taking backhanders, is it? He was protecting his wife from arrest and possibly prison. Wouldn't you do that?'

'Possibly,' conceded Tom, 'but I have no intention of standing for public office.'

'Brian Hilton said that was one of the problems of our system,' she replied. 'He reckons we expect politicians to be morally superior to everyone else but they are just the same as the rest of us.'

'In my experience they are a lot worse.'

'Anyway, whatever happened, it must have shaken them both. He dropped out of the running for the safe seat and eventually became leader of the city council. There were no more rumours about affairs and Mrs Jarvis kept the drinking under control, at least in public. Their marriage has been rock solid since then, apparently. Where are we going by the way?' she asked him.

'I'm off to meet Ian Bradshaw. He's been doing some digging into Lonely Lane for me,' then he added, 'but don't worry, I'll drop you back first.'

'I'm not in any hurry.' Delving deeper into a good story with Ian and Tom was infinitely preferable to returning to her empty flat and worrying about the men out to get her.

'Okay,' he told her, 'then you can ride shotgun. Thanks, Helen.'

'What for?'

'For finding the dirt. I knew there'd be something. There's always something.'

Chapter Twenty-Four

It was hard to meet anywhere in the north-east in the evenings apart from in pubs. Nowhere else was open. Ian Bradshaw was already waiting for Tom at one of his watering holes on the outskirts of Durham city. The detective seemed pleased to see Helen again and they spent a few moments catching up with one another before they got down to business. Like Tom, Bradshaw hadn't seen Helen since the Sean Donnellan case, aside from a few moments at Mary Collier's funeral. Bradshaw proceeded to brief them about Lonely Lane and the negligent attitude of the time-serving police sergeant.

'So Richard Bell was not exaggerating,' said Tom, 'the place really is a magnet for nutters and perverts. It makes me think that anyone could have murdered Rebecca.'

'Not necessarily,' Bradshaw told him. 'Rebecca was killed two years ago and there have been no murders before it or since.'

'Maybe the guy is just lying low,' offered Tom.

'And maybe you're clutching at straws because you're working for Bell's family.'

Helen decided to interrupt before the two men became fractious. 'Why is it called Lonely Lane?'

'It dates back many years,' Tom said. 'Married ladies used to meet their lovers there if they were feeling lonely . . . meaning they wanted sex. Even years ago the place was synonymous with adultery.'

'Oh, I almost forgot.' Helen fished a photocopied article from her handbag and handed it to Tom. It was from her newspaper's archive and showed a man arriving at court for sentencing.

'What's this?'

'A case primarily about money laundering and tax evasion. There were all sorts of scams involving VAT avoidance and phantom employees on the payroll in pubs all over the city. This guy was sent down for a couple of years for cheating the system.' She pointed at the picture of a gloomy man heading into court. 'He took the full rap himself, even though he couldn't have gained much directly compared to the owners and licensees, all of whom were seemingly unconnected. Their only common link was this man, who they all employed as a *consulting accountant*. The CPS was unable to build a strong enough case against any of the licensees individually and they were probably relatively blameless.'

'Because they were front men,' Tom said.

'Exactly.'

'So who was the real beneficiary of this fraud?'

'No one could prove it but the word on the street is they were all pubs controlled by Jimmy McCree. Licences were withdrawn and six pubs closed down. One of them was the Highwayman.'

'So Councillor Jarvis's daughter was working in one of big Jimmy McCree's pubs,' said Tom, 'and she probably never even knew it.'

'I don't suppose the councillor knew it either,' said Helen.

'But did Jimmy McCree?' asked Tom. 'That's the million-dollar question.'

'He had to,' said Bradshaw. 'He must be permanently

worried about undercover cops infiltrating his empire. Everyone who works for him would be vetted, even casual bar staff.'

'McCree has been cosying up to local politicians lately,' said Helen.

'Then hold that thought,' said Tom, 'it could lead us somewhere. McCree is linked to Joe Lynch, who is Frank Jarvis's successor as leader of the city council and Frank's daughter worked for him, albeit indirectly. That could of course just be a coincidence.'

'The north-east is a small world,' Bradshaw reminded him.

'Did you get anywhere with Sandra's university pals?' asked Tom.

'I looked up a few but they all stuck to their original script. In her first term, Sandra Jarvis was a nice, kind, personable soul but when she came back after the Christmas break she seemed different. She was withdrawn and sullen, she missed lectures and tutorials and stopped going out with friends but she never gave a reason for this.'

'No word about drugs?' Tom asked.

'Not a dickie bird,' said Bradshaw, 'but there was one thing that isn't in our case files – unless you found it today in Newcastle.'

'What?'

'Her other job.'

'What other job?'

'One of her mates told me Sandra volunteered at a centre that helps vulnerable kids. It was the first I'd heard of this, so I assumed Newcastle were looking into it as it's on their patch.'

'There's nothing in the case files,' said Tom, 'believe me, I read every bloody word. It took me all afternoon.'

'How could that have been missed?' asked Bradshaw.

'Cock-up or conspiracy?' wondered Tom.

'That's what we need to find out. Apparently Sandra wanted to work with young offenders when she graduated.'

'Rather her than me,' said Tom. 'Where did she volunteer?'

'Her friend reckons a number of places but she'd been helping out at one for troubled teenagers most recently.' He checked his notebook for the name. 'Meadowlands.'

'Why do these places always have such idyllic-sounding names?' asked Tom. 'Bet it's a hell-hole.'

'The kids there are some of the more challenging ones: young girls who got into drugs or prostitution, some of them have been abused by their own family members. Awful stuff, and all before the age of sixteen.'

'Do you think we might be able to speak to the girls there?' asked Helen.

'That's going to be tricky,' Bradshaw told her, 'reporters dealing with vulnerable young people.'

'I'm not a reporter, Ian,' Tom reminded him, 'I've been hired by the police to provide expert analysis.'

'Fair enough,' conceded the detective.

'That wasn't the only thing not in the case files,' Tom said. 'The photograph of Sandra Jarvis buying her ticket at the train station is missing.'

'You mean it's been removed?'

'I don't know, possibly.'

'Like you said, cock-up or conspiracy? It's probably just fallen out of the file. I'll ask them to find it for us.'

Despite his frustration at the lack of clear progress in either case, Tom felt energised somehow. He realised it was because he was no longer digging into the Sandra Jarvis or Rebecca Holt cases on his own. He was part of a team again;

the same team that had blown the lid off the Sean Donnellan and Michelle Summers cases, and their work had already begun to bear fruit. Ian had uncovered the sordid truth about Lonely Lane, following one brief chat with a police sergeant, then he had discovered Sandra's link to the Meadowlands care home. Helen meanwhile had found the reason for the closure of the Highwayman pub then given Tom an intriguing story about Frank Jarvis's private life. Tom felt as if he was moving three times faster now they were both on board.

'What are you looking so smug about?' asked Helen.

'Nothing,' he said.

Chapter Twenty-Five

The foreman made Tom wear a hard hat and high-visibility vest in matching canary yellow before he would let him onto the site that morning. Freddie Holt was waiting for him there. He was standing on a large gantry erected on the edge of a former brewery which was being levelled for redevelopment.

'You're the journalist,' observed Holt, but he was not interested in handshakes or pleasantries. Instead he said, 'Take a look at this. What do you see?'

Tom Carney surveyed the huge expanse of land before him. Aside from rubble poking out of the mud where the brewery once stood, there wasn't much to see. 'A derelict site.'

Freddie Holt sighed, 'Is that all?'

Tom was beginning to get the picture but he felt no great desire to humour the older man. 'A graveyard,' he offered facetiously, 'the wreckage of a once proud industry.'

'Opportunity!' the businessman corrected him. 'That's what I see – but then I have a vision.'

'What kind of vision?'

'Give me one year,' Holt said, as if it was within Tom's power to do so, 'and I will transform this wasteland into a thriving retail park with shops, cafés, restaurants and a multi-screen cinema and you know what that means?'

'Profits?'

'Jobs!' He gave Tom a disappointed look. 'Hundreds of them for local people.'

'Yeah but they're not real jobs, are they?' countered Tom. 'They're McJobs.'

'What?' The businessman either didn't understand the phrase or chose not to.

'McJobs,' explained Tom, 'you know,' and he mimicked an unenthusiastic tone, 'as in, *Do you want fries with that?*' then reverted to his normal voice. 'A McJob — low skill, low pay, no prospects, might as well work for McDonald's.'

'Bullshit.' Holt scowled but he didn't offer a contradictory argument.

'Sorry to rain on your parade,' Tom said, 'but some of us don't buy it.'

'When I look at this site I don't see the demise of a proud industry,' Holt was animated now, 'I see an uncompetitive factory brought low by greedy unions and swept away by economic forces because of their unreasonable demands.'

'You're not fond of them, are you?' asked Tom. 'The unions. I've heard the stories.'

'What stories?'

'The men you use never go on strike,' Tom said. 'There must be a reason for that.'

Freddie Holt eyed Tom suspiciously. 'My secretary said you wanted to write an article about me,' he said, 'but I won't contribute to a hatchet-job, if that's what you're planning.'

'I won't be writing anything bad about your development,' Tom assured him.

'You'd better not be.'

'I'm here to talk to you about Rebecca.'

'What?' The businessman was furious. 'You said . . .'

'I know what I said to your secretary and I'm sorry, but I didn't think you'd see me if I told her the truth.'

'Well you were right about that,' said Holt. 'Now see if you can guess what I'm going to do next.'

'Throw me out presumably, which is fine if you want Richard Bell to be released.'

'Released? What are you talking about? The bastard got life and I hope he rots in there.'

'He's doing life alright, but on the flimsiest of evidence. His family have asked me to look into his case to see if it can be overturned.'

'And you expect me to help you?' Holt's face was reddening.

Tom shook his head. 'No, I expect you to convince me otherwise. I've told them I'll keep an open mind. If you can persuade me he's guilty then I'll leave him in there, as you say, to rot.'

Holt frowned suspiciously. 'Why should I believe that?'

'No reason, but you speaking to me is not going to secure Richard Bell's release and it may just prevent it.'

Freddie Holt hesitated for just a moment 'Then we'll talk inside.' He jerked his head towards a large Portakabin then set off down the metal steps of the gantry, his heavy steel-toed boots clanging ominously with every stride.

Helen knocked on the apartment door and waited, then she knocked and waited some more. She was about to leave when she noticed the spy hole in the centre of the door and got the distinct feeling she was being watched through it. Sure enough, her patience was rewarded when the door opened a fraction but stayed on the chain. A woman in her early thirties peered through the gap at her. Tom had suggested Helen might be the best person to interview Amy Riordan and she had agreed, even though it had meant a drive to Leeds. Tom was right. Amy was nervous enough with a woman standing on her doorstep, let alone a man.

'Amy Riordan?' asked Helen and when the woman did not respond she went on, 'I'm Helen Norton. I work for a local newspaper in Newcastle.' She stressed that part, for she assumed Amy would be less forthcoming if she thought she worked for a London tabloid. 'I'm investigating the Richard Bell case.'

'That case is long over,' said Amy, her voice barely audible, 'why dig it all up again?'

'Because there might be some doubt about the conviction.' It was the shortest explanation Helen could think of. 'I've come quite a long way to speak with you and I was hoping we could talk about Richard.'

The woman shook her head. 'No,' she told Helen, 'I've nothing to say about him.' And before Helen could utter another word, the door was closed firmly in her face.

'So you're interested in the truth, are you?' asked Freddie Holt once they were inside the Portakabin. 'Well, here it is. Richard Bell beat my wife to death. It's that simple.'

'Possibly,' said Tom, 'but there were other suspects.'

'Including me? Oh I've heard it all before, in and out of court,' he sighed, 'and I have to put up with the gossip as well. *Freddie Holt knew his wife was shagging that bloke Bell so he killed her and framed the poor bugger for it.* Isn't that how it goes? I suppose I should be flattered people think I'm capable of something that cunning but Christ, it's fantasy, man!'

'I tend to agree with you.'

'You do?' Holt was clearly surprised by that.

'Yes.'

'Then why are you here?'

'Because I want to know more about Rebecca,' said Tom, 'other than the stuff they wrote in the paper.'

'Most of which was bullshit,' said Holt indignantly, 'particularly the stuff her supposed best friend said. Do you know that bitch Nicole actually wrote to me to say she was devastated by the article? The woman posed in her bloody underwear next to those words. She took that newspaper's money then had the nerve to beg me for forgiveness. She actually said the paper made it all up. Lying bitch!'

Tom decided there and then there would be little point in interviewing Naughty Nicole. 'I hate to break the news to you, Mr Holt, but they probably did.'

'Aye well, I wrote back to her; told her I hope she gets cancer and dies before she has time to enjoy that money.'

'Was none of it true then, the stuff the newspapers wrote about you and Rebecca?'

Freddie Holt sighed, 'Look I am not an idiot. I'm no Tom what's-his-name . . .' He paused to think for a moment before remembering '. . . Cruise. I realise it wasn't my looks that attracted Rebecca. I thought she felt safe with me, stable. She had no worries, didn't have to work, nothing. There's not many can say that these days,' he looked at Tom for confirmation, 'is there?'

'Maybe not,' he said.

'I didn't even need kids. Mine are grown up.'

'Did she want them?'

'No, at least she said she didn't, but if she did want them we could have worked something out.' Freddie made it sound like a business contract that was open for negotiation. 'All I wanted was for her to be happy. I fell and I fell hard. There's no fool like an old fool. I married a woman twenty years younger than me. What did I expect would happen?'

'You sound angry.'

'Of course I'm bloody angry!' He seemed to make a conscious effort to calm down before saying calmly, 'And that's why I killed her.'

Tom said nothing, just stared back at Freddie Holt.

'That's what you want to hear, isn't it? I got into one of my famous tempers and beat my unfaithful wife to death in a jealous rage? That would suit you, wouldn't it? It's about the only thing that would get that toe rag out of his life sentence – if I'd done it and I admitted it to you.'

'So,' Tom asked, 'did you?'

'Kill her? Don't be fucking wet! Of course I didn't. I loved the bloody woman,' he was emotional, 'still do and yes, I know how stupid that makes me sound but . . . I miss her. Or maybe I just miss the way she made me feel,' he offered. 'Perhaps that amounts to the same thing.'

'But she didn't feel the same way?'

'Evidently not.'

'And you never suspected?'

'I told you I was a fool,' Freddie said. 'It does me no credit to admit it.'

'That barrister for the defence,' Tom knew he was about to tread on delicate ground, 'gave you a hard time, didn't he?'

'Thought he could ruffle me, yes.'

'But he didn't?'

'It takes a lot to knock me sideways and Rebecca's death had already done that. He was talking nonsense.'

'Because he said you had a better motive for killing your wife than Richard Bell.'

'Yes.'

'Why was that again?'

'As if you don't know.' Holt gave Tom a dirty look but

continued regardless: 'I was the jealous, controlling husband, wasn't I? The old, bald unattractive man with the beautiful *trophy wife,* as that bastard called her, like that was all she was to me. When I found out about Bell I killed her in a fit of jealous rage . . . except I carefully delayed that burst of temper until I could lure her down a lovers' lane then murder her in a cold, premeditated manner, which sort of weakened his argument.'

'There was also the money?'

'Come again?'

'Your money. If she divorced you, she still would have ended up with some of your fortune, particularly if you couldn't prove adultery.'

'Why would she need to leave me to get my money? I gave her everything she could ever want. She had her own credit cards and a separate bank account with an allowance. I never questioned anything she bought. She lived very well.'

'But she was in love with Richard Bell.'

'She was *screwing* Richard Bell, there's a difference. I don't think for one moment either of them would have left the marital home. I was supporting her and from what I heard his wife was carrying him. The two of them wouldn't have been much cop on their own, would they? He was a bit bloody useless, by all accounts.' It was clear he took some satisfaction from Richard Bell's lack of success outside of the bedroom. 'Just a pretty boy really, though I hear he's not quite so pretty anymore.'

'You heard about his slashed face?'

'Oh yes,' said Holt, 'and no, I didn't pay anyone to do that to him, though I can't say I was devastated when I read about it. I thought it was a form of justice, since looks are all he's got. Look, maybe I did leave myself open but we all have our weak spots, Mr Carney. I loved Rebecca. Why can nobody else see that? They all think it was just about the sex or having the best-looking bird on your arm when you walk into a restaurant but it wasn't. I genuinely loved the girl. The lawyers,' he continued, 'they all wanted me to get her to sign one of those . . . what-are-they-called . . . pre-nuptial agreements like they have in America but I mean . . .' he shook his head '. . . you can't ask your wife to sign something before you marry her in case it doesn't work out. If you do that you're bloody doomed from the start.'

'I still can't see a man like you losing half his fortune and a good chunk of his business empire to a young wife who's been with him for a relatively short time.'

'Look, Rebecca didn't know how much I was worth. She didn't even ask me, not the whole time we were together. She knew I was well off and it ran to millions but even fancy divorce lawyers would struggle to put a value on me.

'I suppose at the back of my mind I knew she wouldn't have been with me if it wasn't for the money. She liked to be looked after, but I thought we had an understanding that included her not screwing another man when my back was turned. I thought she was different – but she was rotten, just like everybody else.'

Until that point Freddie Holt had been kind about his late wife, so the sudden departure from the script was quite shocking. 'You think everyone is rotten?'

'To the core, bonny lad.'

'That's a bit extreme, isn't it?'

Holt shook his head calmly. 'Not at all. It's self-preservation. Think about it. Everybody is out for themselves in the long run.'

'What about people who do genuinely good things – self-less stuff that benefits other people but not them?'

He shook his head. 'They do it so they can feel good about themselves,' he affirmed. 'They like people saying how nice they are so it's just another form of self-interest.'

'That's a pretty fucked-up world view.'

'It's realistic pessimism,' Holt reasoned.

Tom knew it was none of his business but for some reason he was curious. 'What about relationships, do you bother with any of that now?'

'I'm through with all of that nonsense. I haven't got the time or the inclination.' Then he qualified his statement, as if he didn't want Tom to get the wrong idea. 'Everything is still in working order and if I want a woman I have one but there's nothing to it. I don't even take them out anymore.'

'You must know some obliging women.'

'Escort girls.' He said it shamelessly, as if daring Tom to look shocked. 'They know what you want and there's no pretence, you pay them, it's a business deal, the good ones even pretend you're something special for an hour or so, then you leave and you don't take any of their baggage with you. I'm a businessman and I respect the honesty of that transaction. You might be judging me right now but you haven't lived as long as me.'

'I'm not judging you,' Tom told him. 'I read an article on you recently. The reporter said you had an estimated wealth of nearly twenty million pounds. That's bloody impressive . . . if he didn't overcall it, of course.'

'Underplayed it if anything.' Tom correctly surmised the self-made man from Newcastle's mean streets wanted everyone to know just how successful he had been.

'And you built all that from scratch.'

'I've done well, I suppose.' Holt was trying to sound modest but virtually puffing his chest out now.

'Which gives you a pretty big motive.'

'Eh?'

'You just told me there was no pre-nuptial agreement, so if your wife left you for Richard Bell she could have sued for divorce and taken half of it.'

'Now wait a minute,' demanded Holt, 'I had an alibi.'

'Any number of people would be willing to swear they were with you if you asked them to.'

'I didn't have to ask them,' he said and there was anger in those words. Tom began to wonder if he could goad the man into letting his guard down. 'Or bribe them if that's what you mean. I had no reason to kill Rebecca.'

'You had ten million reasons,' said Tom.

Tom quickly realised he'd gone too far. Freddie Holt wasn't the kind of man to accept that kind of insult. Instead he went for the reporter and pushed him hard, crying out in rage at the same time. Tom was slammed back against the wall of the Portakabin. His tape recorder had been sitting unused in his pocket because he didn't think Freddie Holt would open up if his every word was recorded and it crashed to the floor now with an ominous sound of shattering plastic.

'You bastard!' shouted Holt and he immediately grabbed Tom by the throat then started to squeeze, cutting off his air supply. 'I'll bloody kill you . . .' Holt's eyes were wild and there was spittle coming out of his mouth as he let loose a stream of insults. Tom tried to protest but he could barely breathe. He pushed against Holt's bulk, even landed a punch into the man's torso but Holt didn't even loosen his grip. He really is going to kill me, thought Tom and panic gripped him as he realised the man might just be capable of that – and it might not be the first time.

In desperation, Tom did the only thing he could think of to dislodge his attacker. He brought his hand down low, grabbed Holt between the legs and squeezed hard.

Holt's choke hold loosened just a little and he cried out in pain but Tom did not let go.

'We are both going to let go of each other at the same time,' Tom managed to get the words out, despite the pressure on his throat, 'on the count of three.' When Holt failed to agree to this he squeezed harder. Freddie Holt almost doubled up right there and then but somehow he stayed upright and kept his fingers round Tom's throat.

'One . . . two . . . three,' said Tom and he squeezed extra hard then twisted his hand, so that the businessman cried out again and finally let go of him.

Tom released his grip too and Holt buckled. He went down hard, his eyes seeming to swivel as his body hit the floor like a felled tree. The entire Portakabin shook with the impact. Holt lay still for a while, groaning and holding his crotch.

Tom took in a few large lungfuls of air then pressed his own hands to his tender throat gingerly, while checking to make sure his assailant wasn't about to get up again in a hurry. He stooped to retrieve his broken tape recorder and realised it was smashed beyond repair. He surveyed the prone, groaning figure of the businessman, muttered, 'Thanks for your time,' and left Freddie lying there on the floor.

Chapter Twenty-Six

'You want me to write to you?' asked Bradshaw in disbelief.

'New rules,' explained the voice on the end of the line, 'new procedure. You can't just phone us up and ask for a copy of photographic evidence. You could be anyone.'

'I could be,' admitted Bradshaw, 'but I'm not. I told you, I am Detective Sergeant Ian Bradshaw of Durham Constabulary and I am formally requesting to view a piece of evidence in the Sandra Jarvis missing person case. You can easily check if I'm legit just by calling me back on the Durham Police switchboard number so they can put you through.'

'And I told you there's new rules in place and I can't do that.'

Bradshaw had heard about *outsourcing*, which seemed to be the new buzz word at Assistant Commissioner level and above. He knew that certain tasks formerly done by uniformed officers had been taken on by civilians working for private firms in order to 'free up resources and put bobbies back on the beat', as one politician put it. This was the first time he'd been forced to deal directly with one of the androids employed by them. He was already missing the good old days when all you had to do was ring someone you knew and ask them for a favour.

'So I have to put the request in writing?'

'Yes.'

'Is a fax okay?'

'No.'

'It has to be a letter?'

'Yes.'

'Why?'

'It just does.'

'Because that's the procedure?'

'Yes.'

'Okay, let's say I understand I have to actually write to you to request the photograph but at the moment it's missing, so could you at least look for it and call me back if you manage to find it? It could be an important part of our investigation.'

'No, I can't do that.'

'Why not?'

'Because I'm not allowed to look for something that hasn't been formally requested.'

'Again, why not?'

'Because we are very busy here and I can't waste the time.'

Bradshaw wanted to say, 'But you're more than happy to waste mine,' then thought better of it. He was still hoping to get the guy to see sense, though that hope was beginning to fade with every passing minute.

'So you are seriously saying I have to write you a formal letter, put it in the post to you, then wait for it to arrive at your HQ before you'll even start to look for a photograph you might never find.'

There was a deep sigh on the other end of the line. 'That's the procedure.'

'Jesus,' hissed Bradshaw, his frustration bubbling over to the point when his usual discretion left him. 'If the building was burning down would you wait for the evacuation order to arrive in the post before running out of it?'

'Now you're just being objectionable,' the man told him, 'I don't have to listen to this kind of abuse.'

Abuse? I haven't even started yet. 'Alright, okay, I'm sorry. It's just this procedure of yours is very frustrating, that's all.'

'It's not *my* procedure. I don't make the rules. I only follow them.'

That's what the Nazis said at Nuremburg. 'Of course. I didn't mean it like that. I would be very grateful if you could commence looking for the missing photograph upon receipt of my letter . . . please.'

'Of course I will,' he said stiffly.

'Thank you.' *You officious git.*

Helen had been sitting in the café for nearly an hour, sipping cups of tea she didn't really want so she could justify her presence to the owners. She told herself she would give it another twenty minutes before admitting defeat. From her seat by the window she could see the entrance to Amy Riordan's apartment block. She'd hoped her note and the public setting of the café might persuade the woman to join her there.

Helen had not really expected Amy to let her into the flat, which is why she had written the note in advance. She worded it carefully, not knowing how Amy would feel about Richard Bell. True, she had been assaulted by her college boyfriend and forced to call the police on him but they had, presumably, shared some good times together before that point. So despite his inexcusable behaviour, it was possible Amy didn't like to think of her former boyfriend spending the rest of his life in prison.

In her note Helen had chosen a neutral approach and attempted to hand some power back to Amy. Though the judge had, controversially, allowed her history with Richard to be mentioned in court, she had not been called to give evidence for either the prosecution or the defence. Helen wanted to give her the opportunity to speak about the man she had once been intimate with; to condemn him or help to save him but ensure that either way, the choice was hers. She had folded the note, written the name of the café on the blank side and slid it under Amy's door.

The woman Tom described from his interview with Mark Birkett was a free-spirited soul who was too vibrant and carefree for an immature and controlling Richard Bell. Time and circumstances had altered Amy Riordan; Helen could tell that from the moment she first saw the woman and she could see it now as she watched Amy leave her apartment block and make her way cautiously to the café. She was dressed as if to hide her looks in blue jeans and baggy jumper, sleeves pulled down over her hands and balled in her fists. What the hell had happened to Amy in the intervening years? thought Helen. As the other woman opened the door of the café, she sensed she was about to find out.

He drove one-handed, rubbing the chafed skin around his throat with the other hand. Tom kept reliving the moment when Freddie Holt lunged for him. Was it murder he had seen in the older man's eyes and what would he have done if Tom had been incapable of fighting him off? More to the point, had Tom been given a glimpse of what he had done to his wife? Perhaps both Annie and Richard Bell were right about that. Freddie Holt had a strong motive and hadn't tolerated it when Tom reminded him of the fact.

How could he have been so stupid? Tom had been deliberately goading Holt, looking to get a reaction from the businessman, testing his feelings for Rebecca to gauge if they were real. He would surely be more likely to let something slip in an emotional state but Tom had woefully misread the situation. Holt was a street fighter who grew up swinging punches. Tom had meant to press Freddie but only to knock him off balance, not push him right over the edge.

With time before his next appointment, Tom headed back into the city to replace his broken Dictaphone. He'd had a good few years out of the tape recorder and it had seen him through many an interview. Now though it was broken and obsolete. Tom knew just how it felt.

Amy Riordan sipped from a cup of fruit tea and spoke in a very quiet voice, as if Richard Bell was sitting at the next table. Helen had to lean forward to hear her. Amy was still an extremely attractive woman but she looked incredibly tired. 'I'm sorry I didn't let you in,' she told Helen, 'I've had some problems lately.' She didn't elaborate on what they were.

'That's okay,' Helen said, 'thanks for seeing me.' She explained why she was there, including the role Tom Carney was playing in their investigation but stressing that nobody was saying Richard was innocent just yet.

'Richard has a sweet side and a dark side,' Amy told Helen, 'he is capable of love but it has to be on his terms. That's why I broke it off with him, but he's not used to rejection. He takes it very badly. It brings out the worst in him.'

'Richard wanted to control you,' said Helen.

Amy shook her head. 'He wanted to own me. It was great at first but then he started making comments like "You're not wearing that are you?" and "Who was that you were talking to?"' Her face showed her anger now. 'I was nineteen, for God's sake. I was enjoying life and he wanted to keep me tethered to him.' She sat back in her chair and started twirling a strand of hair in a nervous, repetitive gesture. 'It got much worse. I don't think he even realises his behaviour isn't normal.' She shook her head. 'It's always the way; for some reason men get obsessed with me.' This might have sounded egotistical from another woman but not the way Amy Riordan said it, like it was a curse. 'Why can't they just *be* with someone without having to own them?'

'I don't know,' said Helen, quietly. It seemed that Amy Riordan had rarely known anything other than this kind of relationship and it had damaged her.

Amy looked desperate then. 'What's wrong with me?' she pleaded, as if the other woman could provide her with an answer.

The shop had changed since Tom had last been in there. The owner used to provide recording equipment for journalists, secretaries and clerks who took dictation, with a sideline in 35mm cameras and rolls of film, but lately he'd branched out and the small shop looked like something Q from the James Bond films would have been proud of. The technology leap in the past decade meant that machines, which were the preserve of large companies or wealthy individuals in the eighties were now available to anyone with a bit of disposable income.

The Dictaphones, or personal recording devices, as the owner insisted on calling them, were stored in a locked glass cabinet and the prices varied wildly. 'I just want a bog-standard one,' Tom insisted. 'I'm a journalist, not a spy. What's this?' he asked, picking up something that looked like a cross between a chubby pen and a torch.

'A nanny cam.'

'A what?'

'It's the latest thing from America,' the owner enthused. 'You just put it somewhere discreet and you can secretly record the room. It's called a nanny cam so you can check that the nanny is looking after your kids properly and not harming them.'

'So you're filming a young girl without her knowing?'

'Aye,' he admitted.

'Sounds a bit creepy to me. What's all this stuff?' Tom was pointing to a second cabinet.

'Covert listening devices.'

'Bugs?'

'Yep.'

'Everything is so tiny,' marvelled Tom.

'That's the future. We've got high-res surveillance cameras and voice-recognition audio recording devices.'

'I just need something to record interviews,' Tom told him. 'I want an old-fashioned, battery operated, reliable tape recorder with buttons on it.'

'Buttons?'

'*On*, *off* and *record* and possibly *pause* – but nothing flashier than that,' Tom said, 'got it?'

'Aye, I've got it.' The owner did not conceal his disappointment. 'I might still have one of those,' he said gloomily, 'out the back.'

It had taken some time for Helen to assure Amy Riordan she was not the cause of the verbal and physical abuse she had received from several men over the years.

'It's not your fault. You're just very unlucky that's all, but you'll find someone . . .'

'I don't want to find someone,' she said sharply and Helen decided to curtail that subject straight away. She had to remind herself she was here for a reason and needed information from Amy.

'When Richard Bell slapped you . . .'

'He hit me. It wasn't a slap!'

'I'm sorry,' said Helen. 'When he hit you . . .'

'He punched me,' said Amy. 'He was immediately sorry and begged me not to report him but I did. The police were pretty good about it. I think they put the fear of God into him. He never bothered me again. I thought he was going to drop out at one point. He stopped turning up at his lectures or tutorials until Annie apparently dragged him in with her one day.'

'What did you think of her back then?'

'I never even noticed her,' said Amy, 'not at first. Annie seemed to just appear in Richard's life and then she was *there* all the time . . . What kind of woman takes on a man when he has been dumped by his girlfriend for hitting her?'

'Do you think she genuinely loved him?' Helen asked.

'I think she loved the project he became,' conceded Amy. 'She liked to think she was taking on a hopeless case and redeeming him. I don't know if that's love.'

'And did Richard love her?'

'Course not,' said Amy, 'he loved me – or should I say he was obsessed with me at the point she pushed her way into his life. She was picking up damaged goods. He was just grateful because she *saved* him.'

'That's why he cheated on her,' asked Helen, 'because he never really loved her?'

'Possibly. I just think he went back to his old ways. I hurt him so he decided he would avoid emotional attachment. He had his low-maintenance new girlfriend who became his wife and he had others on the side to satisfy his appetite for sex. I think it was all a way to avoid intimacy so he could never get hurt again.'

'But he hurt you, not the other way around.'

'He hit me because I hurt him,' Amy explained. 'He couldn't handle being rejected. Don't you get it? There was no way Annie was ever going to reject him, no matter what he did. She's still standing by him even now, according to the newspapers. When he started seeing her he knew she would never dump him, so he'd never be hurt like that again. Now do you see?'

'I do see. You make him sound very cold.'

'Oh, he can be.'

'Do you think he killed Rebecca Holt?'

'When I broke up with Richard he called me some terrible things, he hurt me, hit me, even wished me dead. Did he mean that at the time? I don't know. Was Rebecca Holt a re-run of our relationship with a different, far worse ending? It seems so. I have spent a lot of time going over all of that in my head. I worry that it's my fault.'

'How could it be your fault?'

'The police asked me if I wanted to press charges when he punched me. I didn't want to ruin his whole life so I let them give him a caution and the university allowed him to stay on. If they'd prosecuted him for assault he might have been convicted. Don't you see? He'd have been kicked off his course and Annie wouldn't have been able to save him. He never would have married her or even met Rebecca Holt so he could never have killed her. That's why I can't help blaming myself.'

'It isn't your fault, Amy. You couldn't have prevented this.'

'Sometimes I worry I will go mad because I find myself wondering . . . all the time . . . if he did kill Rebecca and whether he was capable of killing me back then but just didn't go through with it for some reason. I keep thinking I should have done more to make sure he could never hurt another woman . . . that her death is all my fault.' The tears were flowing freely now.

In her distress, Amy's voice grew louder and other people in the café started to notice the woman who was crying by the window. 'I get so frightened when I think about what he did to her. I keep thinking about it over and over again . . .' she sobbed '. . . because I know it could have been me . . .' She repeated the words in disbelief: 'It could have been me.'

Tom returned home for a while to eat a sandwich and test his new, second-generation Dictaphone, which to his gratification was a no-frills machine similar to his old one. He put it to one side and settled down to make some phone calls.

His first was to the Meadowlands home. Tom spoke to a man called Dean who told him there was no way he would be allowed to interview the girls there, no matter who he *claimed* to be working for. Detectives had already been to Meadowlands following the disappearance of Sandra Jarvis and Dean did not want the traumatised girls in his care disturbed again. Although this was galling, he couldn't actually fault the man. At least Dean was looking out for the girls in his care. However, that didn't help Tom; he would have to figure out another way to get access to them.

There was something else that was troubling Tom after he hung up. If detectives had already visited Meadowlands in connection with the disappearance of Sandra Jarvis, how come there was no mention of this in any of the case files?

His next call turned out to be just as fruitless.

'Physics Department,' answered the man on the other end of the line, 'Doctor Alexander speaking.'

'Professor Alexander . . .' Tom began

'That's Doctor,' he cut in, 'I'm a lecturer, not a professor.' It sounded as if he himself was acutely aware of the importance of this distinction, even if Tom was not.

'Doctor Alexander,' Tom corrected himself, 'I would like to speak with Professor Matthews please.'

'And may I ask why you are trying to get in touch with the professor?'

'I'm afraid that's private.' Tom didn't want to admit he was a journalist following up a murder case, needing to cross-examine its star expert witness. He knew academic institutions could easily be spooked where their reputation was concerned. 'But it is extremely important that I speak to Professor Matthews. There really is a great deal resting on it. Might it be possible to have a quick word with him?'

'Well as a matter of fact,' the tone was indignant, 'it wouldn't.'

'Why not?'

'Because I'm afraid Professor Matthews is no longer with us.'

'Are you saying the professor has left to work at some other university?'

'No,' the tone was blunt, 'I'm saying that he's dead.'

Chapter Twenty-Seven

'Don't call me sir in here,' Kane warned Bradshaw, 'it's my local boozer.'

'Okay,' said Bradshaw but he couldn't ever imagine being comfortable using Kane's first name, even in here.

The mentoring, which consisted of a few platitudes about policing and a number of home truths about the limitations of the legal system, had already concluded by the time the second pint was pulled. DCI Kane didn't seem to mind that he might be almost over the limit but his home was just round the corner.

Bradshaw wasted no time bringing his DCI up to date with both cases but Kane seemed distracted that afternoon. Perhaps he thought he had already done his bit by assigning resources, in the form of Bradshaw and Tom Carney, to assist the councillor. Whatever the reason, he seemed keener to talk about Bradshaw's domestic situation than ongoing investigations. 'You still seeing Debbie Harry?' he asked.

'What?'

'Blondie? You know, what's-her-name.' And he clicked his fingers impatiently for Bradshaw to provide him with an answer for once again he had forgotten her name.

'Karen? Yes, s—' He stopped himself from saying *sir* just in time '. . . I am. She's moving in actually.' He tried to announce it casually.

'Really? I thought you said you weren't shacked up together.'

'We weren't,' confirmed Bradshaw, 'but we're going to be.'

'I'm surprised to hear that.'

'Why?'

'Because when I mentioned it the other day you reacted like a scalded cat. I thought you were more likely to give the poor lass the heave-ho than an engagement ring.'

'We're not getting engaged.' Was Kane being deliberately dim? Bradshaw wondered.

'Well, as good as, if you're moving in together. You can't finish with a lass if she's living with you and you can't date other people either because it would be pretty difficult to bring them back to your place. You might not see it as permanent but she bloody will, so you'd best wise up.'

Bradshaw realised Kane was right. Bradshaw had assumed this was the next stage in their relationship but if they didn't get on she could just move out again, yet Karen had reacted as if he had handed her an engagement ring.

'Yep, it will all change now,' Kane told him.

'How do you mean?'

'Sex will go out of the window for starters. She'll spend all her time sitting on your sofa watching soap operas, dressed in her pyjamas and moaning if you want to watch the football. She won't have to make an effort anymore, so she'll probably put on at least two stone.' Kane saw the look on Bradshaw's face. 'What's the matter, man? I'm only pulling your leg!'

'It's just I never really thought of it as being permanent.' Bradshaw took a long sip of his pint.

'Well that's alright, lad. Most of us blokes don't, do we? That's why we need the women in our lives to give us a bit of a pull in the right direction. Who hasn't been on the receiving end of the where's-this-relationship-going question? If it was down to us none of us would ever end walking down the aisle, but you've got a cracker there. Everyone in the station fancies her.'

'Yeah but . . . what if . . . ?' He couldn't even complete the question.

'She isn't the one?' Bradshaw's silence spoke volumes. 'Ha! Don't worry about that, man. There's no such bloody thing.'

'What?'

'I used to be like you,' said Kane suddenly. 'I know you find that hard to believe but I was, many moons ago. I was the romantic type see. I used to believe in all that guff once upon a time, you know, red roses on her birthday, wining and dining the lady, parachuting down with a box of Milk Tray in my teeth, all that shite.'

'But you don't now?'

'No,' he admitted, 'and I stopped believing in it long before I reached your age.' He regarded the younger man carefully for a moment. 'There's no such thing as the perfect bird, you know. They can be great fun, good company, kind-hearted, beautiful and filthy in bed but you'll still always find something wrong with them if you look for it.'

'So what's the secret then,' asked Bradshaw, 'since you're handing out the advice?'

'Don't look for it.'

'How do you mean?'

'Exactly that. Nobody's perfect so just accept that and don't rock the boat. You're looking at me right now like I am the least romantic bloke in the world but that isn't so. I am telling you that you can set your sights too high and mess up what you've got already and I ought to know. When a man who has been divorced twice gives you some advice, you should listen to it and take heed. It'll spare you a lot of aggro.'

'So, why did you get divorced? If you don't mind me asking?'

'Strictly between us?'

'Of course.'

'Stupid reasons. The first time, with Janet, it wasn't the job or the long hours or all the bad things we see. I'll tell you something shall I. Most of the guys on the job who say that's why their marriages broke up are lying. I mean for some of them it is undoubtedly true that the force caused them marital problems, I'll grant you that, but with a fair few of them it's just a handy excuse because they couldn't be arsed to keep their marriage going and they don't want to admit it.'

'Is that what happened to you then?'

Kane sighed, 'Truth is, I got bored.' He seemed to be reflecting on that for a moment before adding, 'It was fine at first, then, after a few years, I'd come home and she'd be there doing the ironing or cooking the dinner and, I don't know, I just didn't fancy her like I used to and I felt a bit trapped. Then I met this WPC.' And he raised his eyebrows at his own folly. 'She was young and fit and looked bloody good in the uniform, so I gave her the chat. I was older and higher up and she was flattered so I started seeing her on the sly.'

'Did your wife find out about it?'

'Oh yeah but not because I wasn't careful. Things were great with my little WPC for a while but there was something I hadn't bargained for.'

'What?'

'She was a bit of a bunny boiler.'

'Oh.'

'So, once I'd had my fun and the novelty started to wear off I tried to gently kick her into touch. I figured she knew I was married so . . .' and he shrugged to indicate he assumed she would be reasonable about it '. . . but she went ballistic. I mean loopy. Swearing at me in the car park, calling me all sorts while people were walking by.' He still seemed a little shocked at the memory. 'She was screaming, "You bastard, you used me and now you think you can just ditch me when you feel like it and go back to your bloody boring wife."' He exhaled. 'I mean all of that was true if I'm honest but I didn't expect her to tell the whole world about it. It didn't help my career. You can have your bit on the side in our world as long as you're discreet about it. Her screaming at me like a nutter while the Detective Superintendent is parking his car a few yards away isn't discreet. I reckon that cost me a good three years on the promotion front and then of course there was Janet.' He seemed to need to take a sip of his drink to explain that bit. 'My sweet little WPC found out where I lived and went round there to tell her all about us. I don't know what she thought she'd achieve but I came home to find my clothes packed in two suitcases on the door step and I was out of there, no second chances and no get-out-of-jail-free-card. My marriage was over,' he clicked his fingers 'like that. And for what, a few sweaty tumbles in the back of a car and once in a hotel.'

'That's rough,' offered Bradshaw when it seemed some modicum of sympathy was expected from him then, even though Kane had already admitted he deserved everything he got.

'And I still see her around from time to time.'

'Janet?'

Kane shook his head. 'No, the bunny boiler. She's still a WPC, got a husband and a couple of kids now, or so I heard, but every once in a while she'll be in the same crowded room as me when there's some big event or other. I'd love to say she's fat and ugly now but she isn't. She's still quite tidy. Of course I could never forgive her for what she did but you know the really strange thing?'

'What?'

'Despite everything, when I see her, I still get that little surge here,' he thumped his chest with his fist, 'or maybe it's a bit lower down,' he admitted. 'A combination of lust and excitement, which means if the opportunity arose I'd still give her one in the back of my car. Isn't that daft? When I know I should run out of the room and keep going till I'm way over the horizon. I can't help myself. Because I can remember what it was like when it was really good, you know. That lass cost me my marriage – actually no, that's not fair, *I* cost me my marriage – but you know what I mean, she contributed to it and I still look at her and think, "Yep, I would."'

'Blimey.'

'I know, which goes to show how bloody stupid men are. The way we think, even when we know it's going to cost us thousands of pounds and endless grief, we still do these ridiculous things.'

'You said you were divorced twice.'

'Yeah, second time was Carol. It was nowhere near as dramatic. We got on fine at first but I rushed into marriage because I think I was trying to get back what I lost and a bit of me wanted to show the force I was respectable again, you know. I was being considered for promotion at that point, you see. Anyway, it turned out we didn't have that much in common really and, this is the killer, she was nowhere near as good company as my first wife. Neither of us were very happy but somehow we managed five years before we called it a day. No kids, thankfully.'

'You with anyone these days?'

'Nope, I've had enough aggravation for one lifetime, but I can still remember my youthful aspirations, which is why I am counselling you. I used to want the perfect woman too, you see. I was looking for someone who would be a soul mate, a companion, a lover, a friend, someone who could pick me up when I was feeling sad or depressed, someone who needed me but not too much, a lass who was the right height, with the perfect figure and the long hair, the beautiful eyes and legs that went on forever, who would give me blow jobs morning, noon and night then make me bacon sandwiches for breakfast. In short, I was looking for something that didn't exist so, unsurprisingly, both my wives came up wanting. That's why I ended up on my own when it comes down to it, Ian, because I had wholly unrealistic expectations.' He drained the last of his pint. 'These days, I'd settle for the bacon sandwich,' he placed his empty glass firmly down onto the bar, 'and the occasional blow job.'

When he was finally done, Bradshaw didn't know how to respond, so he stayed silent. Kane must have sensed his discomfort so he said dryly, 'Anyway, I've enjoyed our little chat. You mark my words and feel free to ignore them, as I'm sure you will. I'm hardly the best person to give relationship advice now am I?'

Frank Jarvis stopped what he was doing on the allotment when he saw Tom. It took him a while to bring the older man up to date, the two of them sitting together outside Frank's hut while the sky darkened.

'I'm a bit surprised you didn't mention this voluntary work Sandra was doing?' said Tom when he was done.

'Didn't I?' asked Jarvis. 'Isn't it in the case file?'

'No,' said Tom, 'it isn't it.'

'Well it should have been.'

'Interesting,' said Tom and he wondered who might have removed it and why. 'Tell me about this place Meadowlands.'

'I didn't know she was helping out down there. She didn't tell me,' Jarvis said. 'I knew about the volunteering but it was several different places: old folks' homes, kids in care, that sort of thing.'

'Why would she keep it from you?'

'She knew I wouldn't want her working at a place like that.'

'Why not?'

'Because the girls at Meadowlands are very . . .' Frank searched for the right word and finally settled on '. . . damaged. I wouldn't have wanted her hearing about the stuff they'd been through, but that was Sandra. She was always keen to help anyone in trouble.' It was said with a hint of pride.

'Did she go there regularly?'

'A couple of evenings a week, occasional weekends.'

'What did she do?'

'Helping out generally, a bit of guidance, some teaching of basic skills like reading and writing, a little counselling, unofficially, obviously. She didn't tell me much about her voluntary work because everything is meant to be confidential, to protect the girls. You can't chit-chat about it over the dinner table. I found all this out afterwards.'

'Did many people know your daughter was volunteering?'

'I didn't broadcast it and she used her mother's maiden name.'

'Why?'

'Because she didn't want the staff to know her dad was leader of the council. They'd think she was getting special treatment,' he informed Tom, 'or she was a spy.'

Tom admired the girl even more for that. 'I want to go

down there, to speak to the staff and, if it can be cleared, some of the girls.'

'Oh,' said Jarvis, 'why do you want to do that?'

'For the same reason I want to speak to everyone else that knew her,' said Tom, 'to see if they can shed some light on the reasons for her disappearance.'

'Fair enough,' said Jarvis, 'but I suggest you call them first or they might not let you through the door.'

'I already did,' said Tom. 'Spoke to a bloke called Dean and he won't let me in. I can go through official channels, get DCI Kane to phone his counterparts in Newcastle, request formal interviews, but I figured you could use some of that famous influence of yours to open the door for me.'

Jarvis smiled then. 'Consider it done.' Then he regarded Tom for a moment. 'Is there anyone else who's giving you grief?'

'No one whose door you could get me through.' And when Jarvis looked surprised at that, Tom said, 'I went down to that pub Sandra worked at on the Quayside. It's closed now but the police took statements from everyone who worked there with her.'

'I've read them,' said Jarvis. 'There wasn't much there.'

'No, there wasn't,' agreed Tom. 'Nobody even mentioned the owner, Jimmy McCree.'

'Bloody hell,' said the councillor, 'how come the police didn't work that out?'

'I'm not sure,' said Tom, though he had his suspicions, corruption being chief among them. 'I guess it got overlooked somehow.' And Tom told Jarvis about Helen's detective work.

'Very bright lass, that reporter,' observed the councillor.

'Have you met her?'

'No, but I've read some of her recent articles about Joe Lynch.'

'Do you think McCree could have known your daughter was working in one of his pubs?'

'I honestly don't know.'

'But he could have found out,' said Tom. 'It's possible, I mean, probable even?'

'The people who work for him would be expected to pass on information like that but . . .'

'But what?'

'What good would it do him? I grew up in the same streets as McCree, around the same time. He chose one path while I chose the other and I have followed his *career* with interest. I've campaigned against him and folk like him. I've been an ardent opponent of anyone who deals drugs or takes part in organised crime in my city but he has never moved against me before. I can see where you're coming from. Jimmy McCree is not a nice man. I used to think he was the devil . . . but I've since learned there are a lot worse than him out there. I've never heard of him harming innocent members of anyone's family. In a way he's quite old-fashioned about that short of thing.'

'Honour among thieves eh?'

'If there is such a thing.' Jarvis didn't sound sure about that. 'More to the point, why would he do it?'

'I don't know,' Tom admitted, 'but Sandra has disappeared and there must be a reason for her disappearance. We can rule out anything at home and we're drawing a blank at her university so that leaves this Meadowlands place and the fact that she used to work in a boozer controlled by Tyneside's most notorious gangster.'

'You're right about one thing,' said Jarvis. 'I won't be able to get you through his door and I wouldn't want to, for your sake. Jimmy McCree is a very private individual. Oh I know he's seen around town but he won't take kindly to a journalist sniffing about, especially one who's on the police payroll. He'll already know about that, by the way.'

'From his contacts on the force?' asked Tom.

'Exactly,' said Jarvis. 'If you get too near him I'd be surprised if you didn't take a beating. Not there and then obviously but some other time when you were coming out of a pub or your own front door. Jimmy would be miles away when it happened of course and he'd have an alibi.'

'Like you said, not a nice guy.'

'Well a lot of pubs in the Toon have dodgy owners or bent money behind them.'

'And I could be barking up the wrong tree here, but it got me thinking.'

'What about?'

'Who stood to gain?'

'From what?'

'Your daughter's disappearance.'

Jarvis thought for a moment. 'I don't think anybody gained anything from her disappearance.'

'Don't you?' asked Tom. 'Think for a moment. What was the first thing you did when you realised she was missing and wasn't coming back any day soon?'

'I started the campaign to find her,' he said.

'Before that,' Tom prompted Jarvis.

'Before that?' Jarvis wasn't following. 'I liaised with the police as best I could . . .'

Tom shook his head. 'You stood down.'

'Well I had to,' said Jarvis. 'I couldn't carry on doing all that when I had to find my daughter.'

'So you resigned,' said Tom, 'as leader of the city council. You gave up a position of great influence and you stopped campaigning on issues that were once very dear to your heart, like uncontrolled inner city development for example, particularly on publicly owned land on the banks of the Tyne.'

'The Riverside tender?'

'Which you were once very vocally opposed to.'

'I was,' said Jarvis, 'and a bit of a lone voice in the wilderness, I'm afraid. I wanted it to be public parkland surrounded by social housing with affordable homes for public-sector workers. I might as well have asked for Disneyland.'

'But you were still a significant obstacle to the kind of development they are all bidding for now: retail centres with low-paid jobs, restaurants and penthouse apartments overlooking the River Tyne. You got a lot of people questioning the wisdom of that. There would have been some expensive compromises for the developers if you'd have still been in charge.'

'Maybe,' said Jarvis, 'so what's your point?'

'With you gone or at least distracted by the disappearance of your daughter, the way was clear for one of the biggest land grabs in the history of the north-east.'

'You'll forgive me if I view that as a pretty low priority right now.'

'And that's exactly my point,' said Tom. 'You stopped campaigning to make the Riverside development a community asset instead of a licence to print money and started giving different speeches about missing persons instead.'

'So someone harmed my daughter to get me out of the way?'

'It's not inconceivable, is it?'

'And you think McCree could be behind this?'

'When you resigned you created a vacuum,' Tom reminded him, 'and you let someone else take your place.'

'Joe Lynch.'

'Who became leader of the council instead of you,' Tom said, 'and Joe Lynch is a friend of . . . ?'

'Alan Camfield,' said Jarvis, 'according to your reporter friend.'

'Who is working with . . . ?'

And it seemed as if the penny finally dropped. 'Jimmy McCree.'

'Exactly,' said Tom. 'Now you've got it.'

'Who stood to gain?' reflected Jarvis ruefully.

'The answer is, all three of them,' said Tom.

Chapter Twenty-Eight

Since Helen lived and worked in Newcastle and the two men were based in Durham it seemed only fair to split their meetings between the two locations. Helen had given them her address in Jesmond but suggested meeting at the Lit and Phil instead. 'It's more central,' she said quickly, 'and my flat is tiny.'

It had been a while since Tom had been in the ancient library. Its full name was the Literary and Philosophical Society but everyone called it the Lit and Phil. It had occupied the same spot near the railway station for 170 years and held more than 100,000 books between its walls. The place had the atmosphere of a stately home that suddenly decided one day to admit members of the public and allow them to occupy its battered old chairs so they could read in peace. It was an oasis of calm in a bustling city and Tom wondered why he didn't use it more often.

Helen was sitting at a table near a wrought-iron staircase that curved up to the ceiling. Two huge bookcases on either side lent her spot an element of privacy. They could easily talk here without disturbing others, as long as they kept their voices reasonably low.

Helen told them about her meeting with Amy Riordan and the effect knowing she had once dated a murderer had had on her. 'Amy is a damaged individual,' she concluded, 'and some of that has to be down to Richard Bell, whatever else he is guilty of.'

'It sounds like she has had trouble with a number of men,' observed Tom.

'Are you saying that's her fault?' asked Helen sharply.

'No,' Tom retorted, 'I'm saying she's unlucky and so was Rebecca Holt. Richard Bell wasn't the only violent man in her life.' And he told them about his run-in with Freddie.

'So Rebecca went from one angry controlling man to another?' observed Bradshaw.

Again Helen took umbrage: 'Or maybe Tom just brought out the worst in him.'

'How did you get on with Frank Jarvis?' asked Bradshaw, eager to avoid another argument about victim-blaming.

'He's in a state,' said Tom, 'as you would expect,' and he gave them a detailed report on his time with Jarvis. When he was done he told Helen, 'He's a fan of yours too. I think he is quietly amused by the way you are steadily dismantling Councillor Lynch.'

'What about Meadowlands?' asked Bradshaw.

'He says he can get me in there, so we will see if he really can make things happen in this city.' When the detective seemed happy with that answer, Tom asked, 'What about you?'

'Me? The highlight of my day was getting love-life advice from my DCI. Surprisingly, he didn't seem all that arsed about either of the cases we're looking at.'

'Sliding desk,' said Tom. 'The Sandra Jarvis case is now being handled by someone else – you.'

'That's what I figured,' said Bradshaw.

'So we'd better not mess this up if you want a career.'

'I figured that too.' And when no one seemed to have anything to add, Ian said, 'If that's everything, I should really be getting back home.'

Bradshaw and Tom got to their feet then and started to move away from Helen's table as they said their goodbyes. Helen stayed in her seat and seemed to hesitate before speaking.

'Before you go,' she asked Bradshaw, 'could I have a word?' Since they had shared a car both men turned back to join her. 'Er . . . I meant with Ian,' she said awkwardly to Tom, 'if that's alright.'

'Oh,' Tom said, momentarily taken aback, 'of course, no problem. I'll just go and wait in the car then.'

She hated to exclude him but she needed Ian's advice as a policeman. Somehow she knew Tom would be too concerned and protective if he knew what had been happening to her.

Neither Helen nor Bradshaw spoke until Tom had left the room.

'If you won't tell Tom what this is about it must be bloody serious,' he folded his arms, 'so I'm listening.'

In the car on the way back to Durham, Tom didn't ask what Helen wanted to talk to him about, even though he must have been burning to know, and Bradshaw was glad of that. He would not have been able to betray her confidence if Tom had pressed him but it was more than that. He understood why Helen didn't want Tom to know about the attack on her in the car park, the threats over the phone and the vile message sprayed on her car. Tom would want to do something about it but what could he do that wouldn't place him in just as much danger?

Ian Bradshaw knew he should have told her to make it all official; to formally report the incidents and let uniformed officers investigate them, but that would be a pointless waste of time. It would probably only serve to encourage whoever was responsible, since it was proof they were getting to her. Instead he gave her some advice on how to avoid putting herself at risk.

'That's all very useful, Ian,' she told him, 'but what should I actually do?'

'Do you trust me, Helen?'

'I wouldn't be talking to you about this if I didn't.'

'Then leave it with me.'

Tom returned home to find a message on his answerphone. The voice was low and the words reluctant.

'It's Dean, from Meadowlands. Councillor Jarvis called me. We'll let you in tomorrow afternoon,' then he added, 'but you have to bring a woman.'

'Bloody hell,' Tom said aloud to himself because he had only just left Helen. He had a phone number for her flat in Jesmond but didn't want it to seem like he couldn't go a night without calling her. Despite himself, he couldn't help but feel slighted by the way she'd asked him to leave her for a cosy chat with Ian Bradshaw. 'Bugger that,' Tom said and he went off to bed.

Jimmy McCree regarded the man standing on his doorstep that morning with something between amusement and disdain. He turned to call back over his shoulder. 'Put the kettle on, pet,' he told an unseen partner, 'and make a cup of tea for the officer,' then he smirked and walked back into his house, leaving the door open for Bradshaw to follow him inside.

Bradshaw had never met Jimmy McCree but the gangster wasn't psychic. In this part of Newcastle's west end, if you saw someone dressed in a suit and tie he was more than likely a policeman. In some ways the folk that lived here were decent people and the streets supposedly a lot safer than more deprived areas, like the run-down high-rises not so many miles from here. Drugs were less of an obvious problem than feuding between the rougher families. Domestic violence or drink-related incidents were more common in this corner of the city and crime was seen as a perfectly viable career path. For many it was the only option. Jimmy McCree and his family had ruled this part of the world for years and he had never left its terraced streets. Bradshaw wondered what was the point of having all the money he was reputed to have earned if he couldn't spend it on anything, but if McCree did move to a mansion in Gosforth he would lose a good portion of his romanticised, Robin-Hood man-of-the-people image and the protection from the community he lived in would vanish along with it.

McCree sat in an armchair and filled it with his bulk. He was an imposing figure with huge biceps that threatened to rip through his T-shirt. He beckoned for Bradshaw to take a seat. 'I've not seen you before, bonny lad.' His eyes narrowed. 'You didn't come down here mob-handed,' the big man noted, 'so you've obviously got balls.' Bradshaw had heard the stories. If you wanted to arrest Jimmy McCree in his own back yard you turned up with back-up from armed officers and riot shields, because as soon as you knocked on his front door most of the neighbourhood would be out throwing half-bricks at you and simultaneously crying 'Police brutality!' as you led him away.

'And nobody called to say you were on your way, so I'm wondering if this is properly official.' He looked sly then. 'Does anyone even know you're down here?' The implication was that if Bradshaw never returned he might not even be missed.

'Are you finished?' asked Bradshaw, who was in no mood for mind games.

McCree sighed, as if Bradshaw didn't understand the rules of an audience with the King of Newcastle. 'Okay,' he said, 'so what's this about?' And his tone hardened. 'Say your piece then fuck off.'

It didn't take long for Tom to find the faculty building and nobody challenged him as he walked its corridors searching for the relevant room. He was grateful academic people didn't believe in wearing their knowledge lightly, preferring to broadcast their credentials to the world with names and titles on every door, along with the letters denoting their qualifications.

When he found the right door he knocked. 'Come,' was the slightly imperious response. He entered to find a man standing by a blackboard busily scribbling numbers and symbols.

'Looks complicated.' When the doctor turned towards him he said, 'Tom Carney. We spoke on the phone.'

'Everything looks complicated if we have no understanding of it,' said Doctor Alexander. 'French, Swahili, the notes on a music sheet,' the doctor said, and he added some numbers to his work before finishing, 'If someone shows us what it all means, however . . .'

'Yeah,' agreed Tom doubtfully, while hoping the doctor would not try to explain the enormous equation that filled a large section of the blackboard, 'I can cope with a bit of French but I suspect *that* might be beyond me.'

'Please tell me you're not one of those people who

can't comprehend the difference between astronomy and astrology.'

'I think I can at least manage that.' The lecturer peered at him expectantly. 'Astronomy is the study of the planets and the stars,' Tom said, 'whereas astrology is just bullshit.'

The doctor seemed pleased with that answer. 'There is no scientific basis in the notion that the future can be predicted by the position or motion of the stars,' he nodded in agreement with his own point. 'Astrology is often referred to as a pseudoscience but I think that's very generous. I rather prefer your description, though I suspect I won't get away with that in any of my lectures.' Then he seemed to remember something. 'Didn't you call to speak to Professor Matthews?'

'That's right.'

His frown deepened. 'And I did inform you the professor died some months ago.'

'You did,' said Tom, 'but I have a couple of questions and I hoped you might be able to help me with them.'

'I'm afraid I didn't know him all that well.'

'They are about physics actually, not the professor.' The doctor looked doubtful. 'It relates to some expert testimony provided by the professor in a case I am looking into.'

Alexander blinked at him. 'It can't still be a live case. He has been dead for almost a year.'

'It isn't. I am re-examining the case and conducting a thorough review of all of the original evidence.'

'I see,' Tom could tell the lecturer was uneasy, 'but I am not about to assist you in discrediting our former professor.' He folded his arms and glared at Tom.

'Nor would I expect you to,' Tom assured him, 'I just need a better understanding of his findings.'

'Relating to what?'

'The force of a blunt instrument striking an immobile object.'

'Oh,' he unfolded his arms then, 'that I can help you with, I suppose, or I can at least try. What exactly do you want to know?'

'To be specific, I want to understand how you would go about calculating the force of a hammer blow.'

'Oh that's relatively easy.'

'Really?' Tom was surprised to learn this.

'Yes, it's just Newton's equation of motion.'

'I could pretend I know what you're talking about but . . .'

The lecturer reached for a piece of chalk and went back to his blackboard. He grabbed a dusty cloth and rubbed an old equation from the board, leaving a gap large enough to write his explanation, calling out the letters as he wrote them: 'V squared is the final velocity of the hammer, which can be calculated because it is equal to U squared, the initial impact speed, minus 2 AX, with A being the deceleration and X being the distance travelled. You follow?'

'Kind of,' said Tom unsurely.

'It's simple physics.'

'How do you calculate the level of force used if you don't know the impact speed or the distance travelled because you weren't there to measure it?'

'You can't.'

'But Professor Matthews did.'

Doctor Alexander shook his head. 'He couldn't have done. He had to have made certain assumptions, if he wasn't there to witness the . . . er . . . I was going to say *experiment* but clearly it was more serious than that if he was testifying in a court of law.'

Tom explained the circumstances behind Professor Matthews' appearance in court.

'Oh dear Lord,' said Alexander, 'that's truly horrific.'

'So how did he do it?' asked Tom quickly. 'Calculate the force of the blow, I mean?'

'Well the simple answer is he couldn't have done.'

'What?' Tom had been expecting a long discussion about the mechanics of that calculation and, if he was lucky, some small grey area of doubt that could be used to dispute the professor's findings. He wasn't expecting this however.

'Well he wasn't at the scene, was he? He didn't witness the crime and wouldn't have been able to calculate its force just by looking at it.'

'So how did he come up with his findings?'

'I don't want to disparage the late professor,' the doctor said quietly, 'but I am surmising he simply worked backwards.'

'How do you mean?'

'He surveyed the damage caused to that young lady by the hammer then estimated the level of force required to cause it. From that he could extrapolate until he had a series of estimations of velocity, impact speed and the deceleration required to administer the deadly blow.'

'But how could he ascertain whether a man or a woman were capable of delivering such a blow?'

'I don't know.' When Tom seemed dissatisfied with that answer, the doctor felt compelled to add, 'I suppose if it were me I could attempt to replicate those conditions in the lab, using male and female students perhaps, to see how many of them were capable of reaching the required levels.'

'And did he do that?'

'I have no idea but I suspect not.'

'But I don't understand how he could come out with such

a strong opinion. He said that it would be a practical impossibility for a woman to deliver that blow.'

'Did he?' The lecturer bit his bottom lip thoughtfully. 'Look, I've never done that kind of work and I wouldn't want to but if you are called to comment on these cases you are there for a reason. The defence or, in this case, the prosecution, want an expert opinion and it won't be highly regarded if it is something woolly. No one is going to ask you back on the stand if you say, *Having examined all of the facts, I don't know what went on.* Professor Matthews was a favoured expert witness precisely because he was more comfortable making pronouncements based on less comprehensive data than many of us.'

Alexander's answer was a masterful piece of understatement. In short, the professor craved the fame of the courtroom and the accompanying exposure in newspapers more than scientific accuracy.

'So he guessed?' announced Tom, stunned at the realisation. 'I know it was a highly educated guess with a whole bunch of letters after its name but it was still a bloody guess.'

'Er, I'd prefer to call it a supposition but, I suppose, you could, if you wanted, see it as . . . a guess.'

'Christ all-bloody-mighty.'

Chapter Twenty-Nine

Tom's knowledge of physics hadn't greatly improved during his time with Doctor Alexander but his understanding of the world of the expert witness had increased markedly. Their fields of expertise were usually so narrow and specialist that normal members of a jury would be in no position to question the findings of a professor and would simply take their opinions as scientific fact.

Tom wondered how many men and women were languishing in prison because an expert said they must be guilty when they were not. Professor Matthews stood up in court and ruled that only a man could have killed Rebecca Holt. It had taken Tom just minutes with his former colleague to discredit that theory. In that sense it had been a successful morning so far and, buoyed by this, he took a handful of coins from his pocket and fed them into a payphone in the lobby of the university building then dialled Helen at the newspaper. As he waited for her to pick up he wondered again if he should invest in a mobile phone. He could probably justify their convenience but not their cost and though they were smaller than the brick-like unit he'd had when he worked for a tabloid, it was still a pain trying to fit one in a pocket and there were large parts of the north-east where the signal strength made you feel as if you were on the moon.

'Hello.' Tom recognised Helen's voice straight away.

'I need a woman,' he told her.

'Are you always this direct?'

'That depends on how urgent the requirement is and in this case I'm afraid I cannot manage without you.'

'In that case I'm flattered, I think, but what do you want and when do you need it by?'

'A burned girl, you say? Well that's terrible.' Jimmy McCree sounded to Bradshaw as if he couldn't have cared less. 'It wasn't in Newcastle though, was it? I know everything that goes on in my city.' Bradshaw found himself irked by the arrogance of this man. It wasn't *his* city.

'Her body was found in a scrapyard in County Durham but for some reason we've had trouble tracing the owner. Nobody seems to want to tell us who he is.'

'Really? That sounds a bit dodgy to me. Has it crossed your mind that it could just be a front? You know, for criminal goings-on.' Bradshaw ignored him. 'I'm very sorry, officer. I'd love to help you with that one but I can't. Tell you what, I'll ask around though.'

'What about Sandra Jarvis?' asked Bradshaw.

'Sandra Jarvis?' Once again the big man contorted his face but this time it was to feign a loss of memory where that name was concerned. Eventually he said, 'The councillor's daughter?' as if it had suddenly come back to him. 'That's a terrible business. Frank Jarvis must be grieving.'

'She's not dead,' countered Bradshaw, 'unless you are telling me she is?'

'It's just a figure of speech. I meant her unexplained disappearance must be causing him grief. Nothing messes with a man's mind more than problems involving his immediate family.'

'That's true,' said Bradshaw. 'I hear she worked in one of your pubs.' He watched the big man intently now.

McCree regarded Bradshaw innocently as if he had been entirely misinformed. 'I don't have any pubs, detective. Can't imagine where you got that idea from.'

'Of course not,' said Bradshaw dryly and he tried another angle: 'Some folk have profited from Sandra's disappearance haven't they, since Frank Jarvis had to step down as leader of the council?'

'You can hardly blame Joe Lynch for taking over a vacant position. It's not his fault Frank's daughter has gone missing. Since when has ambition been a crime?'

'Know him pretty well, do you? The councillor, I mean.'

'I've *met* him because of my business but I wouldn't say I *know* him. Do you?'

'I know he likes to threaten journalists.'

'I've heard nowt about that.'

Bradshaw knew then and there that he was never going to get the infamous Jimmy McCree to let down his guard. He could have stayed there all day and McCree would bat back all of his questions with the consummate skill of a man who has been questioned countless times by police and never once been convicted. Bradshaw hadn't expected it would go any other way. He simply wanted to be face to face with McCree, to meet the famous adversary at the top of the hit list of every policeman in the north-east of England, and he also wanted a quiet word.

'So Joe Lynch never asked you to terrorise Helen Norton?'

McCree didn't even pretend he wasn't aware of Helen. 'A burned girl, a missing girl . . . and an annoying girl. You've got a thing about women, detective. I'm guessing you're a regular Sir Galahad.'

'I'm here to warn you off her.'

'Oh, really?' And he leaned forward in his chair then,

256

exuding menace, a street fighter who's been challenged. 'Well I've no idea what you're talking about but if I did I'd probably take offence at that.'

'You need to stay away from her.'

'I've never been near the lass, except one time when she took my photograph in a restaurant without asking me, which was an invasion of my privacy, by the way. There was a second time when she followed me to a private charity event at a golf course and that was very rude of her, don't you think?'

'That why you set your thugs on her,' asked Bradshaw, 'and damaged her car – or are you going to say you had nowt to do with that too?'

'I don't know any thugs and I'm not the sort to bear grudges against a woman, even one who seems obsessed with me . . . but if I *was* the type to take exception to someone I wouldn't mess about just spraying their car.'

'Who said it was sprayed?'

'You said it was vandalised. Round here they would key it or spray it. I assumed it was one or the other.'

'You're right though,' admitted Bradshaw, 'that's not really your method. Sickening beatings and the occasional murder are more your style.'

'I've never been convicted of giving anyone a beating. I was arrested once for murder,' McCree conceded, 'but the jury knew it was a stitch-up. The judge was very critical of Northumbria Police in his summing-up. He realised they were trying to frame me because they had a long-standing grudge against me.'

'And why is that, I wonder?'

'When I was a young man I kept bad company for a while and did some things I shouldn't have. I was a bit of a tearaway but I've changed now and I'm a successful businessman.

You lot resent that and you want to put me away for something I never even did. It's scandalous.'

'In that case it might be a good idea to avoid harassing a journalist. You might bring the wrong sort of attention to yourself. So lay off her from now on.'

Jimmy McCree folded his huge arms and stared right back at the detective. 'Or?'

'You'll make an enemy of me,' said Bradshaw, 'and you wouldn't want that.'

When the words came they were a low snarl that reminded Ian Bradshaw of a dog that was only kept back by the chain it was fastened to. 'And I could say the exact same thing back to you, bonny lad. I've been threatened before and you're not the first police officer to do it, but I'm still here and they're all gone. You should bear that in mind. Now get out of my house before I forget you are a guest in it.'

He rose to show Bradshaw his time in McCree's home was at an end. Big Jimmy escorted Bradshaw to the front door and saw him through it. Before he closed the door he said, 'And please give my regards to Miss Norton. Tell her I hope she has a nice day.'

'Yes?' The voice was rasping and disembodied, a Dalek speaking from the intercom on the outside wall of the care home.

'It's Tom Carney,' he said, 'and I brought a woman.'

There was a moment's pause, followed by a buzzing sound from the intercom and the door clicked open.

Tom and Helen stepped inside and walked down an empty, brightly lit corridor until an unassuming man in his thirties emerged from an office halfway along it and intercepted them. 'This is Helen Norton,' explained Tom, 'a colleague of mine.'

The man nodded. 'I'm Dean, pleased to meet you. Councillor Jarvis vouched for you, so that's good enough for me.' Then he said, 'Just a quick word with you before you go in, if you don't mind?' They followed him to his office.

'Thanks for bringing your colleague. No male is allowed in here unsupervised without a female unless he is a member of staff. That's for the girls' protection. I hope you understand. Usually a female member of staff would accompany you but there have been cuts so we can't spare anyone today. We didn't want to delay you, so we'll let you speak to the girls one at a time in their rooms, as long as you stay together. They know you're coming.'

'Fair enough,' said Tom. 'How does it work here? Are the girls allowed out on their own?'

'Of course,' said Dean, 'it's not a prison and the girls here are older but we do operate a curfew. They are expected to be in by nine p.m. We have rules and they lose privileges if they break them.'

'Right,' said Tom, 'we'll begin then.'

'Be careful,' Dean warned, 'all of these girls have had a very hard start to their lives and as a result they are all quite . . .' his eyes narrowed as he searched for the right word '. . . vulnerable.'

'We'll try not to upset any of them,' Helen assured him.

'It's not just that,' he told her. 'I'm sorry to say this, but you can't always trust them. Because of their past and their upbringing, it's in their natures to deceive. Some of them have mothers who are criminals, prostitutes, drug addicts or all three. Many of them never knew their fathers or mothers at all. Some have been in the care system all of their lives and have acquired certain skills along the way.'

'What kind of skills?'

'Well I wouldn't leave any of your belongings lying around if I were you, but it's not just thieving.' Dean lowered his voice in a confidential manner. 'Some of them like to play games. You're clearly both intelligent people but I would advise you not to allow yourself to be manipulated by them. They are good girls for the most part but a past like theirs is bound to affect anyone.'

'Thanks for the warning,' Helen told him. 'Will you be in the room while we talk to the girls?'

'Oh no, they are free to speak their minds. We don't have anything to hide here.'

The girls had their own rooms and each one waited with her door open. The first girl was lounging on her bed, but looked as if she hadn't slept properly in months. She remembered Sandra Jarvis but didn't have much to say about her. Sandra had been here for a while then gone, she said, as if that was a helpful observation. Towards the end of an unsatisfactory conversation, Tom asked her if she liked it at Meadowlands. 'Oh yes,' she said, 'I feel safe here.'

The second and third girls both knew Sandra but said they had not really confided in her, nor had she told them anything about her own life or plans for the future. They didn't know where she lived, who her father was or whether she had a boyfriend.

The fourth girl reiterated the testimony of the previous two but added, quite unprompted by them, that she liked it at Meadowlands.

The fifth girl said she felt safe here.

The sixth refused to speak to them at all, except to say she knew nothing about Sandra Jarvis other than the fact that she had long hair, then she told them to, 'Leave me alone for fuck's sake,' and clammed up.

Girl seven offered very little beyond her assertion that everyone here was well looked-after and she felt safe.

The next room had no one in it.

The last girl in the corridor was slumped on her bed with her head propped up slightly on a pillow and only her eyes moved when they entered the room. Tom guessed she was around fifteen years old but it was hard to tell the exact age of any of the girls. She was wearing faded black jeans and an orange T-shirt with a designer logo, so it was either fake or stolen. The girl had a slim figure and long, dirty blonde hair.

When Helen asked her name she gave it up reluctantly as if it could be used against her: 'Callie.'

'Nice name,' said Tom.

'S'pose,' said the girl without either aggression or any obvious enthusiasm.

'Is it short for Calista?' asked Helen brightly and Callie looked at her as if she had just stepped out of a flying saucer.

'Not short for anything,' observed the girl, 'just Callie.'

'Okay, Callie,' said Tom, 'I guess you know why we're here?'

'You want to know stuff about Sandra,' answered Callie, 'cos she's missing.'

'That's right.'

'How well did you know Sandra?' asked Helen.

'I don't know nothing about her except she used to volunteer. Fuck knows why.'

'What was your impression of her?' asked Helen and Callie looked blank so Tom intervened.

'Did you like her,' he asked, 'or was she one of those stuck-up kids who know nowt about the real world?' He was trying to get some sort of a reaction from Callie, having drawn a blank with all of the other girls.

'She was alright, I s'pose. She actually gave a shit.'

'Do the people that run this place not normally?' asked Tom. 'Give a shit, I mean?' and Callie flared.

'I never said that,' she hissed, 'you're twisting what I said.' She looked anguished.

'You're right,' Tom said, 'I didn't mean to. I'm sorry. It seems okay here.'

'It's great,' she assured them 'We're well looked-after. I feel safe here and I wouldn't want to be anywhere else.'

'That's good, Callie,' said Helen, 'so what was it that Sandra did here, exactly?'

Callie seemed calmer now. 'All sorts. She'd help out with meals and stuff and if you needed something writing, a letter or a form or summat, she'd give you a hand. If you had a problem you could go to her if you wanted to speak to someone nearer your own age.'

'Did you ever speak to her with a problem?' asked Tom, and Callie looked at him suspiciously for a moment as if he was trying to trap her. She must have decided he wasn't because she eventually answered.

'Sometimes; the others are mostly guys and it's easier.'

'To talk to a woman?' said Helen.

'Yeah,' she said.

Tom had previously thought of Sandra as being little more than a girl when she worked here but to a young lass like Callie, she must have seemed like a grown-up.

'Did all of the girls talk to her like that?' asked Helen.

'Some,' she said, 'not all.'

'Some prefer to keep themselves to themselves?' questioned Tom.

Callie shrugged and fell back on her usual answer: 'S'pose.'

'Was there anyone who was particularly close to Sandra?' asked Helen.

'Diane,' admitted Callie, as if they must have known who she was talking about.

'Which Diane?' asked Tom quickly, as if there was more than one. He needed a surname and he didn't want Callie to be suspicious of his reasons.

'Diane Turner,' answered Callie. 'She's my best friend but she's had her problems. She's had a shit life,' and then Callie added quickly, 'before coming here.'

'But Sandra helped her,' observed Helen.

Callie nodded. 'She locked herself in a bathroom, didn't she? Said she was going to cut herself. The staff tried to get her out but she wouldn't come. They was gonna call the police and everything, break the door in, but Sandra said she'd talk to her. She persuaded them to back off for a bit and give Diane some space. She sat on the floor outside and spoke to her through the door. After a bit, Diane opened the door but only to let Sandra in. Then she locked it again and they carried on talking.'

'Do you know what they were talking about?'

'No,' said Callie firmly, 'me and Diane was good mates but she wouldn't even tell me.'

'What happened?' asked Helen,

'In the end they came out of the bathroom but then they went into Diane's room and closed the door. We was about to sit down for breakfast when Diane and Sandra finally came out.'

'So she listened to Diane all night?'

'Yeah.'

'Must have been quite a conversation for it to go on that long.'

'S'pose.'

'How did they look when they finally came out?' asked Tom.

'Knackered,' she said, 'how do you think they looked?'

'Upset? Relieved? Happy? Pissed off? You tell me.'

'Upset,' she said.

'Tearful?' asked Helen and Callie nodded. 'Both of them?' She nodded again. 'And you've no idea what it was all about?'

This time Callie shook her head. 'I told you I tried asking Diane what they talked about but she wouldn't tell me, and Sandra wouldn't be allowed to tell. It's confidential innit. It was like it was . . .'

'Their secret?' supplied Helen.

'Yeah.'

'Must have been a pretty big secret if it took all night to come out?' said Tom.

That was the signal for the shutters to come down again. 'S'pose,' said Callie.

'Is that Diane's room next door?' he asked.

Callie shook her head. 'Used to be. She left.'

Another brick wall, thought Tom. The one person who might have been able to tell them something about Sandra Jarvis was already gone.

'Why did she leave?' asked Helen.

Callie shrugged. 'Got sick of it, wanted to go to London, get a job, get a flat,' she said as if all of those things were easy.

'Did they mind her leaving like that?' Helen probed.

'Who?'

'The people who run this place,' she said. 'Dean,' she offered as an example.

'Like it or lump it can't they?' said Callie. 'Can't stop her, can they?'

'You must have heard from her though,' said Tom, 'if she was your best mate?'

'She sends me postcards.'

'Postcards?' asked Helen.

'From London.'

'Whereabouts in London?'

'Well she ain't gonna write that, is she?' said Callie. 'She was underage when she left. If they found her they'd drag her back here.'

'What does she say on the postcards then? If you don't mind me asking.'

'Wotcha babes,' Callie smiled at the memory, 'she always starts off like that, calls me babes then she tells me stuff.'

'What sort of stuff?'

'What she's up to, you know, stuff,' said Callie but she quickly grew impatient with the line of questioning so instead she rolled across the bed, slid open the drawer of her flimsy bedside cabinet then pulled out a handful of postcards.

Tom took them from Callie. One had a big red double-decker bus on it, another showed the statue of Eros in Piccadilly Circus, a third featured a guard dressed in a red tunic with ceremonial bearskin hat and finally there was an image of Buckingham Palace. They all had London postmarks on them so they really had been sent from the capital and the dates showed gaps of between four and six weeks. The messages on the back were very short and etched in spidery capitals by someone who obviously struggled with writing. One just said 'Miss you babe.' They were signed 'Di' but he supposed they could have been written by anyone.

He turned one of the cards round and asked, 'This definitely her writing?'

'What do you mean?'

'You're sure they are from Diane?'

'Yeah, course,' she sneered at him, 'who else they gonna be from?'

He ignored the question. 'She doesn't say much,' Tom said gently, 'about her life down there?'

Callie finally sat up then and took more of an interest in the conversation. 'She can't, can she? In case they go looking for her. She's keeping her head down, but she's going to get in touch when she can and we're getting a flat together.'

'You're planning on joining her in London?' asked Helen.

'Once I'm older,' said Callie quickly, 'when it's allowed.' Helen guessed she was used to telling figures in authority what they wanted to hear.

'Has Diane got a job?'

'Looking for one, isn't she?' Her tone was defensive now and Tom immediately changed his line of questioning so as not to antagonise the girl.

'When did she go down to London?' he asked.

'A while back.'

'Was it around the same time that Sandra Jarvis went missing?'

'Before that,' said Callie then she frowned, 'no, after,' she thought some more, 'must have been just after.'

'There's no way Diane would have left with Sandra?'

'Diane . . . and Sandra . . . together . . . like a couple of lezzers?' And she laughed as if this was the best joke ever.

'I didn't mean it like that,' Tom told her, 'I mean like you and Diane?' he said. 'Friends.'

Callie shook her head. 'Nah, they weren't mates like me and her.'

'Is this Diane?' asked Helen and Tom realised she had picked up an unframed photograph of Callie and another girl that was propped up on a shelf. They were outdoors somewhere, the local park possibly. Callie was pulling a funny face and her friend was laughing. It must have been a nice moment Callie was determined to keep.

'Yeah,' she said, 'that's Diane,' and she went quiet then, as if seeing her friend made Callie feel her absence more acutely.

It looked for a moment as if that was going to be the end of the conversation but then Callie's eyes seemed to widen and her teeth bared. 'You bitch,' she snarled at Helen, 'you fucking bitch!' Before the reporter could utter a word in her defence, Callie was up on her feet and lurching towards an alarmed Helen.

Chapter Thirty

Tom tried to grab Callie but she shot past him, barged Helen aside and carried on towards the door. They both saw Callie rush for another young girl, who was standing in the doorway. The teenager was dressed in a brown suede jacket and Callie immediately grabbed it in both hands, slammed the girl against the door frame then snatched a clump of her long dark hair and bashed the other girl's head viciously against the wood.

'Callie!' cried Helen, while the other girl screamed and both Helen and Tom went to separate them. Callie had crashed her opponent's head twice more against the frame, raked her nails across her face and was now tearing at the girl's jacket to pull it away from her before Tom managed to grab her.

'Give me that, you slag!'

With one huge tug the brown suede jacket was torn from the other girl, who fell to the floor swearing and cursing. 'It's fucking mine!' she managed between shrieks.

'That's Diane's, not yours!'

Tom wrapped his arms round Callie from behind so he could wrestle her away from her victim. He managed to pull Callie backwards but she let fly with a kick that caught the other girl right on the chin. Tom had seen violence in his time and been involved in more than one fight himself but he had never seen anything like this. Callie's casual savagery was shocking. Helen reached the other girl, who was dazed but still spitting and swearing defiantly at Callie from her position on the ground.

'She fucking stole it!' Callie screamed. 'That's Diane's jacket, the fucking cow nicked it!'

When the two girls had finally been separated, Dean arrived at the scene. 'What's going on?' he demanded and he was greeted by four voices all trying to explain matters at the same time, two of them hysterically. Dean somehow realised the fight was over the jacket and that Callie maintained it belonged to her friend and not the other girl.

'Get her away from here,' Dean ordered, and Helen struggled to steer the other girl from the room. 'Get in there, Susie!' Dean shouted, and between them Helen and Dean managed to manoeuvre the injured but still furious girl into the empty room. There was blood on her face but she was still shouting.

'Calm down, Susie,' ordered Dean, 'and stay in here! Don't let her out,' he warned Helen, who nodded, for she had no desire to witness a repeat of the highly one-sided fight.

Dean closed the door on both of them and returned to Callie. 'You!' he shouted. 'With me now! You're on report.' Callie seemed to slump on hearing those words, giving up the fight all at once.

'That's not fair,' she whined. 'Susie stole Diane's jacket!' Bitter, frustrated tears fell.

Dean snatched the jacket from her then handed it to Tom, who released his grip on the now calm girl. 'Look after it,' Dean said, placing a firm hand on Callie's shoulder before marching her out of the room.

'Don't give it to Susie!' shouted Callie.

'He won't,' said Dean. 'Keep an eye on it till I get back,' he told Tom, who nodded. Anything to keep the peace, he thought.

'It was her favourite,' sobbed Callie as Dean led her away.

'I'll be back in a few minutes,' he told Tom. A moment later, the journalist found himself alone in the room. All was still now; the photograph of Callie and Diane that Helen must have dropped during the scrap the only evidence there had ever been a disturbance here at all.

'Jesus Christ,' he said to himself. Helen was still in the other room with the injured girl. He knew she would look after her somehow and his presence would probably not be welcomed, so he stayed put. He marvelled at the way Susie had taken several blows to the head, some deep scratches and a kick on the chin as if this was just a normal day for her.

And all over a jacket.

He was still holding the offending item and he sat down on the bed with it. The suede jacket was nice enough, Tom supposed, but it looked quite old, probably a charity shop purchase. It had two breast pockets with press-stud buttons and a brown leather collar that matched the colour of the rest of the jacket. There were two further side pockets and one inside.

Tom reached inside the jacket, stopped, paused for a moment then persuaded himself he was doing the right thing. He glanced at the open door and listened. All he could hear was Susie's voice as she protested her innocence and railed at the injustice of the attack from Callie while Helen acted as counsellor. There was no other sound and he knew Dean must have taken Callie to the far end of the long corridor they had marched up to get here.

Tom slipped his hand into the inside pocket but felt nothing. He didn't really expect to find anything. If Diane had been wearing another jacket when she went she would hardly have left anything valuable behind, assuming she actually owned anything of value, which he doubted; and the jacket's new owner would surely have found it by now if she did. Next he checked the open side pockets but all he found was a bus ticket for a local journey. Finally, and with little expectation, he opened the buttons of both breast pockets and fished inside. There was nothing in the first but he felt something in the second and pulled it out.

Tom was now holding a smart and expensive business card. He glanced at the front, which had a black silhouette of a naked woman on a red background. There was one large word printed on it in embossed gold lettering.

'MIRAGE'.

Underneath this in a stylish, italicised font was written, *'Where your fantasy becomes reality.'*

He turned the card over and found an address in Brewer Street and a phone number with a London area code. Brewer Street rang a bell and Tom remembered how he'd once written a piece on Soho clip joints that featured a place on that street.

He heard a door slam and immediately pocketed the card. He listened as footsteps came from the corridor. Just before they reached him he made an instinctive decision. The photograph of Callie and Diane was still on the floor. He knew this was one of Callie's few precious possessions but he bent and quickly snatched it up. He had just finished stuffing it into his pocket next to the Mirage business card when Dean appeared in the doorway looking harassed but a little calmer than when he had left the room with Callie.

'All quiet on the western front,' he said. 'Callie's in the dinner hall and won't be going anywhere. I've got a doc coming to look at Susie, though she's as tough as old boots, that one. Not the first time she's taken a beating,' he observed sadly, 'poor little cow,' then he remembered Tom was still holding the jacket and he stretched out a hand. 'I'd better take that,' he said. Tom duly handed it over.

*

They trudged back to the car together. 'That was . . . unexpected,' said a shocked Helen when they were both inside the vehicle.

'Did Susie say anything while you were with her?'

'Just that Diane had given her the jacket before she left.'

'Why would Diane give it to her and not take it with her, if it was her favourite?' asked Tom. 'Why not give it to Callie instead of Susie if they were best friends?'

'I tried to ask those questions but she just got very irate.'

'Know what disturbed me the most,' he asked her when they reached the car, 'and I'm not talking about the fight?'

'The way they kept telling us how safe they felt?'

He turned to face her. 'And we never even asked them.'

'Sounded like they were all reading from the same script to me,' observed Helen. 'I wonder who wrote it.'

It was DC Malone who answered the phone. 'Yes, he's here,' she said, eyeing Bradshaw. 'Ian,' she called, 'it's the bloke from the garage, about your car.'

'Thanks, put him through.' DC Malone stabbed at some more buttons then waited until Bradshaw's landline began to ring.

He gave Malone a thumbs up before answering, 'Ian Bradshaw speaking, have you found the problem yet?'

'Sorry, pal, she's a total write-off,' said Tom.

Bradshaw swivelled in his chair so he was facing away from his colleagues. 'How did you get on at Meadowlands?' he asked quietly.

'It was . . . interesting.'

'How so?'

Tom briefed Bradshaw on the fight at Meadowlands and the way all the girls there seemed brainwashed, except for one. 'Diane Turner,' Tom told the detective, 'who absconded around the same time as Sandra Jarvis.'

'You want me to some digging about this Diane Turner?'

'Not unless you can do it under the radar. If you start asking questions about Diane it'll be noticed and, forgive my paranoia here, but we don't know who we can trust.'

Tom expected a lecture from Bradshaw about not every policeman on the force being in the pay of gangsters but instead the detective said, 'Just because you are paranoid, doesn't mean they ain't out to get you.'

'Exactly. You can check it out discreetly but something tells me Diane's disappearance wasn't reported.'

'It wasn't,' confirmed Bradshaw.

'How could you possibly know that without checking?' asked Tom, then he remembered the case Bradshaw was working on. 'Because of the burned girl?'

'Believe me, I am familiar with every missing persons report from the past year.' Bradshaw's immediate thought was that if Diane's disappearance *had* gone unreported she might even be the burned girl but he knew that was a long shot and she was probably just another runaway.

Tom must have realised that's what he would be thinking. 'Diane is alive and well and living in London apparently. She's been in touch with Callie but finding her won't be easy. We have no address and she doesn't want to be found.'

'A missing teenage girl in London,' observed Bradshaw dryly.

'I know,' admitted Tom, 'a needle in a haystack.'

'That's alright,' said Bradshaw dryly, 'I'm not remotely busy.'

'There's one other thing,' Tom told him and he reached inside his pocket, drew out the business card and looked at it.

'What is it?' asked Bradshaw.

'Mirage,' Tom told him, 'where your fantasy becomes reality.'

Chapter Thirty-One

Tom's train into London was half an hour late. It was met by an army of impatient cleaners and station staff keen to shoo the passengers from it as quickly as possible so they could turn it around for the return trip that evening. It hadn't taken Ian Bradshaw long to come back to him with information about Mirage. As Tom had guessed from the business card, it was a 'Gentleman's Club'.

Places like Mirage had been springing up all over London lately, thanks to the relaxing of attitudes around the sale of sexual services. Stripping in working men's clubs or the back rooms of dodgy pubs had been replaced by more open, respectable and far more lucrative lap dancing clubs like Mirage, which was owned by a man named Andre Devine. He was seen as 'pretty clean' for that world, with no known connections to organised crime but Bradshaw had stressed the word *known* and warned Tom to be careful. 'So you're off to conduct research into naked women?'

'The things I do to solve your cases for you.'

Mirage seemed like just the place for a troubled young runaway like Diane Turner and if she was there maybe she could shed some new light on the disappearance of her confidante, Sandra Jarvis.

Tom stepped out of King's Cross station and made straight for the Underground, taking the Piccadilly Line to Leicester Square. He cut through Chinatown with its myriad restaurants and exotic grocery stores before entering Soho from

Greek Street. He knew his way around well enough from a six-month stint on the country's biggest-selling tabloid. Soho was always good for stories.

In any other town, a sex shop with painted-out windows would be relegated to a quiet side street. Here, on Old Compton Street, bondage and fetish gear was openly modelled in shop windows by mannequins with loose morals. However, Soho wasn't given over completely to the sale of sex and the contrast was striking. Ronnie Scott's famous jazz club was just a few doors from a scruffy property with a handwritten sign on a wall that offered a 'new blonde' in its cellar and the Groucho Club lay opposite an opened doorway which led to a steep staircase promising a 'model' on the next floor. There was nowhere else like it in England.

Mirage was housed in a large building that straddled a corner of Brewer Street. A big red sign featuring a shapely girl in naked silhouette hung above its door, promising a sexual heaven behind its blacked-out windows. A single finger was pressed to her lips as if to imply Mirage was a secret only a few were permitted to know.

Graham bought Helen a curry. It was to thank her, her editor said, for all of her hard work but he seemed a little nervous and she got the impression he didn't do this sort of thing all the time. He was preoccupied when they ordered but it was a good meal, served at a curry house in a street just off the Bigg Market. They chatted amiably enough and the subjects varied from their families to earlier jobs and he told her some of the war stories he'd accrued during his years in journalism.

'Were you one of the fifteen million then?' asked Graham during a lull in conversation.

'Is that how many tuned in?'

'So they say.'

'Well, it was compulsive viewing,' she said.

'What was that line again?'

Helen recited it for him: ' "There were three of us in this marriage, so it was a bit crowded." '

Graham nodded. 'Devastating to Charles, wasn't it?'

'The woman who would have been the next Queen of England admits adultery in a TV interview? Who could ever have imagined it? Apparently James Hewitt could actually be charged with treason for sleeping with the wife of the monarch. He'd have been hanged, drawn and quartered in Henry VIII's day.'

'So what? The royals have been doing it for centuries. Everybody's at it these days.'

'Not everybody,' said Helen quickly.

When Graham politely enquired about Helen's boyfriend moments later it put her at her ease again. She liked and respected her editor too much to simply brush it off if he turned out to be one of those men whose wives *didn't understand them*.

It was only after he had asked for the bill that his tone turned serious. 'I had an uncomfortable meeting the other day,' he confided, and when she didn't know how to respond to this, Graham expanded: 'The managing director and one of the group's in-house lawyers came down,' he explained. 'I was being warned off. It wasn't as explicit as that but I could tell they were worried.'

'Because of the stories I've been writing?'

'Partly,' he admitted. 'They were careful not to mention specifics and they stressed that I retain full editorial control, but they were very keen to talk about the future and how rosy it could be for me . . .'

'If you didn't rock the boat?'

'You catch on quickly, young lady,' Graham told her. 'We must have stepped on some very important toes lately and that invites scrutiny from worried investors. No one is entirely immune from that in journalism, even us, especially us, since our parent company is losing money hand over fist these days.'

'What did you say?'

'I said they needn't worry about me. I'm in it for the long haul. I said I knew what I was doing. They didn't seem convinced. The stakes are getting higher,' he told her and for the first time he looked genuinely nervous. 'Editors can be dispensed with for any number of reasons. I've seen it happen.'

So this was the reason for the curry and more than an hour's idle chit-chat. Graham was finally coming to the point.

'What do you want me to do?' She expected he would tell her to back off then. Unlike Helen, he had a wife and family to worry about.

'Nothing, for now,' he told her, 'you carry on being our top investigative reporter; just make sure that you're right, that's all – or we could both be out of a job.'

'Right,' she said.

So much for print and be damned.

Tom must have looked respectable enough, as the doorman let him in unchallenged. Getting beyond the girl who took his money was harder; he had to pay her twice. There was a membership fee then a one-off admission charge before he was even admitted to the club. This place was a licence to print money.

The sight that greeted him was a surreal one. Aside from the bar staff, the only men in the place were dressed in suits and surrounded by a large group of girls who played the room. The girls were all dressed in elaborate lingerie but nothing else. A handful of them marched straight up to Tom and encouraged him to buy a private dance before he even had time to order a drink.

'Not just yet.' His refusal was greeted by disinterest or outright hostility from the girls.

'You can't just sit here,' one of them told him, as if he planned to enjoy the view without paying for it.

He ignored her, went to the bar and ordered a single bottle of beer, which cost him a fiver. This was going to be an expensive night and he doubted that DCI Kane would allow any of it to be claimed back on expenses.

Tom sipped his beer and watched the girls coldly. He had no interest in their hustling of the businessmen or the gyrations that followed. He was looking for Diane Turner but none of these girls looked anything like her.

A girl approached him then. She was a strikingly attractive brunette who was less direct than the others. 'Taking your time?'

'I'm looking for a girl . . .'

'Then you're in the right place.' She smiled.

Tom took a chance. 'I'm looking for *this* girl.' He slid the photograph of Diane Turner from his pocket, keeping his hand over the image of Callie so she wouldn't confuse the two.

Her smile vanished. 'You a copper?' The accent was harsher than before, betraying her East End origins.

'No,' he said, 'I'm just . . .' But she was already leaving and he thought he detected a look she had given someone.

Seconds later, Tom's instinct was proved right when two huge doormen appeared out of nowhere, blocking his path. 'Can I help you?' asked one as if that was the furthest thing from his mind.

'Possibly . . .' offered Tom, who was unsure of the best tactic to employ if he was not going to be thrown out on the street, or worse.

'Show me,' demanded the man and he held out a hand. He must have seen Tom show the picture to the girl.

'I'm looking for her.' He handed it over.

The doorman glanced at it for a moment but did not say whether he knew either of the girls and he held on to the photograph. 'Why are you looking for her in here?' There was a definite hint of menace in his voice as if Tom had brought trouble to the establishment.

'I heard she might be working for Mr Devine,' said Tom, 'and I'd like to speak with him if I may.'

'And who the fuck are you?'

'I'm a journalist and I'm investigating the disappearance of a young girl. I think Mr Devine might be able to help me.'

'Doubt it,' said the doorman. 'You wait here.' And he walked away, taking the photograph with him, to Tom's alarm, since he didn't have a copy. The other doorman remained, towering over Tom, who took a long drink from his expensive bottle of beer. He had a feeling that, either way, he wouldn't be standing with it there for much longer.

Moments later Tom was in a first-floor office with his arms outstretched while one of the doormen ran his hands briskly up and down his body. 'First time I've been patted down before an interview,' said Tom, 'but I suppose you can't be too careful.'

'You claim you're a journalist,' answered Andre Devine from behind his desk, 'but I cannot afford to believe everyone I meet.'

'It's still dangerous to own a club in Soho? Well I'm not carrying a weapon, only a pen.'

Devine was a big man with silver hair, which made it difficult to age him. He spoke with a slight accent; he could have been German or Swiss but his English was perfect. 'The pen is mightier than the sword,' he said, 'but not as dangerous as a gun. Sit down, Mr Carney, and explain to me what a journalist is doing in my establishment. This is no brothel. My competitors are the Windmill Club and Paul Raymond, not some low-grade titty bar or coin-in-the-slot peep show. We are high end. I run a respectable place with very lovely girls. There's full nudity, sure, but absolutely no sex on the premises and no soliciting from the ladies off-premises either. Go back out there,' he urged Tom, 'try and get one girl, any of them, to come back to your hotel room tonight for money and see how far you get.'

'I don't doubt it – but I'm not writing a story on prostitution in Soho, or anywhere else. I'm not actually writing a story at all in fact.'

'A journalist who does not write stories?' Devine raised his eyebrows.

Tom explained how he had travelled from the north-east to investigate Sandra Jarvis's disappearance and her link with Diane, though he did not admit he was working with the police. He was a private contractor, hired by concerned relatives in Newcastle. Tom realised the bouncer had given Devine the photograph, which was face up on the man's desk. 'I'm trying to find the girl on the right.'

Andre Devine surveyed the photograph then said, 'I do

not recognise her,' and he frowned. 'This girl is far too young in any case.'

'Even with false documents?'

'You think a fake ID will get her through this door? They would send her away. Nobody works here who is under twenty-one. If you want a teenager to dance for you, we send you a girl who is older but looks younger – and there are plenty of girls to choose from because the money is very good. We have too much to lose using underage girls. They would close me down. Tell me why I would do it? For one punter maybe who likes them very young? No, not here.'

'Then why would she have your business card in her jacket pocket?' asked Tom.

'I don't know,' Devine said. He thought for a moment. 'Maybe someone gave her the card and she tried for a job but was turned away?' He handed the photograph back to Tom. 'Or . . .'

'Or?'

'Someone wants to make trouble for me. Isn't that the most obvious possibility?'

Tom didn't make a habit of betraying his inner thoughts but for once he felt there was no harm in it for he was angry now about his wasted trip. Devine wasn't acting like a man with something to hide. 'I'm beginning to think that it is,' he said. 'Thanks for seeing me. Please call me if she does turn up here.'

Tom knew that Devine could have been lying to him and that Diane might be hiding out back somewhere or just enjoying a night off. She could even be held in the building against her will, but he seriously doubted that. Devine sounded credible and his logic was irrefutable. He was making shedloads of money operating legitimately. Why would he jeopardise all of that to accommodate a teenage runaway?

'Mr Carney,' he said as Tom was making to leave, 'it's still no deal.' When Tom narrowed his eyes at that, confused, Devine said, 'When you are back in Newcastle, tell Mr McCree it's no deal.'

'What?' asked Tom. 'Is Jimmy McCree trying to buy you out? You're a long way from his usual stomping ground.'

'Forget it,' Devine said and he spread his palms as if it was all a misunderstanding. 'My mistake.' He left his desk so he could see Tom to the door and place him in the care of the doormen. 'Safe journey home, Mr Carney. I hope you find the girl you're looking for.'

When he said that, Tom realised exactly what had been going on here.

Chapter Thirty-Two

Meadowlands was veiled in a fog rendered almost impenetrable by the street lamps. Their yellow glow served only to illuminate the moisture in the air, making it thicker and more ghostly. Bradshaw could make out little beyond the building's shape. Meadowlands was a boxy eighties construction that could have been a small school or community hall. It was set back from the road, with a thick barrier of laurel bushes placed between to protect the residents – or possibly the outside world, depending on your point of view. From his car, which was parked in a residential street, Bradshaw could see through the metal gate that kept the entrance secure. The building's windows all had blinds drawn down over them and a single light above the main door illuminated the entrance.

The detective had driven down here on a whim to check the place out but there was really nothing to see, particularly in this fog. He thought of Tom then. The reporter would be in London now, checking out Mirage, and Bradshaw ruefully imagined his friend surrounded by semi-naked girls while he shivered alone in his car. 'Short straw again,' he told himself.

He could have flashed his warrant card and gone in but he didn't want anyone to know that Meadowlands was attracting renewed police attention just yet. Instead he watched and he waited. Half an hour later, Bradshaw was just about to give up and pull away from Meadowlands when he was startled by a sudden thump on his side window. He turned to see a young girl peering down at him and wound down his window.

'Two packs,' she told him.

'What?'

'Of cigs,' she said, but he was none the wiser. 'And a bottle of vodka.' She grew impatient with him then, as if he was supposed to understand her meaning. 'Look, if you ain't got them you can buy them at the shop.' She waited then seemed to get annoyed. 'If you *want* something, go to the shop first. You can't just park here.' Bradshaw belatedly realised his presence in a static car had been misunderstood.

'No,' he told her, 'I'm not looking for that.'

'Ain't you here for . . . ?' She looked flustered then when she realised her mistake. 'What *are* you here for then?' she demanded angrily.

He wasn't about to let her know he was a police officer. 'I was waiting for my girlfriend,' he said as he started the ignition, 'not that it's any of your business.'

'Yeah,' she sneered, 'she stood you up then, didn't she?' She was amused by this but Bradshaw was happy for her to accept the lie. She sauntered off then without a care in the world and when he saw her slim figure more clearly now that she stepped away from his car, he wondered if she could be any older than fourteen.

Bradshaw watched her before driving away. A moment later she reached the bottom of the street and swung the metal gate open so she could walk into Meadowlands.

'We've been taken for mugs, Helen,' Tom told her almost before he was through the door of her flat. 'I've been thinking about it all day.' And he had, apart from an hour's doze

284

on the train back from King's Cross, which partially made up for a sleepless night. The cheap hotel he had chosen was too close to the station and trains had rattled by it constantly. 'Someone has played us.'

'How do you mean?'

'I've been an idiot,' he said and he told her about his meeting with Andre Devine. 'That farce with Callie and Susie.'

'You think it was staged?' she asked. 'It looked pretty bloody real to me.'

'I think the fight was real,' he said. 'Callie would have to be Meryl Streep to fake that level of anger and the violence was all too real, but think about it. Susie said Diane gave her the jacket when she left for London months before, even though Callie said it was Diane's favourite. Callie just happens to see Susie wearing it for the very first time on the day we visit and, predictably, flies off the handle, but Dean quickly intervenes. He puts Susie in her room with you and drags Callie away, leaving me with the jacket.' Tom shook his head at his own stupidity. 'He must have known I'd look in the pockets and he knew what I'd find there.'

'Because he planted it? What makes you so sure?'

'I've been lied to by experts, Helen, including at least one cabinet minister, but this fellah was baffled by my presence in his club. There was I, expecting to see young girls like Callie and Diane being exploited while everyone turned a blind eye, but it wasn't like that. The place was ... I don't know, not *classy* exactly but upmarket and expensive. There was no shortage of beautiful women in their twenties hoovering up cash from business types with more money than sense, and I don't think anyone was being coerced. He doesn't need to use underage girls, the stakes are too high for him to risk it.'

    'Maybe Diane tried to get a job there and they wouldn't let her in?'

    'Perhaps, but I reckon a girl like Diane would have the street-smarts to know she ain't gonna get near the place.'

    'So Dean sent you on a wild-goose chase?'

    'Dean – or someone who controls him.' And he told her Devine's parting comment about Jimmy McCree.

    Helen opened her mouth to speak, but her answer was lost in the loud crash as a window violently exploded.

Chapter Thirty-Three

They would have been showered with broken glass but the debris from the window was cushioned by the curtains. Instead large pieces tumbled loudly to the wooden floor below, breaking into dozens of smaller fragments on impact. The half-brick had been hurled in anger and it parted the curtains, landing on the coffee table between them with a violent thud.

Tom went straight to the window and looked out. As he did so another half-brick shot past him, narrowly missing his head.

'Jesus,' he hissed and the youth outside jeered at him.

'Come on then!' roared the teenager and Tom's first instinct was to run outside and grab the lad until he realised he was not alone. Another half-dozen boys in their late teens were behind him, mostly obscured by the darkness; a snarling pack of animals in jeans and sweatshirts. Another brick thudded against the wooden frame of the broken window. There was a bang on the front door then and he realised there were more of them.

He turned to face Helen, who looked like she couldn't believe what was happening.

'I'll call the police?'

'No time.' He grabbed her by the arm. 'We get out now!'

They ran into the hallway just as one of the glass panels on the front door shattered as a wooden post came through it and landed on the hall carpet. 'Back door?' he asked frantically and she nodded dumbly. Tom started to run but Helen broke away from him.

'My bag!' she shouted.

'There's no time!' But she was already back in the lounge. Tom watched helplessly from the hallway as the remaining glass panel in the front door broke and an arm came through it. A hand snaked round and a palm slapped against the door frame in an effort to find the lock and open it. They'd be inside in seconds and Helen was still looking for her bag.

Tom grabbed the only weapon available, the wooden post used to break through the door. He swung it hard on to the invading hand and there was a gratifying howl of pain from the invading teenager before he pulled his arm away. Tom watched him retreat holding his damaged hand, but others were trying to get through the door now. He backed away just as Helen rushed out clutching her bag. They ran down the hallway and through the kitchen. Behind them someone kicked what remained of the door in. Tom wrenched open the door and pulled Helen through it into the back yard.

Ahead of him was the back street and his car, but before they could reach it another youth stepped out in front of them swinging a baseball bat. Expecting Tom to retreat he raised the bat high but Tom did not stop or go backwards. He knew their only chance was to break though, and tackling one armed man was better than the snarling gang whose noisy, threatening progress through the flat could be heard behind them. As the thug brought the bat back, Tom ran into him, thrusting his head forward hard at the last second right into the young man's face. He cried out in pain and fell to the ground clutching his bloodied face.

Tom didn't have time to take advantage of his felled

opponent or even wrench the baseball bat from him. Instead he powered on through the back yard and out through the open gates, with Helen behind him. The car faced Helen's flat and Tom had his keys out to open it but the mob were too close and he couldn't wait for her to go round the other side. Instead he grabbed Helen and forcefully flung her through the opened driver's door. She landed heavily as he scrambled in after her. They were a tangle of arms and legs now, as she attempted to right herself in the passenger seat and he tried to slam his door behind him. Tom managed to close it and pop the lock just as the first snarling youth reached him. His attacker's face pressed right up against the side window as he tugged hopelessly on the door handle, cursing and spitting at Tom, who thrust his key into the ignition and turned it while the thug banged on the glass. The engine started first time and Tom had never been more grateful, but his relief was short-lived. Just as he was about to put it into gear the youth nearest his window retreated and the face of the man he had headbutted appeared. There was blood all over the lower part of his face and his nose looked broken. The baseball bat came smashing down against the window.

There was an almighty crash and Tom's senses were filled with a combination of noise and pain as he was showered with broken glass, which sliced the skin on his face as he closed his eyes against the fragments. He blinked furiously to try and clear them. The man with the baseball bat struck again, trying to steer it into the gap he had made with the first swing. He narrowly missed Tom's head and caught him a glancing blow on the shoulder. For a moment Tom felt as if every nerve of his body was united in pain. With a cry of rage, he jerked the car into reverse gear and slammed his foot on the accelerator. The car shot backwards and the front wheel ran over his attacker's foot. Tom heard the young thug cry out in agony but they weren't safe yet.

Tom reversed the car a few yards into the dead end in Helen's street so he could drive out the other side. He was now faced with a vicious, screaming gang armed with bricks and bats, and they all descended on the car before he could move it. Blows rained down on them and the sound of denting metal and broken glass was terrifying – then a brick was hurled, causing a spider's web of cracks to the windscreen on Helen's side. Another attacker reached his broken driver's side window now and a punch came through it. Tom ducked but not quickly enough and a hard, bony fist crashed into the side of his head. He instinctively floored the accelerator. The car shot forwards and one of the youths was knocked violently to one side. The car flew past the gang but the back street they were in was short and narrow. Too late, Tom realised he was going far too fast and there was another brick wall straight ahead of them.

'Jesus,' he hissed as he slammed on the brakes just in time. He was forced to reverse a short way, so he could get the angle needed to turn into a tight bend with walls on either side. They were heading back towards the gang now. Tom changed gear and twisted the steering wheel, guiding the car round the bend and down the tiny side street that bordered the block of flats. Heavy objects hurled in frustration by the youths banged against the rear of his car but he didn't care about that now.

Tom sped down the side street and out into the main road without looking or stopping. At the bottom he took another sharp turn, taking them even further from danger.

'Are you okay?' he shouted.

'Yes.' Helen looked shaken. 'Oh my God,' she said, 'your face.'

A quick glance in the mirror made him realise the cause of Helen's alarm. He looked like a gunshot victim. The cut at the top of his forehead was bleeding so much it was in danger of restricting his vision, but he wasn't going to pull over. They'd left their attackers trailing behind but he wasn't going to take any chances in case they were following in a car, and kept going till they were well clear. Only when Tom was convinced they were far enough from the scene with no one behind them did he turn into a well-lit pub car park to deal with the wound.

'Let me see,' urged Helen, concern in her voice, but after a moment's scrutiny she told him, 'I don't think it's as bad as it looks, thank God. You've got one cut on the side of your head and a whole bunch of little ones above your eye. I don't think it needs stitches.'

He swivelled the rear-view mirror, took a quick glance at the cut and said, 'I'll be fine. My thick head took most of the impact.'

'How can you joke about it?' she asked. 'You saw what they did back there.'

'I'm just thanking my lucky stars we got out of there more or less in one piece.'

'I suppose we were lucky,' she admitted. Helen didn't want to think about what would have happened to them both if they'd been trapped in her flat by that mob.

'You got much in the house?' he asked, and when she didn't seem to understand he said, 'You know, stuff.'

'A few clothes . . .' Her voice trailed off. She was relieved she didn't have a lot for them to take. 'But I don't want to go back there.'

'Don't worry, we can phone the police.'

'They never come,' she said quickly, and he wondered how she knew that. Had there been other incidents at her home?

'We can call Ian,' he said, 'he'll sort it. There'll be a phone in the pub but you'd better make the call.'

'Why?'

'I don't think they'd be too chuffed if I walked in there looking like this.'

'Okay,' she said, 'I still don't want to go back there though.'

'You don't have to,' he told her firmly, 'just call Ian and tell him what happened. He'll get someone over there. And don't worry. You're staying with me tonight.'

Chapter Thirty-Four

'I'm afraid the boiler is playing up again but it's a warm house,' he told her when they finally made it back to his home. Tom snicked the top off two bottles of beer, handed one to Helen and took a big swig from his.

'Should you be drinking alcohol after a blow to the head?'

'Probably not,' he admitted cheerfully and he took an even bigger drink. Tom checked his answerphone and there was a message from Bradshaw. He had managed to get someone down to Helen's house to secure it overnight. As expected, there was nobody at the scene to apprehend.

They sat in his lounge and relived the events of the evening. 'Those articles of yours really upset someone,' he said. 'They may have looked like young thugs but you were targeted. They were let off their leash by Jimmy McCree.'

'Or someone who asked him to do it.'

'Is there anybody you haven't fallen out with?' he asked.

'No one that matters.' She drank her bottle of beer far more quickly than usual then said, 'I'm really tired for some reason. Thanks for letting me use your spare bed.'

'I don't have a spare bed.' And he was amused by the look of panic on her face. 'Don't worry, you can have mine. I'll take the sofa.'

'Have you got any blankets?'

'Don't need them,' he said. 'I'll be fine. Haven't you ever slept on a sofa after a party?'

'No,' she admitted.

'I have,' he said, 'loads of times.' *Though not for years*, he thought. 'Go on. Get some sleep. Things always seem better in the morning.'

'I feel terrible, taking your bed.'

'It's no bother.'

They said goodnight a little stiffly and Helen went up the stairs. She sat on the double bed in Tom's room and was about to get undressed when she heard the stairs creak and the unmistakable sound of footsteps coming up them. She instinctively froze.

There was a soft knock on the door. 'Yes,' she said.

'Can I come in?' he asked.

'Yes,' she repeated unsurely.

Tom opened the door and went to a chest of drawers, opened it and pulled out two T-shirts then handed one to her. 'Thought you might need something to sleep in,' he said, 'and there's clean towels in the airing cupboard.'

'Thank you.'

'Night-night pet.' And he left her to it.

Helen immediately felt guilty because she had automatically assumed he was going to climb into bed with her, but she should have known Tom wasn't like that. She felt even worse because of the slight thrill of anticipation that thought had given her.

Helen took off her clothes and pulled on Tom's T-shirt then she climbed into the big double bed and pulled the thick duvet over her. Within minutes she was in a deep sleep but Helen was awakened an hour later by a sudden sound outside. Two cats were fighting. They screamed at one another repeatedly before going their separate ways.

Helen realised she was cold, and then thought of Tom downstairs with no blankets.

Tom was fully clothed, lying on the sofa with his coat pulled over himself, but he couldn't sleep. He had consumed two more bottles of beer after Helen had gone to bed and now he was trying to doze off in a freezing room, but his legs were too long for the sofa. That and the injuries to his face, head and shoulder meant that no matter what position he lay in he couldn't get comfortable.

He heard a click then and a crack of light shone under his door from the hallway onto his carpet-less floor. He sat up groggily as Helen opened the door. She was wearing his T-shirt and he had to make a conscious effort not to stare at her bare legs.

'You're going to freeze,' she announced. 'Come on, you don't have to stay down here.'

Helen deliberately left the light off in the bedroom. She climbed into her side of the bed and turned away from him while he took off his jeans. Somehow she knew Tom would not get the wrong idea about this and he didn't, but she was very aware of the weight on his side of the bed when he joined her and the heat from his body.

'Thanks,' he said quickly.

'No problem,' she said.

When Helen opened her eyes in the morning it took her a moment to remember where she was, then she rolled over and saw Tom Carney sleeping next to her. She tried not to think what Peter would have made of this but soon that thought was banished by the memory of the attack on them at her flat. All of sudden her jealous boyfriend seemed to be the least of Helen's problems. She glanced at her watch on the bedside table and was surprised at how late it was. They had both been exhausted by their ordeal. She left Tom sleeping and slipped out of the bed to use the bathroom. Tom stirred and she watched him as he rolled over without waking.

Helen came out of the bathroom moments later, and when she reached the top of the landing she yelled out in alarm. A strange man was standing at the foot of the stairs, staring back up at her.

The man almost jumped out of his skin when he saw her. 'Sorry, pet,' he spluttered, though he looked at least as alarmed by their contact as she had been, 'I didn't know you were . . . I didn't realise he was . . .' Then he stopped and took a different approach: 'I'll put the kettle on.'

'What's the matter?' asked Tom as he opened the door and blinked at her.

'There's a man . . .' she managed.

'Oh shit, yeah, I forgot about him.' When Helen looked at him disbelievingly he said, 'That's Darren, my brother-in-law. He's a joiner.' And when that proved insufficient he explained, 'He's out of work at the moment. I hired him to finish some of the jobs on the house while I'm busy with these cases.' He then realised the effect that seeing a strange man in the house must have had on Helen, following their ordeal the night before. 'I'm really sorry.'

Now that Helen had calmed down, her first thought was that she had just met Tom's sister's husband for the first time in her underwear and one of Tom's T-shirts.

'Come down,' Tom said. 'I'll introduce you.'

Tom went down the stairs moments later, while Helen got dressed. He found three steaming mugs of tea on the kitchen table and his brother-in-law grinning at him.

'Thanks, Darren,' he said. 'Er, Helen's just . . .'

'It's none of my business, bro,' interrupted Darren, 'but what happened to your face? I hope she didn't do that.'

'It's a long story,' and he was thankful Darren wasn't the kind to insist on him recounting it, 'but do us a favour and don't tell sis about it; she'll only fret.'

'I won't, but I saw your motor on the way in. Looks like you had an argument with a lorry.'

'Is there any chance I could borrow your car for the day until I can get the insurance company to give me a rental?'

'No problem. I'll be busy straightening your kitchen cabinets and sorting these ancient floorboards. Just bring it back in one piece.'

'Thanks.'

'No bother. Do I have to keep quiet about your new girlfriend too?' he asked.

'No, but we're not . . .'

'Course you're not,' he said as Helen, fully dressed now, entered the room. 'Sleep well, did you, pet?' he asked her cheerfully.

Bradshaw was waiting for them at Helen's apartment. 'My landlord's going to go crazy.' She observed the bare wooden boards that had been hastily nailed over the broken windows.

'He's insured,' Bradshaw told her, 'but you might want to think about moving.'

She just nodded dumbly. 'I'm only back here to collect my things.' Though Bradshaw's face betrayed very little, Tom guessed there wasn't much left to collect. They followed Helen into the apartment and Bradshaw left them to it. Tom went with her into the front room. Every piece of furniture had been upended or smashed. She took one look at the scene, turned and left the room.

When she reached the bedroom, the site that greeted Helen stopped her in her tracks. The sheet and duvet had been torn from the bed and slashed with a knife, the mattress had been hacked at with a blade of some kind and its stuffing spread around the room. Helen's clothes had been pulled from her wardrobe; dresses were torn, her coat slashed, jeans and T-shirts were thrown everywhere. Drawers had been pulled out and upended and her underwear scattered around the room. Wordlessly, Helen went to the kitchen and returned a moment later carrying a roll of black bin bags. She tore off the first bag, opened it and began to scoop the nearest debris straight into it. Tom watched her for a moment and when it became clear to him that she no longer wanted to keep a single item from the room, he said, 'I'll help you.'

'No,' she said firmly, 'I'll do it,' then she turned to face him and though she was doing a very good job of keeping it all together, Tom could see in her eyes how much this had hurt her.

'Helen,' he said again, 'I'll help.' He took the bin bags from her, tore one from the roll and began to fill it.

Working together, it didn't take long to clear the room, and once the black sacks were stacked outside by the bins they rejoined Bradshaw in the kitchen.

'This wasn't some random act,' he told Helen. 'I've spoken to my colleagues in Northumbria Police and they've seen this before, but never round here. It's usually a punishment for those suspected of cooperating with the police in rougher parts of the city. Gangs like this start with burglaries and muggings, which gets them noticed by organised criminals, who use them for jobs they don't want to be associated with. Blitzing someone's house like this is designed to intimidate people, and it's often combined with a beating.' He stopped and waited for Helen to speak.

'I see,' she said simply.

'And we all know who you've been upsetting lately.' Ian Bradshaw felt like an idiot. He'd hoped his word with Jimmy McCree might at least have given the man some pause for thought before he targeted Helen again but he had treated it as a challenge to rise to. Now Helen's flat had been trashed and Bradshaw knew it was his fault, but he didn't quite have the nerve to tell her this.

'Come on,' Tom said because Helen looked helpless now the mess had been cleared away, 'let's get out of here.'

'Where are we going?' she asked him.

'To the scene of another crime.' And when she didn't understand he said, 'Lonely Lane. I want to see the spot where that young woman was murdered.'

Chapter Thirty-Five

Lonely Lane was twenty miles from Newcastle and they used the journey time to discuss their options. Tom told Bradshaw his theory that he had been sent to London deliberately by Dean to sidetrack him and how the club owner Devine had mentioned Jimmy McCree on his way out of the building.

'It always seems to come back to McCree, Camfield and Lynch doesn't it?' observed the detective. 'Want me to have a word with Councillor Lynch?' Bradshaw asked Helen, even though he knew the last time he'd had a word it only made things worse. He hoped a councillor, even one in a gangster's pocket, might be made to see sense more easily.

'Don't waste your time, Ian,' she said as they climbed out of the car.

'Talk to the leader of the city council without good cause and you'll be on traffic duty before your feet touch the ground,' Tom assured him. 'I don't think there is much you can do. You have no proof that Jimmy McCree ordered the attack on Helen or that Joe Lynch or Alan Camfield influenced it. I say we keep digging into the Sandra Jarvis case until we find a link to any of them, then, when we have proof, we bring them all down.'

'You make it sound easy,' said Helen.

'It won't be,' Tom assured her. 'It never is.'

They walked down Lonely Lane, which was wide enough for one car to travel along, as long as it didn't meet another one coming the other way. Here and there bushes had been trimmed back and chunks taken out of the banks of grass on the side of the road to create hollows that allowed vehicles to pull in and let oncoming cars pass. Presently they ran out of road and the land changed so that Lonely Lane became a grassy surface between farmers' fields that had been worn down by cars and generations of dog walkers. A low barbed-wire fence separated the fields from the lane but its ancient fence posts sagged in parts and dragged the wire fencing down with them, making it an ineffective barrier to anyone who wanted to roam the nearby woods. The sky was dark and overcast now with the ominous promise of rain. The only building for miles was a single grey stone farm-house that overlooked parts of the lane, but as they walked along it they came across numerous blind spots and shel-tered bits of land, which fell away from the lane to create discreet parking spaces. No wonder this place was favoured by illicit lovers and the voyeurs who preyed on them.

There was no one here today though. Autumn was turning cold, making it a less desirable spot, and the notoriety of the Rebecca Holt killing would have put a lot of people off Lonely Lane as a romantic destination. Tom was willing to bet there were others who were less faint-hearted and still likely to come here once darkness fell.

He turned his attention back to the detective. 'Did you take a closer look at those alibis for me?'

'While you were swanning round the flesh pots of Lon-don? Bradshaw asked Tom. 'I did.'

'And?'

'Freddie Holt was seen by a number of people that day. He visited a construction site, had a meeting with a supplier and signed some papers at his solicitors. Interestingly enough, there are a couple of gaps in his day where the only person who can account for his actions is himself.'

'Are the timings of those gaps significant?'

'I'd say not. If he murdered his wife in between his other appointments he is not only a very cool customer but extremely good at weaving through traffic.' Bradshaw added, 'You look disappointed.'

'I figure Freddie Holt is capable of just about anything, but if he was going to buy an alibi, surely he wouldn't leave any holes?'

'That's what I thought.'

'What about Annie Bell's alibi?'

'Pretty watertight.' Bradshaw found the relevant section in his notebook. 'She went shopping that day and a lot of people saw her. She was in town for hours and can account for most of the time before, during and after Rebecca Holt's murder.'

'How is that possible?' wondered Helen out loud.

'She dropped the kids at school first then parked in the old open-air car park at the edge of town before walking to the shops.'

'Why there?' interrupted Helen. 'Why not the multi-storey?'

'She told us she doesn't like multi-storeys because she worries she's going to scrape her car on the pillars. She prefers the old car park because she has used it for years. We know she was there because her ticket had the entry time on it,' continued Bradshaw. 'We also know when she left because she outstayed the expiry time by twenty minutes and had to go to the office and pay a fine. They slap a ticket on your windscreen but you can settle up with them instantly on the day instead of writing off.'

'She doesn't strike me as the kind of person who forgets how long she's paid for,' said Tom.

'Once in town,' Ian said, reading from his notes again, 'she went to the dry cleaners to drop off some clothes and had the collection tickets to prove it. Then she took a dress back to a store because it didn't fit properly. The transaction showed up on her credit card as a refund, so we know that was legit. Her next appointment was with a travel agent, where she spent half an hour talking to a woman about a package holiday and left with some brochures.'

'Doesn't just browse aimlessly, does she?' remarked Tom. 'Very organised, likes to get things done.'

'She stopped for lunch at a café called Oscars and there was an argument.'

'What about?' asked Helen.

'Her order.' He glanced at his notebook to confirm. 'A jacket potato. She wanted cheese and they gave her tuna.'

'And that caused a row?' asked Helen. 'Couldn't they have just exchanged it?'

'They did offer,' said Bradshaw, 'but only after the waitress had told her she got what she originally asked for.'

'And Mrs Bell didn't take kindly to that?'

'She made a bit of a scene, gave the waitress a right dressing-down and told off the manager, said she'd been coming there for years but the food was always cold or she got the wrong thing and she was never coming back again. There were a couple of regulars and a number of casual diners who witnessed this. We traced some of them. They recognised her photo and confirmed she'd lost her temper with the staff.'

'Interesting,' said Tom. 'Where'd she go next?'

'A bakery, where she ordered a replacement lunch of a sausage roll and a coffee. She ate it in the place, kept the receipt.'

'Why would you?' asked Helen. 'Keep the receipt, I mean. You've eaten your sausage roll and drunk your coffee, what use is the receipt?'

'No use, but she probably stuffed it in her purse with her change and forgot about it. Next stop was the cinema.'

'I'm guessing she had the ticket?' asked Tom and Bradshaw nodded.

'She keeps everything,' said Helen.

'Lucky for us.'

'And for her,' said Helen. 'What did she see?'

'*Schindler's List*.'

'Good choice,' said Helen and Bradshaw suddenly remembered wanting to see it on video with Karen but she said it would be too depressing, so they watched *Mrs Doubtfire* instead.

'A long film too,' said Tom. 'Did anyone ask her about it?'

Bradshaw nodded. 'She'd seen it all right and described it well enough.'

'And after the cinema?'

'Back to the car park, paid her fine for overrunning, then home to see the kids, who'd been picked up from school by the au pair. She confirmed Mrs Bell returned around fifteen minutes after she left the car park.'

'Is there any way she could have driven out of the car park and gone back in again?' asked Helen.

He shook his head. 'That car park isn't automated. It's one of the last old-fashioned ones with an attendant and she parked right by the old guy's booth. Her car never left and he reckons she was very flustered about overrunning and having to pay the fine.'

'Busy day,' observed Helen. 'She packed a lot in.'

'And scarcely a minute of it unaccounted for,' added Tom, 'so, like you say, it's absolutely watertight.'

'Absolutely.' And the detective gave a sly grin.

'What?' Helen didn't understand what was so amusing.

'I know what he's going to say.'

'What is he going to say?' She looked at Bradshaw and then at Tom.

'He's going to say,' Bradshaw began, 'that an alibi that perfect . . .' and he let Tom finish.

'. . . Can't possibly be real.'

'Exactly.' And the policeman's grin grew broader.

They walked in silence for a while until Tom said, 'This is it.'

'Is this the exact place?' Helen asked.

'The case files mention a spot between the river and the woods with a gap in the barbed-wire fence and two felled trees close by,' he said, and pointed out each of those land-marks in turn. 'This cut is where Rebecca Holt used to meet Richard Bell. It's also the spot where she died.'

Helen found it hard to imagine. The location was so peaceful. She realised it was foolish but somehow she expected Lonely Lane to show signs that a brutal murder had occurred at this solitary spot; not ghosts exactly, more of an atmosphere of some kind, but it was as if nothing bad had ever happened here.

'I wanted to see it,' said Tom eventually, 'even though I knew it was probably a waste of time.' But neither Helen nor Ian questioned the wisdom of that idea.

By the time they dropped Bradshaw the rain was coming down hard. Traffic slowed so much Tom wondered if every-one just forgot how to drive once the roads were wet.

'It's time we checked out that alibi on the ground,' Tom said, 'and you could buy a few things in town.'

'Thanks.' Though the prospect of spending money Helen did not have to replace her lost items was galling.

'Darren's letting the plumber in today,' he added, 'so by the time we get home you'll have hot water.'

'Great,' she said, though his use of the words *we* and *home* in the same sentence panicked her a little.

He must have read her mind. 'I'll clear the junk out of the spare room tomorrow and get a bed put in it.'

'Oh, please don't go to all that trouble.'

'I have to do it anyway. I was planning on getting a lodger to help with the mortgage. I figured you probably wouldn't want to carry on sharing my bed for too long.' Tom could also think of someone else who wouldn't be keen on that idea.

'I meant I shouldn't impose on you by staying any longer.' Perhaps she was also thinking of her boyfriend now.

'Where else are you going to go?'

He was right. There was nowhere else. Staying in a hotel for even a few days was prohibitively expensive on a local journalist's salary and Helen didn't know anyone else well enough to stay with them.

Tom seemed to think that was the end of the discussion. 'I am going to park where Annie parked, then I'll walk every yard she walked to see if her alibi really stacks up.'

'According to Ian's colleagues it does.' Annie Bell's alibi was a little too good to be true, but if she really had proof she was elsewhere when Rebecca Holt was murdered, then how could she be in two places at once?

'There are some good detectives working this patch,' Tom admitted, 'but they're not all as diligent as Ian, and you have to remember they weren't looking too closely.'

'What do you mean?'

'The assumption has always been this killing was the

work of a man,' he reminded her. 'From day one it was Richard Bell or Freddie Holt, even a psychopathic stranger – but never a woman.'

'That's because most violence against women is committed by men,' she reminded him.

'True, but that initial assumption was backed up early on by an expert's report, which said the attack could not have been carried out by a woman – and we now know that had no basis in fact.'

'But if virtually every moment of Annie's day is accounted for, what are you actually looking for?'

'A window,' he told her.

The social worker looked weary, harassed and overworked, but she was at least helpful. Ian Bradshaw told her he was concerned about residents of some of the care homes in the area being targeted and used by a gang of professional shoplifters and she seemed to take this at face value. He didn't mention Meadowlands at first because he didn't want anyone to know he was particularly interested in the home. Instead they had a general conversation about the types of young people who end up in care and the merits or defects of the various places that housed them all.

'I'm afraid the stories are often pretty harrowing.' And she proceeded to tell some of them, leaving out names in the interests of confidentiality. She painted a bleak picture of neglect and abuse, and her sympathies very clearly lay with the children she was tasked to protect, no matter what they had done.

Her tone altered slightly when he asked her, 'And what about the Meadowlands home?'

'Oh,' she said, 'that place? A bit of a last-chance saloon if

I'm honest. Meadowlands houses quite damaged young girls who have already been in a lot of trouble. I'm not saying we've given up on them exactly . . .' But it sounded to Bradshaw as if she and her colleagues probably had.

'What exactly is the problem with the Meadowlands girls?'

'They are too difficult to manage elsewhere, so they've been corralled together in one place to prevent them from influencing girls who might still have a chance of avoiding trouble. Unfortunately they tend to egg each other on, so the reoffending rates are highest there. Meadowlands houses teenagers who run away a lot, girls who are violent and are frequently picked up by the local police.'

'What for?' he asked though he obviously had an inkling from the night he watched the place.

'Well, a number of things, but prostitution basically,' she said, 'though I would be loath to call it that.'

'They are selling sex?'

'Sort of,' she said.

'How can you "sort of" sell sex?'

She answered his question with another. 'What kind of women turn to prostitution, in your experience?'

'They tend to fall into a couple of categories,' said Bradshaw, 'the ones who sell sex for cash either because they want to or are forced to, but either way, money changes hands. They work from their homes or rented accommodation. Then there are streetwalkers at the lower end of the scale, who climb into strangers' cars. It's risky and most of the money goes to the pimps who supply them with a fix because they are often dependent on drugs.'

She nodded. 'The girls at Meadowlands are in a different category. They hang around older guys and become friendly with them. Those guys give them cigarettes, booze, weed, small sums of money, a pizza maybe . . . but they expect something in return, not always right away but eventually. The girls get confused and sometimes think of these older guys as boyfriends or at least friends, and the boundaries become blurred, so when one of the men forces himself on a girl they often view it as normal, like it's the price they have to pay for the stuff they've been given.'

'Christ. How old are these girls?'

'The age range is thirteen to sixteen.' And Bradshaw realised the girl who propositioned him outside Meadowlands may have been even younger than he thought.

'That is unbelievable, and you know for sure that this is going on?'

'It's pretty common knowledge.'

'Then why is nothing being done?'

'I could ask you that,' she said, 'since you're a police officer.'

'I'm assuming there have been no arrests because no one knows where the girls are being taken.'

'Oh no,' she said, 'everyone knows. I told you; it's common knowledge. The men involved run a series of businesses in a street just a few hundred yards from Meadowlands. There's a taxi rank, a burger bar and an off-licence.'

'And the men there openly prey on these underage girls?' She nodded. 'But nobody has been punished, why the hell not?'

'You might want to ask some of your colleagues about that.'

Chapter Thirty-Six

Tom arranged to meet Helen later and started to retrace Annie Bell's steps, leaving the car park and mentally totting up the time it would take to do all of her errands as he progressed along the high street: past the dry cleaners, the department store and travel agents then Oscar's café. There was no need to check her story about the row in the café – enough people had witnessed that. Instead he looked through the window and noticed how cramped it was. Causing an argument in a place this size wasn't a very English thing to do, he reasoned . . . unless you wanted everyone to remember you.

When Tom Carney told the young manager of the local cinema he was a journalist, the guy couldn't do enough for him. As he led him into the foyer, Tom realised why he was being so cooperative. The cinema was old, dark and musty. There were even cobwebs in less accessible corners and the place smelt vaguely unpleasant. The manager must have been hoping a journalist might give the cinema a boost, though Tom wasn't sure how linking it to a murder was going to do it any good.

'I'm looking for information on a specific film shown two years ago.' He gave the manager the relevant date, the name of the film and an explanation: he was researching the Rebecca Holt case.

'The police asked us about that,' said the manager. 'I was here then.' He sounded a little despondent as he said that, perhaps realising the amount of time that had elapsed while he was still in the same dead-end job. 'It was to do with an alibi.'

'That's right.'

'That should be easy enough to check. It's all in the logbook.'

Tom watched as he lifted something the thickness of two telephone books from a shelf behind the counter. There was no place for computers here. The manager began to leaf through the logbook, looking for the relevant date. It took him some time but eventually he glanced up at Tom.

'Yes,' said the man with some pride at actually finding what he was looking for. He pointed at the date Rebecca Holt was murdered. 'Screen 2, *Schindler's List*, three screenings: one thirty, five thirty and seven thirty.' He closed the book.

'Do you get many for the early-afternoon showing?'

'It varies. It's never as popular as the evenings but we get a few.' He contemplated this for a moment. 'Or we used to, before the multiplex opened up outside town.'

'What kind of people go to the cinema at that time?'

The manager shrugged. 'Students skiving off lectures, shift workers, people who work weekends so their days off don't match their mates' free time, the unemployed; they get a discount.'

'Bored housewives?'

The cinema manager grinned. 'Sounds like a porn mag.' Tom greeted his feeble gag with a half-hearted smile. 'Some,' he agreed, 'like that Bell woman the police were asking about?'

'You remember her then?'

'It was all over the papers. I don't recall seeing her that

day but I'm not always out front. The police asked the lass who sold the tickets but she didn't remember.' Then he added, 'Mind, you're lucky if she remembers to turn up. There were a few in that day though. It was a popular film.'

'Mrs Bell did have a ticket stub with the date on.'

'She must have been here then.'

'She couldn't have got hold of it any other way?'

'Not unless she asked someone for one on the way out.'

'Which would have been a bit suspicious,' observed Tom. 'I think you would remember if somebody asked you for the used stub from your cinema visit.'

'People drop them in the foyer sometimes,' said the manager. 'She could have picked one off the ground.'

'Not without drawing attention to herself, so we can discount that possibility. So she bought it here? It's the only place you sell them?'

The manager nodded and Tom scanned the room. Once you bought your ticket at the booth by the entrance, you had no choice but to progress into the auditorium. 'Could she have bought her ticket days before?'

'Er no,' the manager sounded sheepish, 'we don't do that here.' He meant they didn't have the technology to allow you to buy a ticket in advance. Tom surveyed the ticket booth. It had a single glass window with a space for one person to distribute tickets from a small semi-circular gap at the bottom of the window, and there was a flat brass counter top that had three slots in it, one for each screen, which spat the tickets out at you. The manager explained that tickets could be distributed on the day of the performance only, because the machine that issued them had to be set at a certain date and it was way too much hassle to change it for one ticket. The whole set-up was like something from the ark and Tom knew the new multiplex would soon see this cinema off.

'What time do you open?' asked Tom.

'Half an hour before the first performance.'

'So she could have bought a ticket thirty minutes before it started and then just turned around and gone out again without seeing the film?'

'She could have,' said the manager doubtfully, but Tom knew Annie Bell couldn't be sure the girl who sold her a ticket wouldn't have noticed her leave, which would blow her alibi right out of the water.

'No, she definitely went in.' Tom said this as much to himself as the cinema manager and his eyes trailed the walls with its posters of the latest releases, the most prominent of which was, appropriately, *The Usual Suspects*. There was a manned sweets kiosk that would have provided another witness to Annie's arrival. At that point the auditorium broadened and there was a wide, sweeping staircase leading to another level. Tom pointed to a dark alcove to one side of the staircase with a faint number three above the curtain. 'So you've got screen three on the ground floor?'

'That's the smallest screen, for the movies that have already been on for a while or the art house stuff nobody really watches,' explained the manager.

'And the stairs take you up to screens one and two?' Tom asked.

'The bigger screens,' agreed the manager needlessly.

'What's through there?' Tom pointed to the dark alcove at the other side of the staircase.

'Toilets,' answered the manager. 'There's an electric sign above the door but it's not switched on just now.'

Tom walked towards it and the manager followed, all the

while keeping up general chit-chat about how good the cinema was and all it really needed was a bit of money spent on it: a lick of paint here, some modern lighting there, to lift the gloom. Tom wasn't really listening. He swept back the red curtain that blocked the entrance to the corridor leading to the toilets.

Tom walked a few feet into the dark corridor then the manager flicked a switch and there was the plinking sound of an ancient strip light trying to fire itself into action. The lights blinked on and off, then one became fully illuminated while the other continued to flash intermittently. 'Bloody thing,' said the manager, 'only changed that the other day,' but his guilty tone betrayed the lie.

Tom could now make out two doors at the far end of the corridor. One had a stick man on it and the other a stick woman. It was the dark shape beyond them that caught his attention.

'What's that?' He pointed.

'Just a door,' said the manager, 'an emergency exit.'

Tom walked down the corridor and approached a large exterior door with a thick metal bar across it.

'This locked?' he asked.

'Never,' said the manager, 'it's a fire escape.'

'Alarmed?' Tom checked, though like everything else in the cinema it didn't look modern enough.

'No.'

Tom pressed down on the metal bar with both hands and it gave way easily, forcing the door to swing open into an alleyway. If you turned to your left you could make your way back to the shops on the high street but the door was shielded from view by two enormous metal wheelie bins. If you turned to the right instead you could follow a narrow litter-strewn alley nobody would usually venture down. A strong smell betrayed its use as a toilet at pub kicking-out time. Tom realised this lane took you towards the quiet back streets used by delivery vans behind the main stores. Go beyond them and you'd be able to creep quietly out of town.

He smiled to himself.

'Like I said,' the puzzled manager reminded him, 'it's only a door.'

'No,' said Tom. 'This, my friend, is a window.'

Chapter Thirty-Seven

Ian Bradshaw and Helen Norton stood outside the cinema, staring at the locked fire exit door. Tom Carney was not facing the door. Instead, he was looking at them.

'How could Annie Bell have known the plot of the movie,' asked Helen, 'if she skipped out of the cinema as soon as she bought a ticket?'

'It had been on for ten days by then,' explained Tom, 'she could have seen it already.'

'A different performance on an earlier day?' asked Bradshaw and the question sounded rhetorical but Tom answered anyway.

'Exactly.'

'So she buys her ticket, heads for the toilets but walks past them, opens the fire exit and slips through it, closing the door behind her, then . . . ?' asked Helen.

'I'm guessing she does a right turn, taking her away from the main drag.' Tom started to walk down the alley. Bradshaw and Helen followed him.

'If she did skip out of the film,' asked Bradshaw, 'how long does that give her for this window you keep talking about?'

'She chose the right film,' Tom said. 'The running time of *Schindler's List* is three hours and fifteen minutes plus trailers and adverts. The average length of a film trailer in this country is two and a half minutes.' He could see they were both looking at him quizzically. 'I've done my homework,' he explained. 'Add in a bunch of adverts for training shoes or the local tandoori and you have around fifteen minutes of extras, so that's three and a half hours.'

'Which gives her enough time to get back to her car and away, except we know the car didn't move so . . .' Helen shrugged.

'She didn't need her car,' explained Tom.

'She couldn't exactly take a cab to a murder,' said the detective and he mimicked that conversation. '*Wait here while I kill someone.*'

'And she could hardly take the bus,' said Helen.

'I never said she didn't need *a* car,' Tom explained, 'I said she didn't need *her* car.' And at that point they reached the end of the alleyway, which opened out into a wide space. 'She had another car,' Tom pointed ahead of them, 'and she parked it right here.'

'Bloody hell,' said Bradshaw, as he realised what Tom meant.

The council had put this open space behind the high street to good use: a car park big enough for around twenty vehicles.

'Annie could have driven a second vehicle down here early that morning or even the night before and left it. She could have jumped on an early bus home if she didn't want to risk a taxi. Who's going to remember one woman on a bus? She parks her own car at the opposite end of town, buys a ticket, does all of her errands then leaves the cinema. She could have driven out of town, killed Rebecca Holt then returned here or left the other car somewhere else. As long as she was back in town to collect her car later, no one is going to question it. She even made sure she was a little late so she had to pay a fine, which went on record and confirmed her alibi so she was in the clear. Her only mistake was making the alibi too damn perfect.'

'That's a bit tricky, isn't it?'

'She has an au pair to get the kids up and ready for school because she runs first thing in the morning. Maybe this time she ran to a car she'd parked a few streets away, drove it to town then got the bus back in time to get the kids to school before heading in again. It's tight but it's possible.'

'How could she have a second car without anyone noticing?' asked Helen. 'Could she rent one? Wouldn't there be records?'

'She didn't need to rent one. She looks after the pool of company cars at her place of work. There are always demos just sitting there. They probably have to be signed out but she is the one responsible for that so I'm assuming she didn't bother.'

'Then how can we prove she used one of them?' asked Helen, 'if she didn't sign it out.'

'I don't know yet,' he admitted, 'but I'll think of something.'

'Okay, it all sounds just about plausible,' admitted Helen, 'but you've not explained one crucial thing.'

'What's that?'

'I understand how Annie Bell could get away to kill Rebecca,' she said, 'but how would she persuade Rebecca Holt to come and meet her?' Helen mimed picking up a phone then and speaking into it. *'Hello, it's Annie Bell here. I know you're having an affair with my husband and I would love to discuss this with you down an isolated country lane but don't worry, I promise not to kill you.'*

'Yeah, yeah, I hear you. I don't know the answer to that question either, but if we do find out how she got Rebecca to agree to meet her we are almost there.'

That night, back at Tom's house, Helen had a hot bath and basked in the heat from fully functioning radiators. Afterwards, she climbed into the big double bed. It was quiet now, the only sound coming from the shower as Tom also took advantage of the hot water. Helen felt warm, safe and drowsy. By the time Tom came to bed she was already fast asleep.

The next morning when Tom visited Annie Bell at her office for a second time it clearly irritated her, though she said nothing. He kept her talking for half an hour, going over old leads and asking questions he'd asked before, just for clarification. Then he asked some new ones, all of which she answered calmly. He told her about his recent meeting with Freddie Holt, which she took a great interest in, but neglected to mention the businessman had attacked him. Tom kept an eye on the time, subtly checking the clock on the wall in her office at regular intervals, because timing would be crucial that morning.

'Oh, I nearly forgot,' he said, 'I do have one more question.'

'What about?'

'Your car scheme.'

'Sorry?'

'The demos on your car fleet,' he said, 'can anyone use them?'

Annie looked confused but replied, 'Theoretically, any-body can drive them. They are insured by the manufacturers for all drivers but we don't permit anyone outside the com-pany car programme to take one for a spin.' She noticed the half-smile on his face and thought she understood now. 'Including you, Mr Carney, if that is what you're asking?'

He held up his hands. 'Can't blame me for trying,' he said.

'I'm thinking of trading mine in for something with a bit more oomph under the bonnet. It's off the road at the moment.'

'Sorry, can't help you,' she told him firmly.

He stole a quick look at the clock again then. It wouldn't be long now, assuming she didn't let him down. 'I suppose you can't let people abuse the system,' he said amiably, 'but how can you possibly control it when the cars are just sitting around here all day?'

'I control it,' she told him. 'If you're a qualifying driver, you can take a demo for a few days or even just a few hours before you order your next car and we sometimes use them as pool cars for off-site meetings, but I keep the keys and they have to be signed out in the ledger.' She tapped her finger against an A4-sized, thick, red, hard-backed book that was on her desk.

'Do you drive them all?'

'Yes,' she said, 'I need to have a working knowledge of them to manage our fleet, in case drivers ask me questions.'

'What's to stop someone just coming in here when you're not around, picking up a set of keys and going for a joyride without you knowing?'

'That couldn't happen,' she said. 'The keys are locked away and when you take a car you have to sign it out.'

'In the ledger,' he said. 'Looks pretty thick. You must have had a lot of cars?'

'We buy a lot of cars,' she told him, 'for managers and the sales force. This ledger contains five years of demonstrators.'

'You're very organised. How many demos do you have at any one time?'

'Usually three,' she said, 'from different manufacturers, rotated every two or three weeks. Why do you ask?'

'You must be an expert then. What would you recommend?'

'That depends on what you're looking for.'

'Something I can count on.'

'German cars,' she told him, 'are usually best for reliability these days.'

'Thanks for the tip. I'll bear it in mind.'

The phone rang then. Right on time, and so loudly that it almost made him jump.

'Excuse me,' she said and picked up the phone. 'Yes . . . what?' A deep sigh. 'What does she want?' she asked irritably and there was a pause while she digested the answer.

Tom frowned his concern. 'Everything alright?'

'There's a journalist at the front desk.'

'Really? What does he want?'

'It's a she and I'm just—' Annie listened for a few moments more then told Tom, 'She's from a newspaper in Newcastle and says she wants to speak to me about Richard's case being reopened.'

Tom shook his head. 'That's not a good idea, Annie. We need to control this story not let every rogue reporter get their hands on it so they can twist things.' He furrowed his brow. 'What's her name?'

Annie asked that same question down the phone and turned back to Tom when she received an answer. 'Helen Norton.'

'Oh, Christ.'

'You know her?' asked Annie.

'We . . .' he paused as if he was trying to put things delicately '. . . worked quite closely together on the case I wrote about in my book, but to be honest I never really felt I could trust her.'

'But how could she know we were looking to reopen the case?'

'Prison guards,' said Tom. 'Your husband warned me one of them would leak it to the press eventually.'

'The bastards,' she said, and it was the first time he'd heard Annie swear.

'Just get rid of her.'

'They've tried but she insists she won't leave until she's seen me. She seems to think I might want to speak to her.'

Richard exhaled. 'Look, I know Helen Norton well enough and she won't budge unless you go out there and tell her face to face to leave.'

'I really don't want to talk to her.'

'Just tell her you still firmly believe in your husband's innocence and are open to any new information that will help to clear his name but you are not actively pursuing any new investigation. That will give her the quote she needs to keep her editor happy but it will kill the story stone dead.'

'Are you sure that will work? What if it makes things worse?'

'It won't,' Tom assured her, 'but whatever you do, don't tell her *I'm* here.'

Annie thought she understand then. 'A woman scorned?'

Tom was evasive. 'It just won't help either of us if she knows I'm on the case.'

Annie still looked unsure. She got to her feet but did not leave the office; instead, she stood there, thinking. She looked at Tom, glanced down at the phone she was still holding in her hand as if reluctant to speak into it again, and then both of them listened as the faint voice at the end of the line began speaking once more. Finally, Annie raised it to her mouth and said, 'Tell Miss Norton I'll be there in a moment,' and hung up without another word. Annie walked out of her office as if sloping reluctantly to the gallows, heading for reception.

Tom didn't move. Not at first. He was mentally tracing the number of steps Annie had to take to reach the end of the room and pass through the door. He had counted them in his head on arrival. She would then march purposefully to reception to meet Helen. A great deal would depend on how long Helen could keep her there but he couldn't rely on it being long. Helen would stall, she would ask questions and demand answers, but Annie would fight her corner and rebuff the journalist. She would regurgitate Tom's statement about believing her husband's innocence then send Helen Norton packing.

Tom had to move quickly and he had to move now. He left his seat and moved to Annie's desk, glancing towards the door to make sure no one was about to walk through it. Outside, the desks were all manned but nobody looked towards him as he bent to slide out the ledger. He ducked back down into his chair and quickly began to leaf through the ledger from the back to the front. There were a series of columns denoting the manufacturer and model, followed by the car's registration number then a time out and a time in to indicate when the car had been taken and returned. Finally, there was a column for the driver's signature, so he couldn't wriggle out of responsibility for an accident or a speeding fine if one landed on Annie's desk weeks later.

Tom knew Annie would be back at any moment. If she had given Helen an unsympathetic hearing, which was likely, she might already be on her way. He thumbed the ledger's pages while he speed-read the dates at the top of each page and drew closer to the date he was looking for.

All too soon he saw the door at the other end of the outer office open. Annie was back already. 'Bollocks.' This was nowhere near enough time. He couldn't afford to be caught leafing through the ledger, but knew he would never get another chance to check it alone.

She was halfway across the room when his eyes settled on the correct page. Three cars were listed there. Tom scanned the notices for the entire week, including the date of Rebecca Holt's murder, but when he reached it he noticed only two had been signed out. The third car must have been the one she took that day, but Annie Bell was almost back at her office door now and Tom had no more time to make a note of it.

Then Annie stopped, right outside the door. At first he thought she had somehow spotted what he was doing and was about to burst in and confront him. Then he heard a voice, but it wasn't Annie's. Instead there was the low murmur of a male employee asking a question. Someone had left his desk and intercepted the boss before she could vanish back into her office. This was Tom's chance. He grabbed a pen and notebook from his jacket pocket and, balancing them against the ledger, hastily noted down the make, model and registration number of the third car.

Tom slapped his notebook shut and stuffed it into his jacket pocket, along with the pen. He could hear Annie Bell giving her employee instructions right outside her door and launched himself out of his seat, pushing the ledger back into its original spot on Annie's desk. He virtually jumped back into his chair and landed on it just as she came through the door. He had to make a show of adjusting his posture and crossing his legs, as if he had grown uncomfortable in his seat.

'Everything alright?' he asked brightly.

'I can see why you don't like her,' was Annie Bell's sole pronouncement on Helen Norton.

When they were done, Annie walked Tom out to the car park. Like Helen before him, she evidently wanted to make sure he was safely off the premises.

'What do you want, Mr Carney?' Annie Bell asked him as they walked towards his brother-in-law's car.

'How do you mean?'

'I'm asking you what you really want out of life.'

'Why are you asking me that?'

'I'm curious,' she said. 'Not this, surely: living hand to mouth, scratching a living from freelance journalism, hoping to land a big story from time to time so you can pay the bills and topping up your income with some investigative work, which must be piecemeal at best. Wouldn't you like something a little more solid?' she asked him.

'Maybe,' he admitted.

'I don't suppose this is what you dreamed of doing when you were a child.'

'No,' he admitted, 'I wanted to be a train driver, an astronaut or a footballer but, like most people, I had to settle for something else. This isn't so bad. I get to choose my own hours, I'm my own boss and occasionally I help to catch some bad guys and put them in prison.'

'Yes, but where is the future in that? Wouldn't you prefer something more stable, a job with prospects and a nicer lifestyle?'

'And where would I get that kind of opportunity,' Tom asked, 'assuming I did like the sound of it?'

'Our company is expanding,' Annie told him. 'I've been talking to my father about new hires, some fresh blood to energise the firm. For a while now we've been discussing the idea of a director responsible for PR.'

'I suppose I do have the skills for that kind of role, but what sort of salary would we be talking about?'

'Seventy K,' she told him.

'Seventy thousand a year, just for handling your company's PR?' He whistled.

'I'm sure you'd have to earn every penny. This company is growing rapidly. We are really going places.'

'That would certainly cure a lot of my problems, but what about my investigation?'

'I'm not talking about right away,' she said, 'I meant afterwards. Once you've seen this through, of course.' And she sighed. 'We both know my husband hired you in desperation, to see if you could uncover something that might win him an appeal. I know you feel beholden to us because you've taken a small amount of our money already and you haven't got anything to show for it, but I just want to say I understand how difficult this is. No one is expecting a miracle from you,' she told him, 'not even Richard.' Then she added, 'Especially Richard. All I'm saying is that, when you do get to the end of this, there could be a very good job here waiting for you.'

'Thanks, Annie,' said Tom. 'That's very kind of you. I promise I'll give that some serious thought.'

And he did give it serious thought. All the way home he wondered why Annie Bell was trying to buy him off.

Chapter Thirty-Eight

The Rosewood café was virtually empty. Rain teeming down outside kept away the faint-hearted but not the detective or the two reporters. They had agreed to meet later than usual to allow Tom and Helen to visit Annie first and now they were bringing Bradshaw up to speed.

'Could you have a word with someone about a car in Annie's ledger?' asked Tom.

'What are we looking for?'

'Proof,' said Tom, 'that she had a demo for her own use on that fateful day.'

'I'm assuming she wouldn't put it in a ledger if she did?'

'She didn't,' admitted Tom. 'Annie is the only one in the company who could get one without signing it out, so I took a look at it around the time of the murder. Soleil had three cars and all three were in constant use for three weeks, apart from a three-day period which overlaps the murder, when only two cars were logged out on the ledger. The third car never left head office during that time.' Then he added, 'In theory.'

'That would make sense,' said Bradshaw, 'if Annie used it.'

'But it doesn't *prove* that she did,' Tom reminded him.

'No,' said Bradshaw, 'but give me the reg number anyway and I'll do some digging.'

'Thanks, Ian.'

'You reckon she did it,' Bradshaw said, 'don't you?'

'Don't you?' asked Tom.

'I don't know. Yes, maybe?' he offered lamely.

'She had a motive,' Tom reminded him.

'Another woman was screwing her husband,' agreed Bradshaw, 'but thousands of women discover that every year and most of them get over it.'

'But Rebecca was one of many and I think Annie always had her suspicions, regardless of what she says now.'

'Then why kill Rebecca, if she wasn't the first he's been to bed with?'

'Perhaps she was the final straw,' said Helen. 'Maybe she'd had enough.'

'Then she should have killed her husband,' observed Bradshaw.

'And done time for it?' said Tom. 'Even with a sympathetic judge and jury, Annie Bell would be a convicted murderer and she'd lose everything: her career, the kids.'

'And this way she gets rid of her rival,' said Helen.

'But she doesn't win,' said Bradshaw. 'She covers her tracks so well her husband goes down for the murder instead.'

'What if that's what she wanted?' Helen asked him. 'We haven't really considered that possibility. We just accepted she is standing by him, but he's going to be away for twenty-four years at this rate.'

'It's his idea to deny guilt, which will keep him in for the full tariff, not hers,' said Tom.

'But has she been arguing that decision with him or is she going along with it?' asked Helen. 'Maybe it suits her just fine for him to be in prison.'

'Not fond of her, are you?' asked Tom. 'If it makes you feel any better, she ain't too keen on you either.'

'I was playing a part,' she reminded him.

'Of an annoying journalist, and you played it very well.' He grinned at her. 'If she really did kill Rebecca, it's two birds with one stone.'

'There is one thing which undermines that theory,' said Helen. 'Why the hell couldn't she just divorce him?'

'Strange as it may sound, she has too much money,' Tom answered.

'How can you have too much?'

'Usually when people get divorced, they sell the house, split the proceeds and argue about maintenance depending on their circumstances. In most cases the kids stay with the mum, the father leaves and pays support to the mother because he is often the one working full time . . .'

'. . . And she is stuck doing part-time, lower-paid work, having sacrificed her career to bring up their children,' Helen reminded him pointedly.

'Pretty much,' said Tom, 'but in Annie Bell's case, it's different. She's a board member of Soleil and a significant shareholder. They have money. Richard Bell on his own is worth bugger all. He has a well-paid job, which he would doubtless immediately lose if he splits from the boss's daughter. With his CV – or lack of it – he'd have very little to offer another employer, so he'd probably end up as a middle-income salesman of some kind, several levels below the false position he found himself in as a family member. Crucially, that means he could take Annie Bell and her dad to the cleaners. He'd be the one who could expect to keep up a lifestyle he has become accustomed to without any of the means. For Annie Bell to give Richard half her net worth she would have to sell her house and shares in the company her father built up. Knowing her, I can't see that happening. Can you?'

'Okay, I agree,' said Bradshaw. 'Divorce would be a

catastrophe for Annie Bell, which gives her a motive to fix things violently, but is there any actual evidence to support this?'

'Let's consider it then,' offered Tom. 'Her alibi was always a bit too damn perfect. We know there is a possible gap around the time the murder was committed and it's sizable. She could have left the cinema easily, giving her around three hours to drive out to Lonely Lane, kill Rebecca then return to town.'

'Why would Rebecca agree to meet her lover's wife at an isolated location without even telling Richard about it in advance?'

'I haven't figured that bit out yet.'

'So what else have we got?' asked Bradshaw.

'We know the expert witness who said the blows could not have been struck by a woman was guessing, so we can disregard that – and there's one other thing,' said Tom, 'today she tried to buy me off.'

'What?' asked Helen. 'She tried to bribe you?'

'Not quite,' he said, 'she offered me a job.'

'What kind of job?' asked the detective.

'PR director with a nice, big salary.'

'Was this dependent on you dropping the case?'

'No,' Tom admitted, 'she was at pains to tell me it was waiting for me once I have given up trying to solve the case. She told me she didn't expect too much from me on that front. It was subtler than that but I got the message.'

'As subtle as a brick,' said Bradshaw then he remembered Helen's window. 'Sorry,' he told her.

'You really think Annie Bell killed Rebecca Holt?' asked Helen.

'I'm starting to,' he said. 'Why else would she try and derail the investigation her husband started? Proving it though, that's another matter.'

That evening, while Tom was reading the paper Helen asked, 'Do you mind if I ring, erm—' and he knew she meant the boyfriend.

Helen was surprised at how easily the lies came to her. She had been forced to leave her flat for a few days while repairs were undertaken on the boiler, an idea that had been planted in her head by the problems Tom had with his own central heating. Then she casually added she would probably use this opportunity to get a different place because her current home was 'a bit grotty'.

Peter had listened to this and, though she was expecting the question, she still felt a slight panic when he suddenly asked, 'So where are you staying now?'

'At a friend's,' she managed.

'A friend? Which friend?' he asked, his tone disbelieving

Helen had always believed honesty was the most important building block in any relationship but she also knew telling the full truth now would be way more damaging than a manufactured half-truth. She *was* staying with a friend; that much was true – but if Peter learned she was not merely sharing a house with Tom Carney but also the man's bed, regardless of the fact that no physical contact had taken place, she was certain this would sound the death knell of their relationship. Peter's jealousy would outweigh any trust he might have had in her.

'Susan,' she told him brightly. 'You remember, I told you about her.'

'No, you didn't,' he said doubtfully, 'did you?'

'Yes.' Susan was a real person from the newsroom. Helen

had spoken to her on a handful of occasions but sincerely hoped her boyfriend would never be in a position to meet her because Helen could easily imagine her blank face when Peter thanked her for helping out his girlfriend.

Helen had told Graham about the attack on her flat, though she played it down considerably. He was still concerned enough to have allowed her a morning off to search for a new place to live. Now she was back in the newsroom looking at old copies of the *Record*. Helen was leafing through one of the heavy old binders with a frown of concentration on her face, oblivious to the chatter and the noise of phones ringing around her. The binder covered the first six months of 1987, around the time Meadowlands first opened its doors, and she examined every page carefully but swiftly, mindful of missing something important. She was searching for a photograph she had never seen before but was confident it would be somewhere in this binder if she looked hard enough. Just when Helen had begun to convince herself her hunch was wrong and this was a fruitless and forlorn exercise, she turned a page and there it was.

'Oh my God,' she said when she immediately recognised the face in the middle of a group shot.

What was it that Graham once told her . . . *A picture is worth a thousand words*?

Chapter Thirty-Nine

With the kitchen finished and most of the new floorboards in place, thanks to Darren's efforts, it was much easier for them to meet at Tom's. Helen was already staying there of course, which Bradshaw found amusing. He arrived before her that evening and, as usual, Tom handed him a beer while they waited for her to join them.

'Brave lass, that Helen.'

'She is,' agreed Tom.

'Smart too.'

'Uh-huh,' said Tom guardedly.

'Bonny lass as well.'

'Paid-up member of her fan club, are you?'

'It's a rare combination,' admitted Bradshaw. 'You don't normally get bright lasses who are good company and that agreeable to look at.' He realised he was comparing Karen to Helen Norton and that was unfair, but he couldn't help himself. He had begun to wonder what it might be like to be in a relationship with a woman like her.

'True enough.' Bradshaw noticed Tom's reluctance to get too immersed in this topic of conversation.

'Ever fancied a pop at her yourself?' asked the detective. 'You seem close.'

'We work well together, that's all.'

Bradshaw nodded slowly. 'And now she's living under your roof.'

'Only till she gets somewhere else.' And when Bradshaw

did not reply he added, 'I could hardly chuck her out on the street.'

'Good of you,' said Bradshaw, 'but I'm surprised you're not tempted. I would be.'

'Sounds like you already are, mate,' and Bradshaw realised he had needled the other man by the way he placed too much emphasis on the word *mate*, 'but I'm sorry to tell you she's got a boyfriend.'

'And I've got a girlfriend,' said Bradshaw.

'How's that working out for you?'

'Good,' he replied quickly, 'very good, thanks.'

There was a tense silence between them for a moment until Bradshaw broke it.

'Don't worry about Helen,' he said. 'I can always tell when a girl is already spoken for.' And Tom noticed the faint trace of a smile on the detective's face as he said that.

Before he could respond they heard a key turn in the lock and Helen came in. 'Sorry,' she said, 'traffic was a nightmare but . . .' she paused to put down her bag and a handful of folders '. . . on a lighter note, I think I found a flat.'

'Oh,' said Tom, 'that's great, Helen,' and ignored the look Bradshaw was giving him. Helen was too busy taking off her coat to notice.

Tom ordered pizza and they argued over who was going to pay. Helen insisted, in lieu of rent for her stay with Tom. While they waited for their food, she showed them her most recent discovery.

'I did some research on Meadowlands. It opened in 1987, so I did some digging into our back copies. It took a while because I didn't have an exact date but eventually I found it.'

'Found what?' asked Tom.

'The picture I was looking for.' She started to remove

the evidence from her bag. 'Places like Meadowlands don't open every day,' she explained. 'They require funding and lobbying plus planning permission and multiple layers of bureaucratic sign-off.'

'It's a wonder they ever open their doors at all,' agreed Tom.

'So when they do finally open,' she prompted, 'what does everyone involved like to do?'

'Pat themselves on the back in a self-congratulatory manner . . .' Tom began and then cottoned on '. . . usually at an opening ceremony of some kind.' And he smiled at her initiative.

'With a local dignitary or two in attendance – and there's nearly always a photo in the local paper.' She handed him a photocopy of the picture she had found in the newspaper's archives.

Tom glanced at the photograph of a small huddle of council officials and child care officers smiling outside the brand new Meadowlands building. One of them was helpfully holding up a length of tape, while another man posed with scissors waiting to cut it and declare the place officially open.

'I wasn't expecting that,' said Tom – for the man with the scissors was none other than Councillor Joe Lynch.

They stared at the photograph for a while, then Bradshaw said, 'What does this prove? Other than the fact Councillor Lynch likes to see his face in the newspaper? They all do.'

'It proves he knows the place,' said Tom.

'It proves he *opened* it,' countered Bradshaw. 'He may never have been back there. I wouldn't say it was evidence of foul play.'

'But we know what he is capable of,' said Helen quietly.

'He does seem to keep cropping up,' said Tom, who was happy to make the link between Joe Lynch's presence at the

Meadowlands opening ceremony and the disappearance of Sandra Jarvis. He was recalling his own conversation with Frank about who stood to gain from the former leader stepping down.

'It *is* something,' said Bradshaw, 'but it's not much.'

'What did you come up with then?' demanded Helen, irritated that Bradshaw could be so dismissive of her detective work.

He seemed almost reluctant to begin. 'I spoke to a lady who works with vulnerable children.' And he told them what the social worker had said about older men preying on the Meadowlands girls.

'Christ, that's terrible,' said Helen, 'but where is this happening? Do they take them to some sort of hideaway?'

'No,' admitted Bradshaw, 'that's the worst part. The woman I spoke to told me there's an office belonging to a small taxi company in the high street, a few hundred yards from Meadowlands. It's in a row of shops next to an off-licence and a burger bar, all owned by the same people. The guys who use it get the girls from Meadowlands to hang out there and that's how it starts.'

'So what exactly are the police doing,' Helen was outraged, 'if everybody knows this is going on?'

'That's what I couldn't understand, but she implied the police don't care. I refused to believe that so I spoke to a uniformed officer who covers the area and he told me they couldn't arrest anyone because it was impossible to press charges. The girls always deny anything bad has happened because they are either too scared of the men or in love with them. He said they were all unreliable witnesses with a history of lying and petty crime and no jury in the world would convict a man on their testimony.'

'That's appalling,' said Tom.

'Are you not bothered that this is going on?' Helen asked Bradshaw when she mistook his calmness for disinterest.

'Of course I'm bothered, Helen,' he told her. 'It made me ashamed to be a police officer.'

'I'm sorry,' she told him, 'it's just . . . I'm outraged that no one is doing anything to stop this.'

'The guy I spoke to literally laughed it off, as if having sex with a fourteen-year-old in exchange for a pizza and a packet of fags was acceptable behaviour. He said if it wasn't those men it would be someone else, because the girls don't know any better. He joked they were doing GCSEs in prostitution and told me there was a place like that cab rank in every town in Britain. He reckons the guys behind it pass the lasses to other men who pay them for the privilege, so not only are they having sex with young girls they are making money too.'

'I can see why the police might have a problem charging the men,' said Tom, 'but there's a simple way to prevent all this. Just make sure the girls don't leave Meadowlands at night. They are all under sixteen so lock the place up at nine o'clock and keep them in.'

'I don't understand why they don't do that,' said Helen.

'I think I do,' said Tom. 'The guys at that taxi rank need at least one man on their side for this to work.'

'Dean,' she said.

'I'm betting he's on the payroll,' offered Tom. 'If police and social services are aware of what's going on, how could he not be? He must let the girls come and go at all hours.'

'There's a lock on the door with a keypad,' said Helen. 'You just need to know the entry code to get in. Dean wouldn't even have to get out of bed. I still don't understand how the police feel completely powerless to arrest men who are having sex with underage girls and treating them like prostitutes.'

'I wouldn't call it prostitution,' said Bradshaw, 'I'd call it rape.' Then he added, 'How can they consent at their age?'

'How many girls at Meadowlands are involved in this kind of thing?' asked Tom.

'I asked that,' said Bradshaw, 'and the answer I got was *all of them.*'

Chapter Forty

When the pizzas arrived they ate them wordlessly, each lost in private thoughts about the girls from Meadowlands and the men who exploited them.

'I'm not hungry,' said Helen, pushing her pizza to one side. 'Does nobody at social services take it seriously when they get a report of child abuse?' she asked.

'I'm assured it does get taken seriously but they've been quite honest with me about it. They are completely swamped. They don't have enough resources to deal with serious cases, let alone all of the frivolous ones.'

'"Frivolous ones"?' He could tell Helen had taken offence at his choice of words.

'Helen, they just can't cope with the workload. They even set up a special phone line during the summer so depressed young girls could call in and talk to a professional if they were experiencing physical or mental abuse and felt suicidal.'

'Well that sounds like a good idea.'

'It was,' he confirmed, 'until they were swamped by hundreds of calls from lasses who simply couldn't go on,' and when she gave him a withering look at his unsympathetic tone, he added, 'because Robbie Williams left Take That.'

'Oh,' she said and reminded herself to be less judgemental in future. 'Do you think this situation with the Meadowlands girls was the big secret Diane told Sandra Jarvis? Is this why they both disappeared?'

'But it isn't a secret, is it,' countered Tom, 'if the police and social services know all about it. They think they're powerless to prevent it, so what could Sandra Jarvis do with that information, except embarrass a few low-level people like Dean? That's not enough reason to kill someone or force them into hiding.'

'You're right,' admitted Helen, 'it must have been something bigger – but what?'

'We may never know,' acknowledged Tom, 'and Meadowlands might be entirely unrelated to Sandra's disappearance, but I think that it is. There's one person who knows a lot more about all of this than they're admitting.'

'Dean?' asked Helen.

He shook his head. 'I'm talking about young Callie.'

'You want me to do what?' asked Helen when Bradshaw was gone.

'Well, I can hardly do it alone, can I?' Tom told her. 'If I'm caught, I'll be arrested. No one is going to believe there's an innocent explanation.'

'And what will they believe if I'm caught?' she asked him, her voice becoming shrill.

'That you're a journalist working on a story,' he assured her. 'Besides, it's a matter of trust and I'm pretty sure she doesn't trust me.'

'Then I'd say she's an excellent judge of character,' she mock-chided him.

'Come on,' he said, 'put your coat on. It's cold outside.'

'It's always cold outside,' she told him and immediately regretted it because that was the kind of thing Peter would have said.

*

He'd managed to sort out a rental vehicle while the garage patched up his own car. 'Bloody hell,' said the mechanic when he surveyed the Renault's cracked windscreen, broken side window, dented bonnet and pummelled bodywork, 'who'd you fall out with?'

'I hit a deer.'

'Looks like you hit an elephant.'

They drove up to the quiet, mostly residential street with its little huddle of shops at one end. It was getting late but the lights were still on in the burger bar, the off-licence and the taxi rank and Tom eased his car into a space where they could see without being seen. The burger bar was dead, as you would expect for a Tuesday evening.

Occasionally a driver would pull up outside the cab office and go inside and once in a while someone went into the off-licence. Racially, they were a mixed bag, with white men and Asians who looked like they had been born locally mixing with other men who, judging by their appearance, may have been from Eastern Europe or a Mediterranean country. They had all adopted the same uniform of T-shirts, jeans and leather jackets or raincoats, which were mostly black. It was hard to tell a criminal from a normal person when everyone likes to dress like a gangster. They all wanted to look like a *face* – even the ones who were just popping out for a packet of cigarettes.

There were no signs of any young girls though.

'It's too early,' Tom said, 'let's go.'

When they parked again it was within sight of Meadowlands, which was barely visible in the gloom. The building was lit by the single large light above its door. Whatever was going on inside was disguised by the thick window blinds. They settled down to wait.

Eventually the door swung open and a young girl emerged. Tom glanced at his watch. 'Ten thirty,' he said, 'so much for a curfew,' and they both watched her walk towards them. Tom had parked on the opposite side of the road under a broken streetlamp and he was pretty sure the girl would not notice his car among the row of others parked outside the houses. Sure enough she walked by without a glance in their direction, heading towards the cab rank.

'What was her name again?' he asked Helen.

'Debbie,' she said, 'the one who told us to leave her alone, "for fuck's sake".'

'You know if a beat bobby stops us we are going to have a lot of explaining to do,' he told her.

'I told you, I am not doing this on my own,' Helen said. 'It's either this way, together, or not at all.'

'Okay, I hear you,' he said.

'Anyhow, have you seen a single police officer?'

'No,' he admitted.

'Exactly. I reckon this place is protected,' she said.

'You mean someone's paying someone to—'

'Turn a blind eye? Yes,' Helen said, 'but I don't know how you keep every police officer in town away from a place like the taxi rank.'

'Aside from the fact that no one seems to give a damn, that's easier than you might think. The boys in blue can be ordered to stay away from certain locations to avoid prejudicing ongoing enquiries by undercover detectives,' Tom explained, 'or a politician can ask a senior policeman to go easy on vulnerable children to avoid a public scandal. Neither party wants to see the crime figures soar because of a raft of arrests of minors on drugs or prostitution charges.'

'What a bloody world we live in,' she said, 'when people put crime stats as their top priority instead of arresting men who use vulnerable children.'

'That's how careers are made.' Tom tensed then. 'Here she comes.' They watched Callie exit the care home and head unhurriedly along the path towards town.

Tom waited till she went round a corner then started the car's engine. They drove into the main road, overtook Callie then pulled over to the side of the road, where Helen got out.

'Callie.'

The girl took a moment to register Helen's presence. 'What do you want?' she snarled.

'I need to speak with you,' she said, but Callie's eyes were already darting around, as if she sensed this was a trap. Tom had not made his presence known yet. He hoped Helen, as a woman, would be a less menacing presence but Callie had clocked him sitting in the car.

'What's he doing here?' she demanded as Tom opened his car window to explain. 'You stole my photo, you bastard!' she shouted at him.

'I did,' he admitted. He handed it back to her through the car window. 'Borrowed it, really.' She marched up to him and snatched the photo from his fingers. 'I'm sorry. I just wanted to be able to identify Diane.'

'To drag her back here?' she accused him.

'No,' he shook his head, 'why would I want to bring her back to this hell hole? Diane is better off in London and we both know it.' That stopped Callie in her tracks. 'I just want to know she's safe and I'd like to speak to her about Sandra Jarvis. I need to find Sandra.'

'Well, I can't help you with that.' And Callie walked away.

'How much do you earn a night, Callie?' he called after her and she spun back round.

'What do you mean?' She looked worried.

'I'll bet it's not that much,' he said calmly, 'so I'll double it,' he told her, 'if you come with us now.'

Chapter Forty-One

It took a moment for Callie to make her decision. He could tell she contemplated denying earning money at the cab rank but she must have reasoned he knew all about that, so there wasn't much point. Offering to double her earnings was the clincher and she told him, 'Forty quid.' Tom knew she was lying.

'I'll give you fifty.'

'You said double.' But she was already getting into the car.

Tom drove them a few miles from town and parked up at the edge of a village in a well-lit side road with neat little houses either side of it. He hoped Callie would feel safe here and be more likely to talk. They both turned to face the girl on the back seat.

'What about my money?' Callie demanded as soon as the car stopped moving.

'Afterwards,' he said.

'When you've answered our questions,' Helen told her. 'That's only fair.'

'Fuck fair,' said Callie.

'Why was Diane so keen to leave?' asked Tom.

When Callie didn't reply, Helen said, 'All the girls seem to like it in Meadowlands.'

Callie turned back to look at Helen. 'You got to say that, haven't you?' she told the reporter as if it was obvious.

'In case Dean and the others get angry with you?'

Callie's silence was answer enough.

'And if they're not angry with you,' Tom said, 'you get to do pretty much what you want,' then he decided to risk it, 'and you can go to the cab rank at night.'

'Are you a copper or something?' barked Callie.

'I told you, Callie. I'm just a reporter who is helping Sandra's old man find his daughter. I don't have any interest in the men that own those little businesses.' He was lying to her about that, for he fully intended to write something about them as soon as he was given the opportunity.

'They're my friends.' Callie was defiant.

'I know you think they are,' said Helen, 'but they are using you, Callie.'

'Don't talk wet,' she told Helen.

'It's none of our business,' Tom told Helen and when she gave him a venomous look he stared right back at her significantly, trying to convey the message that right now this was all about Diane and Sandra Jarvis. 'Callie's a big girl. She can do what she wants. Isn't that right, Callie?'

'Yeah,' the girl agreed and she seemed to calm down a little.

'And if she makes a little money along the way, that's her business.'

'It's not money,' protested Callie, 'well, sometimes, but mostly they just give us stuff.'

'Cigs, booze . . . that kind of thing.' Tom was saying it as if this was all above board and perfectly normal, his tone reassuring her.

'Yeah,' she said, 'all boyfriends do that.' Helen had to restrain herself from telling Callie that this was not how it was supposed to work with a boyfriend but she knew the young girl would clam up again if she tried.

'It's not as if you're the only one,' said Tom, 'we know all the girls at Meadowlands do it.' Callie instinctively avoided that admission but she didn't contradict him. 'You do it, they do it, Diane did it. No big deal.' And he hated himself for saying it. 'Sounds like an arrangement that suits everyone,' he concluded. 'So why did Diane want to leave?'

'It wasn't them,' Callie protested. 'They treat us alright,' she said and Helen wondered about a reality where a young girl could actually be made to believe that sex with a multitude of strangers was alright. 'It was something else.'

'I know, Callie,' he said, 'we figured that out. We know it wasn't the guys at the taxi rank that Diane told Sandra about. Like you said, it was something else.' Callie eyed him warily as he spoke. 'And, whatever it was, it was enough for Sandra to close the door on Diane's room and sit with her all night while they talked about it. You told us they were both really upset in the morning and a little while after that Diane left for London and Sandra disappeared.' He gave Callie a moment to take that in. 'So what was it, Callie? The big secret Diane told Sandra,' he reached inside his jacket pocket and took out his wallet, 'the reason she ran away?' Tom took out the fifty pounds and handed it to her. She took it, folded it and stuffed the money in her jeans pocket but her eyes never left his hands, as he began to count the remaining notes from his wallet. 'Ten . . . twenty . . . thirty,' he began.

'What's that?'

'More money. Forty . . . fifty.'

'What for?'

'Sixty . . . seventy . . . eighty . . .'

'What do you want for it?' And she glanced at Helen. 'I don't do girls,' she told him, 'if that's what . . .'

'That's not what we want, Callie, and you know it. This is

347

easy money . . . the easiest you'll ever make . . . Ninety . . . a hundred . . . there.' He concluded by stacking the money in a neat pile and holding it out for her. She reached for it greedily but he pulled it away. 'It's yours, Callie,' he told her, 'the moment you tell us the little secret you've been keeping all this time. I know you know what I mean. I can see it in your eyes.'

There was a silence that seemed to stretch while Callie weighed up the risks in complying with him.

'We had a problem,' revealed Callie, 'with one of the bosses.'

'What kind of problem?' asked Helen.

'Which boss?' asked Tom at the same time.

'I don't know his name.'

'What does he do, Callie?' asked Helen, but the girl seemed to struggle to say it aloud.

'Does he mess with the girls?' asked Tom bluntly and Callie nodded.

'And you say he's one of the bosses?' Callie nodded again.

'Does he work at Meadowlands?' asked Helen.

'No,' she said.

'For social services then?' said Tom and she simply shrugged. 'Or the council?' He probed further. 'Is he a politician,' he offered as an alternative, 'a policeman or a gangster?'

'I dunno what he does,' Callie told him, 'but he's one of the bosses.' And they realised she used the phrase generically to denote anyone in authority. 'He's high up, you know.'

'And you don't even know his name?'

'No, I don't. He never uses it.'

'I suppose he wouldn't,' admitted Tom.

'But he comes down all the time.'

'Callie,' asked Helen carefully, 'if you don't know this man's name and you don't know what he does, how do you know he's one of the high-up people?'

'Because,' said Callie with irrefutable logic, 'he does what he likes and no one ever stops him.'

'Okay,' said Tom, 'you don't know his name, but presumably you could identify him?'

'Course,' she said, 'but there's no point, is there?'

'Why?' asked Helen.

'No one would believe me.' She said this as if it was obvious.

'What if I said *we* believe you Callie? What if we showed you some photos,' asked Tom and the girl eyed him cautiously, 'and we kept your name right out of this? All you'd have to do is point him out then you'd get your money.' He could tell this idea appealed to her. 'How does that sound?'

There was another long silence.

'Maybe,' she said.

They dropped Callie back on the street not far from Meadowlands then drove away

'You didn't really believe that,' Helen asked once they were alone, 'did you?'

'Believe what?'

'That what the girls are doing with those older men is no big deal?'

'Christ, Helen, how could you ask me that?'

'I'm sorry,' she said immediately, 'it was just . . .'

'I was trying to get her to talk,' said Tom, 'and she did.'

'I really am sorry. I am struggling with this whole thing.'

'What's happening is terrible and we will stop it,' he said, 'but first we have to identify this *boss* who has been abusing the girls at Meadowlands. If we do that, maybe we can bring this all out in the open and then they will have to do something about it. Can you get some photographs of Joe Lynch, Jimmy McCree and Alan Camfield from the newsroom?'

'I think so, yes.'

'Bring a couple of other photographs too,' he instructed her, 'of people who have nothing to do with politics or social services.'

'Why?'

'Because if Callie picks them out, we'll know she's lying.'

Chapter Forty-Two

'There's a message for you,' DC Malone told Bradshaw before he even took his jacket off, 'from a Sergeant Hennessey.'

'Really?' Bradshaw wondered if the message from the time-serving waste of space was to inform him that Hennessey had made a complaint against him. 'What does he want?'

'He said they brought a guy in earlier who'll be of interest to you.'

The man in the cell looked like he had been run over by a Transit van. His face was battered and horribly swollen and as Bradshaw slid the shutter back over the slot in the door the man next to him spoke: 'And before you say anything,' the duty officer told him, 'he looked like that when we brought him in.'

'I never doubted it,' said Bradshaw. 'Who is he?'

'Name's Colin Avery.'

'Tell me what happened.'

'The funniest thing.' The duty officer was trying not to laugh now but the more he kept his voice down so the prisoner could not hear him behind the locked cell door, the more he struggled to keep the mirth from it. 'He's stalked a woman down on some land near Shaggers' Alley, which is why Hennessey said it would interest you. She's been exercising down there, jogging and whatnot. She's about five feet nothing and weighs around seven stone in her bare feet but it turns out she's only got a black belt in karate. He goes up to her, pulls out his percy and starts playing with it right in front of her, but instead of being scared of this pervert she ran at him and she kicked chummy in there right in the balls.' He was laughing uncontrollably now. 'But she didn't just leave it at that . . .' He was fighting to get his breath now. 'She's only gone to town on him . . . That little lass gave him an absolute twatting . . .' And his voice went up several octaves as he wiped the tears from his eyes. 'There's not an inch of him that hasn't got a bruise on it. If a passer-by hadn't come along at that point and suggested she call the police, we'd have probably found his body down there . . .' He made a gasping noise then as he finally managed to bring himself under control. 'We honestly don't know what to do: give her a medal or charge her with grievous bodily harm. I mean, you can't exactly describe *that* as reasonable force,' and he pointed back to the cell which contained the bruised man. 'I have never seen anyone happier to be taken into custody.'

'Has a doctor seen him?' asked Bradshaw, not wishing to question the guy if he had sustained serious injuries.

'Yeah, he'll be fine,' said the duty officer. 'He's got bruises on his bruises but amazingly nothing's broken, though I doubt his percy's still working properly.'

'Thought he might have been released,' said Bradshaw, 'with a caution, for what he did?' He was surprised the man was still in custody.

'He might well have been,' the officer turned serious all of a sudden, 'but we found something in the boot of his car.'

'What did you find?'

'A bag,' said the duty officer simply, 'and you wouldn't believe what was inside it.'

*

'Duct tape . . .' said Bradshaw in a loud and clear voice that seemed to echo and the detained man flinched '. . . hand-cuffs . . .' He let that sink in as he walked round the interview room, circling the table and chair occupied by the balding, chubby man with the vivid bruises covering him. 'A bala-clava . . .' He altered his tone to make it appear as if he was saying that last word with great sadness, as if there was nothing now that he could do for the man. 'And . . .' he was saving the most damning part till last. '. . . an enormous knife.'

Bradshaw stopped walking. 'That's at least ten years right there,' Bradshaw told him, 'even if you don't say another word.'

'But I didn't do anything.' The man's voice was weak, snotty and whiney.

'You didn't do anything?' said Bradshaw. 'You whipped your penis out in broad daylight and started masturbating in front of an innocent woman and you say you didn't do anything?'

'I couldn't help it,' the man whined, 'but I didn't do any-thing with the stuff.'

'The "stuff"?' queried Bradshaw. 'Oh, you mean the highly incriminating items you assembled that could only be used for a robbery or a rape?' Bradshaw bent low so that his face was opposite the man's and their eyes were level. 'I'm assuming the latter. And you say you didn't do anything?'

'I never . . .' the man began but he soon broke down into snivelling tears.

'You never what? Used them? Doesn't matter. The fact that you have them in your possession is enough to prove intent, as is the way you tried to assault a woman . . .'

'I didn't assault her,' he protested weakly.

'Only because she gave you the kicking of your sad and lonely life.' Bradshaw laughed grimly. 'I have to say, Colin, you can't half pick them.'

'I wouldn't have hurt her.'

'No, course not, you just wanted to play with that pathetic thing of yours right in front of her. Normally I might have believed that was all you were capable of, but the items in your car tell me otherwise. I reckon you had something bigger in mind and it involved taking a woman. I think you've been fantasising about this for a while, building up to it for a long time. I think you lost control out there and deviated from your original plan, which was to find the right woman and kidnap her. That's ten years too, by the way,' the man looked even more alarmed, 'at least.'

'I can't go to prison. I can't. I'll die in there.'

'Possibly,' he told the terrified man, 'or maybe someone will protect you, make you their *boy*.' Avery was so scared by that suggestion he had to swiftly bring his own legs together.

'Don't you dare piss on this floor,' Bradshaw ordered. 'Now, you might not have used the items in your bag before but I'll bet you've done lots of other stuff. It's not your first time down Sha— down Lonely Lane, is it,' he corrected himself just in time, 'so if you cop for everything you have done I will tell the judge personally that you cooperated with us and made a full confession. If you don't, we'll make this all formal and we'll charge with you with every rape or attempted rape committed down there in the past five years.'

Now the man was almost hysterical and he began to weep. 'I'm not a rapist.'

'Maybe not,' admitted Bradshaw, 'but you want to be. That much is obvious.'

'It's like you said,' he wailed, 'it's all just a fantasy.' Snot was dripping from his nose now. 'I'd never have done anything, honest I wouldn't,' and Bradshaw had never seen a man look so weak and broken all at once. This pathetic, podgy guy was probably not capable of anything more than publicly playing with himself but Bradshaw wasn't going to let him off the hook that easily. He had to be sure.

'How many women have you groped down there, Colin?'

'None,' and he shook his head violently, 'honest.'

'How many have you tried to rape?'

'I haven't tried to rape anybody.' The words were distorted by his sobbing.

'How many have you actually raped then?'

'None. You have to believe me.'

'No, I don't,' Bradshaw told him, 'I don't have to believe you at all and no one else will.'

'I never raped anybody.' His body was heaving now with the sobs, so every few words he had to take a huge breath to keep going. 'I've never . . . raped a woman . . . I've never *had* a woman.'

'What?'

'I'm . . . a . . . virgin.' Colin Avery broke down then and sobbed uncontrollably.

As Bradshaw watched the man he began to wonder if he had ever seen such a pathetic specimen, but they'd search his home anyway just to be sure. They'd take his photograph and show it to every woman who'd been groped or chased within a five-mile radius of Lonely Lane to see if anybody recognised him, but Bradshaw guessed they would not. He probably lived in a complete fantasy world and there would likely be no physical evidence linking him to any earlier crimes. The most they were going to get here would be possession of a deadly weapon and gross indecency, and the massive beating he took would probably lessen his sentence. The pervert would probably walk free. He might even be awarded compensation. Bradshaw decided Colin Avery deserved to suffer a little more first.

'I reckon I can put you in the frame for at least three rapes,' and then almost as an afterthought he said, 'and one murder.'

The man suddenly stopped sobbing then and looked up into Bradshaw's eyes. 'That wasn't me.'

'What wasn't?' Bradshaw was immediately attentive now.

'The woman who was killed,' said Avery firmly. 'I was there, but it wasn't me.'

'You were there?' Bradshaw was incredulous now. 'What do you mean you were there? What have you done, Colin? Tell me now.'

Avery nodded his head firmly. 'I was watching her from behind the bushes. I saw it but it wasn't me.'

'Who were you watching?'

'That woman who was killed; I saw her sitting in her car. She had the window wound down and she was smoking a cigarette. She looked lovely, so I watched her.'

'What did she look like?' Avery described Rebecca Holt but he could have got that from any tabloid newspaper. Then Avery accurately described the clothes she was wearing that day and the way she'd tied back her hair, which meant he *was* telling the truth.

'What happened then, Colin,' urged Bradshaw. 'What did you do?'

'Nothing! I was just looking that's all.'

'Then what did you see?'

'If I tell you, will you promise I won't go to prison?' He begged, 'You've got to promise!'

Bradshaw leaned closer to the weeping man. 'If you don't tell me everything you know right now, I'll make sure the judge gives you another three years for perverting the course of justice.' Avery looked terrified, so Bradshaw softened his tone. 'If you tell me the truth it will help you, Colin. I'll tell everyone you were a good little boy who cooperated but if you are bullshitting me or I find out you were responsible for this—'

'No, no, it wasn't me. I didn't have the power then but she did.'

'What do you mean, you didn't have the power?' asked Bradshaw. 'You mean the victim did?'

'No, not her,' Avery assured him, 'the woman . . . the other woman . . . the one with the hammer . . . she had the power . . . and she used it . . . I saw her.'

Chapter Forty-Three

'Is he a credible witness?' asked Tom when Bradshaw had recounted the story of Colin Avery's confession. They were at Tom's house again but this time it was fish and chips that sustained them after a long day and the smell of vinegar filled the room as they hungrily ate the food off their laps.

'Well . . . if I'm entirely honest . . . no.' He ate a chip. 'I'm not sure how credible a man like that could possibly be in front of a judge or jury, assuming this ever went to any kind of trial, which is highly unlikely. We arrested Colin Avery down Lonely Lane. At best, he's a perverted fantasist, at worst a clear danger to women. A lawyer would say the whole thing is a hallucination or he is making it up, in return for some kind of deal. I have to say I haven't entirely ruled out that possibility myself, though he's so pathetic I doubt he would have the balls to try and con us.'

'So he is never going to get anywhere near a witness box,' agreed Helen, 'but do you believe him?'

'I'm not convinced I do,' said Bradshaw, 'but I'm far from sure that I don't. Who knows what he actually saw, but when he described the woman who attacked Rebecca Holt it could easily have been Annie Bell.'

'Her photo was in the papers a lot back then,' observed Tom. 'He could have seen her and he would remember the case.'

'I don't think he even reads the newspapers. He looks to

be in his own little world,' said Bradshaw, 'and he knew what Rebecca was wearing that day, which was something we never reported.'

'Even if we believe his account of what happened, it isn't going to be enough to overturn a conviction against Richard Bell or to charge Annie,' observed Helen, 'so how can we use this?'

'The problem is the credibility of the witness,' said Tom, 'or lack of it, right?'

'Yes,' agreed Bradshaw.

'But Annie Bell doesn't know that,' he glanced at Helen, 'which is where you come in.'

Before Helen could ask Tom what he meant, Bradshaw interrupted. 'There's something else,' he told them. 'I looked into that demo car for you. I reckoned Annie might have parked it by the cinema the night before because she wouldn't have time to get two cars down there in the morning,' he reasoned. 'I then figured if she had to drop the kids at school first she probably couldn't get back to it till half nine at the earliest.'

Bradshaw handed Tom a yellow envelope containing some official-looking documentation, which Tom scrutinised. 'Ian, you clever bugger.'

'What has he done?' asked Helen.

Tom grinned. 'Only gone and cracked it,' he told her.

When Tom Carney approached Annie's favourite bench in the park at lunch time the next day, she did not seem happy to see him. 'I hope this is urgent,' she told him as she put her sandwiches to one side.

'It is,' he said and he sat down beside her, waiting until a harassed-looking young mother wheeling a sleeping infant in a buggy had passed them before telling her, simply, 'You were seen, Annie.'

'Seen?'

'That day.'

'What do you mean?'

'The police have a new witness, someone credible. He has told the police he saw a woman walking away from Rebecca Holt's car after she was beaten to death.' He handed her the latest edition of Helen's newspaper. 'The paper doesn't have it all yet but they soon will.'

Annie Bell took the newspaper and read the headline, 'New witness in Lonely Lane murder'. She fell silent and Tom waited while she read the article. Down by the lake an old man shuffled along, one hand gripping his walking stick, his other wrapped tightly round a brown paper bag filled with bread for the ducks.

Helen had done a good job, fashioning an intriguing, if slightly exaggerated news story out of very little. Without naming names, she wrote that a police source (Tom) had revealed to her that police (Bradshaw) were treating a confidential new witness testimony (Colin Avery) as credible. This had shone new light on the case and cast a shadow of doubt over the guilt of Richard Bell. There was even the possibility the case could be reopened, she claimed optimistically. A woman had been seen near the scene of the crime and police were about to appeal for her to come forward to help them with their new enquiries.

Tom realised that all of this would be news to Durham Constabulary, who might not be too pleased with Helen Norton, but it was the only way to frighten the truth out of Annie Bell. He had to get her to admit it somehow.

Annie Bell showed no emotion as she read the story, but

Tom knew her mind had to have been in turmoil. He needed to take advantage of that before she could regain her composure. Annie was devouring the words in front of her, which had been deliberately written in a manner that would cause her maximum alarm. Helen had played her part brilliantly. In a just a few hundred words she spelled out Annie Bell's worst nightmare.

'What witness?' she said without conviction. 'What woman? This sounds like rubbish to me. It's someone trying to get attention.'

'He even described the clothes you were wearing, Annie: dark jogging bottoms and a tracksuit top with a baseball cap. I'm pretty sure he was close enough to pick you out at an ID parade.'

'What are you talking about?' She looked worried. 'Who is this witness and why has he not come forward before?'

'I don't have his name but my source in the police tells me he's married and was meeting someone he shouldn't have been down there. He was terrified if he came forward he would have to appear in court and it would cost him his marriage.'

'Then why would he . . .' Annie's face was a picture of confusion.

'Come forward now? Divorced see, unluckily for you. Him and his missus have gone their separate ways so he doesn't have anything to lose any more, except for one thing?'

'What?'

'It's been eating away at him for more than two years, knowing that an innocent man is rotting in prison for a crime he didn't commit. He never thought Richard would go down for the killing but when he did our man figured he'd get into even more trouble because he didn't come forward sooner. But he rang the police anonymously and they told him it's never too late to do the right thing. They've promised not to take action against him if he tells the truth and that's exactly what he has done.'

'I don't know why he would claim all of this, but it is rubbish. If he saw a woman down there it most certainly wasn't me. I have an alibi,' she reminded him.

'Not any more, I'm afraid,' Tom said calmly. 'You see, I looked into that and I found the exit from the cinema and the car park where the demo car was waiting for you. That's why it wasn't listed in your ledger.'

'What?'

'And something happened today that changed everything,' he told her. 'I think, with my help, the police will soon be able to reopen the investigation into Rebecca's Holt's murder.'

'What do you mean?' She was trying to sound casual, but failing. 'What happened?'

'I found out about the parking ticket.' Tom watched her closely for he could tell she was terrified.

'What parking ticket?' Annie was screwing up her face, trying hard to look baffled.

'You're overdoing it, Annie,' he said, 'the acting. You're not very good at it. You know exactly what I mean: the parking ticket on the demo. You see, at first I assumed you got up early that day and went for your morning jog then collected the demo from some location close by and drove it into town. I figured you parked it up behind the cinema and bought a ticket for the car park before returning home, probably on a bus. Then you took the kids to school in your own car, parked it in the car park at the other end of town – but then I thought otherwise.'

'I'm lost.' And she shook her head as if all of this was fantasy. 'You've completely lost me.'

Tom ignored this and continued. He was taking the credit for Ian's detective work for a reason. 'I figured that might be tricky first thing in the morning so maybe you dropped the demo at the car park the night before. You couldn't buy a ticket until the next morning after you dropped the kids at school but you didn't care about that. No one knew you had the car anyway. You could gamble without any consequences. The attendant came to the car park early that day and issued a ticket for your demo but that didn't matter.

'When I checked your demo log there was one car signed out every day that week apart from the days around Rebecca Holt's murder. I memorised the reg number then went to the department responsible for the collection of fines. Lo and behold, I discovered a VW with the exact same registration number had been parked in the car park behind the cinema without a ticket that very morning. Technically the car belonged to the manufacturer so that's who they eventually contacted for payment but, as much as they want to sell cars to you, Annie, they are not going to pay your parking fines, so they got in touch with you and the fine was promptly paid. Strangely enough however, it wasn't paid by your company or even one of your company car drivers.'

'Wasn't it?' Annie asked in a dead voice.

Tom shook his head. 'No. There's a neat black and white photocopy in the file. It shows a cheque hastily written by a Mrs Annie Bell.' She looked as if someone had punched her then. 'I guess you thought no one would ever find out about that, eh? You figured it would be buried in a file somewhere

363

for years. Well, it was,' he told her, 'for two years, to be exact, until I found it. That's all the proof I need, Annie.'

'It proves nothing!' But her voice was wavering.

'It proves my theory that you slipped out of the cinema through the fire exit then headed for the car park and the second car. I'm assuming you went straight to it before you did anything else that morning, so you could buy a ticket for the vehicle you'd already left there, but you didn't realise the council had privatised the enforcement. A man had already taken a note of your registration number and started the process of sending you a fixed penalty.'

'I'm not even going to answer you,' she said, 'this is such rubbish. I don't even . . .' She shook her head in disbelief.

'You don't have to answer me, Annie. You could just tell it all to the police. They're the ones who will demand answers and you won't be able to explain why you had a second car in town that day. *If* I give it to them, they'll reopen the case for sure,' he said, 'because they'll know the only reason you would need two cars is so you could use one of them to create an alibi and the other to drive out to meet Rebecca Holt and murder her.'

'If?' she asked him.

'What?'

'You said *if* you give it to them – not *when*.'

'Did I?' he asked innocently.

'What do you want, Mr Carney?' Annie's eyes narrowed and she asked, 'Are you recording this conversation, Tom?'

'No.'

She insisted on checking him anyway. He unzipped his jacket, raised his arms and stood there compliantly while she patted his torso and checked his pockets.

'Happy?' Her answer was to sit back down and he joined her.

'So what are you selling, Tom?' she asked. 'You're obviously selling something.'

'Maybe I'm buying,' he told her. 'I'd like to buy your story but I don't know enough of it yet.'

'I don't have a story,' she told him.

'That's a shame,' he said. 'I guess I'll never know why you did it then.'

'Did what?'

'Killed Rebecca Holt. I mean, it's obvious on one level. She was screwing your husband. I wouldn't say that was reason enough to murder her myself but you aren't the first person to lose your mind over an extramarital affair and you certainly won't be the last; but I was hoping you'd have a bit more to you than that.'

'I really don't know what you mean,' she said stiffly.

'I told you the police have a witness. There's also a discredited expert witness, a motive and an alibi that's been totally demolished thanks to a parking ticket that puts you where you needed to be to get at Rebecca Holt. The only thing I really lack is a reason. If I had one of those, I might be able to find it in my heart to understand why you did it. You see, I have a problem, Annie. You were right about me. I am sick of my life. I don't like shuffling from one low-paid assignment to the next. I'm getting too bloody old for that. I could do with a little bit of comfort and that job you told me about sounded pretty good to me but I'm not sure I could work for someone who can kill another human being without a damn good reason.' When she failed to answer him, he added, 'But if you did have a reason?'

'What?'

'Maybe I'd forget to show the police that parking fine. It might easily slip my mind. What's the point in telling them? I mean, it's not going to bring Rebecca Holt back, is it? She's dead and that's that. Maybe she deserved it and perhaps your husband deserves what he got too? Who knows?' he asked. 'And that's my point, really.'

'What are you talking about?'

'I'm saying I can be bought, Annie, but not cheaply. I need a reason to come over to you, something I can live with to convince myself you're not just a bunny boiler. In short, I want your side of the story or we part company now and I turn everything I've got over to the police.'

'You've got it all wrong, Tom. You've joined up some dots but together they don't make any sense and . . .'

He got to his feet before she could finish. 'Enough,' he told her. 'I'm not wasting any more of my time. I thought we understood each other. I'm willing to understand, Annie, or at least to attempt to see it from your perspective, but if you're not even going to try . . .' Tom started to walk away.

He was yards from the bench before he realised the bluff had failed. He'd just played his last card and Annie Bell had trumped it. He would need more than a parking ticket and the testimony of a pervert to prove she had killed Rebecca Holt. Tom was so frustrated he wanted to scream at the top of his voice right there in the park and then, suddenly, he heard Annie Bell's voice behind him, loud, clear but wavering.

'Wait!' she called.

Tom turned slowly back to her then, hoping the truth might finally be waiting for him.

Chapter Forty-Four

Tom walked back and sat down next to Annie on the bench then waited for her to begin. When she eventually spoke her voice was flat. She had finally given up.

'Men are stupid,' Annie informed him quietly. 'They think we don't know, but we always know. They come home then head straight for the shower because they say they got sweaty in the office but they're really trying to wash away the traces of her, whoever *she* happens to be. They say they're late because they've been to the gym or the tennis club but when they throw their sports gear into the washing machine, you go and take a closer look and find it's bone dry.'

Tom stared silently ahead, not moving, barely breathing, because he didn't want to do anything to break the spell. Annie continued to speak in a quiet voice with no discernible emotion as if she was in a trance and the words poured from her.

'So you know, you always know, you just don't know who, not at first, which is why you follow him. You take one of the pool cars and no one notices because there are always new demos coming in and it's your job to try them all anyway. You park it round a corner and you wait until he comes out of that business lunch, the one that finishes early but later he will tell you, in just a bit too much detail, how it dragged on and on because Nick wanted to brag about his new nine iron or Andrew was sleazing over his young PA. You just want to tell him to shut up and stop lying, because you were there.

You saw him leave early and you followed him so you know where he's been and *exactly* what he has been doing.

'You follow him at a distance because women are discreet and you don't want him to see you but you wonder whether he would even notice if you were tailgating him. Eventually he turns off the main road and takes a narrow lane off the beaten track, but you don't follow him down there. That would be too obvious. Instead you park further down on the other side of the road and you wait to see what happens.'

He noticed she was using the word *you* not *I*, distancing herself from her own story.

'Then another car comes along not five minutes after your husband and you wonder what the odds are of that happening. People only go down that track for one reason. Teenagers go there at night to snog and grope one another, though I never did,' she sounded regretful at that, 'but they aren't married and it's their business what they get up to. You only care about your husband and who he's with, but you don't see clearly. The sun reflected off the windscreen so you couldn't make out the other driver but you know it's a woman. You know it's *the* woman. So you wait.'

Annie paused momentarily as if she was remembering how that felt.

'You wait for more than an hour and it eats you up inside because you know what he is doing with her there; you can't help but imagine them together and it breaks your heart, just breaks it.' Tears started to form in her eyes but she angrily brushed them away. 'Finally your husband's car emerges and this time the other car is right behind it. They didn't even wait. They weren't even careful because they thought they were so bloody clever and nobody could ever work out what they were up to. Your husband's car turns right but you don't follow him. You're more interested in the other driver so, when she turns left, you pull your car round and go after her. You follow her for miles, nearly crashing your car on a roundabout because you're so desperate to keep her in your sights. You're waiting for her to stop so you can get a good look at this woman who has been fucking your husband in a car in broad daylight just minutes earlier and you wonder what kind of person she is. Is she single or married, younger than him or the same age; you're pretty damn certain she won't be any older. You think about what she's got that he craves so badly he's willing to risk everything for it.' Then she sighed in a resigned way, 'You already know she's more beautiful.'

She stopped talking then but Tom waited for her to continue. 'Then, at last, she pulls over at a supermarket. You're certain she hasn't noticed you, so you park just a short way from her car. She's taking her time. Maybe she's spraying something on herself to disguise the smell of sex and you find yourself wondering whose car they did it in, his or hers.

'Then finally she's climbing out of her car and you almost duck down but you can't take your eyes off her because you're desperate to know what she looks like. You needn't worry. She's oblivious to the fact you are just a few cars away from her and you get a good long look. She *is* beautiful, of course she is. She's young too and has money for clothes and you're willing to bet the car is all hers, even if she didn't pay for it herself. Somehow you can see right into her and you know she's a clever, cunning, manipulative, ruthless woman who is used to getting what she wants and will happily use each man she meets as a stepping stone to the next one. The reality of it hits you like a punch in the stomach. This isn't some waitress or chambermaid your husband is screwing. This woman is going to take everything from you,' Annie closed her eyes, 'you know that, you just know it.' Then she opened them again and her face bore a determined look. 'Unless you stop her.'

Annie's speech halted then and Tom realised he would have to prompt her to get at the truth.

'So what did you do?'

'I wanted to meet her on the way out of the supermarket. I wanted to grab her and pull her down and smash her pretty face,' said Annie, 'but instead I went home, lay on the bed, cried for a while, then I pulled myself together before the kids came home.'

'Did you say anything to him that night?'

'No, I just listened as he told me all about his day, while I contemplated sticking a kitchen knife between his shoulder blades.'

'But you started to plan?' He was coaxing the story from her, little by little.

'Not then. I felt dead inside at first.' And she exhaled. 'It was a while before I hated him enough to start planning anything.'

'Why didn't you just divorce him?' Tom asked, though he knew the answer already.

'And let him take half of everything? Why should I let him leave and become rich at our expense? Why should we pay him hundreds of thousands of pounds he never earned and damage the company irreparably?'

'Did you think about killing him?'

'Every day for a while,' she admitted. 'Didn't think I'd get away with that. Finally, I started to imagine a way to destroy them. I'd kill her and make it look like he'd done it. Then I'd be rid of them both.'

She'd finally admitted the truth. Tom felt a combination of shock and relief. Even though he had already convinced himself of her guilt it was still incredible to hear it from Annie's own mouth after all of her denials. 'How did you get her to go out there?' Tom had never been able to imagine a way for Annie to lure Rebecca to her death.

'The same way he did.'

'The dead-letter drop?'

'Yes.'

'How did you know about that?'

'I followed him again.'

'And you saw him leave a letter under the stone in the wall?'

'I only saw him park up and get out then head up that little lane but I didn't understand because it doesn't lead anywhere. I drove past him then circled back and when I reached the spot he was already coming out again, so I knew he couldn't have been meeting someone there. When he was gone, I went down the lane myself. I didn't even know what I was looking for and I found nothing that time but I realised the spot was overlooked by Picket Copse. We used to play there when I was a kid.' Annie seemed almost wistful, lost in that memory for a moment. 'I went down there the next day and watched from the copse. I invented meetings so I could catch him out. Then I saw him put a note in the wall.'

She needed a moment then before she could continue. The memory was too raw, even now.

'And that's how you found out where they were meeting and when?'

'Not just that,' she said bitterly, 'they wrote love letters to one another when they couldn't meet. I read their correspondence for two months but there wasn't much love in them. You should have seen the things they wrote about me. They were both so cruel. She said I was fat and looked like a man. I didn't deserve Richard because I didn't have a warm bone in my body and was incapable of real love. She told the father of my children that and he didn't even contradict her.

'He told her I was frigid and he had never loved me, not really. He said he only stayed with me for the sake of the children. I was his biggest regret. He told her he knew he had made a terrible mistake on our wedding day but he went ahead with it anyway. He'd been trapped with me ever since. I don't think you can imagine how that felt.' She sounded at breaking point.

'No, I can't.' And, even though he now knew she must be a killer, for the first time Tom felt sorry for Annie Bell.

'Then she started to persuade him to leave me and soon that was all they ever talked about. If only they could leave us all behind: her jealous, controlling husband, his ugly, frigid wife. If only they could be together forever. I hated her then,' Annie explained. 'I hated him and at first I wanted to die. Then, later, I wanted them both dead instead.'

'But then you had a better idea?' She nodded slowly. 'Kill her and put him in the frame for the murder.'

'That seemed fairer,' she said, 'they both got what they deserved.'

'How did you get her to meet you out there?'

'It was staggeringly easy,' she said. 'I practised his hand-writing and I wrote her a note. I waited till he went down there in the morning and switched his note for mine; same location, just a different day and time. I brought their meeting forward.'

'And you faked the note from the waitress too?'

'Yes,' she admitted, 'I knew something had happened between them from the way she treated him when we ate a meal there. She was rude; dismissive in a way she wouldn't have been with a normal customer and he pretended not to notice. I got her name from her badge then chose a simple, legible hand and gambled she hadn't written to him before. I asked him to go and see her while I was meeting that woman and he fell for it.'

'What did you write?'

'The waitress told him she was pregnant,' she said. 'She was going to tell everyone it was his. I knew that would work. Even if he was convinced it couldn't have been his baby he'd still want to go down there and shut her up or buy her off. I didn't even need her address. I just told him to meet her at her flat.'

'And when he turned up there was no one there.'

'She'd already left the country. I was at the club the week before and I heard one of the barmaids there telling the other she'd gone to Thailand and I thought, this is it, the final piece. Richard will try and claim that a girl who'd already gone abroad asked him for a meeting at her old flat. He'd look like an idiot and a very bad liar.'

'What if he kept the note?' asked Tom.

'She didn't write it,' Annie reminded him, 'so it wouldn't be much of an alibi, would it? The police would think he'd written it. I wore gloves so the only prints they'd find would be his. Anyway,' she said, 'I knew he wouldn't keep it. He'd be too worried in case his frigid wife found it.'

'So he took the bait and drove down there but nobody saw him.'

'Her old flat was empty and he wasn't going to hang

around in case anyone saw him. He still thinks it was some kind of malicious joke by her because he wouldn't see her again. That's how much of an ego my husband has.'

'And you went to meet Rebecca Holt.'

'Yes.'

'How did you get right up to her car without her spotting you?'

'I changed in the demo car. I wore a tracksuit and running shoes, with a baseball cap and my hair tied back. I put sunglasses on. I hardly recognised myself in the rear-view mirror. I parked up some way from the lane then ran to the spot. There was no one around. I had the hammer hidden in the sleeve of my tracksuit top. I thought I'd have to tap on the glass to get her to wind the window down so I could pretend to ask her something but it was already open because she was smoking. It was so easy,' she marvelled. 'I just let the hammer slip into my hand and I hit her hard,' she made a chopping motion with her hand to show Tom the angle, 'right in the middle of that beautiful face.

'She screamed,' said Annie. 'I think she knew straight away that she was done. I hit her again and I just kept on hitting her. She tried to get out of the car and managed to get the door open but she was trapped by her seat belt. I bashed her across the head then . . . I just . . . kept . . . hitting her,' Annie Bell's teeth were gritted now as she relived the moment in her mind, 'until it was over and she was gone.'

'When the police came you acted like Richard was an innocent man who couldn't possibly have committed such a terrible crime?'

'Well, he was,' Annie said, almost gloating, 'and what better way to avoid suspicion than by forgiving your husband and standing by him?'

'That expert witness must have been a godsend,' he observed.

'He was a miracle,' said Annie, looking grateful.

'Why stand by Richard all this time though?' asked Tom. 'Why not just divorce him now he's inside?'

'After standing by him so publicly, I can't do that,' she said, 'not yet. Even Richard would be suspicious. Eventually maybe, when even he would understand that I cannot wait forever. Then I might ask him for a divorce, on my terms. No judge would award a jailed killer half of his poor wife's estate but I'm in no hurry. It's not as if I want to go down that road again.'

'What road?'

'Marriage,' and she added, 'I get more control this way.'

'I assume it's your idea for him to carry on maintaining his innocence so he never qualifies for parole.'

'He thinks it was his idea, but I planted it. I don't ever want him to be free. How could I allow a man like that to play a part in my daughters' lives? He'll never see them again.'

But it's okay for your children to be brought up by a murderer, thought Tom. Her hypocrisy was staggering.

'He might get out eventually,' he said.

'They will be adults by then and it will be too late.'

'It seems like you thought of everything,' said Tom. 'It was very clever, Annie.' He said it like he was congratulating her on a job well done.

'Yes,' she said, 'I'm so clever I married a man who never loved me,' she looked down at her feet then, 'not even on our wedding day.' When her head came back up she turned to Tom. 'Why was I not enough for him?' she demanded, her fists balled in frustration. 'I did everything for Richard. When I met him he was a mess. I saved him. I got him back on his feet, I convinced my father to employ him then make him Sales Director, even to cut him some slack when he began to lose interest in the business. I married him and gave him two beautiful daughters,' the tears began again then, 'why was that not enough?' She stared at Tom as if he knew the answer and was hiding it from her. 'Why isn't that enough for any man?' she pleaded.

'I don't know, Annie.'

Annie Bell did not speak again for some time. Finally she asked, 'What happens now?'

'I don't know,' he said again. 'What do you want to happen, Annie? Should I forget everything you just told me and let you carry on like before? Should we leave your husband in prison for another twenty years, not realising his own wife put him there? Should we let Rebecca Holt's real murderer evade justice?'

'Justice,' she scoffed, 'there's no such thing as justice. Not in this life.' Then she reminded him, 'You told me you'd hear me out. I gave you my reasons, now tell me what you intend to do.'

'Not now, Annie,' said Tom and he got to his feet, 'I need to think.'

'I'll deny it,' she said, 'every damn word I just said, I'll deny it.'

Tom looked down at her then and realised that whatever state she had been in as she recounted her incredible tale, the old Annie had now returned. She was strong, unyielding and very firmly in control just as she had been on the day she beat Rebecca Holt to death.

'I know you will.'

Chapter Forty-Five

Ian Bradshaw had been badgering his counterparts at Northumbria Police for some time. He had called them and written to them twice in an effort to formalise his request but no one had been able to help him.

The photograph of Sandra Jarvis taken from the CCTV camera at Newcastle Central Station had been lost somehow and no one seemed able to find it. A conspiracy theorist might have seen this as proof that someone was attempting to sabotage their investigation but Bradshaw knew the most likely cause was human error or general incompetence.

He had given up asking for a response long before the brown envelope with the Newcastle postmark finally landed on his desk; so much so that he had no idea what it was at first. He opened it to find a compliments slip and a copy of the photograph in question, for someone had finally been able to locate it after all.

He regarded the photograph closely then said, 'Bugger me.'

Tom sat back in his chair, picked up the local paper and examined the front page while he drank his coffee. This was the newspaper he had worked on for six years before moving to London for a short-lived, eventful spell working on a tabloid, which opened up a whole new world of trouble that eventually led him in a full circle back to his home county. That was less than three years ago but it felt like a lifetime. He had been through a great deal since then.

Frank Jarvis was pictured on the front page of the *Durham Messenger* that morning. He had told Tom he was going to attend the opening of the new community centre, even though it was not on his patch and he'd had nothing to do with its development. Jarvis hoped to hijack the local journalist and get him to run another piece on Sandra and it seemed he had succeeded.

Jarvis looked out from the front page under the words, 'Politician appeals for help with hunt for missing daughter'. Tom was a journalist, not an editor, but he knew a crap headline when he saw one. It sounded as if Sandra Jarvis had gone shopping for a few hours and not come home in time for tea. It was typical Malcolm. Tom's former editor had not lost his ability to neuter stories, transforming them into bland accounts of local mishaps. He doubted this would prompt anyone to come forward.

Tom folded the paper in half and dropped it onto the table, leaving Frank Jarvis's face to stare forlornly up at him while he finished his coffee.

He hadn't heard from Annie Bell since their meeting in the park. Tom had thought long and hard about his next move. He considered the nation's legal system, its complex bureaucracy and the way it had of dragging on for years while men and women suffered in the meantime. He went over the evidence he had amassed against Annie Bell and what her lawyers might do with it. He considered the ways in which they would rebuff each point while questioning the validity of everything he had found and his motives for doing so, considering he was on the family's payroll.

Only when he had gone through all of that over and over again did he finally drive out to her home.

*

'We need to talk,' Tom told her when she opened the door.

'What do you want? Have you made up your mind?'

'Yes, Annie, and I'm giving you a chance,' he told her, 'the best chance you're going to get.'

Before Annie could answer, a cry of, 'Mum!' came from the back garden and Annie reacted to it by turning away and letting him follow her through the house. As he had expected, it was a large home with smart, expensive furniture. When they reached the garden it seemed to stretch on endlessly, with three separate areas of lawn, trees, bushes, flower beds and separate play areas for the kids.

'What is it?' Annie asked.

'Holly's biting,' the younger child said, looking on the verge of tears. At first Tom thought she meant the older girl, who was using a swing on a second patch of lawn, then he saw a Labrador that was scampering around trying to jump up and bite the older girl's feet as she swung back and forth.

'Stop that, Holly!' shouted Annie and the dog immediately complied, slinking away to the far end of the enormous garden. It seemed even dogs did what they were told when Annie Bell did the telling.

When the children were calm she led him back inside.

'Go on,' she told him.

'Go to the police,' he said, 'and ask for a detective, Ian Bradshaw. He knows all about the Rebecca Holt case. It won't take long.'

'What won't?'

'Your confession.'

Her breath came out in a rush then and her voice was high but defiant. 'No one will believe it was me,' she told him, 'I can explain the fine for the car.'

'No, you can't, Annie,' he told her, 'and I know it all now. You told me yourself. I know everything you did.'

'I told you because you wanted to understand. You wanted to work for me.'

'I lied, Annie. People do that; just like you lied about the job. You created it and offered it to me to buy me off.'

'I offered it to you because I thought you were different, but I see now that you are no better than all of the other journalist scum I've had to deal with. Whatever you claim I told you, I will deny every word. I'll say it's all fantasy and none of it is true. My husband killed Rebecca Holt. He has been tried and convicted and that's the end of the matter.'

'Except I have your full confession,' he told her. 'I recorded it.'

There was a moment's pause. 'You're lying,' she said.

'No, Annie.'

'You weren't wearing a wire,' she reminded him. 'I checked. I searched you,'

'You're right, Annie,' he said, 'I wasn't wearing a wire, but I got up nice and early that day and went to a little shop I know in the city. I bought something very special there, a tiny, voice-activated, electronic device. Then I drove over to the park and went to your favourite spot, long before you got there. I've got it all on tape, Annie, every word, because I bugged the bench we were sitting on.'

Chapter Forty-Six

Tom played her a short extract of their conversation on the park bench but not before assuring her he had more than one copy.

'Please,' she said as she followed him back through the house, 'don't do this. I'm begging you. Think of them!' She pointed back towards the garden. 'They're only little girls. They need their mother. Don't take me away. I'll do anything you say, I'll give you anything you want but don't do this.'

'You're thinking of your children now, Annie,' he said because he was trying not to think of them, 'but you should have done that before you went after Rebecca Holt. You should have considered the lives of your children before you beat that woman to death and sent their own father to prison for her murder.'

'He doesn't deserve them and they don't deserve a father like him!' Annie screamed.

Tom realised it had been a very bad idea to visit Annie Bell at home. He'd hoped it would be a calmer environment than the office, but the presence of her children seemed to make Annie more desperate. He did not want to hear any more of Annie Bell's protestations so he left as quickly as he could, but she followed him out into the street and began shouting at him as he climbed into the car.

'What would you have done,' she demanded, 'if you were me, what would you have done? The same thing!' she told him. 'The exact same thing!' She slammed her hand on the bonnet in frustration.

'No, Annie,' he told her through the open window of the car, 'I wouldn't. Not everyone is a murderer.' He drove away leaving her shouting in the street.

Tom knew he could do no more now. Annie had been given the facts; only she could interpret them and make her next move. He had fenced her in and left her with only one viable option: phone Ian Bradshaw, tell him the full story and throw herself on everybody's mercy, including her husband's. Would she go through with it or would she force Tom to turn over everything to the police and get them to reluctantly pursue her over a previously *solved* case, while hiring herself the best lawyer money could buy? All he could do now was wait and learn whether Annie Bell had the nerve to see this through.

The next morning get-together at the Rosewood café was dominated by talk of Annie Bell and speculation around what she would do next. It had been almost twenty-four hours and Bradshaw had received no phone call from her.

'I could just arrest her,' he reminded them.

'Then she would hire a solicitor and find out your star witness is a pervert. Let's wait a little longer,' the journalist told him. 'Annie is under a lot of pressure right now and she might just crack.'

Then Bradshaw told them, 'I finally got a copy of the photograph of Sandra Jarvis from the CCTV at Central Station.'

'Great.'

'Maybe not,' said Bradshaw.

'Why not?' Bradshaw handed him the Manila envelope containing the photograph.

Tom slid the photo from the envelope and peered at it. '*This* is Sandra Jarvis?' he asked.

'Yep,' said Bradshaw, 'according to her case file.'

'But . . .' Tom began '. . . it's not Sandra Jarvis.'

'Exactly,' agreed Bradshaw, 'or at least it *might* be her, but it could be practically anybody.'

Helen took the photograph from Tom's hands and looked at it. 'You mean someone spent hours going through CCTV footage and they found this,' she said, 'then they categorically stated that it's Sandra Jarvis?'

'Yes,' agreed Bradshaw and Helen glanced once again at the blurred image of a young blonde woman. Nobody could have convincingly stated it was Sandra. The image was too distorted by distance and the deep grain on the photograph for it to be recognisable.

'But that's ridiculous,' she said. 'Who could have done this and why?'

'Someone corrupt,' said Tom because he realised immediately what must have happened, 'in Northumbria Police who wanted everybody to think Sandra Jarvis got on a train that day and left Newcastle when she didn't. In fact,' he added, 'she may never have left the city at all.'

Annie Bell dressed in a dark suit that morning, but she didn't go into her office. She arrived mid-morning at an office block in town where she was well known. The woman on the reception desk welcomed her warmly and Annie told her she was there for one of her regular meetings with her firm's tax advisor. Other than the woman who asked her to sign into the building when she arrived there was no further barrier between the outside world and the lifts that rose to a number of floors housing different accountancy firms, which was one of the reasons Annie had chosen the site.

Annie Bell signed the entry register while exchanging banal

pleasantries with the receptionist about the weather. She then thanked her and headed for the elevator. The tax advisor was on the third floor, but Annie rode the lift all the way up to the twelfth. She then got out and walked past a number of desks manned by people working for an accountancy firm she had never used. Hardly any of them even bothered to look up but it wouldn't have mattered if they had, because Annie looked like she belonged there and wouldn't have aroused suspicion.

When Annie reached the far end of the room she went through an exit door and found what she was looking for: the long metal staircase that acted as a fire escape. She took the staircase up one more level, pushed hard on the metal bar of the emergency exit door until it swung open, then stepped out onto the roof. The fire alarm immediately went off but she paid it no attention. Instead she walked to the very edge of the building and stopped, then looked down at the concrete surface of the road far below her. Then she took out her mobile phone and dialled a number.

Annie waited as the phone rang and rang. Eventually she was connected to someone on the switchboard. 'I'd like to speak to Detective Sergeant Ian Bradshaw,' she said.

'Please hold.' The phone rang again, three times, and then a male voice came on the line.

'Bradshaw.'

Ian Bradshaw did not say another word during that conversation. Instead, he listened to Annie, who spoke as if she had given a lot of thought to her words before calling him. She told him her name, her whereabouts and her intentions and who she blamed for them. Then she told him to come alone and hung up without giving him the opportunity to respond. As soon as he realised she was gone, Bradshaw raced for the door.

*

When Bradshaw reached the site, a flustered woman greeted him. She was standing to one side of a large group of employees from the office block who had all been evacuated to muster points at various corners of the car park. In the background a fire alarm was ringing incessantly. 'Who called you?' she asked when he showed her his warrant card. 'I was about to phone you. We only just saw her . . .' And she pointed to the figure high up on the roof. Bradshaw couldn't make her out clearly but it had to be Annie Bell. She appeared to be sitting on the edge of the building, legs hanging over the side. 'She told me she had a meeting with her tax advisor,' the woman babbled. 'She's been here before, loads of times. I never thought—'

'It's okay.' Bradshaw held up a hand to calm her then looked back up at Annie. 'Please just tell me how to get to her.'

When Bradshaw entered the building the alarm was still blaring and he had to endure its noise as he hurriedly climbed twelve flights of stairs, eventually arriving breathless at the top and emerging through the opened fire exit door. He hadn't been on the roof of a building since the day his former partner had gone straight through a skylight and broken his back. Detective Constable Alan Carter would never walk again. Never keen on heights, Ian Bradshaw's fear of them had magnified that day.

Now, as he strode across the top of the twelve-storey office building, a bitter northern wind swirled around him. Bradshaw knew the drop from this flat roof had to be over a hundred feet onto merciless concrete below and he had the beginnings of what he preferred to regard as a heightened state of anxiety, as this was something he might be able to control. It made his heart race, affected his ability to breathe normally and created an illogical certainty he was about to drop down dead at any moment. His doctor referred to these spells as 'panic attacks', but Bradshaw didn't like the word panic.

He could see Annie up ahead and wondered if he had done the right thing. He could have ignored Annie's order and mobilised police, ambulance and fire services then sent them to the spot instead of coming on his own, but something told him that would only serve to send Annie Bell quite literally over the edge.

Annie was sitting very calmly, straight-backed, her head up, facing forward. From a distance you might have imagined she was enjoying the view of the city, if it were not for the fact her legs were dangling over the edge and one strong gust of wind would be capable of sending her to her death.

Bradshaw didn't want to think about that. He tried to approach her soundlessly but the roof was covered in a loose gravel surface. She must have heard his tread, for she turned and glanced calmly at him, which had the effect of sliding her even further towards the edge. For a moment Bradshaw thought she was about to jump but she placed a palm on the edge to steady herself.

'You're Bradshaw?' she asked and he nodded, as if the act of speaking might be enough to convince her to jump. 'He asked me to call you,' she said, 'so I did, but not for the reason he imagined. I want you to witness this and tell everyone about it. You can tell Tom this is all his fault,' she announced calmly, 'him and my stupid, selfish husband. I wouldn't be here if it wasn't for them. Richard broke my heart and now Tom Carney is leaving me with no choice.' Annie deliberately slid further towards the edge, using her hands to prevent herself from toppling over the side. They both knew if Bradshaw tried to grab her now she could just let go and her own bodyweight would take her over.

'Annie, don't move,' he told her and he took the tiniest step towards her, intent on narrowing the gap between them. 'You do still have a choice.'

'If you come closer,' she said, 'I'll go now,' and she tensed as if she was about to push herself off.

'Okay,' Bradshaw said, holding up a hand, 'no further,' and he took half a step back. Bradshaw had no plan beyond an attempt to talk Annie Bell down or at least try and delay the woman long enough for her to reconsider. She had called him, but she could have just launched herself from the roof before anyone realised she was up here. Perhaps Annie Bell wanted to be talked out of this. Maybe there was half a chance he could still save her life.

'I realise you can't see a way out just now, Annie, but it doesn't have to end like this. No one is going to like what you did but they may just understand it. If you explain it, they will listen. Think of your children and their futures. Think about what you are leaving behind. Dying isn't the answer.' Bradshaw was close enough to the edge to see the ground far below them and it made him feel sick and dizzy. 'And dying like this is hard.'

'I *am* thinking of my children,' she turned to look at him, 'that's all I'm thinking about and it's why I'm here.' Then she turned back so that she faced away from him and closed her eyes. 'And dying is easy,' she said quietly, 'anyone can do it.'

Annie Bell let go of the ledge, put her arms up and her head back, shut her eyes, slid from the edge and was gone.

'No!' Bradshaw's shout was instinctive and the outstretched hand grasping at the air between them was a useless reflex action, but Annie Bell was already on her way down. By the time Ian Bradshaw reached the edge of the building and peered helplessly over, she'd already hit the concrete.

Chapter Forty-Seven

Tom Carney needed a drink, badly. He'd had several by the time Ian Bradshaw joined them in the pub. His eyes looked a little wild, thought Bradshaw, but he couldn't really blame the guy. This wasn't the way it was supposed to pan out. They had engineered a way to box Annie in and had hoped to resolve everything when she saw no way out. They had entertained images of Richard Bell being freed from captivity while Annie confessed. It wasn't meant to end like this.

Bradshaw managed to get hold of Helen at the newspaper and quickly told her what had happened. It was left to Helen to break the news to Tom. They had gone to the pub to wait for Bradshaw to complete a mountain of paperwork before he could meet them there.

The two of them listened silently while Ian Bradshaw gave them the details: 'Annie Bell calmly walked into an office block, took a lift to the highest floor then climbed a staircase, pushed open a fire exit door, stepped out onto the roof then phoned me on her mobile phone. She sat down on the edge of the building, waited for my arrival so she could say a few last words then launched herself off the edge.'

'Oh my God,' said Helen and sat down heavily, 'did she do this because of us?'

'Because of me, you mean?' snapped Tom and he took a big swig of his drink. 'You're saying it's my fault she killed herself?'

'No.'

'I think that is exactly what you're saying. Do you imagine

I'm not asking myself that too? But what was I supposed to do? We decided to bring her to justice.'

'Yes but is this justice?' asked Helen.

'In the old-fashioned sense it probably is.'

'You don't really believe that,' protested Helen. 'She threw herself off a building.'

'We didn't make her do it.'

'Didn't we?'

'She killed someone, Helen. She planned it meticulously, then carried it out. Annie Bell was guilty of premeditated murder and she couldn't face prison, so she killed herself. That's a choice she made, not us.' To Helen, it sounded as if he was trying to convince himself not her. 'And it's a choice her husband was denied. He's stuck there now, doing life, which is the way she wanted it.'

'Don't you think he is in any way culpable?' she asked.

'No, I don't!' Tom was angry now. 'He cheated on her, so what? No biggie. Rebecca Holt cheated on her old man too, so that's four unhappy people stuck in two crap marriages. They should have all just gone their separate ways, but instead one woman decided to murder another. I'm surprised your sympathy lies with the one wielding the hammer, not the one who had her skull bashed in. Rebecca could have had another fifty years if Annie had just hired a solicitor and divorced her husband instead of hunting her down.'

'My sympathies are with both women. Rebecca Holt didn't deserve what happened to her, but neither did Annie.'

'You're saying he drove her to it, is that it? That it's still down to Richard Bell that his wife murdered his lover. I might have known all this would be the bloke's fault.'

Helen knew he had been drinking but she wasn't going to let that go unchallenged. 'I'm not saying that! It wasn't all his fault, but you seem to think he was blameless! You think Annie Bell should have just calmly announced she was divorcing him and got on with her life like nothing happened? She spent ten years with him and they had two children. How do you think she felt when she found out what was going on behind her back?'

'We know how she felt,' he reminded her, 'and what it made her do.'

'I don't even know why we're arguing,' she said, sounding incredibly weary all of a sudden, 'since we're on the same side.'

'Are we?' He sounded hurt then.

'Of course,' she said, 'and we both agree it's a tragedy.'

'Did Annie Bell mention me?' asked Tom suddenly.

Bradshaw looked at him. 'When?'

'On the roof.'

'I don't think I want to try and recollect everything Annie Bell said before she . . .' He left the sentence unfinished.

'She didn't leave a note?'

'They haven't found one at her home or office. She left the kids with her father, kissed them goodbye like there was nothing out of ordinary and . . .'

'Threw herself off a building.' Tom took another swig of his drink. 'So who did she blame before she jumped?'

'Why would she blame anyone but herself?'

'No reason,' said Tom sharply, 'apart from the fact I secretly recorded her confession and threatened her with a life sentence in prison. She was doing just fine till I happened along.'

Bradshaw's mind was racing and he wanted to buy himself a little time.

'So,' said Tom, 'what did she say before she did it? She must have said something.'

'It was mostly keep back and don't come any closer.'

'That all she said?'

'I was attempting to talk her down,' answered Bradshaw, 'trying to get her to see sense,' and he sighed. 'I feel guilty too, if it's any consolation.'

'What have you got to feel guilty about?'

'I should have called in a professional instead of going it alone. I made a half-arsed attempt to talk a woman out of suicide and she chucked herself off a roof. Whatever I said, it didn't work.'

'Your job isn't to talk people out of suicide.'

'Sometimes it is, Tom,' said Bradshaw firmly, 'I have colleagues who've managed it, but I couldn't.'

'Maybe Annie Bell just didn't see any way back, Ian? I don't think it would have made any difference what you said – a woman like that wasn't going to accept prison and I should have seen it. I was too busy trying to get her husband out of jail to realise she was never going to take his place.'

'An innocent man was rotting in jail before you stepped in. It's not your fault she couldn't accept the consequences of her actions.'

Tom wouldn't let it go. 'But Annie thought killing Rebecca Holt was fair. Someone had stolen her toys and she wanted them back, so Rebecca had to go, but whose fault was it? Certainly not Annie's, I'm betting. She wouldn't blame herself.'

'No, she didn't. The woman was crazy though, wasn't she; at least enough to smash someone's skull in, so what difference does it make what she said?'

'Because I need to know!' Tom thumped his fist down on the table, hard. 'So would you please stop stalling and give me a straight answer for once?'

Bradshaw straightened. 'She did apportion blame.' He saw how intently Tom Carney was watching him then. 'To her husband,' he said. 'It was all his fault apparently, for cheating on her, I assume. Richard was the reason she was up there on that roof, according to Annie.' And that was exactly what Bradshaw had put in his statement. He hadn't lied about that exactly, just omitted Annie Bell's mention of Tom. He had been the only one to hear it and now Annie was dead, so what good could possibly come from including it? What purpose would it serve to blame the young reporter for her death?

'Was that all?' asked Tom. 'What about me?'

Bradshaw realised Tom Carney needed to know the truth. He wanted to hear that Annie Bell blamed him for everything so he could satisfy his own suspicions. Only then could he hope to try and take some sense of responsibility for her actions; for the pressure he had placed Annie under in an effort to exonerate her husband, who may have been guilty of many things, but was innocent of murder. He needed to hear it was his fault, so he could add this to the list of things he'd pretend not to give a shit about; even though he was half drunk already. A suicidal woman had blamed him for making her children motherless. He wanted to argue with the ghost of Annie Bell in his head, tell her he was only doing his job and that it was her fault for killing Rebecca.

Bradshaw knew it wasn't that simple. He had once been exonerated for an act he blamed himself for but, deep down, he still wondered every day what would have happened if only he had done things differently. That thought still tortured him and would until his dying day. But Tom Carney was his friend. He wanted to hear the unvarnished truth and there was no disputing he had the right to it.

'Well?' asked Tom.

'I'm sorry to be the one to break the news to you, mate,' Bradshaw said, 'but you didn't even get a mention.'

Chapter Forty-Eight

You only get one life. That was what he told Annie Bell before she jumped, but she wouldn't listen. He believed it though. Ian Bradshaw was not a religious man. He didn't expect to come out the other side and be ushered up to the pearly gates. He was more pragmatic than that. When it was over it was over, so you had better have made the most of it in the meantime.

Watching Annie Bell go off the side of that building affected him deeply. What must have been going through that woman's mind to compel her to go over the edge like that? Every time he thought about it made him feel physically sick. Though he had not had as many drinks as Tom, he'd sunk enough. He was drunk and knew it, but also somehow clear-headed.

He was sitting at home on the couch when he heard the key turn in the lock. It was Karen back from the gym. 'What's up, babe?' she asked when she saw him sitting there.

'I need to talk to you,' he told her and his face showed Karen he was serious.

'What's happened?' She was next to him then, looking concerned for his well-being, but he couldn't allow himself to be distracted from his purpose.

'Nothing.' He was dismissive. 'It doesn't matter.'

'Then what do you want to talk about?'

'This,' he said and she looked around the room for a clue. 'What?'

'This,' he said. 'Us.' And when she still seemed confused, 'You and me.' Reluctantly he admitted it. 'I don't want *this*.'

Tom was hammered. Helen knew it and so did he. 'Whoops,' he said as he tripped on the doorstep and fell down on his knees in the hallway. 'Sorry.' He staggered to his feet and into the front room then virtually fell onto the couch. 'I'll be fine here,' he slurred, so at least he spared her having to share a bed with him in this state.

'Are you okay?' Helen had drunk a lot more than usual and Ian had matched her, but Tom had drunk twice as fast as them both that day.

'You think I'm a bad person.' His voice was thick with the effect of the alcohol and he was forced to enunciate his words slowly and carefully to avoid slurring them too much.

'No, Tom, I don't,' she assured him, 'I really don't.'

'I didn't mean to kill her,' he said and a part of her heart broke for him then.

'You didn't kill her,' Helen told him firmly, 'she killed herself. Annie couldn't live with what she had done. I feel bad about it too but she is responsible for it, not us.' She picked up a cushion and popped it behind his head and let him fall gratefully back onto it.

'Thanks,' he said and he looked incredibly tired. Simultaneously he closed his eyes and reached out his hand to take hers in it. 'Love you,' Tom said softly, then he immediately fell asleep.

Helen blinked at the sleeping figure below her and wondered if she had heard him correctly. Did he just say . . . ?

'Love you too,' she told him quietly, knowing he couldn't hear her.

*

Bradshaw hadn't necessarily intended it to be a break-up conversation or a break-up row, which is what it very swiftly became. He just wanted to slow things right down and not go straight to the moving-in-together option before they'd had more time, but it soon became clear that, in Karen's eyes, this was make-or-break, love-me-or-leave-me. To his surprise, Bradshaw actually felt quite good about that.

He wasn't enjoying the argument though and he hated to see her so upset. On one level he understood that what he was doing to his girlfriend, who he was already beginning to think of as an ex-girlfriend, was a bad thing. There was nothing nice or particularly noble in giving her the news this way when she wasn't expecting it, but surely it was far better to do this now than years later when they were both trapped.

'Well, thank you very much,' she told him, 'so I make you feel trapped? What am I supposed to do?' she wailed when the argument had been raging for a while. 'I've given notice on my flat! All my stuff is packed up or here already. Where am I supposed to go?'

'Your parents' maybe?' This suggestion just elicited a groan of frustration from her. 'But you can stay here as long as you need to. I'll sleep on the couch,' he added quickly, 'obviously.'

'Don't be bloody stupid!' she shouted. 'I'm going to Mum and Dad's and I'm going there right now, you arsehole!' Bradshaw was mightily relieved to hear that.

She made for the door, then turned back and gave him a withering look.

'If you had doubts you could have told me before,' she bawled at him, 'you fucking coward!'

And Bradshaw had to concede she was absolutely right about that.

'Are you alright?' Helen asked him as she drew back the curtains. Tom winced at the morning sunlight as it streamed through the window, then he groaned.

'God, my head.' He brought a hand up to his forehead. 'How much did I drink?'

'A lot, but that was understandable.'

'I don't remember coming home,' he said and she had to assume he also didn't recall saying 'Love you' either, so it was the drink talking – but did that make it more or less true? She banished that thought before it had time to take hold.

'I'm off to work now but I'll be back later and I'll bring those photographs you asked for.'

Tom managed to sit up. He twisted his face. 'The whole room is spinning.' Then he seemed to register what she had said. 'Don't you think we've done enough damage for one week?'

She rounded on him then. 'No, I do not! Listen to me. I know you are upset about what happened to Annie Bell. Ian is too and so am I, but this is different. We have to help those girls at Meadowlands and that means finding this man and stopping him. So you need to get a shower, make some coffee and sort yourself out, because tonight we are going to find Callie again.'

Tom held up a hand to placate her. 'You're right, I'm sorry. I'm getting up now. I've got things to do too.'

'What kind of things?'

'Well, I have to go and see Richard Bell for starters,' he told her, 'and I'm not exactly looking forward to that.'

*

The governor had already informed Richard Bell of his wife's suicide, so at least Tom wasn't forced to break the news to him. Because she had chosen to throw herself off a tall building in front of a police officer, there was little room for ambiguity. Tom had driven there in a state of high anxiety made worse by the colossal hangover he was enduring. He had been so shocked by Annie's death because, whichever way you looked at things, it was largely due to his actions. The only coping mechanism he could think of at the time was alcoholic oblivion. That was fine yesterday, but now he had a burning stomach, a severe feeling of nausea and a pounding headache that showed no sign of abating.

By the time Tom arrived at HMP Durham, Richard would have had hours to digest the news about Annie, but when he walked into the room it didn't look as if he had been able to accept it.

'I'm very sorry about your wife,' Tom told him.

'What did you say to her?' Bell was ashen-faced and looked like he was in deep shock. Had he taken Tom's apology as some form of acknowledgement of responsibility? 'What did you say to my wife?'

'I told her what I found out, Richard, that's all. I did what you asked me to do,'

'What did you say to her!' He roared the words this time.

'Hey!' shouted the prison guard. 'Calm down, Bell,' he warned but did not take further action, presumably cutting the grieving widower more slack than usual for his loss.

'The truth. I told her the truth. I said to you when you started this that I might uncover something you didn't want to hear.' Tom hesitated while he tried to find the right words but ended up choosing the most direct approach. 'She did it,

Richard. Annie killed Rebecca and I can prove it.' He went on to tell the disbelieving man everything. Bell didn't speak for a while. He just listened but his face was a picture of disbelief.

'I can't accept this.' He shook his head. 'You say you've got all this on tape?' Tom nodded.

'We can use this. I've given my recording to a Detective Sergeant Ian Bradshaw. I'm certain they will reopen your case. I think, Richard, that it could even be enough to get you out of here.'

Surely that would bring the man some comfort.

'Jesus Christ,' mumbled Bell and he began to cry. Tom couldn't tell if it was relief or sadness at first, then Bell mumbled, 'What difference does it make?'

'What difference? I thought this was what you wanted. You'll be freed. You'll see your daughters again . . .'

'And how am I ever going to explain to them their mother killed herself because of me, because of something I did? I don't care anymore. Don't you get it? This is all my fault. Rebecca died because of me. Annie is dead . . . because of me. Oh God.' And he wept once more.

Tom could think of nothing to say to console the man, for he knew exactly how he was feeling. Only Richard Bell's guilt was magnified because he had the deaths of two women on his hands, not just one.

Chapter Forty-Nine

Callie stopped in her tracks when she saw Helen standing in the street up ahead of her. 'I told ya I don't do girls.'

'Please get in, Callie,' urged Helen. 'We can help you, we really can.'

Callie snorted, 'Yeah right.' Whatever had happened since their last conversation, it seemed the girl was having second thoughts about cooperating.

'You want to help us find Diane, don't you? I thought she was your friend.'

'She *is* my friend,' answered Callie firmly.

'Then help us to find her,' said Helen, 'please.'

'Fuck off,' snarled Callie and she began to walk purposefully away from Helen.

'Callie, please don't do this.' Helen had no idea how to stop the girl from going to the cab rank but she was determined to try, so she went after her. 'We both want the same thing. We both want to find your friend.'

'That why you ain't been back since?'

'I'm sorry,' Helen told her, 'we've been looking for her.' She didn't want to reveal the reason they had not been back sooner. Annie's death was too recent, too raw.

Helen drew alongside Callie then and the younger girl stopped. She turned towards the reporter and shouted, 'Fuck . . . off!' then started walking again. She'd barely gone three yards before the car moved off and pulled in next to her.

Tom leaned out of the window and in a loud and aggressive tone called, 'Callie!' She spun round to face him. 'Get in the car!' And when she hesitated for a second, 'Do you want to earn this money, or what?'

Without another word Callie went to the car, opened the back door and climbed in. Helen followed and Tom drove them away.

'What do you want from me?' Callie asked them. 'I told her before I don't do . . .'

'Shut up, Callie,' Tom ordered her, 'just shut up,' and she fell silent. He was angry and tired and was gambling that poor Callie was used to being told what to do by men. He felt bad about that and knew Helen, the voice of his conscience, would probably give him a hard time afterwards, but she had tried to reason with Callie and it simply hadn't worked. 'We told you, we just want you to look at some photos then pick out the man you told us about,'

'Oh,' she said, looking nervous now, 'him.'

'No one will ever know it was you. We won't need you to do anything except point at a picture and say, "That's him." It'll be the easiest money you ever earned.'

They took Callie into the front room of Tom's house and sat her down. Helen took the file from her bag and drew out the photographs she had brought with her. She now understood why Tom had wanted to bring the girl back here to his home, away from the taxi rank and Meadowlands; places filled with threatening figures who would view what she was about to do as treachery. Now that Callie was in his home, she felt safer. Helen could sense it.

She knew there was a strong chance that Callie would

identify Jimmy McCree, Joe Lynch or even Alan Camfield. If she really opened up about the abuse going on at Meadowlands they had agreed to phone Ian Bradshaw, who could immediately take Callie into protective custody.

Helen spoke to Callie before letting her see the photographs: 'I want you to take a look at these men, Callie. I want you to tell me if any of them have ever . . .' she hesitated for a moment while she chose the right words '. . . been with you or hurt you in any way? I want you to tell me if the man who hurt your friend Diane is here. Will you do that for me?'

'Okay,' said Callie, who did at least appear to be taking this seriously.

Helen realised she was holding her breath as she removed the first photograph from the file and placed it face up on Callie's lap. The first image was Alan Camfield.

Callie leaned forward, took her time examining the photograph then said, 'No,' and she shook her head, 'not him.'

Both Helen and Tom were watching her, searching for any sign she might be lying or was simply too scared to implicate anyone, but neither of them detected any hint of evasion from Callie.

Helen placed the second photograph face up on Callie's knee. This time it was a stranger Helen had fished from the newspaper's photographic archive, a head-and-shoulders shot of someone who had been awarded the MBE for services to charity. Callie shook her head, so Helen withdrew the photograph and produced another.

The hard face of Jimmy McCree stared up at young Callie but the girl didn't flinch. She just shook her head. 'No, I never seen him.'

Helen and Tom exchanged glances before Helen showed Callie a fourth photograph. It showed the smiling face of a local fireman in civilian clothes and Callie immediately said, 'Never seen him before either.'

Helen reached for the last photograph and placed it in Callie's lap. The sly face of Councillor Joe Lynch looked out at them from the picture. Callie leaned even further forward now and stared at the face intently. Both Helen and Tom held their breaths.

'No,' she said simply, 'it ain't him neither.'

'You're sure?' asked Helen disbelievingly.

'Don't you know who that is?' demanded Tom with a stern enough tone to ensure that Callie took a second look. Perhaps she thought he was about to deny her the money.

She took a long hard look and confirmed the worst of their fears: 'No, it's not him. Definitely not. I'd know the guy who hurts us anywhere.' And when neither Helen nor Tom could think of anything to say at that she protested loudly, 'I would!'

'Alright, Callie,' Tom held up a weary hand, 'we believe you.' And he looked at Helen in disbelief. He did believe the girl, but all of their theories involving McCree, Camfield and Lynch were wrong. He knew Helen was thinking the same thing. *Where the hell could they go from here?*

'What now?' asked Helen helplessly.

'I don't know.' Tom sounded desolate. He slumped back into his chair and closed his eyes. 'Get her home, I suppose.' *If you could call it home*, he thought.

'It's late,' Helen said to Callie, 'we'd better get you back.'

'Dean won't care,' said Callie, 'as long as I'm earning,' and she looked at Tom significantly. He reached for his wallet and handed her the money she'd been promised.

'You can tell Dean it's from your usual contacts,' he said.

'I'll tell him what I like,' she said firmly. She stuffed it in a pocket then got to her feet and stood there impatiently.

Helen and Tom took longer to rise, for they were both devastated. Tom had been convinced that Diane's flight from Meadowlands was linked to the disappearance of Sandra Jarvis and that, in turn, Joe Lynch's connection to Meadowlands and his friendship with McCree and Camfield must have played a part here. He'd been convinced they had somehow used Frank Jarvis's daughter to get what they needed.

Tom fumbled in the wrong pocket for his car keys then found them in the next pocket. He fished them out, just as Callie spoke.

'That's him!' she said firmly. '*That* is definitely him.' She was staring down at the coffee table where Helen had placed the photographs.

Tom immediately felt a surge of anger towards Callie, for she was obviously messing them around now. She'd already had a long look at the photographs then denied any of the men were responsible. Now, moments later, she claimed it was one of them.

'Come off it, Callie, we're not bloody stupid,' he told her.

'It's him!' She was animated now.

'You just said it wasn't any of them,' Helen answered sharply. She was even beginning to think there might be some truth in what Dean had said about not being able to trust a word these vulnerable girls said.

'I'm telling you, *that's* him!' She pointed down at the table and was so angry now that Tom paused.

'Who,' he demanded, 'which one of them?'

His aggressive tone seemed to aggravate her. 'It's none of *them*!' she shouted. 'It's *him*!'

Tom and Helen followed the direction of Callie's finger and both of them realised the truth at exactly the same time.

Callie was not pointing at any of the photographs but at something else close by, the folded copy of the local paper Tom had left there that morning. Looking up at them from a half section of the front page was the picture of Councillor Frank Jarvis appealing for information on his missing daughter. 'He's the one!' shrieked Callie.

She grabbed the paper, turned it towards them, jabbed a finger into Frank Jarvis's face and said, 'That's him!'

Chapter Fifty

'Callie,' asked Tom, 'are you absolutely sure about this?' but he could tell by the look in her eyes she was certain. 'Do you know who that man is?'

'He's one of the bosses I've been telling you about. He gives Freak Boy money to let him in,' she explained. 'He's been doing it for years, since before I was there.'

Tom and Helen looked at one another in disbelief then they glanced back at Callie.

'You're certain it's this man?' demanded Tom.

'Yes.'

'And he makes you do things?' asked Helen.

'Yeah,' Callie said quietly, 's'pose.'

'You suppose?' questioned Tom, gently. 'He either makes you do things or he doesn't, Callie?'

'He makes us do stuff! If we do what he wants he says we're *good little girls* but it ain't like we've got a choice. We can't say no.'

Tom sat back down heavily then, with a sick feeling in the pit of his stomach. Helen took the newspaper from Callie's hand and stared at the image of Frank Jarvis on its front page. She sat down on the sofa, leaving Callie as the only one still standing. She looked at the two reporters with confusion now.

'I did what you said,' she reminded them. 'I told you what you wanted to know!' Callie couldn't understand why they were reacting this way. 'This is what you wanted to hear,' she protested, but she did not how wrong she was about that.

'What the hell are we going to do now?' asked Helen when the enormity of Callie's accusation had finally sunk in.

'I don't know.' Tom was reeling from the realisation that, if Callie was telling the truth, he'd been working for a child rapist.

He tried to tell himself the possibility still remained that Callie was wrong or maybe she'd been got at. Was this all a plot by Joe Lynch and Jimmy McCree to discredit their former nemesis? But even as he was thinking this he had to ask himself, why they would even bother? Frank Jarvis had already stepped down and given up his opposition to the Riverside tender. The clincher for Tom was Callie herself, who was entirely believable. No way could she have faked this.

Then Tom remembered how Sandra Jarvis had spent the whole night locked away with Diane Turner, emerging the next morning looking upset and emotional. Tom had always had an instinct that this was the reason for Sandra's disappearance. He believed Diane must have confided a big and damaging secret to Sandra. Only now did he finally realise what that secret was. Diane had told Sandra about the powerful man who'd been abusing her, not realising that all the while she was doing this, she was describing Sandra's own father to her.

If Sandra believed Diane Turner, this would surely be enough to drive a once-happy, high-achieving young girl into despair and send her off the rails. Small wonder there were missed lectures, erratic behaviour and whispers of drug abuse – but there were no drugs, only the truth about her father.

It must have been too much to take on board at first, and

she did nothing. Then, when she had taken some time to decide what to do about Diane's allegations she must have finally confronted her father, which led to the row between them at the allotment.

Diane Turner could have not have realised she was telling Sandra about her own father because Sandra used her mother's maiden name at Meadowlands, so nobody realised she was the politician's daughter. Tom froze then and looked closely at Callie.

'What?' she asked.

'You said you didn't know his name. The guy in the newspaper, the one who abused you.'

'I didn't,' Callie said. 'I don't.'

'Did Diane know his name?'

'No. I said. He never used it.'

'Then how could she have told Sandra who he was?'

'Eh?'

Helen cut in then: 'Do you know who that man is, Callie?'

'I told you,' she snarled, 'no.'

'He's a politician, who's well known in the city government.'

'I said he was one of the bosses.'

Helen looked at Tom to see if he had any objections to her revealing the whole truth to Callie. He nodded.

'He's also Sandra's father,' Helen told the young girl.

'No fucking way!' Callie protested as if she couldn't believe what they were telling her. 'He can't be!'

'He is,' said Tom, 'and we think Diane must have told Sandra when they stayed up all night together – but she couldn't have done that if she didn't know his name.'

'Well she must have shown Sandra . . .' And she stopped herself.

'What?'

Callie shook her head. 'Nothing.'

'What did Diane show Sandra?' Helen asked her.

'I don't know.' But it was obvious Callie was lying.

'A girl like Sandra wouldn't believe her father was guilty of something like this,' Tom said, 'not unless she had proof. So what was the proof, Callie? What did Diane have on Frank Jarvis when she couldn't even tell Sandra his name?'

'Come on, Callie,' Helen urged her. 'If you tell us we can protect you but we need to know the whole story or we can't do anything to help you. How did Diane make Sandra believe?'

'The photograph,' she blurted suddenly, 'she's got a photo of him. She must have shown her that.'

'You've got a photo of Frank Jarvis?' asked Helen.

'We're not stupid,' Callie told them. 'We know no one's going to believe us against one of the bosses. That's why they pick girls like us in the first place. They can do what they like to us. Me and Diane both knew if we told anyone we'd be in even bigger shit, but Diane wanted to run away. She said they'd come after us but not if we had something on them, so I took a picture of him and Diane together.' Callie said that as if it was such a simple thing, like a holiday snap. Helen tried to comprehend a way in which Callie could have taken an incriminating photograph of Frank Jarvis without his knowledge. 'He didn't know about it but she did,' confirmed Callie. 'She asked me to take it. We figured if he ever tried to do anything to us we could tell him about it and he'd back off.'

'You took a photo of Frank Jarvis,' Tom asked in disbelief, 'with your friend?'

'Yeah,' she said, 'while he did it with her.'

'How?' he demanded.

'There's a vent between our rooms.'

He hardly dared to ask the next question. 'Where is this picture? Have you got it, Callie, or did Diane take it with her when she ran away?'

'I haven't got it,' Tom's heart sank, 'but I don't think she could have taken it either. She went in a hurry and left most of her stuff behind.'

'Where is it?' Tom asked her. 'Where's the photograph now, Callie?'

'I'm not sure,' she told him, 'but I think I can get it.'

Chapter Fifty-One

'Detective Sergeant Ian Bradshaw,' he said, holding up his warrant card for the briefest of moments before pocketing it again. 'I'm here to speak to a Miss Callie McQuire.'

'Er.' It wasn't just hesitation Bradshaw saw in Dean's face that morning but alarm. 'I'm not sure if . . .' he mumbled and he looked behind him into the corridor, as if he expected to see Callie standing there. Bradshaw had been well briefed by Helen and Tom and he found himself enjoying the man's panic.

'I know she's here,' Bradshaw told him, 'so please let me in,' then he added a respectful but firm, 'sir.'

'We don't let people in,' Dean said unsurely, 'not without an appointment.'

'I'm not people though, am I? I'm a police officer and your refusal to let me in could lead to a charge of obstruction.'

'Of course, sorry, officer.' Dean stepped to one side to admit the detective. 'Please come in. I have to follow procedures. They get very sensitive, what with all the rules these days on child welfare.'

'I'll bet they do,' said Bradshaw.

'But like you said, you're police so . . . I'll go and get her.'

'I'd rather see her in her room, if that's alright with you?' Bradshaw's tone indicated he would do this whether it was alright with Dean or not.

'Okay,' he said, looking flustered, 'may I ask what this is all about, officer?'

Bradshaw was already marching off down the corridor

while Dean trailed in his wake. 'Down here, is it?' he asked, though he already knew it was because Tom had described the home's layout to him. 'What's your name again, sir?'

'Er . . . Dean.' It came reluctantly. 'Dean Anderton.'

Bradshaw slowed his pace halfway down the corridor then stopped and turned towards his host. 'Dean Anderton?' he said, like he was recollecting something. Dean watched the detective with his mouth open, looking worried, and Bradshaw wondered what he might find if he delved a little deeper into Dean Anderton's past. 'Well, Mr Anderton, I'm assuming these young ladies are all in your care?'

'Yes, they are.'

'In that case, I don't mind telling you that there have been some very serious allegations involving young Callie.'

'Really?' Dean's voice went up several octaves. *He's shitting it*, thought Bradshaw. 'What kind of allegations?'

Bradshaw wanted to say, 'Soliciting, sexual abuse, rape, kidnap, possibly even murder,' but instead he leant in confidingly. 'Theft.'

'Theft?'

'Yes,' confirmed Bradshaw, 'multiple counts from several retailers.'

'Shoplifting?' Dean's relief was tangible.

'You don't sound too concerned.'

'No, of course I'm concerned, it's just, I'm glad it's nothing too bad, you know.'

'What were you expecting? Theft is serious.'

'Of course it is,' said Dean, 'but when you work with vulnerable kids like these you do tend to fear the worst.'

Bradshaw deliberately narrowed his eyes at Dean. 'I'll bet you do, Dean,' he said, 'you must fear that every day. Of course, it's a vocation.'

'Eh?'

'Working here with, as you say, *vulnerable* kids. You must be very dedicated.'

'Well, I do my best,' and with the threat of immediate arrest having been lifted, it was as if Dean was suddenly able to think straight again. 'I'm surprised they sent a DS down here for this. We usually just get a bobby from the local nick if any of the girls step out of line.'

Bradshaw had anticipated this. 'The allegations against Callie are part of a wider, ongoing investigation into a criminal syndicate exploiting young people. Callie's information could be priceless.'

'I see,' said Dean, who was hardly comforted by this admission, and he looked away.

'Which one is it, then?' asked Bradshaw and when Dean looked confused he added, 'Callie's room?'

Dean took Bradshaw to the end of the corridor. Callie was awake and dressed but sprawled lethargically on her bed in jeans and T-shirt.

'There's a police officer here to see you, Callie,' announced Dean, 'so sit up now like a good girl eh?'

Callie obeyed him, but Dean didn't move.

'I'm sure you'll understand that this part is of course confidential, Mr Anderton.'

Dean couldn't resist a last sidelong glance at Callie as he left her room. 'I'll be in my office at the end of the corridor, if you need anything.'

'I'll leave the door open,' Bradshaw said as Dean sloped away. 'I can call if I need you.'

Callie was sitting up now on the edge of her bed, looking groggily at the detective.

'Right then, Callie, I am Detective Sergeant Bradshaw

and I am here to talk to you about some allegations of a criminal nature that have been made against you,' he said and listened for a moment in case there were any sounds that might give away Dean's presence in the corridor. 'I'm sure you are aware that theft is a very serious matter.' Then he heard Dean's door open and close, its hinges squealing. Bradshaw took a step back and leaned out to survey the empty corridor. Now he could talk freely to the girl.

He knew he had to move fast. 'You know why I am here?'

'Ian, is it?' He nodded. 'What we waiting for then?'

'Show me,' he demanded, and she rolled over on the bed and slid her pillows to one side to reveal a metal grille in the wall close to the spot where Callie laid her head each night. Bradshaw realised you could probably hear a lot of what went on in the next room but he couldn't work out how you could see anything, let alone photograph it. Callie snatched a nail file from her bedside cabinet and used the thick end to work at one of the screws on the edge of the panel until it came free. She repeated the exercise until there were four screws on her bed and the grille came away from the wall. She moved out of the way to allow Bradshaw to bend down and take a look.

Behind the grille was a space and on either side of this was a cavity that ran through the wall. Directly in front of him was a second grille that was the twin of the one Callie had removed. There were sizable gaps between the slats for ventilation, which meant Bradshaw had a reasonably uninterrupted view of the next room and its contents, including the bed which, crucially, was set against the far wall. Anyone doing anything there could be easily observed thanks to the gaps between the metal slats on the grille, which would prevent someone on the bed from noticing they were being spied upon.

'I was just messing about one night and I realised the

screws came off if you turned them. I thought it would be a laugh for Di and me to have a chat in the middle of the night.' She looked sad then. 'The other thing was her idea.'

'Taking the photograph, you mean?'

'She asked me to get some proof, so I did.'

'So you took a photograph and this shows . . . ?'

'Him on top of Diane.'

'But Callie,' he asked, 'how the hell did you get a photograph like that developed? Who in the world would process something like that and not immediately phone the police?'

'I didn't,' she said, 'Diane did.' She smiled at his naïvety. 'She took it to the guy who runs a little shop at the end of town. He does all sorts.' Bradshaw knew the kind of place: a store that stays open all hours and does everything from dry cleaning and clothes mending to photocopying documents and taking passport photos. 'She gave him a handy,' said Callie matter-of-factly, and there was his answer. He'd processed a photograph showing the rape of an underage girl and kept it quiet in return for a hand job from that same young girl. Bradshaw made a mental note to reckon with that guy before this was over.

At Bradshaw's urging, Callie screwed the metal grille back in place. By now she had convinced the detective she wasn't making this all up. 'Can we get the picture?'

'I think so.' But she didn't sound certain.

'Come on, we've haven't got long,' he said, 'and grab your bag.' He didn't want anything to delay them.

'If I can get the photo,' she threw the bag on her shoulder, 'you can't leave me here.' The fear in her eyes was genuine.

Callie was right not to trust anyone. Once that photograph was filed as evidence its presence could be leaked; then someone might try and silence Callie.

'Get me the photo and I won't leave here without you,' he promised her, 'but hurry.'

She sprang from her bed and rushed to the door, but paused while she leaned out to check for Dean's presence. When she was satisfied he wasn't there she whispered, 'Come on,' and led Bradshaw into the room next door, which used to be Diane's. They already knew it was empty thanks to the grating, but Bradshaw wanted them to be in and out of there straight away. They couldn't afford to let Dean know about the photograph.

Callie went to a corner of the room and dropped her bag. 'Lift me up,' she said to Ian and angled her head towards a ceiling tile that looked like all of the others.

Bradshaw heard Dean's door squeak open. 'On my shoulders.'

He bent low and the girl clambered on him, then he straightened with her on his shoulders. Wasting no time, she pushed the ceiling tile upwards and it came loose. Callie moved it to one side and reached in. 'I can't feel it,' she said. 'It's not there.' She sounded panicked.

She looked down at him then. 'Move me,' she demanded and he walked in the direction she indicated so she could reach another tile, which she pushed upwards before scrabbling around beyond it once more.

Bradshaw knew Dean would be there any moment and he didn't want the carer to find him standing in the wrong room with a young girl on his shoulders. 'Got it?' he asked.

'No,' she hissed back, 'over there.' She replaced the second tile and waved an arm once more so he could steer her to the opposite corner and another ceiling tile which she pushed up. 'It's not . . .' She didn't need to finish. She clearly couldn't find the photograph. Not for the first time, Bradshaw wondered if she had made the whole thing up. Even if she wasn't lying about the existence of the photograph, it wasn't here now. Someone had taken it. Diane maybe, or perhaps someone else had found the incriminating evidence and destroyed it. He could hear Dean's footsteps coming closer.

'Take me back there,' she demanded and he realised she wanted to try the first ceiling tile again. His first instinct was to say no, particularly when he heard Dean's footsteps draw even closer.

'Be quick then,' he whispered and he let her have one last go at the opening behind the first tile.

There was a knock at a door then and Callie was still scrabbling around above him.

A second knock, firmer this time.

He was about to let her down when she said, 'Got it.' It must have been pushed too far back for her to reach at first.

A door opened then and Callie was still on his shoulders.

She withdrew an envelope and he lowered her to the ground as swiftly as he could without dropping her.

'Callie?' Dean's voice, close by but muffled by a wall and sounding confused. 'What are you up to? Where are you?' Dean was in the wrong room. Naturally he had walked into Callie's room, not Diane's, and this had given them precious seconds to retrieve the photograph. 'Detective?' shouted Dean. 'Where are you?'

'Just a moment,' called Bradshaw as Callie straightened her clothing then he noticed something. 'The bloody tile,' he told Callie desperately when he realised she hadn't put it back properly and there was a noticeable gap in the ceiling.

'Shit,' she hissed.

'With no time to put her on his shoulders, he grabbed Callie round the waist and hoisted her into the air like a ballerina. She stretched out an arm, pushed up the tile then let it fall back snugly into place. Bradshaw dropped Callie back onto her feet just as the door opened.

'What is it now, Mr Anderton?' asked Bradshaw irritably. Then he realised Callie had dropped the envelope on the bed when she replaced the tile and it was still sitting there. He prayed Dean wouldn't notice.

'What are you doing in here?' demanded Dean. 'You can't just walk into another girl's room like this.'

'I can if I have reason to believe a crime has been committed,' Bradshaw told him. 'Don't think for one moment that Callie is the only girl involved in this.'

'Fuck off,' sneered Callie. 'I told you I ain't done nothing.'

'Callie,' warned Dean.

'Right that's it,' Bradshaw said, as if his patience had finally deserted him. 'Callie McQuire, I am arresting you on suspicion of theft.'

'What?' she cried in protest, playing her part. 'You can't do that!'

'No,' said Dean, 'you can't.' He seemed very sure of that all of a sudden, which troubled Bradshaw.

'And why not?' the detective demanded.

'Because I phoned Northumbria Police and they have no record of a detective Ian Bradshaw.' He eyed Bradshaw contemptuously.

'Well they wouldn't, Mr Anderton. I'm with Durham Constabulary. Did I not make that clear to you? Do you wish to see my ID again?' He took out his warrant card and pressed it close to Dean's face. 'Now is that all, or perhaps you'd like to come along as well to assist me with my enquiries?'

'No,' said Dean in a very small voice.

'Okay then,' he turned back to the girl, 'let's get this over with, Callie.'

'This is a fucking joke!' shouted Callie. 'You can't do this. You've no right!'

'I have every right, now move it!' He guided them both towards the door, ensuring Dean went through it first and, as he did so, he used Callie's exit to scoop up the photograph and tuck it under his jacket before leaving, then he marched her off down the corridor.

As they left the building, Bradshaw made a point of holding on to her arm and steering her towards the back seat of his car. He opened the door then pressed down on her shoulder, so it looked as if she was being coerced into the vehicle. He climbed into the front seat, then started the engine. Bradshaw glanced back at the care home and saw that Dean, as he expected, was watching from a window.

'Oscar winner or what?' asked Carrie exuberantly.

'Sorry?'

'We totally fooled Freak Boy. Good, wasn't I?'

'Exceptional,' he told her as he drove away.

He bought Callie a can of Coke and some crisps then took her to the interview room. He didn't tell any of his colleagues why she was there. He let her eat the crisps while they waited for Helen and Tom to arrive. Once she was settled, he picked up the envelope and withdrew the photograph and looked at it.

When Callie finally spoke, he almost started, for he had forgotten she was in the room with him by then. 'Told you,' she said matter-of-factly.

'Yes,' he said, 'you did,' and he slid the photo back into the envelope. 'Do you have any other photographs?' asked Bradshaw, not that he needed further proof.

Callie rummaged eagerly in her bag and handed him a

yellow envelope with a Kodak logo on it. She must have misunderstood him. When he opened the envelope, all that was revealed was a handful of snaps featuring Callie goofing around in town; sometimes on her own, but on occasions with another girl. Bradshaw didn't bother to tell her he meant other photos of the Councillor. She was watching him intently so he skimmed through them dutifully, taking the time to look at each one. If you didn't know anything about Callie's life or what she had been through you might have imagined she was a normal fifteen-year-old girl hanging out with ordinary friends just like thousands of others her age, but Bradshaw knew she had already been abused by countless men. It was heartbreaking.

'This your friend?' he asked as he came upon a photograph of the two girls sitting on a wall together and laughing.

'That's me and Di.'

A thought struck him then. 'When did Diane disappear?'

'She didn't disappear,' and he regretted using the word, 'I get cards from her.'

'Cards?' He recalled Tom mentioning something about this.

'Postcards,' she said, 'from London.'

'Okay,' he said, 'so when did you last see her?'

'The day before she left.'

'Did she tell you she was going to leave?'

'She told me loads of times she was going to London.' Callie was evasive. 'I'm going too, when I'm sixteen.'

'But did she tell you she was about to leave that day?'

Callie hesitated for a moment. 'No,' she said and he could tell this admission hurt her for she would have expected Diane to confide her plans to her best friend. 'As soon as she had the chance to get away from Freak Boy she went. She had to go when she could.' Callie was defending her friend's actions but he suspected she was also justifying them in her own eyes. 'That's why she sends me the postcards,' Callie said, 'so I know she's okay and she's waiting for me. As soon as she tells me where to meet her, I'm gone, out of there.'

'And when exactly did she leave?'

'I don't know the date,' she said, 'but it was a Friday. I remember that.'

'How many months ago,' he asked in as calm a voice as he could manage, 'would you say, roughly?' He shrugged as if it was no big thing.

'Five?' she offered. 'Six maybe.'

There was no trace of anxiety, for Callie knew her friend was safe; she'd had the postcards, but the time frame she now described forced Bradshaw to take a long hard look at one of the photographs of Callie and Diane. He zeroed in on it and had to force himself to mask his emotions then. What he was looking at still wasn't entirely clear however.

Bradshaw took a moment to compose himself. 'There's something I need to ask you, Callie,' he said carefully, trying to make this sound as routine as possible. 'It might help us to find your friend when all of this is over.'

She nodded her understanding.

'Does Diane have a tattoo at all,' he pointed to his own neck, 'just here?' He traced the spot where the tattoo would have been if it hadn't been scorched from the skin of the burned girl.

'Yeah, she does,' said Callie, 'she's got a tattoo of a little blue bird,' and she smiled at the memory at first but then she regarded him oddly. 'How'd you know that?'

Chapter Fifty-Two

Bradshaw walked to his desk very slowly. The look on his face was enough to attract interest from several of his colleagues. Even DC Malone asked, 'You alright, Ian?' but he didn't reply. He didn't even hear her.

He was about to sit down when a familiar voice called his name: 'Bradshaw! Get in here,' and he looked up into the unsmiling face of his boss. DI Tennant did not look happy but, unlike Malone and the rest of Ian's colleagues, she was too angry to notice the almost robotic way Bradshaw moved from his desk to her office.

'Ma'am . . .' Bradshaw began listlessly but she cut him off before he could continue.

'I don't know what you're playing at . . .' Tennant told him '. . . but I'm not putting up with it any longer.'

Bradshaw failed to comprehend her meaning but for once he wasn't unduly concerned about his boss's opinion of him. He was preoccupied with thoughts of the young girl in the interview room and how he was going to find the words to break the news to her that her best friend was dead. DI Tennant's foul mood was of minimal concern.

'Ma'am?' he offered again but he had to make a conscious effort to concentrate on the conversation because he was in danger of zoning out.

'This charade you are conducting with DCI Kane . . .' she began.

'Oh,' Bradshaw said, 'that,' because it really didn't seem remotely important any more.

'Yes,' she said, 'that!' Kate Tennant couldn't understand why he was being so calm. She had known they were up to something ever since Kane asked Bradshaw to drive him home. Her suspicions were intensified by the ludicrous mentoring programme Kane had signed Bradshaw up to; as if the older man even knew the meaning of the word. 'At least you're not denying it . . .' She launched into a lecture about Bradshaw having the bloody nerve to ignore the chain of command, spy on her, go behind her back and undermine her authority all at the same time. When Bradshaw failed to respond to this she asked him outright what he had been up to and whether he had anything to say for himself.

'Up to?' he asked dumbly.

'Bloody hell,' she hissed through gritted teeth, 'I'm trying to give you a bollocking here, Bradshaw, and you're just standing there like a spare prick at a wedding. You don't even have the decency to look embarrassed. What have you been doing for fuck's sake?'

'Following a new line of enquiry,' he told her blandly.

'What?' she asked and she looked as if she was about to completely lose it. 'Is that all you have to say for yourself?'

'Yes,' he said simply, 'and I know who the burned girl is.'

DI Tennant didn't quite hear him at first. Her mouth was already open as she had been about to administer an arse-kicking of immense proportions in which trust, honesty, integrity and professionalism would have played a major part. 'What did you just say?' she asked him instead.

Later, when Ian Bradshaw released Callie McQuire without charge, she went straight to the car where Helen was waiting for her. He had not yet found the nerve to tell her about Diane and reasoned it was best to leave this till their investigation was concluded. Ian beckoned Tom over and told him everything he had learned from the girl.

'And the photograph?' asked Tom.

'Looks genuine,' said Bradshaw.

'Christ,' hissed Tom, for even now he half expected it all to be some kind of con, or a case of mistaken identity, 'it's definitely Jarvis?'

Bradshaw nodded.

'Were is it now?'

Bradshaw patted his chest to show it was safely in his jacket pocket.

'Anything else?' asked Tom when his instinct told him Bradshaw was holding something back.

'Yeah,' he told Tom quietly, 'I'm pretty sure Diane Turner is the burned girl.'

'Oh dear God,' said Tom and he instinctively turned to look at Callie in the back seat of the car. 'She doesn't know? Let's keep it that way for now. If she finds out . . .' He didn't need to complete his sentence. Both men knew there was no telling what Callie would say or do if she discovered her friend had been murdered.

'Let's get her away from here,' said Tom.

They drove to Tom's house and went inside.

'Let's see it then,' said Tom.

Helen and Tom stared at the photograph for a long time without comment. There was a single grey line across the middle of the picture where one of the slats on the ventilation grille had obscured Callie's view but she had done a good job with the camera. The top left-hand corner of the photograph showed the face of a much older man forcing himself upon an underage girl. Her face was pressed downwards and to one side so she was facing the camera in the bottom left-hand corner of the photo. There was no doubt that this was Frank Jarvis and the girl he was raping was Diane Turner. Helen and Tom exchanged looks, both of them deeply affected by the image.

'Callie?' asked Helen eventually, 'did Diane show this photograph to Sandra Jarvis?'

'I dunno.' The denial was automatic, a reflex action Callie always employed to avoid trouble. Perhaps she belatedly realised she was with the only people in the world she could trust, for she opened up then: 'Yeah, she must have done.'

'What did Sandra say she would do?' asked Tom. 'For Diane, I mean.'

'She said she would try and help her,' said Callie.

'But she didn't, did she?' said Tom. 'Not at first.'

'Did she hell. She went back to uni,' admitted Callie, 'but Diane didn't expect Sandra to help her. How could she?'

'She just wanted to tell someone about it,' said Helen.

'Yeah,' said Callie, 'she told me she felt like she was going to explode if she didn't tell somebody. She knew Sandra was alright, see, so she could tell her.'

'A few weeks went by,' said Tom, 'then Sandra got back in touch with Diane.'

'How'd you know that?'

Tom didn't want to admit it was obvious from the timeline. Diane had told Sandra about the abuse during the Christmas holidays; Sandra had gone back to university in January and completely fallen apart. By the end of February, she had decided to do something about it. She was going to confront her father and rescue Diane. It was the only explanation for their joint disappearance.

'How did Sandra get in touch?' said Tom.

'She came up to the burger bar and bought Diane some chips.'

'Just an old friend from Meadowlands meeting up with the girl she used to help out?' Callie nodded. 'So the men in the place didn't mind,' Tom said, almost to himself. They probably thought they would get their hands on Sandra too if they let her hang out there, he reasoned. 'But Sandra had a plan, didn't she?'

'She knew Diane was going to be sixteen soon. Sandra told her she could leave Meadowlands and she'd arrange it so that no man ever hurt her again.'

'And not long after that Diane left for London.'

Again Callie nodded. 'She got away real easy and no one ever went looking for her. Sandra was right. Even Dean didn't kick off about it, so whatever Sandra did must have worked.'

'Then Sandra disappeared too,' said Tom. 'What do you think happened to her, Callie?'

'I dunno.'

Tom could have pressed Callie further but she knew far less about Sandra's disappearance than he did. Why upset the girl by telling her the truth: that Diane Turner was dead, her face sickeningly disfigured so that her secret would die with her. If Diane Turner really was the burned girl, they now knew the reason she was killed – but not who did it. Frank Jarvis was the reason behind Diane's death, but was he capable of such savagery on his own? Did Sandra Jarvis suffer the same fate, Tom wondered and could her own father really be responsible for it if she had?

*

They needed a babysitter for Callie and Bradshaw figured it ought to be a woman, so he asked DC Malone to stay with her at Tom's house. He could have asked Helen but she had no power to prevent Callie from running off and she had every right to be there. They drove out to confront Councillor Frank Jarvis together, with Bradshaw at the wheel, Helen and Tom in the back seat. They all agreed it was better this way. He wouldn't know they were coming, and if Bradshaw dragged him in for questioning at the station, he'd be on his guard or he'd simply clam up and demand a lawyer without telling them anything.

'He might give something away,' said Bradshaw, 'if we can rattle him.'

'Oh we'll do that alright,' said Tom.

As Bradshaw drove, nobody said anything for a while. They were still trying to accept what they had learned. Whatever any of them had expected to find, it could never have been as devastating as the truth.

Helen was trying to comprehend what it must have been like to be Sandra Jarvis, a young, good-hearted woman willing to stay up all night and listen to a damaged girl and offer her comfort. Then she had been shown a photograph of her dad raping an underage girl in her care. Helen wondered how she had been able to hold it together, without blurting out that it was her own father who was abusing Diane. Her entire world must have tumbled down around her.

Tom spoke then. 'I understand why Sandra Jarvis confronted her father. She must have threatened to expose him or tried to convince him to hand himself in. I can imagine him denying everything and her not buying it because she'd seen the photograph; all of that I can visualise . . . just . . .'

426

he said, 'but I still can't comprehend a world in which a man would kill his own daughter to cover this up . . .'

'I know,' said Bradshaw. 'I keep going over the exact same thing. Jarvis killing his own little girl? It seems impossible.'

'Fred West did,' said Helen, for the infamous serial killer had recently hanged himself while on remand.

'But West was a maniac,' said Bradshaw, 'he murdered twelve people. West *enjoyed* killing. This is different. We're talking here about a man murdering his daughter to protect his name.'

'It goes against everything,' said Tom, 'it goes against nature. As a father, wouldn't he be more likely to kill himself than his own little girl?'

'But surely she can't be alive somewhere,' reasoned Helen, 'after all this time?'

'I don't know. Maybe she just ran off to get away from all of this and she's working behind a bar somewhere in Ibiza.'

'And maybe I'm mistaken and Diane really is alive and scratching a living in London somewhere,' said Bradshaw, 'but we both know that isn't true.'

'So who murdered Diane Turner?' said Tom. 'Did Jarvis do that too?'

'Why would he hire you,' asked Helen suddenly, 'to look for Sandra, if she was already dead and he did it?'

'I keep thinking about that, and there is only one explanation. I never thought for one minute that the grieving father so desperate to find his daughter could ever be responsible for her death,' said Tom, 'and that's exactly how he wanted it. No one suspected him: not the police, the press or any of us. Frank Jarvis came up with the perfect mask for his actions, a campaign to find the missing woman he already knew was gone,' he shook his head, 'and I was taken in by it, just like everybody else. What an idiot.'

'That is so cold,' Helen shook her head in disbelief, '*if* he killed her.'

'Maybe he didn't do it himself; maybe someone else did it but she died because Diane told her secret to Sandra. That much I am certain of. It's too big a coincidence.'

'Agreed,' said Bradshaw, 'so now let's sweat the bastard.'

Chapter Fifty-Three

They drove quickly and Bradshaw explained why he was breaking every speed limit along the way: 'He could run. They do sometimes if they are fenced in. He might even have run already.'

'Why would he run?' asked Helen. 'He doesn't know we are on to him.'

'Dean will have called Frank Jarvis the moment I took Callie away. Jarvis knows I've been asked to help Tom locate his daughter so I doubt he'll believe the story about the shoplifting gang, do you?'

'I'm not convinced he'll run,' said Tom. 'It will be the word of one respectable pillar of the local community against a teenager who has been in trouble with the police for most of her young life.'

'There's the photograph,' Bradshaw reminded him.

'But he doesn't know we've got that. If he knew about the photograph, wouldn't he have found it before now?'

'Maybe.' But he still overtook the car in front of him at speed. 'Let's not leave it to chance. The one thing I have learned is that nobody really knows for sure what anyone will do under pressure.'

Their thoughts turned to Annie Bell then, and no one contradicted Bradshaw.

They were thankful for fine weather and light traffic, which combined to make their journey to Newcastle an easy one.

Bradshaw didn't even bother to park outside Frank Jarvis's house, he simply halted the car in the middle of the road and the three of them got out. The detective banged on the door.

Frank's wife answered. 'Is he in, Mrs Jarvis?' asked Tom.

'No.' Her head lolled slightly as she took in each of them sluggishly.

'Then would you mind telling us where he is?' Bradshaw didn't try to disguise his impatience with her.

She looked at Tom then. 'Where do you think he is?'

They had to leave Bradshaw's car outside the Methodist chapel and trek on foot up to the allotments. Bradshaw had a strong premonition he wouldn't be there. He was convinced Frank Jarvis knew everything they had been doing and he'd fled, so he would never have to face them or the truth. Bradshaw was mentally preparing himself for the manhunt that would follow Frank Jarvis's disappearance, then they rounded a corner and there the man was, sitting on a bench as if all was well in the world.

'What's this?' asked Jarvis, his suspicions immediately aroused by the presence of all three of them. Maybe Dean had not been able to get hold of the politician to warn him if he had been here for a while. No one answered, just continued to walk towards him.

Bradshaw wordlessly handed him the envelope. Jarvis looked at him expecting an explanation, but when he received none he opened it. He slid the photograph out, looked at it for a second and his eyes widened in shock. The photo fell to the floor.

'It's all over, Frank,' Bradshaw told him. 'We know everything.'

'That's not me,' Jarvis managed, but the shock of seeing

himself in such a damning photograph, whose existence he clearly wasn't aware of, was affecting his ability to lie with any credibility.

'How many of those girls have you raped over the years, Frank?' asked Tom.

'No,' gasped Jarvis then he contradicted his claim of mistaken identity, jabbing a stubby finger at the photo: 'That's a fake, is that.'

'We have a credible witness who says otherwise,' Bradshaw explained as Jarvis continued his panicked denials, 'someone who can confirm you have been going to Meadowlands and abusing those girls for a long time.'

'Dean is a liar!' shouted Jarvis.

'Is he?' asked Bradshaw. 'One of my colleagues is on the way to arrest him right now. Something tells me he is likely to fold under questioning. I wouldn't want to rely on a man like Dean to back me up. He'll sell you straight down the river.'

If possible, Jarvis looked even more panicked. 'I haven't done anything. This is blackmail! Someone is trying to ruin me! Who took this picture? Can't you see it's a fake?'

They let him ramble on then and the denials kept coming, interspersed with wild accusations. He was not a child rapist, he didn't know anything about any girls at Meadowlands, this was blackmail, someone was trying to destroy him. Every time he came out with another flustered rebuttal, Bradshaw met it with a cold, hard question. How could he explain the photograph? Why would anyone wish to destroy a man who had already stepped down? What really happened to his daughter? Who killed Diane Turner?

Tom took a step back and left the two men to argue it out. He knew Jarvis was never going to confess and they were still no closer to understanding what really happened to his daughter. All the while Bradshaw was talking, Tom Carney remained quiet, even as Councillor Jarvis's denials grew ever more desperate.

Tom felt they were still missing something. Each time he tried to visualise Sandra's murder at the hands of her own father the whole scenario seemed to break down in his mind. There were cases of a man killing his own daughter but these were incredibly rare and always seemed to involve the father's loss of control over his offspring, where a man was unable to accept that his child was an actual person, with the freedom to make her own choices – but Frank Jarvis had made a point of instilling independence in his daughter and encouraging her to question authority. Sandra's school career, her tutorials at university, her work with damaged children all spoke of an independent young woman free from the shackles of her parents. Of course if she had confronted her father about Diane Turner and her knowledge of the photograph, it would have been a shock. Flustered by her accusations he might have snapped and . . . what? Murdered his own flesh and blood?

That was what Tom kept coming back to. The one, simple phrase that reverberated with him and contradicted everything else: Sandra was Frank Jarvis' flesh and blood. It was beyond dispute that not many men could bring themselves to kill their own daughter. Their first reaction would be to protect a daughter beyond all sense of personal safety. Tom was going round in circles. Jarvis had an evil secret; his daughter had discovered this and confronted him then Jarvis snapped and . . . once again the train of thought broke down. How could he have done it to his own flesh and blood?

That thought triggered a memory, something Tom had been puzzled by at the time so he had stored it away in a recess of his mind. Until now, when all of a sudden it broke free and he finally understood.

He could picture her now. The mad old lady, Frank Jarvis's mother-in-law, sitting in her armchair with that sly look on her half-senile face as she told Tom, 'That one, she's a little cuckoo.' Jarvis's wife had snapped at her to shut up. Tom had not understood her then. He thought she was questioning the sanity of her own grandchild – but no. He finally realised what she meant and the mist began to clear.

'Oh my God,' he said aloud and because this was the first time he had spoken in a while, both men stopped and turned to listen. Tom looked Jarvis in the eye then said, 'She's not yours.' He spoke the words quietly but they landed on Jarvis like a blow.

'What?' asked Jarvis as if Tom had said something ridiculous, but his voice wavered and it was enough to give him away.

'Sandra is not your daughter,' and Tom shook his head at his own foolishness, 'even the dates add up. All this time, I thought that affair years ago was you cheating on your missus but it was the other way around, wasn't it? Sandra wasn't the happy outcome of you patching up your marriage. She wasn't born prematurely. She was the product of your wife's affair, not yours.'

'That's a damned lie!'

'Is it? We'll ask your wife then shall we?' and Frank Jarvis opened his mouth to protest but he couldn't think of any response. 'That's why she drinks, isn't it? I don't mean she feels guilty because she slept with another man and had a daughter by him. That's a common enough tale. Every extended family has at least one *cuckoo*, as your mum-in-law eloquently put it. I thought she meant your daughter was mentally unstable, but what the batty old dear was really trying to say was that Sandra had been planted in the nest by someone else. So who was he, Jarvis?'

But Jarvis had run out of words all of a sudden. He shuffled towards the bench and seemed to slump into it.

'It will be simple enough to fill in the blanks. We'll just ask your wife. I'm pretty sure she'll be very forthcoming once we tell her you're the prime suspect in her daughter's murder.'

'Shut up!' yelled the politician and he got to his feet angrily then. 'I did good by her! I stood by my wife when many a man wouldn't have! Christ almighty, she made me look like a fool!'

'No, she didn't,' Tom told him, 'but she would have if you'd kicked her out. You couldn't get a divorce back then if you wanted to succeed in politics, and you knew it. You had to keep your family together at all costs. You didn't stand by her; you convinced her to stand by you and give your marriage another shot. The price you paid was a daughter who wasn't your own.'

'I brought that girl up! I treated her like my own daughter. I turned a blind eye to everything my wife had done.'

'But you didn't care about that, did you, Frank? You weren't too bothered when she went elsewhere for what you couldn't give her,' and Tom shook his head. 'What was she: seventeen or eighteen when you started walking out with her? She was already too old. You're only interested if they're very young and you enjoy it a lot more if they struggle. Christ, your wife must have been so lonely.'

'Shut up,' hissed Jarvis.

'All the way up here I kept on thinking, *He can't have done it. He can't have killed his own daughter.* Oh I knew what you'd done to Diane and Callie and God knows how many other girls, but I kept telling myself murdering Sandra was against nature. The truth is, you could kill another man's child when she was threatening to destroy you – and Sandra would never have seen it coming because she didn't know, did she? Did the poor girl turn her back on you, Frank? Is that what happened?'

'Shut up,' he said again.

'When did you kill her? During the argument up here, or was it later? We know she never left Newcastle. That was one picture that *was* a fake. When we find out which bent copper identified that girl at the railway station as your daughter and derailed a massive missing person's enquiry, he'll be arrested too. Maybe he'll have a story to tell. Perhaps he'll do a deal.'

'What did you do with the body?' asked Tom. 'How did you get rid of it?' And then Tom remembered something else, something someone had told him before his first meeting with Frank Jarvis. 'She never left, did she, Frank?' He looked round the allotment. 'That's why old Harry never saw her come down off the allotment that day. You killed her here, didn't you?'

'Shut up!' he roared. 'Just shut up, for God's sake!'

'No, Frank, I won't shut up. Harry caught you out, didn't he? You didn't see him creep up here while you were digging a trench to bury Sandra. You panicked and told him it was for your potatoes but it was the wrong season. Harry thought you were a poor gardener but you were so proud of growing all your own vegetables you wouldn't have got that wrong. Was Sandra's body in the shed? Did you wrap it up in something and bury her here? I'll bet you did, and Harry will be able to tell us exactly where, won't he?'

'I'll get a team up here now,' Bradshaw told him. 'If you've got something to say, any mitigation you want to give before that happens, then now is the time to tell us.'

Jarvis turned slowly back to the bench and sat down.

'Suit yourself, Jarvis,' said Bradshaw. 'You're on your own now.'

'Alright,' Jarvis said wearily, 'I'll tell you. I'll tell you everything.'

Chapter Fifty-Four

Tom, Helen and Bradshaw formed a semicircle around Jarvis.

'Where is she?' asked Tom, and the councillor answered by pointing to a rough area of overturned soil where nothing grew but weeds.

'What happened?' asked Bradshaw.

'You may as well tell us,' Helen informed him, 'we know most of it already.'

'I was sitting here that day,' he began, 'when Sandra marched up to me. She was angry. She said she knew about Diane Turner. I didn't even know who she meant.'

'You never bothered to learn their names,' said Tom.

'I didn't want to know their names,' Jarvis corrected him.

'That made it too real.' Helen hissed the words at him angrily.

'Sandra told me she knew all about me,' he said. 'She called me such terrible names, used words I'd never heard her say before.'

'And of course you denied everything,' said Tom.

'What choice did I have?' Frank reasoned, 'but Sandra wouldn't believe me. She said it was true and she'd get this Diane girl to tell everybody about me. She said they would put me away. I didn't think she was capable of that much hate. I tried to explain it to her. The lasses at Meadowlands are not like other girls.'

'Bet she didn't take kindly to that,' said Tom.

'She kept saying Diane was *innocent*.' He shook his head. 'I told her she was a long way from innocent.'

'Why didn't Sandra just go to the police about you?'

'She wanted me to admit it all. Sandra told me I had to go to the police and tell them what I'd done. If I didn't, she'd produce this girl who'd tell the whole world about it. Nobody would believe a girl like that but if my own daughter was standing next to her when she said it . . . they'd think I was a paedophile and a rapist.' Jarvis snorted at the absurdity of that description.

'Well, you are,' said Helen.

'I'm not a paedophile!' he raged, 'I've never harmed innocent children.'

'But you raped underage teenagers,' said Tom quietly.

'If you think I'm the first man to lie down with that Diane then you're a bloody fool. She's been with dozens of men.'

'So that makes it alright? We know you raped her when she was fifteen. She was probably a lot younger than that when you started.'

'Oh come on! You keep calling it rape and it's far from it. They'll sleep with you for a packet of fags!'

'What is wrong with you?' asked Bradshaw. 'They are just kids.'

'I have a weakness,' admitted Jarvis, 'that's all.'

'A weakness for young girls?' asked Helen and he nodded.

'Did you tell your daughter that?' asked Tom. 'Because I'm guessing she was about as sympathetic as we are.'

'She didn't understand,' said Jarvis. 'She told me she would ruin me, said she was ashamed of who I was, told me I was no longer her father. I had to laugh at that one. I was never her father.'

'And that's why you could bring yourself to kill her,' said Tom.

437

'I had no choice!' roared Jarvis. 'She left me no option!'

'There's always a choice,' said Helen. 'You could have let her go.'

'You should have killed yourself,' observed Bradshaw.

'What happened?' asked Tom.

'She said her piece then tried to leave.' Jarvis spoke so quietly he was almost inaudible. 'I knew I couldn't let her go. She turned her back on me so I grabbed that.' And he glanced at a large shovel that was sticking out of the ground nearby. They all stared at it. 'And I hit her.'

'You hit her round the head?' asked Bradshaw and Jarvis nodded. 'And that's what killed her?' Jarvis nodded again.

'Then you buried her out here and started the biggest cover-up you could,' observed Tom, 'but you couldn't have done that alone. You were in the deepest shit imaginable, Frank, and you needed a powerful friend. It had to be someone who knew people, somebody who could fake sightings of a missing girl all over the city, so no one knew the last time she was alive was up here with you. He could even get a bent detective to say he'd found Sandra on CCTV at the railway station. Most of all, you needed someone who could find Diane Turner and make her disappear.'

'I didn't know what to do . . .' he protested.

'What else could you do,' asked Tom, 'except go and see someone you've known all your life who didn't mind doing your dirty work: Jimmy McCree?'

'There wasn't anyone else who could . . .'

'Tidy up your mess?' asked Bradshaw.

'Where did he find Diane?' asked Tom.

'That bit was easy,' said Jarvis. 'She was in my daughter's room at her lodgings in Durham. There was nobody else there because it was reading week.'

'So she was on her own when they took her,' said Helen, 'poor thing.'

'She didn't stand a chance,' said Tom, 'did she?'

'I didn't know they were going to . . .'

'Kill her?' asked Helen angrily. 'What did you think they would do?'

'I don't know,' said Jarvis. 'I just wanted all this to go away.'

'You did know,' said Bradshaw. 'As long as Diane was alive she'd be a walking, talking threat to you and a link to Sandra. When you got Jimmy McCree involved you knew there was only one possible outcome.'

'Did you pay him?' asked Tom and Jarvis shook his head. 'No, you didn't have to. You just stepped down as head of the council and walked away from the planning committee and the Riverside tender. Then you backed Joe Lynch as your successor, because he was already on McCree's payroll. That's how McCree managed to get in with Alan Camfield. He brought the leader of the city council with him. You stepping down was the price you paid for cleaning up your mess, wasn't it?'

'He made me do that. I had no choice.'

'So the city got saddled with Joe Lynch.'

'That's not my fault. McCree insisted on it. Joe Lynch is the corrupt one and I tried to expose him.'

'You haven't said a word against him since he became leader of the council,' said Helen.

Jarvis looked at Helen as if she was simple. 'Who do you think has been sending you your tip-offs on Lynch?' A chill went through Helen because she knew she'd been played then. 'I love this city and Lynch isn't worthy of it, so I helped you with your articles and they have done him some real damage.'

'Lynch might be a bad man,' Bradshaw told him, 'but as far as I know he never asked Jimmy McCree to kill a young girl.'

Jarvis shook his head. 'We never had that conversation. He said he would make sure the girl never said a word against me. I thought he might pay her off or . . .'

'You knew he would never do that,' said Bradshaw.

'What about the photograph?' asked Tom. 'Didn't you try to get it?'

'I didn't know anything about it. I never knew there was a photograph.'

'Sandra must have been keeping that up her sleeve in case you wouldn't admit everything. McCree had Diane Turner killed before she could tell anyone about the photograph,' Tom said, 'but someone must have found out who her best friend was so he could arrange those fake postcards to be sent to Callie from London and nobody suspected she was dead.'

'Then you started the campaign to find your daughter,' said Tom. 'I have to hand it to you, Frank – of all the cynical, soulless, ice-hearted exercises I have ever come across, this one takes the absolute prize.'

'I . . .' he began.

'If you tell us you had no choice one more time, so help me . . .' And Tom balled his fist in readiness.

Jarvis shook his head. 'Don't you see, I only did what I would have done if Sandra really had disappeared. That's all.'

'To alleviate suspicion?' asked Bradshaw.

'If I had sat back and done nothing, everyone would have wondered why. I had to quit because McCree made me but this campaign was the excuse I needed to step down from the leadership.'

'So nobody suspected you'd been got at,' said Helen, 'and no one assumed you'd killed your own daughter.'

'Killing one girl in a fit of high emotion is a terrible thing,' Bradshaw told him. 'You'll get life for that but it might not mean life,' he told the councillor and Tom was immediately back in the world of Richard Bell and his tariff. 'The other girl, however.'

'But that wasn't me,' protested Jarvis, 'that was McCree.'

'Only because you begged him,' said Bradshaw. 'The leader of the council in his back pocket? It must have been like Christmas for Big Jimmy. He won't be so happy once he hears you've been arrested for murder though Frank, because he'll know the only chance you have left is to make a deal.'

'A deal?' Helen was shocked. 'He doesn't get any deals.' She jabbed a finger at the distraught councillor. 'He's a bloody murderer!'

'And so is Jimmy McCree,' Bradshaw told her, 'and I want them both.'

Jarvis seemed to snap back into reality at the mention of McCree's wrath. 'I want a lawyer. I'm saying nothing more.'

'You'll get one,' Bradshaw told him. 'They'll be queueing up for a high-profile case like this one.' He turned to Helen and Tom. 'I think we're done here. I'll call this in,' he glanced at Sandra Jarvis's burial site, 'and get a team out here.'

'Read him his rights,' Tom told Bradshaw, 'then bring him down the hill.' And with that, Tom turned and started to walk down the hill himself.

'Where are you going?' asked Helen.

Tom turned back to face them. 'Me? I'm going on ahead so I can knock on every door. I'm going to tell everyone to come out and watch Frank Jarvis being led away in handcuffs.'

'Don't,' pleaded Jarvis, 'please. I'm begging you.'

'Fuck you,' Tom told him and he carried on walking.

Frank Jarvis looked completely destroyed at that moment, so Helen told him, 'You deserve this.'

Chapter Fifty-Five

It didn't take long to find her. Sandra was buried right where Frank Jarvis said she would be. The team who scraped away the soil found a badly decomposed body wrapped in plastic sheeting a few feet below the surface.

Sandra Jarvis was no longer missing.

News that Frank Jarvis had been arrested on suspicion of his own daughter's murder spread quickly through the city. It wasn't long before Jimmy McCree was tipped off by one of his police contacts but he didn't run. Maybe he reasoned he could clear his name one more time. Perhaps he thought Jarvis would be too scared to do a deal with the police or he could silence the councillor before he did. Maybe he just didn't fancy trying to hide on the Costa del Sol for the rest of his days. Either way, they found him sitting quietly in his armchair when they broke down the door.

The police had taken the usual precautions but the crowd that gathered outside McCree's home that day was strangely subdued as they watched their 'community leader' being marched away in handcuffs. They were used to seeing him arrested when a rival had been brutally beaten or even killed but the general consensus was always that he was just protecting his turf from outsiders. If you were daft enough to try and take on Big Jimmy you were asking for trouble and at least McCree was one of their own, which partly explained the usual hostility towards the police when they came to take him.

Not this time though. Word had spread that McCree had done some kind of deal with a local politician. They were despised as much as the police round here. The whispers on the street were that two young girls were the victims this time and a collective shudder seemed to go through the community.

So much for Robin Hood.

Ian Bradshaw was standing on the pavement outside McCree's home as he was led away. He had been invited to tag along by his colleagues in the Northumbria force, since he had brought them such a huge scalp and there was no way he was going to turn down the opportunity to see Jimmy McCree in handcuffs.

McCree stopped when he saw Bradshaw. 'You again?'

'Your luck finally ran out, Jimmy.'

'We'll see about that,' the big man retorted but he didn't look quite so sure now. The two burly officers escorting him dragged McCree away.

After he was gone, Bradshaw heard an old lady whisper to her neighbour, 'They say one of them was nowt much more than a bairn,' and she shook her head sadly at the state of the world. Bradshaw knew then that no matter what happened in court, Jimmy McCree would no longer enjoy the indulgence of a community that had finally learned just who they had been protecting.

It had been a very long day. Graham Seaton had overseen the publication of the newspaper's biggest edition in years. Then he fielded calls from other news outlets around the country, desperate for the inside track on a series of stunning news stories written by reporter Helen Norton. The newspaper devoted a series of pages to several related articles.

The body of Sandra Jarvis had been discovered on land a short distance from her home and a man arrested on suspicion of murder. That man was her own father and the former leader of the city council. If that were not enough, police raids had been carried out on the Meadowlands children's home where Sandra had worked as a volunteer and a number of other properties in the area, including an off-licence, burger bar and taxi rank. A total of thirteen men had been arrested, including a male care worker from Meadowlands. The girls had all been removed for their own safety then placed in care elsewhere and it was rumoured Meadowlands was likely to close for good.

In a separate article, Helen reported the arrest of well-known local businessman Jimmy McCree, on suspicion of a second murder linked to an unidentified body with a burned face, discovered in a scrapyard on the outskirts of the city. Readers were gleefully reminded that McCree's security firm was part of Alan Camfield's current bid for the Riverside tender and both men recently met with Councillor Joe Lynch in a city-centre restaurant.

Between them, Helen and Graham managed to draft each article so that readers would be in little doubt all of these events were linked. The edition was a chronicle of crime and high-level corruption that was the basis of radio and TV news broadcasts all over the region and beyond.

Graham left the office later than usual that evening but with the pride of a job well done. He was exhausted but his mind was buzzing. He was in a state he would have described as 'wired'. This was what journalism was all about. Seaton even allowed himself a quick daydream about the possibility of an award for their coverage as he drove his car out of the car park.

He felt bad that he wouldn't get to see his kids tonight; his wife would have packed them off to bed hours ago but she'd understand. He'd managed a brief phone call home to explain things to her but had to cut her off in mid-sentence so he could take yet another call from a London tabloid keen to hear his views on the situation, in exchange for a mention that would reflect well on both him and his newspaper. He hadn't even had time to end the call with his usual, 'I love you.'

He was on the dual carriageway heading north when it happened. He couldn't have been more relaxed about his career at that point. Every newspaper in the country was reporting on their exclusive and he felt vindicated at last. Helen Norton deserved a lot of the credit too. She'd done a great job and he saw her as a future Chief Reporter for the paper.

That was his last thought before the other car hit him. Seaton hadn't even seen it until the final moment because it drew up alongside his vehicle at great speed from the inside lane and as it reached the mid-point of his car it suddenly sent him barrelling into oncoming traffic.

Afterwards, there would be much discussion about the driver of the other car failing to stop. There were no cameras on this stretch of the road, so the car that hit his would never be traced and the accident – because it was still officially classed as an accident in the absence of concrete evidence indicating otherwise – happened on a part of the dual carriageway with no crash barriers in the central reservation. Graham Seaton's car ploughed through to the other side, unopposed by anything until it smashed into a car travelling at eighty miles an hour in the opposite direction.

The other driver was killed instantly, while three people

in the second car that clipped the spinning wreckage of Seaton's escaped with serious, life-changing injuries, but none of them was able to give police much of an account afterwards of what actually occurred that night, since it all happened so fast.

Seaton's car had rolled twice before it smashed into trees by the side of the road. Everyone, including his closest friends and family, prayed he had been killed instantly when he hit the other vehicle, before the spilled petrol ignited and flames took hold of the car, sweeping through it and charring everything inside.

Chapter Fifty-Six

Helen was running late, but she had good reason to be. She had just spent time with Graham Seaton's widow, who looked like a hollowed-out shell with nothing left inside her now but pain. She had gone round to the house out of respect for Graham and a duty to the wife she had never met. She had thought that offering words of admiration for her late editor might provide some small crumb of comfort to his widow, but regretted her visit almost immediately.

Though Helen's grief at poor Graham's awful, premature death could never have been as deep as his wife's, it still burned intensely within her days after news of the so-called accident was broken to them all at the paper. Now she found herself stumbling to say anything worthwhile, when all she really wanted to do was express her anger at the men who killed him and rage at the unfairness of it all. Instead she had a solitary cup of tea with the devastated woman and ended up offering up weak platitudes about how proud his children would be once they were old enough to understand what their father had done with his life.

'They'd rather have their dad back,' snapped his wife.

'Of course,' said Helen, 'I'm sorry.' And she left as soon as decently possible after that.

On the drive back she had an awful sick feeling that Mrs Seaton suspected she and her husband might have been something more than just colleagues, but how the hell could she put that idea from a widow's mind without being hugely insensitive? Either way, it had been a terrible decision to go round there and all of a sudden the tears that Helen had been too shocked to shed on first learning of Graham's death finally came. She had to pull over by the side of the road and wept openly until she was finally done.

All of this meant she was very late when she parked in the dedicated space outside her newly rented flat and climbed out of her car. She would have a quick shower, change and be on her way again before too long. She had almost reached her front door when she spotted the note, which had been folded and pinned to the wood with a drawing pin. She looked around but there was no one near.

Helen pulled out the pin and the note fell to the ground. She picked it up, unfolded the paper and read the words.

ROSES ARE RED, VIOLETS ARE BLUE
YOUR EDITOR GOT BURNED
NOW WE'RE COMING FOR YOU

'DCI Kane sends his regards,' said Bradshaw as he handed Tom a pint. 'What the hell have they done to this place?'

'Mexican theme, dinosaurs in the garden, jelly beans on the bar.' Tom was dismissive. 'So Kane actually sent his regards, or are you making that bit up?'

'He did.'

'I'd have thought you and I were both *persona non grata* these days.'

'Well, we have caused him an absolute mountain of paperwork,' admitted Bradshaw, 'and he did say we were both pains in the arse, but we resolved the disappearance of Sandra Jarvis and cleared up the burned girl case. Jimmy McCree is in custody for that one, which is a major win, and he'll stay there if Frank Jarvis testifies against him.'

'What about Annie Bell?'

'I try not to mention her name around Kane,' said Bradshaw. 'It tends to affect his mood if he's reminded that every journalist in the country wants to ask him if he sent the wrong guy to prison, but it could be worse. They could be asking who was the young bobby that allowed Frank Jarvis's missus to walk away from a drink-driving charge twenty years ago,' and he regarded Tom carefully. 'You knew, didn't you?'

'I guessed,' Tom admitted, 'and you worked it out too.'

Bradshaw shook his head. 'He told me. He said he was wet behind the ears back then and you didn't do anything without asking the grown-ups first. He'd seen Frank Jarvis on the local news, saw Mrs Jarvis's name on her licence and asked if they were related. Then he called it in and the adults told him to give her a bye so he drove her home.'

'Then all of a sudden he had friends in high places.'

'That was how it worked back in the seventies but I still think Kane isn't corrupt, not really. You must think that too or you would have exposed him.'

Tom shrugged. 'No one's interested in all that. They want to read about murder and high-level corruption.'

'Right,' said Bradshaw but he didn't sound convinced. 'On a lighter note, how's Helen?'

'Gone,' he said.

'Oh.'

'Found a flat and moved out days ago.'

'Sorry to hear that,' said Bradshaw. 'It must have been nice having her around.'

'My place was a little cramped,' he said. To change the subject, Tom asked, 'How's Karen?'

'Gone too.'

449

It was Tom's turn to say, 'Oh.'

'It's fine,' Bradshaw sipped his pint, 'it was my decision.'

'Right.'

'Of course every guy in the force thinks I'm stupid or gay but you can't have everything.'

'At least you've got your freedom,' Tom observed. 'How'd she take it?'

'Not well,' Bradshaw admitted, 'but then she got all her stuff, moved back into her mum and dad's and now she's seeing her ex again.'

'Blimey,' said Tom, 'that was quick.'

'Karen doesn't like to be on her own,' observed Bradshaw, 'and he'd been hanging round. I'm happy for her.'

'Really?'

'No, not really,' admitted Bradshaw. 'I've woken in the night in a panic a couple of times wondering if I did the right thing. I almost rang her once . . .'

'Then you realised you didn't really want her back.'

'Yeah.'

'I reckon you liked the idea of being with her more than the reality, that's all.'

Bradshaw thought for a moment. 'You know, that's probably as good an explanation as I've managed to come up with.'

Helen walked into the pub then and they took their drinks to a table by a window and sat down.

'Are you okay?' asked Tom.

'No,' she said calmly enough but he realised it was a stupid question. How did he expect her to be when her editor had been killed? 'I went to see his poor wife . . .' Her sentence remained incomplete. 'The funeral is on Monday.'

'I'll be there,' Tom told her and she squeezed his shoulder in gratitude.

'Is your newspaper sorting out something for you?' asked Bradshaw, and when she didn't comprehend his meaning he explained: 'Protection. Graham was the editor but you wrote the articles.'

'Oh,' she said. 'Well they've asked me not to come in for a while, so I suppose I'm not suspended exactly but kind of on gardening leave.'

'Is that all they are doing?' asked Tom.

'I think everyone there is in shock,' Helen explained. 'They've never had a situation like this before. I suppose they think I'm responsible.'

Tom was angry. 'That's ridiculous.'

'No, it's true. I *am* responsible. Like you said, Ian, I wrote the articles.'

'I didn't mean . . .'

She held up her hand. 'I know you didn't. I'm just saying that if I hadn't written those stories, Graham would still be alive, and I have to live with that.'

'Here we go again,' said Tom, 'blaming everyone but the people who actually do the killing.'

'It's okay,' she said. 'I'm not sure I want to go back there anyway. I'll need some time.' She smiled grimly. 'I'm hoping you two have happier news.'

'Not really. I saw Richard Bell again today,' Tom told them.

'How was he?' she asked.

'Not great. He's even talking of copping for it.'

'What?' Helen was shocked. 'But he didn't do it and everyone knows he didn't. Annie confessed!'

'Says he doesn't care anymore one way or another. He still

blames himself for Annie's death and Rebecca's and reckons he deserves whatever he gets. He thinks his request for an appeal will drag on for months anyway, possibly even years, and he mainly clung to the innocent plea because he didn't want his little girls believing he was a murderer. Now he thinks that might be better than knowing their mother was, so he's trapped in another dilemma. His legal team aren't helping.'

'I thought they'd be going all out to get him released.'

'They think it could be claimed Annie was depressed and suicidal, so maybe she wanted to take the blame to get the man she loved released from prison. That's why she allowed herself to be taped confessing to me.'

'But that's ridiculous.'

'Helen, I bluffed her. She thought there was a witness but there wasn't, not a credible one. She thought the police were coming to arrest her but they weren't. We might have got somewhere with her if Ian had brought her in for questioning but she killed herself.'

'Isn't that evidence of a guilty conscience?'

'It only shows she wasn't of sound mind, which doesn't help his cause.'

'But what about the parking fine?'

'He parked the car there and drove it to meet his lover then he killed her. She quietly paid it to suppress the evidence of his guilt.'

'But that's crazy!'

'It's what any lawyer worthy of his profession will tell a judge,' said Tom. 'Richard Bell is going nowhere in a hurry. There's no real incentive to reopen the case.'

The barman called Ian Bradshaw to the phone then and he went, muttering to himself about being foolish enough to have told people he was going to the pub, by which he meant DCI Kane.

'Richard Bell is faced with a pretty stark choice. One I wouldn't envy,' said Tom. 'Continue to deny guilt and face a full twenty-four-year sentence, by which time his kids will have grown up and forgotten him, risk everything on a new appeal or admit he did it, even though we all know that he didn't, and hope he can get out in another six or seven years. Then of course he'll have no job and no home and there's no guarantee he will ever be allowed to see his children again.'

'Who's looking after them?'

'Annie's father, who would probably like nothing better than to see his son-in-law suffer, since he probably blames Richard for the death of his daughter. Do you really think he'll allow the man to see his granddaughters?'

'But he'll have some rights, as their natural father.'

'I suspect those rights will be eroded by the fact that he's a convicted murderer. It could reasonably be argued he isn't safe to be allowed near his own children.'

'Does he know this?'

'We talked about it, yes, but I don't think he has the energy left to keep on fighting.'

'But he's not guilty,' she protested.

'That's what I said.'

'And what did he say?'

'"We're all guilty of something."'

Bradshaw rejoined them and his face was white.

'You okay?' asked Helen.

'Not really. I've just been given some news and you're not going to like it.'

Tom couldn't recall the last time he'd received good news. 'Go on.'

'It's Councillor Jarvis,' said Bradshaw. 'There's no pleasant way to tell you this so I'm just going to say it.' And he took a breath. 'He's dead.'

'Dead?' said Helen. 'How?'

'Found hanged in his cell.'

'He killed himself?' she asked the detective.

'Doubt it somehow,' said Bradshaw.

'That was no suicide,' snapped Tom. 'He was killed to shut him up, just like your editor.'

'Guards found him,' said Bradshaw, 'with sheets knotted round his neck and the other end tied to the metal bar in the window.'

'Does anybody really believe it was suicide?' asked Helen.

'There's plenty that want to believe it,' admitted the detective. 'It would be a lot more convenient.'

'So who did it?' asked Helen. 'McCree?'

'Who else has the contacts on the inside?' Tom asked. 'Where does this leave your case against Jimmy McCree?'

'In tatters,' admitted Bradshaw. 'The only evidence we have linking Jimmy McCree directly to the murder of Diane Turner is from Frank Jarvis, who is no longer in a position to testify against him. McCree's lawyers are already petitioning for his release from remand. They said all along Jarvis's claims were a ludicrous attempt to avoid taking the full blame for his daughter's murder and their client knows nothing about the other girl. The CPS won't be able to pursue it now.'

'So he gets away with it?' said Helen.

'Not quite,' said Bradshaw. 'We've been assembling quite the dossier on Jimmy over the years and his recent arrest on suspicion of murder gave us new warrants to search his home and a number of places associated with him.'

'What did you find?' she asked.

'There's enough to bring charges for money laundering and possession of illegal firearms at the very least plus tax evasion and possession of a small amount of class A drugs but not enough to do him on supplying. He's probably looking at a couple of years inside if he pleads guilty.'

'He'll do that with a smile on his face now he's avoided life,' commented Tom.

'But it will be his first actual criminal conviction. That'll cost his new security business a lot of money. Alan Camfield has already slammed the door shut on him and pulled out of the Riverside tender, which has been ripped up so they can start it all over again without him. Joe Lynch is vulnerable too. He may have to stand down as leader of the council because everyone is openly talking about how corrupt he is. This is all very far from over. Every police officer in the north-east is in full agreement that Jimmy McCree is now our number one priority and he'll slip up again one day. We'll be waiting when he does.'

'In the meantime, he gets away with murder,' said Helen.

'Believe me I am as pissed off about that as you are, Helen, but there's nothing we can do about it.'

'There is one thing I can do,' Tom told them both. 'I'm going to write about it. I'm going to put all of this down in a way no one can bloody ignore. I'll tell the story of the man who's rotting away in jail even though it was his wife that really murdered his lover. I'm going to tell the world about the politician who abused his position to prey on young girls nobody would ever believe. I'll write about his murdered daughter, how he was forced to end his political career and who gained because of that, then I'll say how bloody convenient it was for everyone when he was found dead in his cell.'

'You don't mind who you upset, do you?' said Bradshaw but he was smiling now.

'I've still got contacts who love stories like these. There'll be banner headlines on the front pages of some very big newspapers and some people won't like that,' agreed Tom, 'but by the time I'm done there'll be dozens of other reporters queueing up with some very awkward questions for Alan Camfield, Joe Lynch and Jimmy McCree.'

When Tom was finished, Bradshaw regarded him closely. 'I quite like the sound of that.'

'The power of the press,' said Tom, 'and no, I don't expect to change the world, not even a small corner of it, but it's a start.'

'I'd like to help you,' Helen told him, 'but I may need a change of address,' and she handed him the note that had been pinned to her door.

He read it then gave the note to Bradshaw. 'You sure about that?' Tom asked. 'They are already gunning for you.'

'So I may as well fight back. Are you still looking for that lodger?'

'Not anymore. The room's yours.'

'So it's print and be damned?' Helen asked him.

'Print and be damned,' he said emphatically and Helen smiled. She knew this time they both meant it.

The End

Acknowledgements

Thank you to everyone at Penguin Random House for publishing *Behind Dead Eyes*. In particular, a huge thank you to my editor Emad Akhtar for all of his great ideas and hard work helping me knock this book into shape. Thanks also to Viola Hayden for all of her help.

I would like to thank the legendary 'Agent Phil' my literary agent. Phil Patterson at Marjacq has represented me for quite some time now. He is a huge support and an all-round top bloke. Thanks also to Sandra Sawicka at Marjacq for ably handling my foreign rights.

Behind Dead Eyes enabled me to work with the amazing Keshini Naidoo for the fifth time now. Once again thanks for helping me get to the end of a book, Keshini.

Thanks to Peter Hammans and all at Droemer Knaur, my publisher in Germany, and a very big thank you to the brilliant Ion Mills at No Exit for getting me started.

Mark Birkett made a very generous bid at an auction to support a fine charity, the Alan Shearer Foundation, for which we all thank him. In return he is now immortalised as a fictional character in this book.

Aspiring authors only ever become published authors with a lot of help and support along the way. I am lucky enough to be able to thank the following people for believing in me at key times, which kept me going: Adam Pope, Andy Davis, Nikki Selden, Gareth Chennells, Andrew Local, Stuart Britton, David Shapiro, Peter Day, Tony Frobisher, Eva Dolan, Gemma Sealey and Dave Nellist.

Anyone who has ever lived with a writer will know why I must say a massive thank you to my lovely wife Alison for putting up with me. We are a weird bunch in general and our idiosyncrasies must be quite hard to tolerate at times. I couldn't have done this without you, pet. Thanks for all of your love and support.

Saving the very best till last, my wonderful daughter Erin keeps me going. Thanks for making absolutely everything worthwhile. Your dad loves you more than anything, Erin, and he always will.